# Praise for the novels of Candace Camp

"A truly enjoyable read."  —*Publishers Weekly* on *Mesmerized*

"Fun…frothy…entertaining."
      —*Smart Bitches, Trashy Books* on *His Wicked Charm*

"A smart, fun-filled romp."  —*Publishers Weekly* on *Impetuous*

"Alex and Sabrina are a charming pair."
      —*BookPage* on *His Sinful Touch*

"Those who have not discovered Camp's Mad Morelands
are in for a treat… Camp is a consummate storyteller whose
well-crafted prose and believable characterization ensure that
this intriguing mystery…will utterly enchant readers."
      —*RT Book Reviews* on *His Sinful Touch*

"From its delicious beginning to its satisfying ending,
Camp's delectable [story] offers a double helping of
romance."      —*Booklist* on *Mesmerized*

"[A] beautifully written charmer."
      —*Publishers Weekly* on *The Marriage Wager*

"A clever mystery adds intrigue to this lively and gently
humorous tale, which simmers with well-handled sexual
tension."      —*Library Journal* on *A Dangerous Man*

"Delightful."  —*Publishers Weekly* on *The Wedding Challenge*

T0198092

## Also by Candace Camp

For additional books by Candace Camp,
visit her website, candace-camp.com.

# CANDACE CAMP

## A SCANDAL AT STONECLIFFE

CANARY STREET PRESS

CANARY
STREET
PRESS™

Recycling programs
for this product may
not exist in your area.

ISBN-13: 978-1-335-51313-7

A Scandal at Stonecliffe

For questions and comments about the quality of this book, please contact us at CustomerService@Harlequin.com.

TM is a trademark of Harlequin Enterprises ULC.

Canary Street Press
22 Adelaide St. West, 41st Floor
Toronto, Ontario M5H 4E3, Canada
CanaryStPress.com

**Printed in U.S.A.**

This book is dedicated to all of my wonderful and loyal readers. Writing is solitary work, but knowing that you will soon be rooting for (or against) the people who populate my stories makes this job anything but lonely. I love the characters who have unfolded in my work, but getting to share them with you is the real joy of writing. I think of every one of you readers as my partner in crime! Thanks so much for accompanying me on these journeys.

I wish I could list all of you by name, but I'd like to say an extra big special thanks to my Candace Camp Ladies for your great insights, suggestions, and support. Thank you so much for your time and positive energy: Kat, Lori D., Brenda, Candace N., Maria, Alison, Monika, Lori Q., Suzannah, Megan, Michelle, Barbara, Kelly, Kari, Chasity, Karen, Amy, Marina, Sherry, Anna Katharine, Niki, Jennifer. You ladies are the best!

# CHARACTER LIST

## DUNBRIDGE FAMILY

**Nathan Dunbridge**—gentleman, neighbor to the Stonecliffe estate, friend of the Rutherfords

**Rose Dunbridge**—Nathan's mother

**Jocelyn Dunbridge**—Nathan's aunt

**George Dunbridge**—Nathan's deceased father

## COLE DETECTIVE AGENCY

**Verity Cole**—detective and former spy

**Mrs. Malloy**—bookkeeper

**Lady Bankwater**—Verity's client

**Lord Arden**—subject of one of Verity's cases

**Lady Arden**—Arden's wife and party hostess

## RUTHERFORD & LOCKWOOD FAMILIES

**Lady Lockwood**—mother of Adeline, grandmother of Annabeth

**Petunia**—Lady Lockwood's pug

**Thomas Rutherford**—deceased former Earl of Drewsbury, Adeline's husband, Marcus's brother, Sloane's uncle

**Adeline Lockwood Rutherford/Lady Drewsbury**—Countess of Drewsbury, widow of Thomas, daughter of Lady Lockwood, aunt of Annabeth Winfield Rutherford

**Marcus Rutherford**—father of Sloane, younger brother of Thomas

**Sloane Rutherford**—Nathan's longtime acquaintance and former rival, former spy and smuggler

**Annabeth Winfield Rutherford**—Sloane's wife, close friend of Nathan's

**Adam Rutherford**—deceased first husband of Noelle, son of the Earl and Countess of Drewsbury

**Noelle Rutherford Thorne**—widow of Adam, mother of Gil, now wife of Carlisle Thorne

**Gilbert (Gil) Rutherford**—current Earl of Drewsbury, six-year-old son of Adam and Noelle

**Carlisle Thorne**—husband of Noelle, guardian of Gil, son of Horace Thorne, raised by Adeline and Thomas

## DOUGLAS FAMILY

**John Douglas**—head of the family

**Flora Douglas**—John's wife

**Robert Douglas**—John's brother

**Margaret Douglas**—John and Flora's daughter

**Malcolm Douglas**—Margaret's son

## OTHERS

**Harold Asquith**—Verity and Sloane's former spymaster

**Basil Stanhope**—aristocrat

**Jonathan Stanhope**—Basil's son

**Parker**—Sloane's old rival, current owner of Sloane's former illegal businesses

# CHAPTER ONE

NATHAN LOOKED AROUND the crowded ballroom. Lady Arden's yearly ball was a must for anyone with any pretensions to the *ton*. Frankly, he couldn't understand why; he had always found the affair deadly dull. But its size was precisely why he'd chosen it for his first foray back into London Society, hoping that among such a large group of people, his own presence would be hardly noticed.

He'd known that there was bound to be gossip about him and Annabeth. Even though their engagement had been known only to the families, everyone was aware that Nathan had been head over heels about Annabeth for years. Her wedding to Sloane Rutherford and Nathan's subsequent departure to the Continent had doubtlessly set tongues clacking.

Nathan had spent six months touring Europe, most of it visiting a friend who had moved to Italy. When he had returned three months ago, he had avoided London, going straight to Dunbridge Manor, his home in the country. Unfortunately, his mother and aunt had left Bath and moved into the manor during his absence, and fond as he was of them—even Aunt Jocelyn—there was really only so much cosseting, sweetness, and concern a man could bear. He loved his mother dearly, but they fared better if he didn't actually have to live with her.

So a few weeks ago, he had returned to his flat in

London, with its blessed silence and a complete lack of maternal worry. He had stayed away from parties, however, going only to his club or joining friends at horse races, or contests of pugilism, or nights of drinking.

Those activities had grown boring, as well. He hadn't felt any need to drown his sorrows in months—absence, he'd found, didn't make the heart grow fonder; it eased the pain—and he didn't enjoy waking up the next morning with a pounding head. Moreover, it seemed as if nearly all his closest friends, like Carlisle, were now married or engaged or pursuing a lady. Life had become rather lifeless, somehow, so he had decided to return to the *ton*.

His hope that he could escape gossip at a large ball was clearly unfounded. As soon as he stepped into the ballroom, seemingly every eye in the place turned in his direction. There was nothing to do now but face the whispers and sly glances.

As he started forward, Lady Arden swept up to him, smiling. "Mr. Dunbridge! I was hoping you would attend my little party. It's been ages since I have seen you." Her last statement rose questioningly.

"Yes, I have been out of the country for some months now," Nathan replied with a polite bow.

The small woman looked up at him with sympathy. "I am so sorry. I fear Miss Winfield will regret her decision."

"*Mrs. Rutherford* is quite happy," he replied, putting an emphasis on Annabeth's new name. "And I am very happy for both of them. As you probably know, we all grew up together." No need to mention that being near Sloane while he was still engaged to Annabeth hadn't meant warming up to him.

"Well, I have just the thing to brighten your day." Lady Arden ignored Nathan's statement. "You must allow me to introduce you to Mrs. Billingham. Such a charming woman." Her eyes lit up with a matchmaking zeal that Nathan was all too familiar with. From the moment he left university, half the matrons in the *ton* had been trying to find him a wife.

He knew it was useless to attempt to escape a matchmaker, so he let her lead him across the floor toward a knot of people. The group, mostly men, were clustered around a woman with dark red hair. She was dressed in a black ball gown with a wide neckline that showed off her lovely white shoulders, and though her back was turned toward him, Nathan suspected that she was equally attractive from the front, given the looks on the men's faces.

"Mrs. Billingham." Lady Arden determinedly moved into the group, forcing a few of the men to step aside. "Please allow me to introduce you to—"

The woman turned, and Nathan saw her face. It was a fox-shaped face dominated by expressive golden-brown eyes. A familiar face, more intriguing than beautiful, and one he had expected never to see again. *What the devil was Verity Cole doing here?*

He stopped abruptly, jaw dropping. "Good Gad. Veri—" Nathan broke off and cleared his throat. "That is, um, *very* pleased to, um—"

"Oh," Lady Arden said in disappointment. "You already know each other."

"Yes. I, well," Nathan floundered. He could hardly deny recognizing Verity, given his reaction, but what was he to say? God only knew what sort of masquerade she was carrying on now. "Mrs.—ah—" *What had Lady Arden said Verity's "name" was at the present moment?*

Fortunately, Verity spoke up to save him. "Mr. Dunbridge and I are acquainted. Not well, of course—it was my dear Hubert who was his friend. They went to school together." Her eyes twinkled.

Naturally Verity would find it amusing to cast him unknowingly into her sea of lies.

*Well, I can play at that game, too.* "Yes, indeed. Splendid chap, Hubert. Where is he? I must chat with him." Nathan made a show of surveying the room.

Verity made a choked noise and whipped out a handkerchief, raising it to cover her mouth. To Nathan's amazement, tears welled in her eyes. "Oh, my poor Hubert."

The other men scowled at him, and Lady Arden told him quietly, "Mr. Billingham passed on a year ago."

"Oh. Beg your pardon, ma'am." It was a struggle to keep his face sober as Nathan met Verity's gaze above her handkerchief. He wondered if anyone else noticed the mischief in her gaze.

She dabbed artistically at the corners of her eyes. "Of course. How could you have known? Dear Hubert and I have been living in Russia for some years now."

"Russia?" *Where did she come up with these things?*

"Yes. You know how it was with poor Hubert."

"Mmm," Nathan said gravely. "Indeed." *Clearly, my school chum had been obsessed with tragic literature, ballet, or, perhaps, snow.* At least the party was not as dull as it usually was.

"I knew you would understand."

Nathan still wasn't certain what relation Hubert was supposed to be to her. Husband seemed likely, given the show of tears, but then one would cry over the death of a brother, too, wouldn't one? Although Verity apparently could cry over anything…or nothing at all.

He sketched a little bow to her. "Do say you will take a turn around the room with me, Mrs. Billingham, and tell me what misfortune claimed poor Hubert."

"Yes, that will be a great comfort to me," Verity replied, taking the arm he offered. "Gentlemen. If you will excuse us."

Nathan nodded to the others and started away, bending his head a little toward Verity in what he hoped looked like sympathy. "What the devil are you doing here? Pretending to be…whatever it is you're pretending to be."

"A widow," Verity supplied. "A wealthy widow, which is why you saw all the men hovering about like bees."

"I daresay that's not the only reason." He cast his gaze down at the neckline of her dress, which skimmed across the top of her full breasts. "That's scarcely what I'd call mourning."

She hid her laugh behind her widespread fan. "That's because poor dear Hubert died over a year ago."

"And your hair is red." *What a perfectly ridiculous thing to say. As if that had anything to do with anything*, Nathan admonished himself. It was just that she looked so different with her hair that rich dark auburn instead of the dull brown that he'd seen before.

"Yes, it is." Her voice brimmed with amusement.

"Is that the real color? Do you even know the real color?"

"Honestly, Nathan, you sound as if the color of my hair offends you."

"No. Of course not." He wasn't about to tell her how far from offended he was by the sight of her hair. "It's just…one never knows what's real with you and what is not."

"Well, my hair is red, and I cannot disguise the color of my eyes, so you see me as I am. Except for the jewels, of course." She touched the diamond studs in her ears. "They are as false as my name."

"Verity." Nathan sighed. "You are going to get yourself in trouble. What are you doing?"

"My job."

"Don't tell me you're spying again."

"Don't be daft. I have been hired to find some jewels."

"You're stealing?"

"You would jump to that thought first, wouldn't you? I don't know why you have such a terrible image of me."

"You don't know why!" His voice rose on the words, and two of the guests turned their heads toward him. He lowered his voice, though it lost none of its indignation. "You wormed your way into Lady Lockwood's house by pretending to be a maid—from Yorkshire, no less."

"I don't know what's so terrible about Yorkshire."

"It's not Yorkshire, it's you—with your costumes and accents and pretenses. You pulled all of us into a bizarre scheme to recover some document because, oh, yes, it turns out you're actually a spy."

"I *was* a spy," she corrected him. "Not anymore."

"No?" He remembered too clearly getting shipped off to Stonecliffe with Verity as part of a plot to keep Annabeth safe. "Then why did I endure a week of escorting you around the garden while you pretended to be Annabeth, all the while criticizing my acting?"

"Well, you must admit you weren't saying anything very lover-like."

"As if some chap up in a tree peering at us through opera glasses could tell what I was saying to you!"

"To be fair, I never claimed there were men in trees with opera glasses. That would be quite silly. A spyglass would be much more practical for the purposes."

Nathan hissed. "Which made the fact that you were pretending to be Annabeth even more unnecessary. Now you pop up in the midst of the *ton* as a 'widow from Russia.' And you wonder why I think you're up to something illegal?"

"I'm not *from* Russia. I never mastered that accent, and I can't speak a word of the language. I've been *living* in Russia the past few years with Hubert, which was rather foolish of him given, you know, his condition."

"No, I don't know," Nathan responded. "Who in Hades is Hubert? And what was his 'condition'? I ought to know, seeing as how I was such good friends with him."

"Hubert was my poor departed husband, who died of consumption."

"Consumption? He had consumption and he moved to Russia so he could live in all the ice and snow?"

"I never said Hubert was an intelligent man," Verity replied confidingly. "I married him for his looks. I have a weakness for handsome men, I'm afraid."

"You or Mrs. Billingham? You talk as if you actually *are* her."

"I need to maintain the role, it helps prevent slips. So if we're through with your questioning…" Verity raised her fan and sent him a laughing look over it.

*Those eyes…*

"Stop pretending to flirt with me," he snapped.

"Who says I'm pretending? Like Mrs. Billingham, I, too, appreciate a handsome man."

"Verity…"

"You're no fun at all." She sighed. "Very well. I chose Russia because it's so far away that I would be unlikely to run into anyone who had actually been there."

"I don't believe you. I think you made it all up on the spot just to drive me mad."

"While that did provide me some satisfaction, I did not make it up on the spur of the moment. I've been Mrs. Billingham for two weeks."

"Two weeks?" Nathan groaned. "This is getting worse by the moment."

"I don't know why you'd say that." Verity paused at an open doorway to let in a maid carrying a tray of glasses.

"Champagne, ma'am? Sir?" the girl asked.

"Why, yes," Verity said, taking two glasses and handing one to Nathan. Verity took a sip of her drink and glanced around in a seemingly casual way.

Nathan had seen that watchful look in her eyes before and was not fooled by it. "Verity, what are you—"

She gave him a bright smile and slipped out the door.

"Verity!" he hissed. "Wait. Come—oh, the devil." Nathan went through the doorway after her.

They were in a back hallway, its narrowness and lack of decoration indicating that it was for the servants' use only. Verity's champagne glass sat on a table, and she was already halfway down the hall.

"Verity!" Nathan raised his voice a little.

She turned around, her eyebrows going up in surprise, and held her forefinger to her lips in a silencing gesture. "Shh."

"We're out of earshot," he said.

"The walls have ears," she said lightly. "Meaning the servants. You people never consider that—and then you wonder why the servants have all the gossip immediately."

"You people," Nathan muttered. Verity had an unwavering dislike of the *ton*. But it was pointless to get into that. Instead he set aside his own glass and caught up with her as she continued on her way. "What are you doing? Someone is going to find you out."

"Well, yes, if you keep nattering on." She turned right at an intersecting hall, and they were back in the public area of the house, the corridor laid with carpet and containing portraits of various grim-looking people from an earlier time.

Only a few steps took them to the entry hall. On one side lay the ballroom, which they had just left, and opposite it was a corridor. There were a few people scattered around the entry. Suddenly Verity moved closer, her hand slipping into the crook of Nathan's elbow, and she gazed up at him, plying her fan flirtatiously. She was, he thought, a master at flirting. *No doubt it was all those years of living in France.*

Nathan felt his heartbeat speed up; it was damned difficult not to react as if that subtle, seductive quirk of her lips was real. Of course, *she* wasn't wrestling with distraction, she seemed firmly on task, propelling him down the hallway, then turning her head slightly to cast a cautious glance over her shoulder. Her fingers dug into Nathan's arm, and she ducked into the next room, pulling him with her.

"Verity…" he began in exasperation—more at himself for falling so easily into Verity's scheme.

She touched her fingers to his mouth, stopping his speech. She was wearing lace evening gloves, and the texture of the lace felt odd against his lips…and somehow tantalizing. He could feel the heat of her skin beneath the lace. The touch was gone in an instant, and she eased the door shut and started walking around the room, lifting the corners of paintings to look behind them.

"Why are we in Lord Arden's study?"

"Looking for a safe," she replied, as nonchalantly as if she'd said she was looking for a dropped fan. "The study seems the most likely place." She glanced at him. "If you'd help, we'd be done much faster you know."

"Blast it, Verity." Nathan joined her in searching. Irritating as it was to do as she said, Verity was right. The key thing was to get her out of here as soon as possible. He might be able to talk himself out of it if they were caught, but he actually *was* who he said he was and a well-known member of London Society, whereas Verity was anything but that. "Tell me why I'm risking jail, or at least my reputation."

"Lord Arden has a valuable brooch that belongs to my client." Verity turned away from her fruitless search of the walls and bent to pull up a corner of the rug to peer beneath it.

"Arden *stole* a piece of jewelry?" Nathan half turned to throw her a skeptical glance.

"No. Well, not exactly. My client gave it to him. It fastened at the top of her frock, and he apparently removed it in the course of, um…"

"Yes, I understand," Nathan said quickly, feeling his

cheeks heating. How was it that Verity always managed to make him feel like a green schoolboy? "So Arden pocketed the brooch?"

"Yes—a playful sort of thing, you understand. She was moved that he wanted a sign of her affection, so she gave it to him."

"And now the affair is over, and she wants it back." Nathan lifted the end of the rug closest to him to peek under it.

"She *needs* it back," Verity replied. She moved to the desk, opening and closing drawers and, when one would not open, she pulled something from her hair and inserted it in the lock, manipulating it until the drawer opened.

Nathan was impressed by her skill. Completely illegal, of course, but he couldn't keep from wondering if she might be willing to teach him how to do it.

As she carefully picked through the drawer, Verity went on, "The brooch is apparently part of a set of jewels that belong to her husband's family, and she is supposed to wear the entire set next week when she sits for a portrait."

"Seems like a foolish thing to give away, then."

Verity flashed him a quick grin. "Yes, doesn't it?" She shrugged. "But they say love makes people foolish."

Nathan made a noncommittal noise in response. He suspected Verity was shooting a barb at him for his long and unrewarding pursuit of Annabeth. There wasn't much he could say to that. It had been a mistake. But at least he'd finally realized it.

"Not, of course, that I would know anything about that," Verity went on. She closed the drawer and, hands on hips, cast an encompassing look around the room.

"Well. If there's a safe here, he's disguised it too well for me to find." Her eyes twinkled. "And there's little chance of that."

"Then we're finished. Good." Nathan smoothed down a rumpled corner of the rug with his foot and started toward the door.

"Yes." Verity joined Nathan as he cracked the door a fraction.

He listened for any sounds of people in the corridor outside and, hearing nothing, carefully opened the door. The hallway seemed empty for the moment, and he breathed a little sigh of relief and stepped out, Verity behind him.

Nathan started back toward the party, but Verity grabbed his hand and tugged at him, nodding her head in the other direction. "Take the back stairs. It's less noticeable."

"You're going up to the family's rooms?"

"Of course. The next most likely place for a safe is his bedroom."

"Verity, really..." But Nathan went with her. He told himself that he had to do what he could to keep her from getting into trouble, but the truth was he couldn't deny a tiny thrill of excitement as they sneaked up the servants' stairs.

The corridor on the floor above was empty, and Verity hurried through it, looking into the darkened rooms as she went. Suddenly, there was the sound of voices on the main stairs.

Verity grabbed Nathan's lapels and yanked him to her so hard that they stumbled back against the wall. "Seduce me."

## CHAPTER TWO

"What?" Nathan's eyebrows shot up.

"Sh!" Verity hissed. "*Pretend*, Nathan. As if you want me in your bed."

*Well, that wouldn't be difficult, pressed against her this way.* Nathan braced his forearm against the wall and half turned to shield her from the view of whoever was climbing the stairs. He lowered his head, bending toward her and setting his other hand on her waist. "Wonderful," he groused. "Now everyone will say I'm a lecher."

"More acceptable than everyone saying you're a thief."

Verity curled one hand around the back of his neck, and a frisson shot down his spine like a bolt of lightning. *Heaven help me, she smells good.* It wasn't the bold provocative fragrance he would have expected her to wear, but a light, elusive floral scent that was somehow even more stirring to his senses.

They were so close he could see each individual eyelash, the smooth texture of her skin, the curve of her lips. He had a mad urge to trace that curve with his finger. Her supple body was molded to him all the way down, and he had the embarrassed certainty that Verity could feel his body move in response to her. There was a little glimmer in her eyes that he knew was amusement.

To avoid her gaze, Nathan pressed his cheek to the

side of her head. Her hair was soft, a few fine stray hairs tickling his nose. He slid his head down and found that her cheek was as soft and smooth as it looked. He stopped short of her shoulder so that he would appear to be nuzzling her neck. He resisted the temptation to actually press his lips to her skin.

The voices had been growing louder, but now they stopped abruptly. There was the distinct sound of a snicker and someone cleared his throat, followed by a low murmur of voices.

"Are they coming this way?" Nathan whispered.

"Hmm? Oh." Verity shifted so that she could see around his arm. "They're just standing there grinning."

He let out a little huff of exasperation. "How long are we going to have to keep this up?"

"I know it must be a trial to be this close to me," she told him tartly. "Perhaps I should end the scene by slapping you for making improper advances."

"I'd rather you not." Nathan managed not to add that the only trial was not acting on his impulses. Continuing the pretense but removing himself somewhat from danger, he straightened and cupped her face in his hands, gazing down at her. Her eyes were fascinating, somewhere between amber and whiskey and always alight, whether it was with amusement or anger or curiosity.

"Or maybe we should slip off the other direction and go into a bedroom," Verity suggested.

"Verity..." Nathan sighed. "They may have recognized you. Your reputation would be in tatters."

"No. *Mrs. Billingham*'s reputation would be in tatters." Her eyes sparkled. "Ah. There they go." An instant later, she added, "We're safe."

Nathan relaxed, realizing only now how taut his entire body had been. He moved away, tugging at his lapels as if he could pull himself back in order as long as his clothes were straight. "I'd hardly say we're safe."

"Of course you wouldn't." Verity seemed—as usual—irritated with him. She started away. "You needn't stay, you know."

"Ah, but then who would you have to play your wicked seducer?"

Verity made a show of rolling her eyes, but the corner of her mouth deepened into a dimple. And her dimple was lethal. She set off down the hall and Nathan fell into step beside her. "I suppose I must keep you in that case." She continued looking into rooms, then stopped at a doorway and peered more closely. "I think this is it."

"You must have the eyes of a cat if you can see anything in that darkness."

"Didn't you know? That's what I am." Verity cast him one of her sly sideways glances. Nathan had to admit that she did look a bit like a cat, golden-eyed and complacently mysterious, as if she knew things you could never possibly guess, but she would tolerate you anyway. She certainly moved as silently as a cat. He suspected her claws were equally sharp.

She picked up a candlestick from the hall table and led him into the room. It was a spacious chamber with a massive bed of black walnut, obviously inhabited by a man. Verity began the same sort of search she had downstairs, though here she added opening drawers and going through their contents, careful not to disturb them.

This time Nathan joined her without having to be asked, looking behind pictures and under the thick rug.

He was not expert enough to riffle through the drawers without leaving any trace of a search, but he opened the doors of the large armoire to peer inside. One side was lined with widely spaced shelves holding hat boxes. In the other half, shirts hung from pegs.

There was something odd about the cabinet. Nathan frowned, studying it for a moment. Then it struck him that the floor of the side where clothes were hung was several inches higher than the floor of the shelved half. His mind went to the secret drawers and puzzle boxes where Annabeth's father had hidden things.

Nathan went down on one knee and ran his hand across the floor of the armoire. There was a joinder line near the back of the floor. Farther back, in the corner, he found a slight depression, and he pressed against it. Nothing happened. He tried pushing it to the side, and there was a faint click, and the front portion of the raised floor tilted up slightly.

Sliding his fingers under it, he pulled and the section opened easily. Beneath the floor lay a metal box. "Verity."

"What?" She must have heard the tone of barely repressed excitement in his voice, for she was at his side immediately. "Oooh. Clever lad."

Nathan was annoyed by the gratification he felt at her approval. He lifted the box from its hiding place. It was locked, but Verity made short work of the lock and opened the lid. Inside was a jumble of objects—folded pieces of paper, a monogrammed handkerchief, a pair of spectacles, and several bits of jewelry. Verity pounced on an emerald brooch, but Nathan was more intrigued by a silver disc, engraved with something that resembled a family crest, but which, on closer inspection, proved to be a graphic phallic symbol emerging from flames. Nathan hastily closed his fist over the token, his cheeks reddening, and cast a sideways glance at Verity.

She was watching him, a frown starting to form between her brows. "What's that? What are you hiding?"

Nathan sighed. Of course she had seen it. Indeed, it was probably his attempt to conceal it that had drawn her attention. "It's, um, well a sort of coin. A kind of badge, as it were. A token…though it's usually called a key because it gains one entrance."

"Entrance to what? Nathan, you're babbling," Verity said crisply. "And you're blushing. What is it?" She reached over, trying to pry his fingers apart, and, with another sigh, Nathan opened his fist. Verity plucked it from his hand and looked at it. The other side of the coin was facing upward. "Lord Arden's initials—did you notice that the monogram on the handkerchief was not his? But wha—"

She turned over the disc and sucked in a small breath, her eyebrows vaulting up. Her reaction gave Nathan some satisfaction. He wouldn't have been surprised if she had said, "Oh, that," and tossed it back. And, though the light was dim, he was almost sure that was a hint of red staining her cheeks.

"The Devil's Den. It's, um, a certain sort of club where men and women engage in certain—" Nathan began. Good Lord, how was he supposed to explain this to a lady—even one as lacking in delicacy as Verity?

"You mean it's like the old Hellfire Club? The Marquis de Sade? That sort of thing?"

*Well, apparently not so difficult to explain, after all.*

"And you know this place?" Verity stared at him. It was the first time he had ever seen shock on her face.

"No! I mean, not personally. I've never been there. I wouldn't—it isn't the sort of thing that I—I've simply heard of it. I wasn't even sure if it actually existed."

"Rumors around your gentlemen's club, then." No one could put as much scorn into the word "gentlemen" as Verity.

"Well…yes."

Verity frowned, rolling the coin back and forth between her fingers in a way he'd seen street entertainers do. "Are they willing? The women, I mean."

"Yes, of course. At least, I've never heard anyone say otherwise. Like-minded women. Or, um, women who are, uh…"

"Prostitutes?"

Nathan simply nodded.

"Just because a woman is paid for her services, it doesn't mean she wants to be hit for some man's pleasure." Verity's tone was bitter and she continued to hold the token, looking at it but not, Nathan thought, actually seeing it.

Nathan had never seen this expression on Verity's face before, either. He wasn't sure what it was—anger? Sorrow? Regret? Whatever it was, it was a deeper emotion than she usually showed. Obviously the conversation had touched a nerve somewhere, and he realized suddenly how very little he knew about this woman, even though they'd spent a fortnight or more around each other.

"Verity," he said softly, reaching out toward her.

Verity quickly swiped a hand under her eyes, then stood and tossed the token back in the box. "We have the brooch. It's time to go."

Obviously, whatever emotion had touched her, Verity wanted no sympathy for. Or, at least, none from him.

Nathan closed and relocked the box and returned it to its hiding place, sliding the wooden covering back where it was before. Just as he stood up, footsteps rang in the hallway. *Good Lord. Did no one stay in the ballroom at this party?* Though he couldn't exactly blame them—he himself had been thinking how very boring it was until Verity showed up and turned it into a whirlwind of intrigue.

Verity gestured at him and jumped into the wardrobe. Nathan followed, closing the door behind them.

"I have it here somewhere," a man said, entering the chamber. An indistinct murmur followed in reply. There was the sound of the man—Lord Arden, presumably—rattling around, opening and closing drawers.

It was cramped, hot and dark in the wardrobe. Nathan imagined Lord Arden opening the door and finding them hiding in the furniture. *What could he possibly say to explain that away?*

Nathan turned his head to look at Verity. The thin line of light between the doors fell across her face, lighting the dried track of a tear on her cheek. Sympathy stirred in him again, and he took her hand in his. This time she didn't pull away, but closed her fingers around his.

Arden apparently found the object of his search, for the other man laughed and thanked him, but the two men lingered, chatting about some bet. Finally they left the room, but Verity and Nathan remained where they were until the sound of the steps faded away entirely.

Then Verity eased open the door and they surveyed the room before leaving the wardrobe. They paused once more at the doorway, listening for a long moment before slipping out into the corridor. The hall was blessedly vacant, and they walked quickly toward the servants' staircase. It wasn't until they started down the narrow steps single file and Verity dropped his hand that Nathan realized that they had continued to hold hands ever since they left the armoire.

The staircase eventually opened up into a hallway and Verity stopped so abruptly at it that Nathan, lost in his own thoughts about what exactly the handholding had meant, almost ran into her. A large man, presumably a guard hired specifically for the party, had spotted them. There was no time for a thrown-together pretense. In the seconds it took for the man to turn his head as if to call to someone, Verity launched herself at him. Her raised knee caught him square in the solar plexus. Air whooshed out of the guard's lungs. He fell to his knees, and swiped at Verity's leg on his way down, but she easily sidestepped his clutches. In one smooth movement she slid behind his torso and locked her elbow around his neck, using her other hand to pull her binding arm tighter until the man's eyes got hazy.

"What are you doing?" Nathan hissed.

"Just knocking him out," Verity said, letting up pressure the second the guard's lids fluttered closed. His limp form slid down to the floor as she moved to listen at a doorway nearby. Seemingly satisfied by what she did, or didn't, hear, she peered inside.

"Here. Drag him into this closet." She waved Nathan over. "It'll give us enough time to escape before anyone knows something is amiss."

Nathan looked at the large man's form and back at Verity. Had it really only been an hour that she'd been back in his life? He'd already committed more sins than he cared to count. At this point what was one more?

"Fine." Nathan hooked his elbows under the arms of the guard and started dragging him over to the door. "How exactly do you propose we keep him in?" he asked after the guard's large frame had been folded away into the rather small space. "It's not as if we have the means to lock this door."

"We just need something to wedge it closed." Verity tapped her finger against her bottom lip in thought. Suddenly her golden eyes lit with a gleam and she pulled out her fan, jamming it under the door until the folds of the handle forced it to a stop.

"That's not going to hold him for long."

"We're not trying to trap him forever. Besides it'll likely take him a minute before he has his wits about him enough to realize he just needs to push the fan out to be able to open the door."

Verity looked over Nathan with a critical eye. "Now straighten your cravat before we enter the ballroom. You look as if you've been ravishing someone or committing a crime of some sort."

Nathan opened his mouth to tell her that, thanks to her, he had done something akin to both those things tonight. But before he could get the words out, there was a stirring in the closet. Verity gave him a pointed look and headed off to the ballroom.

THE POLITE CONVERSATION and blandness of the party was even more noticeable to Nathan after all they had done this evening. It seemed almost farcical how Verity tucked her hand into his arm, and they walked around the dancers, with her chattering about utter nonsense and nodding to this person and that. *Surely she didn't know all these people.*

Then Verity turned to him and smiled in that way of hers that left Nathan wondering whether she was pleased or merely laughing at him. "I'm leaving."

He felt oddly deflated. Just the aftermath of all the tension, he supposed. "I'll escort you."

She nodded. "That will make it more noticeable that we've been here all the time."

"Glad I could be of service," he replied drily.

Every man to whom Verity gave her bright smile as they passed beamed back, a little envy in their eyes as they glanced at Nathan. He couldn't help feeling a bit of satisfaction at the envious glances—and even more pleased, somehow, that he knew Verity was thinking nothing of the men, except for how their eyes lent her an alibi. Once outside the ballroom, she dropped her hand from his arm and quickened her pace. She went to the cloak room to retrieve a filmy evening wrap that was completely useless to ward off any evening chill, but had the effect of drawing one's eye even more to the décolletage of her gown.

She glanced at Nathan in surprise as he accompanied her past the footman and out the front door. "You're not going back in to your friends?"

None of the people inside were really friends, just people one saw at parties. But all he said was, "I'll walk you home."

Her smile this time was softer, more real—or perhaps that was just because it was too dark to see well. "That's kind of you," she said as a town carriage pulled up in front of the house. "But I have my carriage."

And before he could speak she was down the steps and climbing up into the carriage. She looked back at him through the window and gave a small wave as the vehicle took off. Nathan stood for a moment, watching it disappear.

Everything seemed deadly dull again. There was clearly nothing else that could compare to the excitement of an evening with Verity. Nathan had no interest in going back inside. He might as well go home. He wondered if Verity meant to continue her role as Mrs. Billingham. Would she go to other parties? For a moment, he thought about remaining in London for a while instead of going back to the manor.

But, no, Lady Drewsbury and Noelle were having a party at Stonecliffe for Lady Lockwood's birthday in two days. He had to be there for that. And there was no real reason to stay here.

Nathan turned and walked away.

# CHAPTER THREE

VERITY SETTLED BACK against the cushions of her carriage. It was a small town coach, seating only two, and quite ordinary on the outside, but inside it was plush, with thick cushions covered in darkest red Moroccan leather. Verity had learned that in her line of work, it didn't do to stand out. But she could enjoy comfort and beauty where it wasn't obvious—and she had frankly delighted in her disguise as Mrs. Billingham, wearing the vibrant frocks she usually had to eschew.

She smiled to herself. Mrs. Billingham was enjoyable, but never so much so as tonight. She hadn't seen Nathan Dunbridge in at least seven or eight months. Annabeth had said once that he was visiting someone in Italy. *Nursing a broken heart over Annabeth was more like it.*

Verity hoped he was over that now; he deserved something better than unrequited love. Verity had forgotten how handsome Nathan was—slender and tall, with that tousled, wavy brown hair and those hazel eyes. Or were they green? Verity had always had trouble telling which they were. They seemed to change with his mood.

Nathan was remarkably fun to tease, and now that he was no longer mooning about after Annabeth, he wasn't so annoying. Granted, he was an aristocrat and therefore not someone Verity could fully trust, but still…he was terribly easy to like.

He'd even proved to be handy for providing an excuse for her presence upstairs. It was unexpectedly unnerving to pretend a seduction with Nathan. He'd been warm and enveloping, the scent of him enticing, and really, he had a very kissable mouth. When he had whispered to Verity, his lips hovering only inches from her neck, it had sent a thrill through her. She could only hope he didn't notice.

She had thought he might actually kiss her, but Nathan was too much the gentleman to take advantage. It was somewhat concerning that she wasn't sure whether she was pleased or disappointed by that fact. For that reason Verity hadn't suggested she give him a ride home—she wasn't about to make the mistake of getting caught up in her own charade of seduction.

It had been too happy an evening to risk that. Nathan had broken the dullness of the ball, and there had been the thrill of the hunt, the gratification of discovering the brooch. There had been that one moment when her mask slipped as she'd looked at the club insignia coin, but it had been very brief, not enough to spoil things. And surprisingly Nathan's hand on hers had been soothing.

It didn't take long to reach her home, a narrow terraced house, attractive but indistinguishable from the others in the row. It was a lucky break that it was in a fashionable enough area for Mrs. Billingham, but Verity had bought it solely for her own enjoyment. Like her carriage, the inside was of higher quality than the outer shell, tastefully though somewhat sparsely furnished—too much clutter simply got in the way in an emergency. And Verity always allowed for emergencies.

The house was silent and empty. No servants lived here; even Mrs. Masters, her housekeeper, arrived in the morning and left at night. There was only one maid, Mrs. Masters's daughter. Verity had no need for a personal maid—she rarely bought anything that did not fasten in the front, and the fewer eyes in the house the better. And it was one less person she had to protect.

Verity had no expectation of danger, really; it had been several months now since anyone had tried to kill her. But old habits lingered. She'd stayed alive throughout the war by exercising caution, and she saw little reason to stop. For the same reason she followed her nightly routine, picking up the small lamp she'd left burning low and walking through the house to check all doors and windows and places where someone might lurk unseen.

Upstairs in her room, she took down her hair and undressed, changing into a silky soft nightgown. Her outer clothes were normally plain and practical, but like her undergarments, her nightclothes were of the finest quality and designed for beauty. It was another one of her secret treasures.

She took the brooch she had removed from Arden's house and slipped it into a shallow drawer of her dresser, locking it afterward. Her lips curved up as she thought again of the evening. And Nathan. If she continued her charade a bit longer, she might run into him at another party. Mrs. Billingham was a handy disguise to use for her clients. Of course, it wouldn't do to keep it up *too* long. Mrs. Billingham would have to disappear—go off to Bath or Brighton or, better yet, the Continent. But another few days shouldn't hurt.

Not, of course, that she would do that in order to run

into Nathan again. She was still looking for another client's stolen silverware—Verity was growing more and more sure that it was the woman's granddaughter who had taken it, but in that sort of situation one had to be absolutely sure.

But having a chance to tease Nathan and perhaps manage a dance with him certainly added to the appeal. She had realized tonight how nice it was to have someone for whom she didn't have to put up an act.

VERITY'S CHEERFUL MOOD continued the next morning as she went to work. Last night had been a success, made all the more enjoyable by the opportunity to banter with Nathan. Verity was always buoyed by giving a client a positive report, and she especially looked forward to returning Lady Bankwater's brooch to her. Verity liked Lady Bankwater, and the woman had been most agitated about her missing jewelry. Besides, Verity had taken a strong dislike to Lord Arden, and sneaking something away from him right under his nose added an extra fillip.

As was her usual practice, Verity disembarked from her carriage a street or two away from her detective agency and walked the rest of the way. Another old habit, she supposed; it was easier on foot to spot anyone following her or watching her from a building.

A discreet brass plaque beside the front door of her building read Cole & Son. There was, of course, neither a father nor a son, but clients found the notion of there being a man in charge—especially an older man—reassuring.

The door opened only to a straight flight of stairs into an entry area containing a sofa and chairs. Blocking any entrance into the hallway was a high counter, where a woman sat, knitting. Mrs. Malloy knitted every moment she wasn't busy with company papers and books. Verity wasn't sure who the beneficiaries were of her office manager's products.

"Hello, luv." Mrs. Malloy beamed at her. Mrs. Malloy was a customarily jolly soul. She had a ready smile and her eyes twinkled behind a set of spectacles, the lines beside her mouth and eyes indicating that her frequent smiles were nothing new. A white cap trimmed with lace sat atop her salt-and-pepper hair, completing the picture of a plump and pleasant grandmother.

No one would have suspected that beneath that graying head lay one of the sharpest financial minds in the country. Verity's business had been starting to thrive three years ago when boredom had driven Mrs. Malloy to apply for a job, but it was Mrs. Malloy's expertise at investments that had made Verity's money mushroom into its current very healthy state.

"You're looking quite sharp this morning," Mrs. Malloy went on.

Normally the dress Verity wore to work was a plain brown frock with a decorous lace fichu at the neckline, and her hair was covered by either a dull brown wig or a white cap of the sort Mrs. Malloy was wearing. She made it a point to look as serious and professional as possible when she was at her office.

Today, however, Verity intended to call on Lady Bankwater in her role as Mrs. Billingham, so that required a fashionable afternoon dress and hat, along with green half boots and matching gloves and pelisse—Mrs. Billingham favored a bold style.

"I'm feeling quite sharp," Verity replied and related

last evening's successful recovery, and they continued to chat for a few minutes before Verity went into her office. The first order of business was to send a note to Lady Bankwater requesting to call on her this morning. It was inappropriately early for a social call, which would mean that Lady Bankwater should be both free of visitors and still at home.

Verity had only enough time to read a report from an employee guarding one of their clients before the messenger lad returned with Lady Bankwater's acceptance, as well as the woman's carriage. It was a kind gesture but also indicative of Lady Bankwater's eagerness to get her hands on the brooch.

Lady Bankwater was in a cozy sitting room when Verity was shown in, not the large and formal drawing room. Her face was taut, and she jumped to her feet, coming forward to take both Verity's hands.

"Dear girl, do come and sit down." Her eyes flickered to Verity's reticule, but she was too trained in courtesy to ask for the jewelry outright. Social niceties must be observed first. "I'll ring for tea."

They kept up a light chat until the tea cart was rolled in, and Lady Bankwater closed the door behind the butler. Verity reached beneath the neckline of her dress and pulled out a rolled-up handkerchief. Unfolding it, she revealed the emerald brooch, holding it out in the palm of her hand.

Lady Bankwater pulled in a sharp breath. "You have it!" She reached out, almost snatching it from Verity's hand. "I'm sorry, I know you said you had it, but I didn't dare believe it. I was afraid you'd found some other brooch."

"No. I recognized it immediately. You described it perfectly."

The other woman folded her hand around the brooch. Tears filled her eyes. "You don't know how much it means to me. How afraid I was that I would never get it back."

"I know it's very important to you." Verity didn't understand exactly why. It was an expensive item and no doubt her husband would be upset about a piece of family jewelry disappearing, but it seemed that Lady Bankwater could have simply said she'd lost it. Her anxiety made Verity wonder just how far Lord Bankwater's displeasure would take him. "No doubt Lord Bankwater would be most upset. Some men can be quite violent about such things."

Lady Bankwater looked at her blankly. "What? You thought Bankwater would…would hit me? No, no, you mustn't think that. My husband may not be exciting or sentimental and he is more interested in researching odd animals—kangaroos and such—than in spending time with me, but he is the kindest of men. He would have regretted its absence, but he would not have even taken me to task for it."

"I see." Verity, in fact, did not. Why had Lady Bankwater been so anxious, almost fearful? But she could scarcely press her client for details.

Lady Bankwater's expression of alarm turned to one of guilt. She sighed, her shoulders slumping. "I'm sorry. I fear I haven't been quite honest with you." She looked down at the brooch, rubbing her thumb over the settings, then raised her head and gazed straight at Verity, her jaw setting. "I didn't need it because of the portrait. The truth is Arden was blackmailing me."

"Ah." Now Verity did fully understand. "He threatened to show the brooch to your husband. To tell him about your affair."

"Yes." Her eyes welled over, silent tears running down her cheeks. "My Jasper is so good, so honest—our match was not based on love, but it has grown to be a warm union despite our different dispositions. I could not bear to have him hurt like that. To look at me with such disappointment. I'm sorry." Lady Bankwater pulled out a handkerchief to wipe away her tears.

"It's all right. It would have made no difference to me. I would have retrieved it anyway." *Though it would have been nice to know that the man who might catch her was a villain.* "You're not the first client who has been embarrassed to reveal the truth."

"That's very good of you. I feel like such a wretch. I care for my husband, I really do. But Jasper is not a passionate man even when he is here. He was gone so long on that trip to Australia, and I was so lonely. And Lord Arden was so attentive, so…thrilling." She shook her head. "I was horridly foolish. I realized it almost right away. I saw that I was risking all my future happiness for such fleeting pleasure." Lady Bankwater's cheeks colored, and she looked down again, picking at the embroidery on her handkerchief. "I ended it. And when Jasper returned, everything was right again, and I thought it was all over, but…"

"Lord Arden started blackmailing you," Verity supplied.

Lady Bankwater nodded. "It isn't only the money—though I can't imagine how I could have kept on paying him without Jasper noticing. But Arden took such pleasure in it. He loved being in control. Humiliating me. He insisted that I give him the money in person. I think he wanted to see how much he was upsetting me." She looked up sharply at Verity. "He's wicked. Frankly, he frightens me. He doesn't know that you are the one who took this, does he? I would hate to think that I put you in any danger."

"Don't worry." Verity smiled reassuringly. "He doesn't know. And I can handle a dangerous man."

"I wish I never had to see him again," Lady Bankwater said. "But he'll probably be at Mrs. Dedham's gala tonight. And I must attend it, she's Jasper's cousin." She sighed. "Besides, I'll have to face him sometime."

Verity left soon thereafter. There was still time to go to the park. It was bittersweet, that moment of mingled love and pain; she tried not to indulge in it too often. But she felt too good today to dampen her mood. Instead she returned to her office.

She thought about Lady Bankwater's words during the afternoon. Verity now saw Lord Arden as he was—a blackmailer. One who took pleasure in his victim's pain.

Verity wondered about the other things she and Nathan had seen in that hidden box. Perhaps they were all things Arden used to coerce money out of people. She wished she'd read the notes at the bottom of the box. Who else might he be targeting?

It wouldn't hurt to go to the gala Lady Bankwater had mentioned and see whom Arden talked to and how they responded. Besides, Lady Bankwater would be there and she might be glad of some protection from him.

The gala would be large. Perhaps Verity would see Nathan again. The thought made her smile a little. Not that she was going because Nathan might be there. She would be there because she liked Lady Bankwater—and despised men like Lord Arden.

Verity thought of what she might wear tonight. Since Mrs. Billingham had been in mourning for a year, she could wear her new peacock-blue dress. And perhaps a different hairstyle. It rankled that Nathan had first known her in her dowdiest state, in costume as a mousy lady's maid. Though, she had to admit, imagining his expression as he took in her new frock was further inducement. Verity wanted to look her best around Nathan, and the idea that she even cared what he thought stunned her.

MRS. BILLINGHAM HAD not received an invitation to the gala, but it was easy to get in, as she had thought it would be. There was a crush of guests and no checking of invitations. There wasn't even a need to find someone to chat with and slip in as one of her party, as she had done when she first set out as Mrs. Billingham.

Casually Verity strolled about, unobtrusively searching the area. It was second nature to note the doors and avenues of escape, even as she smiled and nodded at some admirers—but she was more interested in finding her quarry. She soon spotted Lady Bankwater chatting with several people, one of whom was clearly her husband. He was a short, balding and bespectacled man—no one could ever have mistaken him for handsome—but the way he beamed at his wife when she laughed made Verity extremely glad she had been able to help Lady Bankwater. *A poor decision made in the heat of the moment should not cast a pall on one for the rest of one's days.* A little while later, Verity caught sight of Lord Arden. His eyes were also fixed on Lady

Bankwater, though there was none of the same warmth the woman's husband had in Arden's expression.

After more than an hour there had still been no sign of Nathan Dunbridge. It seemed unlikely he was attending after all. Verity sighed, the evening suddenly feeling flat. Her beautiful blue dress now felt uncomfortable and she wished she could go home and change into her night clothes. However, she had come here to make sure Lady Bankwater was safe, and while Verity had been gazing into the distance wondering about Nathan, Arden had cornered his prey. They were talking furtively, somewhat hidden by a potted plant. Lady Bankwater's face was pale, and she clutched her fan as if it were a lifeline.

Verity started in their direction, but before she could reach them, Lady Bankwater abruptly left. Arden turned. His gaze stopped at Verity. His eyes were flat, his face expressionless. Verity wondered what Lady Bankwater had said to him. Did he suspect Verity?

She felt a little rush of excitement. Verity hoped he would come after her; it would be a pleasure to put his arrogant arse on the pavement. He approached but kept his eyes averted. Verity was unsure if he was actually seeking her out or if she was merely in his path.

But as he passed by, he uttered in a harsh tone, "I'm not someone to be trifled with."

He strode away before she could respond. Verity picked up her skirts to follow him.

"Oh, Mrs. Billingham," a voice trilled behind her, and Verity turned, smiling a greeting.

The woman began to chat away as Verity wracked her brain to remember the woman's name. Verity was good with names usually and she'd met the woman only last night at Lady Arden's ball, but that had been right before Nathan was "introduced" to her, and the surprise had driven the woman's name right out of her head.

"You must come call on me one day," the woman was saying now.

"How very kind of you." *Cathcart, that was the name.* Verity's gaze went past the woman's shoulder. A tall man with cropped dark hair stood in the doorway, surveying the crowd with disdain.

Verity froze, unable to speak or even to think. It was *him.*

"Dear? Are you all right? You have gone quite pale," Mrs. Cathcart said anxiously.

*No, it couldn't be him. He was dead.*

Mrs. Cathcart turned to see what had so riveted Verity. "Ah, I see. Jonathan Stanhope. He's a very eligible young man. However, he lives at his country estate mostly. Well, ever since that tragedy with his father."

*Of course it wasn't him. It was his son. It was just that he looked so much like his father now—that coldly handsome face, that haughty stance.*

"Do you know him?"

"No," Verity managed to get out. She was acting like a terrified little girl. She had to pull herself together. "I just—suddenly I felt a trifle faint." She whipped open her fan and began to ply it. "I should sit down a moment."

Mrs. Cathcart took her arm, guiding her over to the nearest seat. She bent over Verity solicitously, suggesting smelling salts and a glass of wine. Verity just wanted the woman to leave her alone. But at least her incessant hovering blocked Verity from Stanhope's view.

She stole a look around Mrs. Cathcart's skirts. He

was no longer by the door. *Where was he now?* Verity knew she had to get out of there. The only question was in which direction.

Verity took the other woman's hand and smiled at her. "You are so kind. But I am keeping you from the party. It's best if I just go home now."

After she managed to get rid of Mrs. Cathcart, she took an encompassing look around the room. Fortunately Stanhope was tall enough that she could see his head above most of the others. His back was to her, so she hurried out the door farthest from him. She didn't bother to retrieve her light evening wrap, but went down the stairs as quickly as she could without looking as if she was fleeing.

It wasn't until she was in her carriage that she felt safe. She took a steadying breath and leaned back, willing away her nerves. That initial bolt of fear had been natural and, of course, she'd remained shaken even after she'd realized her first impression was a mistake. But she wasn't the girl she'd been all those years ago. She wasn't about to run scared. Why, just a few minutes earlier she had been anticipating a confrontation with Arden with relish. She must regard the situation calmly, rationally, as she usually did.

She wondered if Stanhope had seen her. For a moment Verity would have been as visible to him as he had been to her. But even if he had noticed her, he might not have recognized her. Supposing Stanhope had though, she still didn't know what he would do. *Was he like his father? Would he come seeking revenge? No, of course he would not.* She was being foolish. He thought she was dead.

*They all think I'm dead.*

# CHAPTER FOUR

Not for the first time this weekend, Nathan wished that he had stayed in London. It wasn't so much that he kept thinking about Verity Cole, although he did, or that he dreaded enduring Lady Lockwood's acid tongue—he'd been astonished to find that he had actually missed the old dictator at times in the past few months he'd been away. Nor, even, was he unhappy at the thought of seeing Annabeth and Sloane together.

What *was* driving Nathan mad was his mother's conviction that seeing Annabeth with Sloane would cause him anguish. For two days she had been alternately assuring him that she knew he would handle the situation like the gentleman he was, then asking him if he didn't want to stay home so he wouldn't have to see his former love.

"I do hope everything goes smoothly," his mother was saying now as their carriage lumbered toward Stonecliffe.

Aunt Jocelyn let out an inelegant snort. "If Lady Lockwood is there, I can guarantee that things will *not* be smooth."

"Oh, Jocelyn." Rose Dunbridge patted the other woman's hand. "How you love to tease. You love Lady Lockwood, as we all do."

That was an egregious whopper. Jocelyn was almost

as sharp-tongued as Lady Lockwood herself, and there had been several instances where a verbal battle between the two had lasted for hours as neither woman would concede her position. But Nathan didn't point out the error in his mother's memory. She somehow managed to actually believe whatever cheerful comments she made.

"It is too bad, though, that Annabeth will be there," Rose went on, dogged in pursuit of her theory. "I know how painful that will be for you, Nathan."

"Mother, I promise you. I am no longer in love with Annabeth. I saw her when I first returned from Italy, and it wasn't painful in the least."

Nathan had realized that he was no longer in love with Annabeth while he was still abroad. It was odd how pressing the ache for her had been for years, yet when Nathan had first ceased to feel it, he hadn't even noticed that the pain was gone. In fact, thoughts of Annabeth had been absent for quite some time before he'd become aware that she only sprang to mind now and then as memories of an old friend.

Despite all that, some part of Nathan had dreaded their first reunion. He had feared that he'd just tricked himself into believing he was no longer in love with her and that when he was confronted with her again, happy and in love with her new husband, his old feelings would come rushing back. Or that the situation would be so awkward that they'd never be comfortable around each other again.

Surprisingly, after an initial hesitancy in their greeting, seeing her had turned out not to be difficult at all. She was just Annabeth, and he was just Nathan, friends since he was six. Nothing had stirred in him but the pleasure of seeing an old friend, and they had chatted together easily.

"Yes, I know you felt that way *then*, but she wasn't in a 'delicate condition' at that time," Rose Dunbridge said. "It's altogether different now."

Nathan wasn't sure what Annabeth's pregnancy had to do with what he felt for her, but he was too wise to follow that subject.

His mother went on, "She and Sloane should have stayed in Dorset or wherever it is."

"Cornwall, Mother. And Annabeth is Lady Lockwood's granddaughter. Of course she would come."

Jocelyn laughed. "Adeline is Lady Lockwood's daughter, and *she'd* move to Northumberland if she thought it would keep Lady Lockwood away."

"Oh, Jossy…" This was one of Rose's frequent refrains.

Aunt Jocelyn and his mother were as different as could be, Rose being as sweet and flighty as Jocelyn was sharp and practical, but they had been the best of friends since their first Season. Jocelyn was Nathan's aunt on his father's side, and it had been through Jocelyn that Nathan's father, George, had met Rose. Jocelyn had been a frequent visitor to their house all of Nathan's life. She had never married, and after George died of jaundice several years ago, Rose had moved in with her sister-in-law. It had been a pleasant situation for all concerned…until Jocelyn had sold her home in Bath, and the two women both moved into the manor. Luckily, Nathan liked his flat in London.

"It will all turn out well, though, dear." Rose patted her son's arm. "I'm sure of it. You'll meet another splendid young woman who loves you."

"Preferably one with money," Jocelyn inserted.

And here was his aunt's favorite topic.

"Oh, Jocelyn, that doesn't matter," Rose protested. "What's important is love. Why, look at George and me. We were so very happy."

"Be that as it may, it doesn't alter the fact that there's woodworm in the railing and you've had to close off the east wing entirely."

"I realize that, Aunt Jocelyn," Nathan said, doing his best not to snap at her. "We'll find some way to deal with it." Though he had no idea what that might be. The estate was mortgaged to the hilt, and even if they sold it, it would do little more than pay off their loans and they would be left with no income from the farms. He couldn't help but wish that a few of his ancestors had, at least every now and then, had some sort of financial sense.

"Oh, let's not talk about such gloomy things now," Rose said as they reached Stonecliffe. "This is a day for celebration."

Escaping the carriage seemed cause enough for celebration to Nathan.

Everyone was gathered in the larger assembly room, for Lady Lockwood's entire family was there, even down to her dead son Sterling's daughters, who contributed little other than to giggle and keep Petunia running in excited circles—*as if Lady Lockwood's demon dog needed anything to stir him up.*

It didn't surprise Nathan that the pug was the first to see him. It was typical of his luck. The little dog launched into her peculiar barking and made a beeline for Nathan's shoes.

"Hah, outsmarted you," Nathan told the dog. "Wore

my oldest pair." Petunia sent him an aggrieved look, but carried on her attack with only slightly less enthusiasm than she would have no doubt shown for a more expensive target.

Everyone turned to see them, and Adeline rushed forward, hands outstretched. "Nathan. Dear boy. It's a delight to see you again." She turned to Rose. "And you must be exceedingly happy to have him home."

Adeline chatted with the three of them until there was an imperious thump of a cane across the room. "Don't just stand there talking, Adeline. Let them in."

Adeline quickly stepped aside and everyone else parted like the Red Sea before Moses, forming an aisle straight to an ornate chair where Lady Lockwood sat. Nathan started forward, dragging Petunia, who remained firmly latched onto his shoe, along with him.

"For goodness' sake, Annabeth, come get that dog," Lady Lockwood ordered.

Annabeth hurried forward, but Nathan hastily grabbed up Petunia before she could bend down to pick up the pug. She smiled as Nathan passed the animal off to her. "Sorry."

Nathan stared at her. His mother had said she was pregnant, but he had not expected her to be so well along. When he'd first seen her after he got home only three months ago, she hadn't been showing at all. Still, even if hadn't seen her swelling stomach, he would have known the truth by her face. Her skin shone, her eyes were alight, and her joy was palpable. Any lingering worry Nathan had that she might be unhappy with Sloane was thoroughly resolved. Everything was just as it should be, however painful the road to get there had been.

"Take your time, Dunbridge," Lady Lockwood said in a tone that was in direct opposition to her words. "It was a shock to us all to see Annabeth. I'm sure you didn't expect her to be quite *this* pregnant. I was too polite to say anything, of course, but one can't help but wonder if she will eventually birth a house."

Annabeth deposited the wriggling pug into Lady Lockwood's lap with perhaps a bit more force than was necessary.

"It's a good thing you are so polite," Nathan recovered enough to tell Lady Lockwood, then turned to Annabeth. "I see you're still spry enough to chase Petunia, though."

"Yes, for my sins," Annabeth chuckled. "How are you? It seems forever."

"I'm quite well. Married life is obviously agreeing with you."

Annabeth laughed. "I'm as wide as a barn, and you needn't pretend otherwise. Sloane is convinced I am going to have twins."

"But you're glowing," Nathan replied. "I know you're happy. And I couldn't be happier for you."

"Nathan Dunbridge," Lady Lockwood trumpeted. "You can chitchat later. Come here, boy, and let me look at you. I may have forgotten you after all this time. Your absence has been almost as irksome as your former omnipresence at my home used to be."

Nathan went up to the Lady Lockwood and bowed. "My lady. It's so good to see you again." It was the truth. In some strange way, he was fond of the cantankerous old woman.

"Humph. You still make an elegant bow, Dunbridge. Welcome home." She gave a regal nod of dismissal, and Nathan stepped back. Everyone else moved in to greet him. Sloane's father, Marcus—*what was he doing here?*—was first, followed by all the others in an almost dizzying array.

Even Sloane had a grin and a pleasant greeting for him. If marriage and impending motherhood had made Annabeth glow, it had clearly softened Sloane's personality. Nathan doubted that they would ever be good friends, but he'd known Sloane forever, and now that they were no longer snarling over Annabeth, Sloane seemed like less an enemy and more like one of those annoying sort of cousins that one can't get rid of.

"Nathan! Nathan!" a boy shouted, tearing into the room and running at him.

Nathan laughed and picked him up. "Oof. My goodness, Gil, you've become big."

"I'm six now," Gil explained. "I can ride my pony without any leading rein. And I can read and do sums."

"I can see you're practically grown up," Nathan said.

Gil leaned in and said in a reassuring voice, "But I still like to play with my soldiers."

"Excellent. Then we shall have a battle next time I come, eh?"

"Yes." Gil nodded and jumped down, announcing to the room at large, "I'm going to dinner and bed now." He went first to Lady Lockwood and made a proper bow, then kissed her cheek.

Gil made a tour of the room then left, taking Petunia with him. And, much to everyone's relief, Sterling's giggling girls were shepherded out by the eldest daughter. The group was further reduced when Adeline took Rose and Jocelyn for a tour of her gardens, and at last it was possible to carry on an actual conversation.

Nathan was talking to Carlisle and Noelle about his stay in Paris when Bennett, the Rutherfords' dignified butler, came into the room and said in disapproving tones, "A Mr. Malcolm Douglas asking to speak to you, Mr. Dunbridge."

Everyone there turned to look at the man who had followed Bennett into the room. He was blond-haired and had a pleasant, open face. Mr. Douglas looked puzzled but smiled, and said in a Scottish brogue, "I'm afraid there's a mistake. I came to see George Dunbridge. I inquired at his manor, and they said Mr. Dunbridge was here."

"I am Nathan Dunbridge, George's son. I'm afraid my father is deceased." Nathan came forward. "Perhaps I can help you. Now is not a good time, but we could talk tomorrow if you would like to come back to the manor."

The visitor's look turned mulish. "I won't be fobbed off. I'll have my say."

Nathan suppressed his irritation. He figured it might be easier to let the man say whatever it was so he would leave. "Very well. Why was it you wished to speak to my father?"

"I am his son."

## CHAPTER FIVE

THE MAN COULD not have tossed in a more explosive conversational bomb. Nathan's jaw dropped, and for a moment, the scene was frozen in silence. Then Lady Lockwood thumped her cane and exclaimed, "What impertinence! Toss the charlatan out."

That was very much what Nathan would like to do, but the last thing he wanted was to have a brawl in Adeline's house. The important thing—the only thing—was to get this fellow out before his mother and aunt came back inside from the garden.

"I don't know what you want," Nathan said firmly and stepped up to grip the man's arm. "But we are *not* speaking of this here and now. I will return to London tomorrow, and we can discuss the matter."

Douglas jerked his arm away. "I'm not taking orders from you. I mean to be heard."

"And I will listen. You have my word. Contact me, and we will set up a meeting." Nathan gave him the address of his flat, then went on firmly, "But *now*, unless you want to get tossed into the nearest pond, you will leave. Immediately."

For a moment, Nathan thought the man would refuse, but when Carlisle and Sloane came up to stand with Nathan, Douglas shot him a final glare and stormed out of the house.

Nathan turned to the others. "Please don't say anything to my mother and aunt about this. It would be most distressing to them. I'll take care of the matter, and Mother need never hear of it."

"Of course, we shan't say a word," Lady Lockwood said stoutly. "I'm sure the scoundrel is lying. He's not George's son. He's *Scottish*."

Marcus, standing beside Lady Lockwood, cleared his throat. "George *was* friends with that chap—what was his name—whose family had a lodge in Scotland. Used to go there for the fishing and whatnot. George visited him there a summer or two."

Lady Lockwood sent Marcus a quelling look. "*I* never heard of this. And I don't know any Douglases, either."

"Well, that should settle the matter then," Sloane murmured.

"What are you going to do?" Carlisle asked Nathan.

"I'm not sure. I'll make some excuse to Mother and return to London tomorrow and see what it is this fellow wants."

"Money," Sloane said drily.

"I'll need to look into Douglas's background, see if there's any truth to his story."

"There are some Douglases in the *ton*," Carlisle offered. "A chap named Robert, I believe. I don't know him, but I'm sure some of those Londoners who have estates in Scotland would know more about any Douglases."

"Why would someone in the *ton* be claiming to be illegitimate?" Nathan said.

"Again," Sloane said drily. "Money. There are a number of penniless second and third and fourth sons running about. They may be unwilling to lower themselves by working, but swindling would be acceptable."

"Ever the cynic, I see," Carlisle told Sloane. He turned to Nathan. "If there's any way I can help you, you know I'll be more than glad to do it."

Nathan shook his head. "No, though I thank you for the offer. But I would ask a favor from you, Sloane. I need to find Verity Cole."

Sloane's eyebrows slid up in surprise, but he made no comment, merely gave Nathan directions to Verity's detective agency. Just as he finished, Adeline and the Dunbridge women returned from the garden, and all discussion of Malcolm Douglas ceased.

NATHAN LEFT FOR London early the next morning despite his mother's protestations that he should stay. He found the office easily enough, but when he walked inside, there was no sign of Verity, only a pleasant grandmotherly sort of woman who sat behind a counter, placidly knitting.

Her eyes were filled with curiosity when he asked for Verity. She hesitated for a moment, studying him, then, apparently deciding he wasn't dangerous, directed him to a particular bench in Hyde Park, adding, "She often goes there around this time."

Nathan found Verity right where the woman had said. Today she looked more like a governess than the lively widow of the other night, her red hair covered by a bonnet and her dress an unremarkable brown, with a decorous white fichu at the neckline. She didn't see him at first, her gaze directed across the park to the wide walkway, where two women were walking, pushing a baby carriage.

As he came closer, Verity turned her head sharply and looked his way. She smiled—not one of her repertoire of smiles, carefully orchestrated to suit her needs, but a sweet curve of her lips and a certain warmth in her eyes that conveyed surprise and welcome. *Or perhaps he just liked to think it meant that.*

"Miss Cole." He swept off his hat to bow slightly to her.

"Mr. Dunbridge. This is a surprise. We seem to have a habit of running into one another."

"Well, this time I was looking for you."

"Indeed. How did you know where to look?"

"I asked Sloane where your office was, and that very nice woman there sent me here."

"You asked Sloane? I *am* impressed."

"That I asked him or that he told me?"

Verity laughed. "A little of both." She gestured to the bench beside her. "Please, have a seat, and tell me what sent you searching for me."

Nathan sat down beside her. Verity was just as lovely in her plain clothes...though he did wish he could see her hair. "I have a bit of a problem, and I hope you can help."

Verity glanced back at the two women, then turned to him. "How might I help?"

"Do you know them?" Nathan asked curiously, nodding toward the pair. "I'm sorry. I didn't mean to interrupt. If you're here to talk to them, we can do this another time."

"No." Verity gave him her cocky grin. "I'm just spying. You know, that's what I do. I've seen enough. Now... tell me all."

"I—there's a chap I need to find out something about. His name is Malcolm Douglas. He's—" Nathan paused. He hadn't really thought about how embarrassing it would be to talk about this, especially to a woman. His cheeks warmed.

"He's what?" Verity gave him a flat look. "Nathan, you know I don't have delicate ears. Tell me."

"He claims to be my father's son."

"Ah. So it's a matter of family honor?"

"No. I mean, only partly that. It would upset my mother greatly if she found out my father had been unfaithful. They always seemed very much in love. I wouldn't have thought my father would have an affair. But…" He trailed off.

She nodded. "Gentlemen stray."

"Not every gentleman," Nathan protested.

The corner of Verity's mouth curved up. "No. Not you, I would think."

Nathan wasn't sure whether she was complimenting him or thinking him a joke. "I would have said the same about Father." He shrugged. "But the past year I've found that he did keep secrets. Nothing horrifying, just…well, I'm not sure I knew him as well as I thought I did."

"Do you believe what Mr. Douglas told you? Does he have any evidence?"

"I don't know," Nathan admitted and told her what had happened the day before. "When I got back to my flat in London, he'd already called on me. He left me the name of his inn, and I need to reply. Set up a meeting. I would appreciate it if you could go with me when I talk to him. I'm not sure I can deduce whether he's telling me the truth. I thought you'd be more able, that you've dealt more with…"

"Mountebanks and other liars?" Verity's eyes twinkled. "You're right. I have."

"I'm not sure what you charge. Should I pay you now or—"

"Pay me?" Verity eyebrows shot up. "I'm sorry. I didn't realize this was a business transaction. I thought I was doing a favor for a *friend*. But apparently I was mistaken."

"No!" Nathan was taken aback. "You aren't—I mean, of course you are more—I just didn't want to, to take advantage of our relationship—that is, our friendship. Naturally I regret..." How was it that he invariably said the wrong thing to Verity, even when he was trying his best not to offend her? And then he always turned into a blithering fool trying to get out of the mess he'd made.

"Your fumbling and agitation is apology enough." Verity's face softened. "Though I will downgrade you to mere acquaintance if you ever propose paying my fee again." She reached out to put her hand lightly on his arm.

Nathan was terribly aware of her touch, and for a moment it drove all else out of his mind. But when she pulled back, he wished she'd left her hand on him.

She went on, "Of course I will help you. Now, tell me. Where and when are we meeting this man?"

"Tomorrow afternoon? I'd like to get rid of him as soon as I can. I had thought of going to the inn where he is staying." He frowned. "No, that won't do, I'm not familiar with it. I'm not sure it's an appropriate place for a lady."

Verity grinned. Nathan was sure she found him laughable. *No doubt she never thought of such things as propriety.*

"Not there," she agreed. "We don't want to meet him on his ground."

"But we can't meet him on *my* ground. It would be disastrous for your reputation to come to my flat." It didn't matter if she thought he was an old-fashioned prude. She might not care, but he refused to be the one to involve her in a scandal.

"Then let's do it on *my* ground. We can meet at my house. You gentlemen can call on me." Her eyes lit up. "Of course! That's it."

Nathan looked at her warily. "What is it?"

"You can pretend to be courting me."

"What?" Nathan felt a flush rising up his neck. "But that's—it—we couldn't—"

Verity cocked one eyebrow, saying coolly, "You think it would be outlandish for you to court me?"

"No!" Nathan scrabbled for something to say. He was never sure when Verity was teasing him or genuinely upset. There was a light in her eyes that made him suspect that at this moment she was only trying to get a rise out of him, but he had to come up with an answer anyway. And, really, he didn't know why he had reacted so strongly to her suggestion. "It's not that. It's just that, um, I'm no good at pretense. I'm a terrible liar."

"You'll get more comfortable with it, I promise." She grinned. "And you did fine at Lady Arden's party the other night. The thing is we will be spending time together, perhaps a lot of it, working on this. This would be the perfect excuse. I am supposed to be a wealthy widow, remember. And you are wooing me for my money. No one will think anything of it. That's what a gentleman does when his estate is deep in debt. And, not to boast, but I am quite sought after in that regard."

"Verity! I wouldn't marry you for money." Nathan

was shocked. He couldn't believe she thought that was the sort of man he was.

Verity's eyes flashed, but she kept her movements measured as she rose to her feet almost calmly. Even so, there was no doubt in Nathan's mind that she was genuinely angry now.

"I am well aware that I am not a suitable wife for a *gentleman*." The word dripped from her mouth as if it was an obscenity. "But others will believe the charade. Unlike you, they don't know enough of who I am to have a low opinion of me." She whipped around and started off.

"No. Verity, wait."

"I can't. I have a previous engagement." She turned back to him, her gaze now as cool as her tone of voice. "I will see both of you at my house tomorrow at four. Good-bye."

"Verity, I didn't mean—" Nathan started after her, then stopped. She wouldn't listen to him now, no matter how much he explained. She was the most hardheaded woman he'd ever met.

Nathan turned and walked away in the other direction, irritation bubbling in him. *Blast it. Verity is the one with the issue. She takes every utterance I make in the worst way possible.* He had been appalled that she could think he would marry *anyone* for money, but of course she had decided he meant only that he would not marry *her*.

This time he would just let her stew about it, if that's what she wanted. It was bloody tiring, always having to watch his words with Verity. And, really, what could he say to her? *I will marry you?*

Of course he wouldn't marry her. She was annoying and impulsive and did such outlandish things. The fact that she was alluring, that it had aroused all of his senses just to sit close to her, that her laugh made him feel warm inside—none of those could counter all her other exasperating qualities. Being with Verity would never be dull, but marriage to her would be absolutely exhausting. And just imagine the children she would have—fiery-haired moppets all tearing around, getting into trouble. *She*, of course, would just encourage that sort of behavior.

*Why am I even thinking about this?*

Verity had the most absurd effect on him. It would have been better if he had not asked her for help. It had seemed quite logical when he thought of it. She would be better at all this than he was. But she was simply too captivating, too lively, too exciting, too…*everything*.

Nathan sighed. But he couldn't back out of it now. It would only confirm her opinion that he was a snob and a dullard, deceitful and unfeeling like all upper-class gentlemen—*and why did she have such an antipathy for gentlemen, anyway?*

He had to meet her tomorrow, had to include her. He would show her that he wasn't any of those things, that she didn't know him as well as she thought she did. That *he* would not let her down. Because however much it should not matter what Verity thought of him, the truth was that it did. It mattered a great deal.

Verity admitted that she had been a little hasty in storming off yesterday. Nathan hadn't done anything wrong; of course he wouldn't want to marry her— though his being horrified at the idea of pretending to court her was rather unflattering.

She wasn't sure why Nathan so often aroused irritation in her. It wasn't his fault that he had been raised an aristocrat and imbued with aristocratic ideals of class and behavior. He was in general a very nice man—courteous and thoughtful, but with a sense of humor and quick retort, as well. He wasn't arrogant or cruel. He would never intentionally hurt anyone's feelings.

She liked him. In fact, Verity sometimes thought she could like him more than was wise. And that might be the very reason she was so often upset by him. It was clear that far from liking her in return, he usually regarded her with disapproval, even horror. There was a bit of desire there, as well; she was aware of his reaction to her when they were pressed against each other. But that was just his body—and he had probably been aghast at his response.

He loved Annabeth. *She* was the sort of woman he wanted. And Annabeth was in no way like Verity.

Annabeth was tall and slender and had silky-straight locks, and Verity was small and curvy with an unruly mop of red hair. The differences went far beyond that, of course. Annabeth was easy to like—indeed, Verity was friends with her—and Verity knew that she herself was often not likable. Annabeth was a lady. Her lineage was impeccable, and her past unblemished. She knew exactly how to act. Verity possessed none of those qualities.

Being quick and stronger than she looked or possessing the ability to use a small blade to incapacitate but not kill were hardly attributes known to inspire romantic feelings. Nor was having a past that kept her looking over her shoulder still.

Verity wouldn't have been surprised if Nathan had

decided to deal with his problem without her, so it was some relief to her that he arrived at her house the following afternoon well before the appointed time. Verity said nothing about the way they had parted yesterday, and Nathan seemed equally disinclined to mention it.

As she led him into her parlor, Nathan looked around him with interest. "The house you rented is lovely."

"I own it," Verity replied. She couldn't keep the pride out of her voice. She added in a joking tone, "I am a woman of property."

"A very nice property." Nathan smiled. Verity wondered if he actually liked her home; it was hard to tell with Nathan because he was always so polite. Another thing that irked her about him. Verity had dealt with many a rude man and while she didn't enjoy their company as she did Nathan's, at least she always knew where she stood with them.

"The agency has done well," Verity said by way of explanation.

"I've never known a woman who had a business," Nathan said. "Come to think of it, I don't know any man who has a business. Well, except for Sloane."

"It's not quite the thing, you know, old chap," Verity drawled in that lazy public school style many young gentlemen affected.

Nathan chuckled. "I suppose not. But I think a business would be rather interesting."

"You do?"

"Yes. It gives one something to do, doesn't it?" Nathan said. "Sometimes the days seem somewhat empty."

"What? You mean dressing and going to your club and making calls isn't enough to fill one's life?"

"I am aware you're making fun of me, but...yes,

sometimes I think so. Sloane has accomplished things, however illegal some of them might have been. He has something to show for his life. You have something to show for yours." Nathan shrugged. "You're proud of this home—you're proud of your business."

"I am." Verity couldn't help but be pleasantly surprised by Nathan's remarks. Not only had he noticed the pride she took in the things she valued, but he seemed genuinely interested in them, as well. It was hard to write that off as just genteel courtesy. "The agency has done very well, better than I anticipated. Especially the last few years, once I realized what a good market I have in wealthy women."

"They need a lot of jewels returned, then?"

Verity laughed. "No, not that often. Though one of my clients has a granddaughter who has been pocketing things. It would be embarrassing to hire a Bow Street Runner for the theft, you see. But I can get the goods back without drawing any unwanted attention."

"It seems hard to imagine you not drawing attention." He added hastily, "Not to imply you aren't good at what you do. I just mean I noticed you even when you were Annabeth's maid."

"Ah, yes. One usually notices an irritation." Verity smiled to let him know she was teasing. As much as she liked watching Nathan twist himself into knots when he spoke without thinking, it seemed cruel to never give him a break. "Sometimes I work for people who are being blackmailed—as it turned out, my client from the other night was. Her lover had threatened to show the brooch to her husband."

"Lord Arden?" Nathan asked, astonished.

Verity nodded. "Genteel manners can hide a great

many sins." She heard the bitterness in her tone and pushed it down, going on quickly, "Sometimes I'm tracing someone. But most often I do jobs like I did with Annabeth—though usually the person is aware that I've been hired to keep them safe. A woman doesn't want to have a guard hanging about her all the time—sometimes it's her husband she wants protection from. But a maid or a companion can be close to her without any questions asked. My secretary, Mrs. Malloy, is quite good at that, too—you've met her."

"Mrs. Malloy? But how—I mean, she doesn't look like she would provide much protection."

"You'd be surprised how lethal a pair of knitting needles can be. Trust me, Mrs. Malloy knows how to handle troublesome men. She used to own a brothel."

Nathan's jaw dropped. "That grandmotherly woman in your office?"

Verity laughed. "Yes. She's also good at keeping the books and making sure all our accounts are in good standing. Not to mention quite expert in investments."

"Good Gad."

There was a knock on the front door, clearly audible in their room, and a moment later the maid ushered in a man. Verity studied him quickly. He was blond-haired and blue-eyed, unremarkable but not unattractive. Of medium height, he was dressed in gentlemen's clothing, his hair styled in a popular Byronic fashion. In short, he looked to be the sort of man who would be acceptable at any *ton* party or dinner.

He spoke like an educated man, as well, though he had a Scottish burr. "Sir. Thank you for seeing me." The man looked curiously at Verity. "Ma'am." He turned to

Nathan, his expression uncertain. "I thought we were to meet, just the two of us."

"You may speak freely in front of Mrs. Billingham," Nathan said airily. "Mrs. Billingham, allow me to introduce you to Mr. Douglas."

"Yes, well, as to that…" Douglas shuffled his feet a little, looking embarrassed. "I—ah, this is rather a delicate subject." He glanced again at Verity. "Not fit for a lady's ears."

"Please, don't worry about me," Verity told him. "I am aware of gentlemen's proclivities. Illegitimate offspring are not uncommon, I fear."

She could sense Nathan squirming inside at her frankness. But Verity saw little purpose in standing about trading euphemisms and hints.

"I am *not* illegitimate," Douglas snapped. "George Dunbridge married my mother."

"What!" This brought forth an exclamation from Nathan. "He couldn't have. He was already married. I know this much about my father's character. He would never have deceived any woman by pretending he had no wife."

"Yes, well." Douglas glanced down at his hands, nervously turning the brim of his hat. "I don't know about that. I never knew the man. But you have it backward. It was *your* mother he deceived. He married mine two years before he married yours. I'm not really Malcolm Douglas, though I was raised as such. I am Malcolm Dunbridge. Your father's eldest son."

## CHAPTER SIX

"You LIE!" Nathan exclaimed. He had gone white around the lips, and his hands clenched. Verity had never seen him look or sound so fierce.

"I do not," Malcolm shot back. "I'm speaking nothing but the truth." He took a step forward, his hands doubling into fists, as well.

*Wonderful.* That was just what she needed—two men brawling in her parlor. She would have to be the one to break it up. *And in this pretty new frock, too.*

"Gentlemen, please," Verity said, stepping between the men and calling up her best imitation of Lady Lockwood's daughter, Adeline, whose gentle, sweet manner she had studied a few months ago when she was staying at Stonecliffe. If that failed, Verity would have to resort to her imitation of Lady Lockwood herself—which was, when one thought about it, a role she was more adept at playing. "We need to look at this calmly, with courtesy and thoughtfulness. Like the gentlemen you are."

Both men relaxed a trifle, though neither looked particularly pleased with the idea. "Let's sit down," she suggested, gesturing toward the sofa and the chair that sat across from it, several feet away. She took her seat in the chair between them.

"Now." Verity turned to Malcolm, resuming her own demeanor. "Mr. Douglas—" She held up a hand as if to stop him. "For the moment, I will call you that, for I have no way of knowing whether you are telling the truth. Do you have any proof that George Dunbridge married your mother?"

"I don't see how it's any of your concern," Douglas said irritably and looked over at Nathan.

"Mrs. Billingham is here because I value her advice," Nathan said in a tone that brooked no argument. "And I promise you that we can both rely on her utmost discretion."

Malcolm looked at him for a long moment, then shrugged. "If this is the way you want to handle it, then…my parents were married here in London at Saint Agatha's. The church will have the records of it. July 29, 1787."

Verity glanced at Nathan. It was clear from his face that he was stunned. However little Douglas wanted to talk to her, she had to take the lead in questioning him.

"I'm a mite confused," Verity said. "You seem Scottish. I assume your mother is Scottish, as well. How did she and Mr. Dunbridge come to know each other? Was she living in London then?"

Fortunately, Malcolm seemed to have given up his resistance to Verity's inclusion in the conversation. He simply shook his head and said, "Nay. She's a Scot— Margaret Douglas, a respectable girl from a good family. It was Dunbridge who came to Scotland. He met her when he was spending the summer visiting one of his friends. They fell in love and married."

"But surely the wedding would have been in Scotland, where they were, rather than in London." Verity adopted an innocent frown of puzzlement.

"They eloped. My grandparents were dead set against

the marriage," Malcolm explained. "My mother was young and the Douglases dinnae like the English, so they went as fast and far away as they could." He looked at Nathan. "I know this is a shock to you, and I am sorry to lay this problem in your lap. But I'll not forego my heritage."

"What is it you want, Douglas?" Nathan rose from his chair.

"My birthright." Malcolm stood up to face him. "I'm a reasonable man, as I believe you are, too. I am only asking for what's right and fair. No doubt you need time to think it over, so I'll take my leave of you now. We'll discuss this matter further another day. Good day." Malcolm gave them a sharp nod of farewell, then turned and left the house.

"Well." Verity left her chair and went to Nathan. "That wasn't what I expected."

"It rather took me by surprise, as well." Nathan still didn't look quite like himself, but the stunned expression had vanished. "I thought that he would make some claim of illegitimacy and ask for money to keep him silent. Not that he would try to take my…well, *everything*. Even my name." He stood up and began to pace. "Not that it would do him much good, given that the estate is mortgaged to the hilt, and the rents barely keep our heads above water."

"That was a bit of a miscalculation on his part."

Nathan set his jaw, his expression stony. "I cannot believe it of my father. To have wed my mother, knowing that he already had a wife—no, it's impossible. Not just because he would not have committed bigamy. He would never have done such a thing to my mother. He loved her, I'd swear that on anything you like." His expression changed from belligerent to worried. "Mother will be devastated if this is true."

"*If* it's true. All we have is this man's word. I think he's a charlatan."

"He seemed sincere to me. Insulted even, that we thought him illegitimate."

"I'll admit that he is good at lying," Verity told Nathan. "But he's not telling the truth."

"How can you tell?"

"His story sounded rehearsed to me. His answers were *too* quick, as if he'd thought up all the responses to any possible questions beforehand and memorized them. And there was just something in his manner, in the way he watched you. I was the one questioning him, but he kept looking at you. Judging your response. He wanted to see how rattled you were."

Nathan let out a little huff of a laugh. "Well, I am rattled by him. He seemed very confident to me—giving us the name of the church and the date. Surely he must know we'll check it."

"That's exactly what I plan to do, and I suspect we'll find no record of the marriage. But that doesn't *prove* that they hadn't married. He could claim the record had been lost or perhaps he'd got the church wrong."

Nathan hesitated for a moment, then said, "The thing is, my father apparently did spend the summer in Scotland a time or two when he was young, according to Sloane's father. Marcus said George had a friend who owned a lodge up there."

Verity shrugged. "I think someone could find that out without too much trouble. Maybe Douglas grew up in the village where the lodge is and heard that George Dunbridge used to visit there, then decided to put that knowledge to use and wove this fanciful story. Why did he wait so long to inform you that he was the heir? Given the date of the marriage, I would think that he's at least a year older than you. Indeed, he looked older than that to me. Why would he go along, content with being Malcolm Douglas, making no effort to find you until he was thirty-four or -five?"

"It does seem odd," Nathan agreed. "And why did he come to *me*? Why didn't he simply hire a lawyer and pursue his legal rights in court? I could understand if he wanted to get to know our side of the family—I am his half brother if what he says is true. I could even see him shoving it right in my face because he was angry and resentful. But he didn't convey either of those feelings in his manner. He seemed most interested in trying to come across as reasonable and genteel."

"Precisely. My opinion is that he wants to blackmail you. That conciliatory manner…giving you time 'to think about it' and then 'discuss it later.' Saying he only wants 'what's fair.' He wants you to brood about the scandal, about your mother's feelings and the horror of a public lawsuit. About having everything, as you said, snatched away from you. He's counting on your being willing to make any immediate financial agreement with him in order to avoid it all. He will come to you and offer to settle the matter like a gentleman and accept some amount of money, and no one will ever need to know. He'll call it a reasonable agreement. It's blackmail."

"I'm not about to give in to blackmail." Nathan's eyes flashed. "Malcolm's fair and far off if he thinks I won't fight him on this. I don't believe him. I *can't* believe it of my father. Yes, perhaps he kept a secret or two, but they were minor things, things he would have told me if he hadn't died so young. But deceiving everyone for thirty some-odd years? He couldn't have carried it off even if he'd wanted to. Even Lady Lockwood knew nothing about it."

Verity smiled faintly. "Then it couldn't have happened."

Her statement won a rueful smile from Nathan. "Indeed."

"I'll go to this church tomorrow. Even if—"

"*We'll* go to this church," Nathan put in. "I'm going with you. It's my mystery to solve, after all."

Verity would enjoy his presence, but she wasn't about to let him know that. "Oh, so you don't trust me?"

He scowled. "Of course I trust you. What a thing to say. *I* was the one who stood up for you when Sloane and Annabeth were wondering whether you were the traitor. I told them you were trustworthy. I would have thought that would have given me some credit with you."

His response surprised Verity. She had expected to rouse in Nathan the usual sort of polite irritation at her needling him. But this had obviously touched a sore point. "I'm sorry. You're right. I should not have said that."

Now he was the one who looked astonished. "You're apologizing?"

"Yes, I know. It's a once-in-a-lifetime event, so you should enjoy it," she told him wryly.

"Verity. I am aware that you don't like me, but surely you know that I am not untrustworthy or deceitful."

"No! I don't dislike you. I've never dis—" When he raised an eyebrow, she went on, "Yes, all right. Maybe I didn't like you much when I first met you. But that was just because you were a member of the *ton*. And you were always so amiable and polite."

"Yes, those are qualities that often offend people."

The corner of her mouth twitched. "You know what I mean. You were too proper. You never raised your voice, you were never mean or petty. You didn't even tell Lady Lockwood to fire me for my impudence even though I was a bit rude to you."

"A bit?" Nathan rolled his eyes, but he was smiling. "You were the most unmannerly maid I've ever seen, but I wasn't going to try to get you tossed out just because you didn't like me. Besides, one doesn't tell Lady Lockwood to do anything."

"True." She smiled. "I thought you must be hiding something, acting a part. But after a while I realized that you simply *were* that kind—I am sure your servants must take terrible advantage of you."

"Nonsense. I'm a tyrant at home."

"Mmm-hmm. You keep believing that," Verity said, feeling relieved. They were back on an even keel. "I am sorry I took that jab at you. I know you stood up for me back then, and I appreciate that now still."

"Well, it was simply the truth." He seemed a trifle embarrassed now. "Besides I'm aware of how unfair it feels to have people believe you are capable of misdeeds that would never even cross your mind."

"You'd be amazed how little the truth factors into what people say," she told him. "Anyway, I was only teasing you." She wasn't going to tell him that she'd teased him mostly to hide her pleasure that he wanted to accompany her to the church. Showing one's emotions always meant giving some part of one's power over to another, even if it was only a small measure. But that was not the sort of thing that Nathan Dunbridge would understand. He was always so authentically himself. Not trying to posture or put something over on her. It was refreshing. "And what do you mean? Who has ever thought you capable of misdeeds?"

"When Gil, Noelle's son, was being targeted, it was by my solicitor. The man did his best to make people believe it had been *me* trying to harm the boy." Nathan's brows knitted together.

"Someone thought you could harm Gil?" Verity goggled. "What idiocy. You're like an uncle to him."

"The evidence pointed to me. I can't really blame them."

"Annabeth doubted you? Mr. Thorne?"

"No, I don't think Annabeth believed it for a moment. Carlisle said he didn't, but I could see the lurking doubt in his eyes. No one wanted to believe it. They were torn. But still they suspected me. And Carlisle is my oldest friend. The fact that the thought even crossed his mind...it was logical, though."

"He is a fool, then. *I* wouldn't have believed you'd hurt Gil for a second, and *I* haven't known you all my life. You know, I could have Mrs. Malloy put the fear of God in Carlisle if you want."

"I wouldn't want her to damage a knitting needle." Nathan's eyes twinkled. "Besides, he was only following the direction the clues led—it's understandable."

"You can understand something and still be angry about it." Verity reached for Nathan's hand.

"I suppose I never thought about being angry."

"You don't think about being angry. It's something you *feel*. Like a ball of fire in your chest." She gestured at her own body with their clutched hands, almost touching Nathan's skin against the bodice of her dress. Suddenly she was very aware of how warm his hand was in hers. She let go of it, busying herself with an invisible wrinkle in her skirts. "I could see suspecting someone like *me*," Verity explained. "Or perhaps Sloane. It would be foolhardy not to consider most people. The human race is a deceptive and sometimes violent group. But not you."

"Because I am too staid and boring?" Nathan teased.

Verity did not return the light tone but instead said with frank honesty, "No. Because it's simply not in your nature."

He smiled faintly. "I believe that was precisely the argument I used for your innocence."

Verity laughed. "Then either you and I are upstanding citizens...or we're setting ourselves up for disappointment."

Though she made the statement in jest, the more time Verity spent with Nathan, the more she worried she was doing just that: setting herself up for a devastating fall.

# CHAPTER SEVEN

VERITY'S COMMENTS ABOUT trust had stirred such feelings in Nathan that even after he was home for the evening and enjoying a brandy, he couldn't seem to fully pull his mind away from their conversation. He had thought he'd put that whole issue with Carlisle to rest. But had he really? Ignored it, perhaps, but he'd never acknowledged what had happened. Talking to Verity about it made Nathan wonder—had he done his relationship with Carlisle a disservice by not speaking with him about it? It had felt like the polite thing to do at the time; the easy thing, the gentlemanly thing. Verity may have had issues with gentlemen that Nathan still didn't fully understand, but he was beginning to think there was some validity to the way she saw things. Perhaps polite and easy wasn't always best.

*What am I thinking?* He pulled himself up short. There was nothing to be gained from telling Carlisle how he had felt. It was over and done with, and bringing it up again would just be uncomfortable for both of them. It was a little frightening the way Verity crept into Nathan's mind and made his thoughts branch off in directions they had never gone before. Her effect on him was confounding—and who she was as a person was even more so.

Nathan had no understanding of Verity; she fit into

no neat category. She was always verbally poking at him, and he was usually clueless about whether she was teasing or serious. She had an unerring ability to get under his skin, and yet he enjoyed her company. She was bold and outspoken, but somehow wrapped in secrecy.

Worse, Nathan had no understanding of himself when he was with her. He would have said he was a fairly sophisticated man, someone who talked smoothly; there were women who even said he was charming. Yet with Verity he immediately became a bumbling, incoherent fool—blushing like a schoolboy and falling into every verbal trap she laid.

He wasn't the sort of man to run about stealing jewels. He had told himself he had joined her in order to keep her out of trouble. But that would be an impossible task, and anyway, Verity could protect herself—probably better than he could. Nathan knew, deep down, that he had wanted to be part of her adventure, that as uneasy as he'd been during the whole process, he had also found it exciting.

Formerly Nathan would have said that Verity was the last person he would turn to for help, yet he had run back to London to involve her in his problem. He could have hired a Bow Street Runner, but instead he had chosen this unorthodox woman who thought he was naive and foolish.

Of course, she would think that of him. Verity was a woman accustomed to men who were privateers and spies, daring men who risked their lives on a daily basis, not caring whether they operated within or outside the law. She would scarcely be impressed with a man whose skills were dancing, good manners, and affability. Even

Nathan's love for Annabeth had been a slow and patient thing.

Verity was no more the sort of woman for him than he was *her* sort of man. But somehow he couldn't stop thinking about her. Those golden-brown eyes. That thick auburn hair. He kept remembering those moments in the Ardens' corridor when he had been so tantalizingly close to her and wondering what it would have been like if his lips had actually touched her skin, if he'd kissed her neck and worked his way up to her mouth. Would she have kissed him back? And if she had, would she have been Verity, or some character that suited her purpose?

Verity could play dozens of roles—how did one know the real her? Was there a real her? Perhaps there was no essential Verity, just a compilation of pretenses. Nathan didn't know if it was wishful thinking, but he thought that he had seen the real her several times. When they were alone together there was an ease, a calm, a comfortableness. It had not felt as if she was trying to do or be anything but what she was. It had felt as if they were old friends…but also somehow more. Like they had met in many lifetimes in the past. Drawn together again and again. A silly, impossible thought that never would have entered Nathan's mind if he hadn't been spending so much time with Verity.

It would be wise not to go with her on the search tomorrow. Give himself a chance to recover from this momentary madness, to return to his usual equilibrium. But once again he could not force himself to be wise.

THE FOLLOWING DAY he was on her doorstep at ten o'clock. And just as it had the day before, his pulse sped up at the sight of Verity. And thundered even more when they sat down together in the close confines of her town carriage.

"I still don't understand why your father and Margaret Douglas married in London," Verity said as the carriage made its way through the traffic of London. "Couples usually elope from England to Scotland, not the other way around." Verity paused. "But that is assuming that Malcolm's story is true and there is a record of their marriage at Saint Agatha's. If he is lying, then why did he choose that church?"

"You're right. Father could have brought Margaret home and had the wedding at the manor. Or chosen any church in the country—one in Newcastle or York or some obscure village. A place where it would be more trouble for us to check the records." Nathan was intrigued by the puzzle for a moment before his spirits fell. "But that makes it more likely his story is true, doesn't it? Knowing how easy it would be for us to check."

"Perhaps." Verity shrugged. "I still don't trust him."

"What if he isn't lying? I don't know if I could face Mother."

"In that case I suppose I'll simply have to make him disappear," Verity responded lightly.

"Verity!" Nathan gaped at her.

"Well, I can't let him turn you out of your home, can I?"

"What is wrong with you? You can't go about killing people willy-nilly."

"It wouldn't be willy-nilly. It would be quite specific. But I wouldn't have to kill the man. I can 'persuade' him to go away." Her mouth curved up in a wicked smile, and her hand slipped under her long sleeve, showing the hilt of the knife in a sheath strapped to her arm.

"Verity!" Nathan's voice rose in alarm. "No. No persuading, either."

"Very well." She heaved a sigh. "You take all the fun out of things." Her eyes twinkled merrily.

"You were joking!" *Hopefully.* "Good Gad, Verity. You realize, I presume, that you are absolutely mad."

"I thought you were in need of cheering up."

"So of course your thoughts went to murder." Nathan grinned.

"It distracted you, didn't it?"

Nathan thought how very much he would like to pull her to him and kiss her. Instead he said grumpily, "Do you always go about carrying a knife?"

"Usually."

"You had one the other night? At Arden's party?"

She nodded. "Though I had to strap it to my calf. The dress didn't allow for much concealment."

"That's the truth." His blood flooded with heat at the memory of her low-cut gown and bare arms. He scrambled to distract his thoughts. "Are you always in danger?"

"No. I very rarely have to use it. But I find it's better to have it and not need it than to need it and not have it."

Nathan had not been involved in Verity's world long enough to fully understand it, yet he had to admit what she said made a certain sense.

When they reached Clerkenwell Green, the driver stopped to ask a passerby for the directions to the church. The man looked back at him in surprise. "Saint Agatha's?"

"Yes. Saint Agatha's, the church," Verity leaned out the window and added.

This caused the man to turn his head toward her and then whip off his cap and begin to stutter. Nathan sympathized.

Finally the man burst out, "It's down the road past that alehouse and turn to the right. At the end of the lane. But you'll not have any luck there. The church burned down, oh, two or three months ago."

"Thank you," Verity almost purred. She settled back in her seat, turning to Nathan with a satisfied smile. "I think we've discovered why Malcolm Douglas chose this church."

The blackened stones still stood, but the inside had been gutted by fire. There was a cemetery beside the rubble, and a man with the collar of an Anglican priest was occupied with pulling up weeds from around the graves. He straightened and smiled when they approached.

"I am sorry to hear about your church," Nathan began.

"Ah, yes, it was a terrible thing. They had to pull down the manse to keep it from spreading to the other houses." He gestured toward a ruin beyond the church. "It will be a good while until it's rebuilt."

"Did anything inside escape the blaze?" Verity asked. "Were you able to save the church's records?"

"No." The man sighed deeply. "It happened in the middle of the night, and by the time I realized it was on fire, it was too late. Everything in the vestry and the office—the chalices, the candles, the vestments—all burned. They can be replaced but the records cannot. All that history lost."

"What started the fire?" Verity asked. "Was it set?"

"On purpose, you mean?" The priest stared at her,

shocked. "No, of course not. I mean, well, we're not sure what caused it. But why would anyone set a church afire?"

"No doubt you're right," Nathan said soothingly. "Thank you. We won't bother you any further." They left the man frowning at the building.

"I knew it!" Verity declared triumphantly as they climbed back into the carriage. "Douglas made sure we couldn't disprove his story."

"Burning down the church seems a bit extreme." But Nathan couldn't help but smile at Verity. He felt elated, too. Surely this meant Malcolm's story wasn't true.

"Perhaps he had nothing to do with the fire, he just looked for a church that suited his needs."

"I still don't understand what he hopes to do. He has no proof," Nathan said. "Even if his story were true, if my father really had married his mother, the record of it is gone."

"He could still sue. His mother could testify. Perhaps they could bring in a false witness to the ceremony."

"But the vicar who performed the ceremony…"

"It was almost thirty-six years ago." Verity raised her eyebrows. "What clergyman would remember a ceremony he performed that long ago, much less the names of the witnesses?"

"So what are you saying? You think one witness would be enough to sway a judge?"

"I think that would be enough to have a big messy public case about it. With all the gossip that would entail. That's the leverage he's going to use against you." She went on in a deeper voice with a thick Scottish burr, *"This would be so terrible, so public, I dinnae want to do that to ye, lad. So if ye'd just give me a few thousand pounds, I'll give up my claim. Ye can avoid all that."*

Nathan's mouth twitched up at her imitation. "Well, I'm not going to do that. So what can we do to thwart him?"

"We need to investigate Malcolm Douglas. Find out where he's from, who knows him. Who his real father is. And who he's working with. He's bound to know we would go to the church, so he would have made preparations for false witnesses. He must have accomplices somewhere. We can follow him and find out who they are. Talk to them…"

"Are we back to bashing people about?" Nathan grinned to show he was teasing.

"Nah. Money always loosens lips, I've found." She winked, and something turned in his chest.

Verity was so different, he thought. So unorthodox. *So tempting.* "I think we should go to a party," Nathan said.

"What?" Verity stared at him.

"Well, we *are* supposed to be in the midst of a courtship, aren't we?"

"You have been a little light on the gifts for one of *my* suitors, but yes…" A sly smile spread across her face.

"I do beg your pardon, Mrs. Billingham," Nathan replied in the same teasing tone. "I fear that's one of the drawbacks of being wooed by a genteelly impoverished aristocrat. However, I *do* have an invitation to a party tomorrow evening. I hadn't planned on going. But it just occurred to me that the host has family in Edinburgh. Alan might know something about the Douglas family."

"Oh. I see. Yes, you're right." Verity dropped her teasing tone and became all business. "That would be productive. Will it be a large party? Elegant? I must decide the appropriate attire, you see."

"No, it won't be a grand ball. I am sure there will be dancing, but Alan Grant and his wife are younger and less formal than Lord and Lady Arden, and their house is smaller. It will be mostly friends and family, probably a number of Scotsmen."

"Very well." The carriage rolled to a stop in front of Verity's house, and she and Nathan climbed down. Turning, she held out her hand in farewell and said briskly, "I'll see you tomorrow evening, then."

"Yes. Of course. Till tomorrow." Nathan tipped his hat to her and walked away. He knew that he'd made a mistake, though he wasn't sure what it had been. Had he stepped outside the boundaries of their relationship by suggesting they attend the party? Did she feel that his case was taking up too much of her time—time she could have spent working on other cases that actually brought in money? Indeed, *was* he taking advantage of her?

There hadn't really been a need to ask her; Nathan could have gone to Grant's party on his own—it might have been wiser to do so. Verity was more experienced than he in questioning people, but she was also likely to say something outrageous or make up some fiction that Nathan would have to then go along with. One never felt quite easy when Verity was around.

He had to admit that he simply wanted to have her with him. He wanted more time with her. He wanted to waltz with her—to hold her close, her hand in his, as they glided across the floor.

He felt that he was getting himself into a different sort of trouble, one much riskier than keeping his inheritance.

Nathan was so lost in his thoughts that he didn't notice the man standing near his flat until the man stepped into his path. Nathan pulled up short. "Mr. Douglas." *Well, this is interesting.*

"Mr. Dunbridge." Malcolm nodded in greeting. "I apologize for calling on you again, but I thought…well, charming as Mrs. Billingham is, there are certain matters that are too indelicate for feminine ears."

Nathan almost smiled at the idea of offending Verity's "delicate" ears. "Indeed? I would have thought the subject of philandering fathers and illegitimate sons was indelicate enough."

"Yes, of course." The other man gave him a rueful smile. "It was rather difficult for me to discuss such things in front of a lady. I thought that we could talk more easily, just the two of us, gentleman to gentleman."

*Just as Verity had predicted.* Nathan looked at him coolly. "What more is there to be said? Unless, of course, you'd like to talk about the matter of the church you named having burned to the ground, along with all its records."

"Did it?" Malcolm carried off a good show of surprise, Nathan thought. He suspected Malcolm was well prepared for the news. "I say, I am sorry to hear that."

"No doubt," Nathan replied drily.

"I assure you, I had no idea that it was gone," Malcolm replied. "But it does not change the facts of the case."

"You don't *have* much of a case without the records," Nathan pointed out.

"There are other ways to prove the marriage."

"How?"

"I would hope we will not have to go so far. I have

no desire to cause you—or your mother—any pain. We both know that *she* is the one who will suffer most from the scandal."

Nathan itched to plant a hard fist into the man's jaw, but he maintained his poise, crossing his arms to make sure he didn't do exactly that. "I assume you have some proposal to make—out of the goodness of your heart, of course—to save my mother from suffering."

Malcolm's eyes hardened. "Aye, scoff if you like. But I've no desire to have my name dragged through the mud in the courts, either. I am willing to settle this thing between us."

"Gentleman to gentleman," Nathan echoed, his voice acidic. He dropped his arms and took a step forward. "Mrs. Billingham was right—you're nothing but a swindler. And I have no intention of becoming your next victim. I will not pay you blackmail. I have a counter proposal to make—you go away, and I won't report you to a magistrate."

"Blackmail? I am the party who has been wronged in this matter, not you. Clearly I should not have come to you—a man who can't even speak for himself, but lets a woman do it for him. I should have dealt with your mother instead."

With a snarl, Nathan grabbed Malcolm by the lapels and shoved him back against the side of the building. "Don't you dare go near my mother. You take your tale to her, cause her any distress, and I will hunt you down." He gave Malcolm a shake for emphasis. "Do you understand me?"

Malcolm tore out of Nathan's grasp. "I understand that you're a bloody fool. You think I'm scared of a man who hides behind a woman's skirts? You understand *this*, Dunbridge." He jabbed his forefinger in the air at Nathan. "You consider my offer very carefully. Think how much your mother's tears are worth to you." He turned and started away, then swung back and added, "And how much you want to keep Mrs. Billingham. If news of this gets out, she won't stay around to let your scandal taint her, as well. You'll lose her as surely as you will your good name."

FOR A MOMENT Verity had thought that Nathan simply wanted to take her to a party, that he wanted her company. But of course there had been a practical reason for it. It was in aid of what was truly important to him. It was irritating, even maddening—to know that she wished he had had no such motive in mind.

Still, she couldn't help but feel eager for tomorrow. She had attended parties before, usually in one guise or another, but she had never enjoyed them in the same way she had the other evening at the Ardens' ball. Men had flirted and danced with her, done their best to charm her. But they had been doing those things to an illusion. Nathan had been bantering with *her*. And that made all the difference.

However, much as the thought of a party appealed, Verity could not ignore the difficulties. Not that she thought she and Nathan couldn't carry off the roles— she had no doubt of that. But there was the worrisome issue of Jonathan Stanhope.

She had come to decide that her fears of Stanhope recognizing her were groundless. He had glanced in her direction for only an instant, and it was as likely as not that he hadn't even noticed her to begin with. Verity had

not recognized *him*, really; it was just that he looked
enough like his father to make her blood run cold.

It had been many years since they'd seen each other,
and the sophisticated Mrs. Billingham did not look the
same as Verity had sixteen years ago. Her form was
more curvaceous, and the soft girlish face had been
honed by time and experience. Her hair had been red
then too, of course, but even it had turned a darker shade
as she had grown older.

But Verity could not simply dismiss the possibility,
either. She had to be practical, had to consider the risks.
However impulsive and incautious someone like Nathan
might think she was, she had not stayed alive all those
years as a spy in an enemy country without considering the dangers and making plans to circumvent them.

Right now she needed to consider that she might be
pressing her luck to continue to attend *ton* parties. She
could not let her desire to go to a ball with Nathan over-
rule her common sense. The more often she appeared
in London Society, the more likely she was to run into
Stanhope again.

On the other hand, it seemed most unlikely that the
grand Lord Stanhope would be attending a party that Nathan had termed small and consisting primarily of friends
and family and Scots. Besides, Verity would know to
watch out for him now; she would not be taken by surprise as she had been the other night. She would make
sure to attract no notice until she had made a survey of
the guests at the party, and she would keep an eye out
for his arrival all during the party, ready to slip away at a
moment's notice—on the off chance he even showed up.

There was no reason to deny herself a dance—maybe
two—with Nathan.

VERITY SLEPT POORLY and awoke early the next morning doubting her decision. Not one to waffle usually, she also wasn't one to distrust her instincts. She was still contemplating whether she was being wise, and felt she needed to investigate further.

Throughout the past few years that she had spent in London, Verity had not seen or heard any mention of Stanhope, even in the cases she had taken that involved members of the *ton*, which had reinforced her opinion that, like his father, Jonathan preferred to live at the family's country house. The fact that he had been at one party did not mean that he would continue to remain in London.

With this thought in mind, Verity went to the flower market, where she astonished a flower girl by purchasing her flowers, basket and all, as well as the girl's discolored and fraying straw hat. Returning home, Verity darkened her eyebrows, brushed a yellowish powder over her face to make it appear sallow, and pulled on a drab worn gown and old scuffed half boots. She tucked her hair under the ragged straw hat and finished off the transformation by scrubbing her hands with dirt and adding a smudge to her jaw.

Then she set out for the Stanhopes' townhome. She considered it a testament to the accuracy of her disguise that a gentleman stopped her to buy a posy for an afternoon call. As she neared the house, Verity's steps became slower, and when she reached the end of its block, she stopped.

It had been many years since she last saw the place, but still it set the nerves jittering in her stomach. She realized with a touch of surprise that for the last few years, as she built her life in London, she had avoided any route that would take her past the Stanhope home.

It was an ordinary enough dwelling for a wealthy man, one among a row of houses the color of pale butter, lying in a crescent across the street from a quiet green park that completed the half-moon shape. On the back side of the park lay a busier thoroughfare, but here everything was peaceful and pristine. Except for her memories.

Verity drew in a little breath. She was no coward. She didn't balk at doing things just because they were hard. *Don't be a ninny, girl. Move.*

She started forward, her eyes scanning the area. A lady, carrying a parasol and followed by her maid, turned into the little park. A footman at the end of the curve came out of the house to water the pots of flowers that bracketed the front door. Verity slowed her pace. There was no sign of anyone at the Stanhope house.

She crossed the street, reminding herself that it was unlikely the same servants would still be there, and even if they were, no one would recognize her as a Cockney flower girl. Before she reached the steps down to the servants' door, a maid emerged from it, carrying a bucket of water and a scrub brush.

"'Scuse me, miss," Verity called. "Buy a flower?"

The girl goggled at her. "What would the likes of me do with a flower?"

"Brighten up the 'ouse, they do," Verity said. "Go on, 'elp a poor girl out."

The maid laughed. "I don't buy the flowers."

The door opened and an older woman emerged, frowning. "Em, quit dawdling and get to work." She looked up and saw Verity. "Here! Who are you? What are you doing peddling flowers here?"

Verity did her best to look abashed, ducking her head. "Truth is… I come to see…is Lord Stanhope still here?"

"Lord Stanhope!" Em exclaimed. "'Course not. He went back, soon as the doc—"

"Hush, Em," the older woman interrupted sharply. "How many times have I told you not to talk about your betters?" She moved in front of Em to face Verity. "As for you, you impertinent girl, it's no business of *yours* where his lordship is. Now be on your way."

"I was 'oping, I mean, I'd like to get out of the city, I would," Verity said. "I thought I could 'ire on to work in the country."

"What for?" Em asked in a stunned voice, and the other woman looked equally astonished.

Verity shrugged. "I don't know. I 'eard as it was an easy job."

"Well, it's not," the older woman, whom Verity had privately labeled the housekeeper, said flatly. Her expression softened a little. "I promise you. You don't want to work for his lordship."

Behind her, Em nodded her head in emphatic agreement.

"Now, go on home, girl," the housekeeper told Verity, crossing her arms in a manner that said the conversation was over. She turned and went back down the stairs with Em following.

Verity was happy to comply. She whipped around and walked away, barely able to keep the bounce out of her step. He was gone. It was safe for her to stay in London. The pair of servants had confirmed that Jonathan was like his father with the warning that she wouldn't want to work for him. And while that was anything but good news, the fact that he had left the city most definitely was.

After she had returned home and washed the flower girl disguise from her face and hands, Verity went through her clothes. She pulled out a dress of shimmering bronze moire. It was a simple style, a slender column falling from the fitted bodice, without fussy ruffles and only a bit of blond lace at the neckline, but the color emphasized her eyes, and it was a gown she had chosen for herself, not for Mrs. Billingham.

Verity wanted to feel like herself tonight. She wanted one evening where she could enjoy dancing with Nathan and not think of playing a role. And she wanted Nathan to think twice about the validity of their courtship. Even if it meant running the risk of Verity forgetting the pretense herself.

The way Nathan's eyes widened when he saw her was proof that her dress had succeeded. As he laid her gossamer wrap around her shoulders, his fingers grazed her skin. They were hot and a little unsteady.

They left the house and Verity took her usual look around at their surroundings, but her gaze did not linger. She wasn't worried about anyone attacking her here, and she felt much more relaxed now that she knew Jonathan Stanhope had gone back to the countryside.

As soon as they walked in, Verity and Nathan greeted their host and his wife, but it would be awkward to start asking about the Douglases immediately.

Nathan offered Verity his hand, and they joined the dancers on the floor. Nathan was as adept at waltzing as Verity had thought he would be, but she had not envisioned how breathless she would feel this close to him, only inches from touching, or how lost the rest of the world would be to her.

She gazed up into his face, contemplating the color of his eyes. *Were they green or hazel? Mostly green*, she thought, *but with a ring of gold around the pupil that changed their color.* This close, she could see the little curved scar on his cheek and she wondered how it had happened. A childhood accident, she imagined; it was merely a thin white line now.

The music stopped, and they came to a halt, but for a moment, they still faced each other, her hand in his. Then Verity stepped back, and he released her hand. They walked from the dance floor and made a wide promenade around the room. Nathan paused to speak to a friend, and within moments, there were three men around Verity, vying for her attention. One offered to get her a refreshment, another asked for a dance, and the third assured her that she was even more lovely than usual tonight.

Nathan deftly moved into the group, scowling at the men and offering Verity his arm. "Mrs. Billingham, I believe you wished to speak to Lady Hornsby."

Verity looked up at him, her eyes dancing, but she said only, "Yes, I did. Please excuse me, gentlemen." She nodded at the other men and took Nathan's arm. They walked away, and Verity said with a grin, "Are you trying to scare away all my beaux, Mr. Dunbridge?"

"Upstart puppies," Nathan grumbled.

Verity laughed. "You sounded just like Lady Lockwood."

"Egad." Nathan glanced around the large room. "Ah, there are Alan and Charlotte. Let's see what we can discover."

He threaded his way through the guests to where the Grants stood talking to another couple. There were greetings all around and introductions to the other man and woman, followed by a good deal of chatting about nothing. Nathan took the lead; Verity was happy to simply listen and store away bits of information for any future forays into the *ton*.

Finally, when there was lull in the conversation, Nathan said casually, "I was hoping I might see Malcolm Douglas here. Do you know him?"

Alan shook his head. "Douglases are pretty thick on the ground in Scotland. Which family does he belong to?"

"I've no idea," Nathan told him. "I've only met him once, and we talked briefly. He's a little shorter than I and blond. Blue eyes. About my age."

"That, too, fits a very large number of Scotsmen. Or Englishmen, for that matter." Grant shrugged his shoulders and looked over at the other couple.

"I'm always in London," Grant's friend replied. "I don't know any Malcolm. I know a Robert Douglas, but he is a good bit older than that. I saw him here just a moment ago, if you would like to meet him."

"Why, yes, that would be nice," Nathan told him.

Verity glanced at Nathan as they followed the man through the room. Though his air remained nonchalant, she could see the same light in his eyes that she knew burned in hers—the same eagerness for the hunt.

Robert Douglas turned out to be a large, jovial man, his hair mostly gray, but with blond strands mingled in. His eyes were light-colored. Verity's hopes rose at the similarity of coloring to their quarry, but they were immediately dashed when the older man greeted them in a voice utterly devoid of any trace of Scotland.

Grant's friend introduced them, then said, "My friend Nathan was asking about a fellow named Douglas. I told him you were the man to see."

Douglas chuckled. "Well, there are a number of us around, but I'll be happy to help if I can."

"I'm trying to find a man named Malcolm Douglas."

Nathan started to describe him, but Douglas burst into a grin, exclaiming, "Malcolm! You know my nephew?"

"I believe I may," Nathan replied, his voice admirably calm and casual. "I met him the other day."

"He's in London?" Robert said in surprise. Then he chuckled. "That young rascal. I invited him for a visit, you know. He said he would come, but then he never did. Ah, well, young men…no doubt he didn't want a stodgy old uncle hanging about."

*Or he didn't want his uncle to know he was working a blackmailing scheme.*

"Perhaps it was not the same man," Nathan hedged. "He sounded much more Scottish than you."

"Ha! That's Malcolm for you. I imagine he does his best *not* to sound like an Englishman. It's a point of honor for the Douglases—I am something of an outcast in my family, you see. They're all living in the past, don't you know—dead set against the British."

"Not so set against British money," Verity whispered out of the corner of her mouth and was rewarded with a smile that Nathan tried to hide from Robert.

"I am sorry I can't be of more help," Robert went on. "If you do find the boy, I hope you will let me know— don't worry, I don't plan to check up on him. He gets enough of that from his mother. But I would love to see him again. He could visit me at my club—I can always be found at White's." He chuckled, then hastily added, "Of course, you are quite welcome by yourself, as well."

"That's very kind of you, sir. If I see him again, I will let him know."

They stayed for a few minutes longer, then bade Douglas a polite good-bye.

"I think we've accomplished all we can here," Nathan said as they walked away.

"Yes, it sounds unlikely that anyone else here would know Malcolm if he and his family are that reclusive."

One of Verity's more persistent suitors intercepted them. "Mrs. Billingham, would you honor me with a dance?"

"Mrs. Billingham and I were just leaving," Nathan told him, giving him a hard stare.

The other man took a step back, looking at Nathan with surprise. "Yes, of course. Your servant, ma'am. Dunbridge." He walked off.

"Well, that was a bit peremptory, wasn't it?" Verity said mildly but made no effort to resist as they headed toward the front door. Frankly, she found Nathan's unaccustomed rudeness rather appealing.

Nathan merely gave a noncommittal grunt, but as they left the house and started toward Verity's home, he said, "None of them are worth your time. They're all penniless youngsters. Viscount Sperle has a title, but his lands are in terrible shape—he's not done a thing to improve them. Westerbridge is a wastrel."

Verity let out a little laugh. "Nathan, you *do* realize that I am not actually in the market for a husband."

He assumed a haughty look. "I was merely supporting your story."

"Well, you may want to stop. You'll have everyone
thinking you're jealous. There will be gossip all over
London tomorrow."

"Isn't that what we want?" Nathan gave her a reckless grin. It was a look that suited him. Had he changed
or had she never had an accurate view of Nathan?

"You wouldn't want to carry it too far," Verity told
him.

"How far is too far?" He quirked an eyebrow at her.

A little ball of heat gathered in her abdomen. Nathan
was flirting with her without anyone there to witness
it. *Had that even occurred to him? And am I actually
blushing?* She turned her head away, and they walked
on in silence for a moment.

Nathan must have realized that he was being unlike
himself, for after a moment he said a little stiffly, "I only
meant that you shouldn't become too…um, attached."

Verity stopped, gaping at him. "Attached? To one
of *them*?"

Nathan let out a laugh, and he seemed to relax. "You
know what I mean."

"Not really. Perhaps you should explain."

He started to speak, then shook his head and sighed.
"Yes, well, I don't know what I mean, either."

They started walking again. Verity mulled over his
words. "Nathan, if you are thinking that I believe any
of these men would actually marry me, you needn't
worry. I am well aware that none of them would court
me if they knew, as you do, how unacceptable I am."

"I never said you were unacceptable," Nathan protested.

"You didn't have to say it. We both know it."

"I don't," he said stubbornly.

Verity looked at him. The mulish look on his face was somehow endearing. "Nathan...you don't have to be polite with me. You cannot deny that a man like Viscount Sperle would never marry a former spy with no name or family."

She could see Nathan struggle to come up with a reply that was neither a lie nor a hurtful truth. Finally he said, "Well, Sperle certainly wouldn't marry you if he knew how well you can handle a knife."

They had reached her house, and Verity unlocked the door and went inside. Nathan followed her. A lamp burned with a low light on the hall table. The rest of the house loomed dark and silent around them. Verity turned to face Nathan, acutely aware of how alone they were. She wished for an instant that she and Nathan were not so different, that they had no pasts. But, of course, that was silly and naive.

"Thank you." She smiled at him. "I shall see you tomorrow then? We'll put a watch on Malcolm Douglas?"

"Yes. Of course." Nathan paused, then said in a rush, "Verity, I don't think you're unacceptable. Any man should be proud to marry you."

Verity melted inside. "You are such an honorable man, Nathan. Probably too much for your own good." She reached up and cupped his cheek with her hand. "But I'm very glad you are."

Nathan gazed at her for a moment, his eyes dark. Verity found herself stretching up toward him. And then he kissed her.

## CHAPTER EIGHT

NATHAN'S LIPS WERE warm and soft, and Verity gave herself up to pleasure. A faint voice in the back of her mind whispered that this was a bad idea, but it was easy to ignore that warning when Nathan curved his hand around the nape of her neck, his fingers stroking across her skin. Desire rippled through her, and she pressed herself up against him, reveling in the pressure of his firm chest against her breasts.

At her response, his kiss deepened, his tongue tangling with hers in a delightful dance, and heat bloomed between her legs. His hands slid down her sides, thumbs brushing the edges of her breasts, and rounded over her hips. She was all heat and hunger as his fingertips trailed over her, and she ached to have the barrier of clothes between them gone, to feel his skin on hers.

He lifted his head, sucking in a breath, and gazed down at her, his eyes wide and dark. They remained in that position for a moment, as if the heat inside them had melded them together. Then Nathan jerked away.

"Oh, God. Verity—I—I—forgive me."

Verity stared at him, for once unable to toss back a saucy retort—or, indeed, any response at all. Nathan turned and rushed out of the house.

Shocked, Verity shut the front door after him and

leaned back against it, sliding down to sit on the ground. *Dear heaven, what had just happened?*

Nathan Dunbridge—polite, proper Nathan Dunbridge—had just lit a fire inside her. *And not some small fire dancing on the hearth, but a great blazing Guy Fawkes Day bonfire, flames leaping toward the sky.* Forgiveness was the last thing she wanted to give him, she thought. What she wanted was to chase after him and wrap herself around him and— She stopped herself thinking too far ahead. The fantasies tumbling about in her head shocked even her.

Verity was not without experience—she had kissed a number of men, some in deception and some in passion—but none of those kisses had ever shaken her like this one. She felt suddenly as naive as any young lass, her body a storm of sensations.

How could she feel this way about Nathan? She didn't even like him. *Well, that wasn't true*, she admitted in her mind. She did have a certain liking for Nathan and always had, even in the beginning when she'd been caustic with him. She enjoyed teasing him and flirting with him. She liked to ruffle his feathers, to shock him until he exclaimed "Verity!" in that way of his.

But this! This was a thing altogether different. This was a feeling very close to need. And Verity did not need. Anyone. Ever.

She rose to her feet and shook her skirts into place, bending down to pick up the gauzy shoulder wrap that had fallen to the floor in the storm of that kiss. She started up the stairs and was almost to the landing before she remembered that she had not gone through her nightly security check.

Irritated, she trotted back down the stairs. Telling

her heated body to cool down and her buzzing brain to turn off, she went through the checks of doors and windows with exaggerated care. Unfortunately neither her brain nor body complied.

She wondered what Nathan thought. It had been obvious that he'd felt the same passion—her lips curved with satisfaction as she remembered just how that desire had evidenced itself. But what did he feel now? What did he think about what had happened between them? Verity had the lowering suspicion that he regretted it.

After all, he doubtless still yearned after Annabeth. *What if he had imagined it was her, the great love of his life, that he'd been kissing?* That was a thoroughly depressing thought.

It wouldn't happen again, she was sure. Nathan was too gentlemanly to run about kissing ladies willy-nilly. Of course, he didn't consider her a lady, but still, she was too connected to his inner circle for him to think she was someone he could trifle with. That was why he had apologized; he considered kissing her a social breach.

Which meant he would be careful not to indulge in that again. She might not be a woman to be trifled with, but neither was she a woman whom he would court. Verity let out a little sigh. Nathan had denied that she was unacceptable, but they'd both known that that was a lie of kindness. No gentleman of his status would offer her marriage.

Not that she even *wanted* marriage. She was an independent woman and meant to remain one. Verity would never submit to being ruled by a husband—not even a charming one who gave her magical kisses.

Tomorrow, they would go back to the way they were,

this episode forgotten, and that would be for the best… but tonight she was going to luxuriate in the memory of that kiss.

NATHAN AROSE EARLY the following morning—though he had spent very little time sleeping. He had left Verity's house in a sensual haze that even the brisk walk back to his flat had not dispelled.

He was shocked that he had wanted Verity so much. She wasn't traditionally beautiful—though God knew her sly smile beckoned a man and one could get lost in those golden eyes, not to mention that her form was deliciously curved and for days his fingers had itched to pull the pins from her rich red hair and let it cascade across his hands.

*Well, perhaps it wasn't such a shock, after all.* He'd been suppressing his hunger from the first moment he saw her at Lady Arden's ball.

Still, she was not the sort of woman he usually desired. He had been in love with Annabeth, but he hadn't been a monk, and the women he'd admired and the lovers he had taken were mostly tall, willowy, ladylike and…*well, much like Annabeth.*

Verity was none of those things. Rather than serenely beautiful, Verity's good looks were vibrant and unavoidable. She was flamboyant, one might even say brassy. He never knew what was going to come out of her mouth or what she might do. She annoyed him; indeed, she seemed to enjoy annoying him.

Yet, still, he had abandoned all reason and kissed her as if he wanted to consume her. It had been the merest wisp of rationality that had pulled him back before he did something irredeemably foolish.

It wasn't that he had thought Verity wasn't willing. She had returned his kiss with equal heat. Nathan smiled to himself, thinking of her response. The little shiver that he'd felt run through her as he caressed the tender skin at the back of her neck. He could still feel the wisps of hair that escaped her chignon softly teasing his fingers. Her mouth hot and seeking. Her body pliant beneath his hands as they moved down her back.

With a little growl, he pulled his mind back from the seductive memory. It was no help to dwell on it. It wasn't her response to his kisses that was the problem. It was what would happen after them.

Neither of them would ever fit in the other's life. They had nothing in common; Malcolm Douglas was the only reason they were together right now, and that would soon be resolved. There could never be anything between them but a tempestuous affair. And, appealing as that sounded at the moment, it would be bound to end badly, and Nathan didn't want that. He didn't know what to make of the relationship he had with Verity, but he was sure that he wanted to hold on to it.

Nathan dressed and ate his breakfast, then walked over to Verity's. It wasn't until he got there that he realized that it was far too early to make a call. And he hadn't thought of anything to say; their first meeting after last night's kiss was bound to be awkward. He turned aside and started to leave, but halted on the pavement and walked back, trying out a few phrases under his breath.

Just as he raised his hand to knock, the door swung open and Verity frowned at him. "What on earth are you doing, whirling around out there? Come inside."

He gaped at her, any phrase of apology or greeting flown from his mind. Verity's abundant hair was braided and wound into a tight flat knot atop her head. But that was the least of it. She had on a rough grayish shirt of the type workmen wore, and below that she was wearing breeches, the ends loose and rather ragged, as if a pair of men's breeches had been cut off. Below that, her feet and a good portion of her calves were bare.

To put a final touch on the ensemble, she had wrapped a slender rope around the waistband of the trousers, which were clearly too large. It was all astonishing, but it was her bare feet and shins that captured his gaze. He had never before realized how tantalizing the sight of a woman's bare feet could be.

Letting out a little growl of irritation, Verity grasped him by the arm and pulled him inside. "Whatever is the matter with you?"

"What—how—why are you wearing that?" Nathan couldn't quite pull his thoughts together. Why was she dressed as whatever she was—a man? A street urchin? Perhaps an escapee from an asylum?

Verity let out a little laugh and answered his tangled question in order. "They're boy's clothes. I had them tucked away in a trunk. I am going to pose as a beggar in order to spy on Malcolm Douglas."

She turned and walked back to the stairs, where she sat down on a step and began to pull on a pair of small battered brogans. "I had to purchase the cap and shoes from the chimneysweep's boy. I think he found me suspicious."

"Imagine that," Nathan retorted acidly. He had found his tongue again. "What the devil do you think you're doing? No one will believe you're a lad."

"Yes, they will." Verity shrugged. "People see what

they expect to see." She stood up and pulled a too-large waistcoat over her shirt.

He was sorry to say, it did serve to conceal her breasts. "They aren't your only curves." He looked pointedly at her shapely bottom, which even the loose trousers could not hide.

"Hmm." Verity twisted to look down at her backside. "Perhaps you're right." She pulled her shirt out from the breeches, so that it hung down over her hips. "There. That'll do."

"Verity…"

"Have you ever noticed how long you can stretch out my name?"

He ignored her remark. "Why in the name of all that's holy do you need to dress up as a street urchin for us to keep watch on Douglas's movements?"

"We can't very well just hang about on the street waiting for him to come out, can we? Even if we sat in the carriage, people would find it odd. He might notice us. But nobody notices a lad sweeping the crossings or begging."

"I find it hard to believe they wouldn't notice a beautiful woman pretending to be a boy."

Verity's cheeks warmed a little, but she only said, "I'll take that as a compliment. However…" She turned and picked up a creased and dirty cap that hung on the newel. After putting it on and pulling the bill of the cap down low on her forehead, she crossed her arms and planted her feet apart, her face surly. "A tuppence to clear the way, guv? Wot do ye say?"

"I'd say you're charging entirely too much," Nathan replied drily. There was no point arguing with Verity, she always did as she pleased. Besides, she had managed to look amazingly like a lad. "What am I supposed to do while you're cavorting about as a street sweeper—and, just a word of caution, you look more like a pocket-size bruiser than a sweeper."

She laughed and studied him. "Yes, a gent like you can hardly stand on the corner all day. I suppose you could go as a beggar too—I have some other tattered clothes and bandages upstairs."

"I'm sure you do." Nathan grinned. It was hard to hold on to a grievance with Verity.

"I could be a pickpocket and you could be my kidsman," Verity suggested merrily.

"Just what I want to be seen as." But Nathan couldn't keep from laughing with her as he took her arm and steered her toward the door.

"I could put a mustache on you." Verity's eyes lit up. "Let me put a mustache on you."

"No. Out." Nathan started to pull her outside, but Verity resisted.

"Whatever would people say if they saw a street urchin leaving my home?" She fanned her face comically as if the mere thought gave her vapors. "I'll leave through the servants' quarters and meet you in the carriage."

They started toward the inn, with Verity proposing schemes, each one more outrageous than the last, and Nathan dismissing them with a smile. It occurred to Nathan that he hadn't felt this light in months.

In the end, Nathan wound up strolling past the inn a few times, keeping an eye on Verity as much as on the inn, and finally just going into the public room of the place and sitting down in the dimmest corner. He pulled his hat down to partially conceal his face and began to nurse one pint after another. He was going to get bosky doing this if Malcolm Douglas didn't show up soon.

What was the man doing? Did he intend to spend the day locked up in his room? Of course, there was always the possibility that Malcolm had left the inn before they arrived, but if he had, surely he would return soon.

Nathan wondered how Verity was doing out on the street. She had shown how well she was able to take care of herself, but he couldn't help but worry. If her hat somehow came off, her bound-up hair would mark her as a woman.

After a while, he got up and strolled outside to see her. She was in fine form, naturally, chattering in an almost unintelligible Cockney accent as she vigorously swept the dust from the pavement in front of a lady and her maid. She glanced up and saw Nathan, but made no sign, and after a moment he returned inside.

Clearly, there was no need to worry about Verity. She took to any role like a duck to water. Though he had spent a good bit of time with her the past few days, and Verity had learned a great deal about him, Nathan realized that he knew almost nothing about her. However, he was aware from their time at Stonecliffe that she had a very healthy appetite. So later in the day, after Nathan finished a light luncheon at the inn, he wrapped a hunk of bread and some cold meat and cheese in a napkin.

Verity wasn't busy with a customer this time, just roaming up and down the road. He walked over to her and handed her the bundled napkin. She unfolded the cloth and hesitated for a second, then looked up at him with a smile. "You brought me food."

"Well, I thought you might be hungry. I suspect the innkeeper would not let a street urchin in."

"You are right about that," she said, grinned, and thanked him. She stuffed an inelegantly large piece of bread in her mouth and turned away, keeping watch on the street.

Nathan had no reason to stay, but he lingered for another moment. "I take it you've seen nothing of our quarry." When she shook her head, he went on, "Has anyone been suspicious of you?"

Verity swallowed and cast him an amused glance. "No, but they will be if you keep popping out here to talk to me." She handed back the napkin, grinning.

Nathan rolled his eyes, determined not to rise to her teasing for once. "That's gratitude for you." He glanced about and sighed. "I fear this is getting us nowhere. I'm going back in to question the innkeeper."

"You think he'll tell you anything?"

"My dear boy," Nathan drawled in a haughty voice. "Money will open nearly all mouths." He flipped a coin to her and strode off.

Behind him, he heard her let out a crack of laughter and call out, "Thanks, guv!"

The innkeeper was pleased to see both Nathan and his money, and within minutes, Nathan was walking back outside. He looked at Verity and nodded in the direction he was proceeding, then crossed the street.

Verity caught up with him as he turned the corner. "What is it? What did you find out?"

"According to the innkeeper, Mr. Douglas gave up his room yesterday."

"He's scarpered?" Verity exclaimed.

"Apparently. Suspicious, wouldn't you say?"

Verity nodded. "He's looking more and more a villain. Why go to the trouble of moving unless it's to keep *you* from knowing where he is."

"What are we to do next?" Nathan went on. "We can't check every inn in London. Besides, he could have rented a flat or a house. Or moved in with his uncle—he said he'd been expecting Malcolm."

"Why go to his uncle now? He didn't before, and I can only assume that it was because he wanted to keep this scheme a secret from the man."

"Yes. Robert Douglas seemed a decent sort."

"And talkative," Verity pointed out. "The fewer people know a secret the better—and especially a man prone to chat."

"Still, that doesn't narrow our search much."

"No. But right now, I think the only choice we have is to wait and see what Malcolm's next move is. A black-mailer always turns up again," Verity said.

"Oh. Well…then I suppose we won't be together. That is, I mean, getting together to search or…whatever." Nathan's spirits fell. Sitting alone in his room for days waiting seemed a dismal prospect.

"I suppose not."

He couldn't tell from her tone whether she was glad or sorry. "Although…you know, isn't it possible he might prefer to contact us somewhere other than our homes? He doesn't want us to know where he is, but he wouldn't like meeting us again on our territory, so to speak. We could continue our charade, go to a play or ball or so on."

"Make it easier for him to approach us?" She smiled up at Nathan, her eyes twinkling in a way that told him she saw right through his excuse. They had no way of knowing where Malcolm was or if they would run into him. Nathan didn't mind; actually finding the black-mailer seemed less fun than the chase.

They strolled back to her house. Nathan knew they must look extremely odd, the gentleman and the urchin, but it was too enjoyable. He bought Verity a Banbury cake from a street vendor, and she ate it as they walked, seemingly undeterred by the dirt on her hands that she'd acquired in her role.

As they turned a corner, a lady and her maid emerged from a house down the street. Nathan narrowed his eyes, peering at the woman. "Isn't that the woman you were watching in the park?"

Verity choked on her bite of cake and her head snapped up, her eyes going to the woman. She whirled and walked quickly back the way they'd come.

"Verity?" Nathan gazed after her for a moment, then turned to look again at the women walking toward him. He was certain that it was the same pair, though without the baby. He followed Verity. She was walking so fast, it was almost a run, and Nathan had to break into a trot to catch up with her. "Verity? What was that all about? Who is that woman?"

"It's not important." Her voice was a trifle shaky. "Just business. You know."

"Not really." Nathan regarded her curiously. He could not remember ever seeing Verity this rattled, her cheeks flushed and her breath uneven. And he was certain these signs didn't come from exertion. "You think she would have recognized you? You're in disguise, after all."

"Well, um, I have spoken to her up close, you see." She added, "And I was dressed like a man then, as well."

"You're not lying as well as you do normally."

Verity looked at him, her eyes filled with a sorrow

and regret that he had never seen there, and she said, "You don't carry any secrets, do you?"

She seemed so lost and vulnerable in that moment that it pierced him. Nathan was sure that the woman they'd just seen was more important than someone Verity was being paid to watch. "Verity, if there's something wrong, if you need help, I would do whatever I could to—"

"I don't need help." Her face set into stubborn lines. "And there's nothing you can do."

"I know you think I am incapable," he returned, nettled. "But I'm not entirely without skills."

"There's nothing *anyone* can do. And it has no bearing on what we're doing."

"So now you're the one who says we're only business, not friends."

She cast him an exasperated glance out of the corner of her eye. "I didn't say that."

"Then I *am* your friend?" Nathan wasn't sure why he was pressing the issue. Verity had every right to not tell him anything. But somehow it rankled—she knew all sorts of things about him, but now that she was feeling something true, something deep, she wouldn't share that part of herself.

*"Yes,"* she replied in a goaded voice. "You're my friend."

He smiled to himself, inordinately pleased at her admission. "Well, some people find it helpful to *talk* to their friends."

Verity rolled her eyes as they rounded the corner to her flat. She marched inside, and Nathan followed. "I don't have that kind of friend," she said over her shoulder as she started up the stairs.

"What kind? The kind who care?" Nathan asked behind her. "The kind who'd like to help?"

She stopped halfway up the flight and turned to face him. "The kind who stick their nose where it doesn't belong."

Nathan stiffened. *Why am I pursuing this?* It should make no difference whether she shut him out. "You're right. I haven't any right to inquire into your life." He turned around, cursing himself for being a fool, and reached for the door handle.

"Wait, Nathan."

Nathan turned to look up at her. She looked very pale, almost frightened, and Nathan felt he had been a brute to push her to speak about something that shook her like this. "Verity, you needn't tell me."

"No." Her chin was set, her hands clenched at her sides. "You are connecting yourself to me in this pretense. It could reflect on you. You deserve to know." She drew a breath. "I murdered a man."

# CHAPTER NINE

VERITY WHIRLED AROUND and ran up the rest of the stairs. She didn't want to see the look on Nathan's face. Nathan would be far too polite to follow her upstairs. She hurried into her room and closed the door. She wanted to burst into tears, but she refused to do that. Damn him for pressing her on this.

She stripped off her clothes and threw them on the floor and started over to the wash basin to clean off her disguise. Behind her there was the sound of hurried steps in the hallway, then a pounding on her door. "Verity!"

*Obviously he's not as gentlemanly as I thought.*

"Don't you dare come in here," she called to him, and for good measure, she slipped over to the door and turned the key in the lock.

"Damn it, Verity, you don't have to lock the door. I wouldn't come into your bedchamber without permission," Nathan said gruffly.

She didn't answer, pouring water out into the basin and setting to washing her face and hands. Verity wondered why he hadn't left the house after that confession from her like any other gentleman concerned for his reputation. *Nathan is simply the most annoying of men.*

"You can't expect me to just depart after an announcement like that," Nathan went on.

"Anyone with any sense would have," she snapped back.

Ripping out the hairpins, she let her braid fall down her back and then pulled on an old morning dress that was easy to wrap around herself and tie on her own. She glanced at herself in the mirror and grimaced. She looked her worst. But what did it matter? She couldn't get away without telling Nathan the whole story, and surely after she did that, no trace of their little flirtations would be left. But at least he would leave after that.

Verity unlocked the door and opened it, gesturing for him to enter. He stepped inside, glancing around the room a trifle uneasily. "Um, Verity, perhaps we should go to another room."

"Oh, what does it matter? The story won't sound any better." Her voice was bitter, which she regretted. She didn't want him to know how much it hurt to tell him. She gestured toward the comfortable chair beside the fireplace. "You might as well sit down."

"I can't sit down while you're still standing," he protested.

"Oh, for pity's sake, Nathan, can you not abandon courtesy this once?"

He sat down. "Verity, you were a spy, and I understand that you might have done things in the name of the Crown that—"

"I'm not talking about that," she said impatiently. She linked her hands in front of her, like a schoolgirl about to recite a poem. "My mother was French. Her parents were émigrés when the Revolution happened. She married my father, who was handsome and penniless—

she had an unfortunate romantic streak. I was their first child and several years later, my sister, Poppy, was born. Mama grew tired of being dunned by creditors and having to sneak out of our lodgings in the dead of night to avoid paying the rent, so when our father died, she chose her next husband for his wealth."

"Understandable."

"Yes. I have no quarrel with her pragmatism. It was the man she chose. He was a rigid man who brooked no opposition. He was at best unkind and cold. At worst, he was given to punishments."

"Verity, no." Nathan rose and went to her, taking her hands in his. "I am so sorry."

His sympathy put her perilously close to tears, and she pulled away. "It wasn't just with us, but also with his own son."

"Did he…hurt you?"

"At first he was inclined only to break our spirit. He was given to furious lectures or locking us in our rooms for the day or denying us supper for our transgressions. Standing in the corner. That sort of thing." She wasn't about to recount to Nathan the pain of standing motionless for hours until her back tensed and her knees ached or she fainted. "The worst thing was having to apologize to my stepfather and ask his forgiveness. You can imagine how well I liked that." She cast Nathan a little smile.

"He should have been taken out and thrashed." His eyes were dark and glittering, his voice clipped.

Verity warmed a little inside at Nathan's outrage. "He didn't strike Poppy or me. He was harsher with his son, but the boy spent most of his time away at school. It was my mother who took the brunt of his wrath." Ver-

ity's eyes flashed, the familiar cold iron of anger forming at her core. "We had always lived in the city—that
is where he courted my mother, where we first went to
live with him. But soon we were spending more and
more time at his country house, and before long that is
where we lived. I missed the city, but it was more than
that. In the country we were completely under my stepfather's control. We had no friends. He used to say to
my mother, in a lover-like way, that he wanted her all
to himself. But it wasn't that. He wanted her alone and
unable to rely on anyone else. I hated him with all my
being. Then my mother died."

"He killed her?" Nathan exclaimed.

"No. A fever took her. But my stepfather had killed
her soul first—she had no will to live, and she went
easily."

"I'm so sorry." Nathan again reached out to Verity.

She took a step back with a sharp shake of her head.
She could not bear the kindness in his eyes. It threatened the steel box she'd locked up this part of her
life in. "Naturally, he was named our guardian after
mother died. And we had nowhere to go, in any case.
My mother's parents had returned to France, and my
father's family had not acknowledged us after he eloped
with Mama. We were solely dependent on our stepfather, with no one to turn to."

"What happened?" Nathan asked grimly.

"Once, I went into his private office for paper and
an envelope. He found me writing a letter to our grandparents in France about how scared I was for Poppy.
He ripped it out of my hands and tried to hit me, but
I dodged the blow and ran into the adjoining sitting
room." The memory flooded through Verity now, more

charged and immediate than it had any right to be after so many years. "My defiance would flip this switch in him and his eyes would turn dark and deadly, like there was no person behind them—just pure rage. He started after me and I threw his porcelain snuff box at him. It shattered and he charged at me, furious, so I grabbed a fireplace poker and swung it across a table, sending everything crashing to the floor. He yelled that I was crazed, and I said I was—and vengeful, as well. And if he touched me or Poppy, it would be last thing he'd ever do. After that he left us alone. I believe he was a little frightened of me."

"Can't imagine why." The hint of a smile tugged at the corner of Nathan's mouth.

Verity answered with a tiny smile of her own. It was going better than she'd expected. But she hadn't reached the worst part. "I was careful to always be with Poppy. She was only seven years old and more sensitive than I ever was. I was helped by the servants, who loved her and knew our stepfather for what he was. But then one day the headmistress of a school came to our house, and I was told he was sending me to finishing school. I refused. At one point I believe I kicked the woman in the shins."

"A natural reaction."

Verity nodded faintly. "Needless to say, she refused to take me. But I suspected that was not the last of his tricks to get rid of me, and I was afraid one of them might work and Poppy would be left alone. So I told the vicar in town." Verity's sour expression did not go unnoticed.

"What? Did he not believe you?" Nathan asked.

"I'm not sure. Either way, he was beholden to my

stepfather—his job depended on keeping him happy. The vicar told me I should honor my father, as the Bible instructed. I said he wasn't my father. It went downhill from there. I thought about running away, but we had nowhere to go. I didn't know how we'd survive. And then..."

Verity paused to take a breath, the years-old fear tugging at her chest again.

"Verity, if this is too much..." Nathan looked regretful. With anyone else, Verity would have assumed it was because he wished he never asked, but Nathan just seemed sad she had gone through all this.

"I want to finish." Verity's eyebrows knitted together. "I want you to know...me. Our stepfather took us back to the London house. I was glad until I realized why. He had decided to put me in a madhouse."

"My God."

"They didn't get me. I saw them and their wagon, and I knew what he planned. I had to escape, but I couldn't take Poppy with me. But I wasn't about to leave her alone with him, either—I knew what would happen. So I opened a window and made it look as if I'd gone out that way, and I went up to the attic and hid. They took the bait and went running out after me. That evening, I crept down, intending to gather Poppy and a few belongings and run. He was already there in our room."

Verity's hand started to tremble and before she could even think to pull away, Nathan was holding it. His palm was warm and comforting so she let it be.

"Poppy looked so small and pitiful, quaking with fear and crying, as he thundered at her. He told her that he would make sure she didn't grow up like me, that she would learn obedience. But she stood there like a little soldier and told him she was just like me." Verity's voice thickened with unshed tears at the memory. "He raised his hand to hit her, but I got there in time, and I whacked him over the head with the closest thing at hand. It was, ironically enough, a Bible. He was so startled by my attack that it sent him stumbling back. He fell and hit his head on the marble top of a dresser. I remember the awful crack it made. The blood soaking into the rug. I grabbed Poppy, and we ran."

"But that wasn't murder," Nathan protested. "You were a child. And you were defending your sister from a monster."

"Oh, Nathan," Verity said sadly, shaking her head. "Spoken like a gentleman who has rights. Poppy and I were his wards. He had complete control over us, and we had nothing. We had no defender. Just like my mother. A wife and children are completely in a father's power, he can beat them bloody if he wishes. You must know that."

Nathan flushed and said quietly, "Yes, I know. I'm sorry. It's wrong. But, still, it wasn't as if you meant to do it."

"It's true that cracking his skull on the marble was an accident. My blow wasn't hard enough to kill him. But I *wanted* to kill him. I would have struck him the same if I'd had that fireplace poker in my hand instead of a book. I was glad he was dead." She looked straight into Nathan's eyes. "I'm not like you, Nathan. I can be savage inside. Perhaps I *am* a bit crazed."

"You're not," Nathan told her flatly. "And everyone can be savage inside sometimes. If he were here right now, I'd beat him to a bloody pulp."

"Yes, but you wouldn't kill him."

"I would if it was to protect someone I love."

*To protect Annabeth.* But she didn't echo her thought aloud. Nathan was still being so kind to her, so understanding. And Verity knew the pain that would twist his expression if she mentioned his former love. Nathan didn't deserve that. "Even so, it would haunt you."

"It has haunted you."

"No. I was *hunted*, not haunted. I've never felt remorse over it. I was scared afterward, but I didn't regret what I'd done. I searched his desk for money and took my mother's jewels with us. I knew they'd be after me. No one would have believed I was innocent of cold-blooded murder. After all, I'd told him I would end him if he touched Poppy. I have little doubt he told others of my threat when he was constructing an excuse to put me in an asylum. My kicking that headmistress wouldn't have helped my case, either. The vicar's opinion probably would have weighed against me, too."

"How did you live?"

"Very poorly. We managed to lose ourselves in the East End. That's where I picked up the accent. I was always good at imitating voices. The money ran out and I couldn't get much for my mother's jewelry—everyone assumed I'd stolen it. After that I stole food and anything I could pawn. Poppy caught cold, and I wasn't that good at thievery—nor with defending us. I was having to pick all that up as I went. I was close to despair. And that's when Asquith showed up."

"Asquith? The spymaster?"

She nodded. "Yes, Spider himself. I told you that he had a finger on every pulse, spies all around. He had noticed me, and he had decided I was trainable. I spoke

French like a native because I learned from my mother, which was also useful. He offered me a job."

"Spying? You were a child!"

"I was fourteen. And killing a man and surviving in the stews of London makes one grow up quickly. To me Asquith was a gift from heaven. The chance to flee England, to have my tracks covered by a man with power. Training, food, a roof over my head, security. It was work I was suited for. I was angry and I wanted the danger. But, of course, I couldn't take Poppy. I didn't think about it at first, but as I went along, that became clear to me. Asquith said he knew a couple—good people with money and education and kind hearts. They were unable to have children and wanted to adopt a child. It was a perfect situation for both them and Poppy."

"But not for you." Nathan watched her.

"No. Not for me. But I knew I could not take care of her. Obviously I couldn't take her with me to France, and without Asquith's offer, I'd have no money. How was I to raise her? I dreamed for a while that I could let her live with them and still stay in her life—come back to see her from time to time, maybe get enough money to create a home for the two of us someday. But Asquith made me see that was folly. A spy cannot afford attachments."

"Asquith is another man with a great deal to answer for," Nathan said grimly.

"Yes. But he was right—about that, at least. It would have been unkind to both Poppy and her new parents if I had popped back into her life now and then, keeping alive her old memories. Not to mention the fact that I might have led my enemies to their doorstep. Spying was not a position with a long life. I figured it was better for Poppy to grieve me while she was still so young. I thought maybe, in time, she would forget about our childhood—even if that meant also forgetting me. So I handed her over to the couple and told her I loved her but I could not stay. A few months later Asquith spread the rumor that I had been killed in France. I don't know exactly what Poppy learned, but the Bow Street Runners stopped searching for me. I haven't seen Poppy since the day I left. Except from a distance."

Nathan wrapped his arms around Verity, holding her close. The embrace was warm and comforting, and she leaned against him for a moment, soothed by the steady thump of his heart beneath her ear and the encircling protection of his arms. It would be so nice, so easy to give in to this feeling. To depend on him.

*Easy and wrong.* Nathan was staunchly loyal and his sympathy so easily aroused. She could not entangle him further; she had to give him the chance to free himself of her past.

Verity put her hands against his chest and stepped back, gently but firmly pulling out of his arms. "There. That is my tale. Poppy is the woman you saw me spying on. No doubt that is reprehensible."

"No. It's tragic."

Verity shrugged. "As I said, I realized that you have a right to know that the woman you are pretending to woo is a murderer. If someone were to recognize me and discover what I've done, you would be embroiled in the scandal. At the very least, you would be made a laughingstock for being duped by me."

"I will be embroiled in a scandal if Malcolm Douglas tells *his* tale, and I suspect I was laughed at often enough before," he said lightly. "You're not getting rid of me that easily. Perhaps *I* should offer you the chance to avoid being connected to *me*."

Unexpected tears caught in her throat. Verity wanted to return to his arms, but that, she knew, would be a bad idea. Their former embrace might have been mere friendship, but Verity knew that right now she wanted to kiss him, and this was the worst place to indulge herself.

She shook her head. "Really, Nathan, you all but ask others to take advantage of you." She turned and started for the door. "Come. I think a spot of tea is in order. Or perhaps something stronger."

As they went down the stairs, she went on, "You really should take better care. Your kind heart will get you into trouble one day."

"I shouldn't like to be the sort of man who measures his friendship by whether it is an advantage or detriment to himself."

"That's a very 'Nathan' way of looking at things."

"Unfortunately, I don't really know any other way." He grinned.

"No. I don't suppose you do. And the world is a better place for it."

## CHAPTER TEN

THE FOLLOWING DAY, Nathan and Verity each took a section of London and went around to the inns, looking for Malcolm Douglas. It was, Nathan soon decided, a fool's errand. There were far too many places to stay in the city, and the odds of stumbling on the man were exceedingly slender. For all they knew, he was staying under an assumed name.

Searching by himself was tedious. Whatever one might be able to say about Verity, that was not an adjective that would apply to any task done with her. Things were often outlandish, tense, surprising. But never boring. Nathan had the uneasy feeling that when this was all over and he returned to his everyday life, it, too, would feel humdrum.

He spent much of the day thinking about Verity— about the kiss the other night and all the reasons he should not continue down that path. And when he wasn't daydreaming or lecturing himself, his mind went to Verity's past. He hated what had happened to her, and he hated just as much that there was nothing he could do to make it better.

Of course, Verity would dismiss with scorn the idea that Nathan should do anything for her. She was above all self-sufficient. She needed no one. He'd been taken aback by her attitude at first, but he'd never really thought about what in her life had led her to be that way. Verity had had no one to depend on, no relative or friend, not even a clergyman who should have given her aid. She had earned her independence in a hellish crucible.

It was no wonder Verity found Nathan rather useless. She was right in saying he viewed the world from a far different perspective. His father had been a good man, with whatever discipline he doled out tempered by love. George had set the example for honor and loyalty that his son had followed. Whatever money problems the Dunbridges had, there had always been enough to get by, and it had not affected their status in the *ton*.

Nathan had been an only child, but he had had good friends who had been as much family as friends, and there had been Lord and Lady Drewsbury, adults whom Nathan could always turn to in times of trouble. He had grown up knowing his place in the world was secure. In short, he had never really had to face any adversity. His worst problem had been his years of unrequited love, and his hardest decisions every day were what waistcoat and jacket to wear.

He had to wonder how he would have fared if he had grown up in Verity's situation. *What sort of man would I have become?*

When he arrived at Verity's that evening to escort her to a *musicale* at Mrs. Hargrove's house, such thoughts—indeed any thoughts—flew out of his head. She came down the stairs toward him, a vision in her gauzy gown of sea-foam green. The wide neckline was low, and the supposedly concealing lace that bordered it only made the swell of her breasts more seductive. Her hair was pinned up in a style many women wore, but somehow on Verity it was far more entrancing. The knowing little smile that played at her lips added to the rush of hunger that swept through Nathan.

It was clear she knew the effect it would have on him. Which meant she had intended to cause that effect. Which meant...what? Nathan really wished he knew whether the teasing look in her eyes was an invitation or merely Verity having fun at his expense.

The *musicale* they attended was uninteresting, as such entertainments invariably were. Nathan would have preferred not to have to listen to the five Hargrove daughters' musical talents—or lack thereof—but it had been the only invitation he'd found for this evening. However, Verity enlivened it with whispered comments behind her fan, which Nathan returned in full measure, until the matron behind him rapped him sharply on the shoulder and advised him to be quiet. After that Verity leaned over closer to whisper her remarks to him, and her breath brushed Nathan's ear and neck, sending frissons of sensations through him.

As soon as the hosts' daughters had finished their recital, Nathan and Verity excused themselves from the assembly room.

"Thank God, you had that 'headache' come on," Nathan laughed. "I'm not sure what I could have said to Violette's parents about her personal interpretation of what can only loosely be described as a melody."

Though there was a heavy mist hanging in the air outside when they emerged, Nathan and Verity decided to walk back to Verity's house. It wasn't far, and it was a pleasant walk. The evening air was soft and warm, and the enveloping fog made it seem as if they were in a place apart from the rest of the world. Even Verity was content to merely stroll along, her hand tucked in his arm.

"I discovered nothing today," she said.

"I'm not sure searching inns is a good use of our time," Nathan agreed. "Maybe we should redirect our efforts."

"You're right," Verity said.

He sucked in a breath of exaggerated surprise. "You agree with me? Has the world tilted on its axis?"

For answer, she jabbed a finger into his ribs. "Hush. I always agree with you when you're right."

"You mean, when I think the same thing you do."

"Exactly." She flashed him a smile. "I have business scheduled tomorrow morning. A client is donating a certain ring to the British Museum, and she wants protection while she carries it. It's some ancient thing her husband dug up on their land, but apparently she's decided that it is bad luck to possess it."

"So she's giving the bad luck to the museum?"

Verity laughed. "Hopefully not."

They crossed a street, and suddenly two figures burst out of the fog. One was tall and thin, the other short and square, and they would have looked comical together if they had not been wearing hats pulled down low and scarves wrapped around the bottom halves of their faces like highwaymen. They took Nathan and Verity so much by surprise that before they could react, the short man knocked Nathan to the pavement, and the tall thin one grabbed Verity from behind, wrapping his arm around her waist and pinning her arms to her sides.

She twisted and kicked back with her heels and Nathan sprang up to go to her aid, but the man whipped out a wicked-looking knife and laid it against Verity's throat. Verity went still, and Nathan halted. The other man moved close to Nathan, taking his arm, but it was clear the threat to Verity was all that was needed to stop him.

The man holding Verity growled, "Giv'm to me."

"What?" Nathan looked at him blankly.

"Bleedin' 'ell." The robber raised his voice. "Are ye a bloomin' idiot? Tell me or I'll cut 'er throat."

A thin red line formed across Verity's throat as the man pressed the knife against her a little. Verity was staring daggers. Nathan was certain she wanted him to refuse, but he decided to take a different tack.

"No, don't!" Nathan's voice rose in agitation, and he waved his hands helplessly. "I'll give you whatever you want! Just don't hurt her! Please, she is so dear to me…such a delicate flower. You must not harm her!" He stepped forward, wringing his hands.

Verity sent him a deadly look, but she began to cry, great tears rolling down her cheeks. "Please, sir, please, don't hurt me. Give him your money, darling." Her words ended in a high wail.

"Shut yer bonebox, woman!" Verity's captor barked.

"Tell me." The man took his hand from Nathan's arm and jabbed him in the ribs. "Go on."

"Yes, of course, of course. Anything. I'll give you anything." Nathan made a show of searching the pockets inside his coat. "Oh, dear, did I not bring it? I couldn't have left my coin purse at home."

At that, Verity began to wail again, her voice so high and fraught with tears she was unintelligible.

"Stop that!" The ruffian's arm loosened as he pulled away to escape her cries. "Where the hell—"

"Aha!" Nathan pulled out a coin purse with a flourish. "Here. Take it all. Take everything!" He started forward, opening the pouch and holding it out in his palm. He stumbled, and the coins tumbled out, rolling about on the ground. Nathan crouched down, picking up coins and moving yet closer. The other thief went down on his knees beside him, also grabbing at the coins.

"What the bleedin'—get up, Shoe, ye daft—" The man gestured at his comrade with his knife.

In that instant, Nathan's fists clenched around the pouch, and he shot up, slamming his hands into the robber's groin as he rose. At the same moment, Verity drove her heel back hard against her captor's shin, and bent forward, twisting, using the man's own weight as momentum to flip him to the ground. More coins rained down on the lane from the man's pockets as he was momentarily in midair.

The second ruffian jumped forward, swinging his fist at Nathan, but he blocked the blow with one arm and drove his other fist into the man's stomach. The man staggered back, and took one glance at Verity charging at him, wielding his companion's knife, and he took to his heels.

Verity and Nathan wheeled around to the other robber, only to see that he had managed to jump up and run, as well. The thick fog had already swallowed them.

"We'll never catch them," Verity said in disgust. "But at least we're not entirely empty-handed…" She bent down and retrieved a small bag that had fallen out of the man's pocket along with his coins. It had Fairborn's Confectionary stamped on the front. Opening it, she took a little sniff, "Fancy a lemon drop?" She popped one in her mouth.

Nathan turned to her, and she looked so incongruous,

standing there in her evening dress, holding the large knife, chewing on a lemon drop that he began to laugh. Verity let out a giggle herself and dropped the knife, running to him. And then she was in his arms, and he was kissing her.

Rationality and circumspection fled from his mind as desire flooded through him, mingling with the excitement of the fight and the anger that had surged in him at the sight of the ruffian's knife against Verity's slender white throat. In this fragment of time, all that he knew was Verity and the sweetness of her mouth, the soft curve of her body pressed against his.

"Verity," he murmured, his voice thick with passion as he sank his hand into her hair, sending hairpins flying. The soft curls twined around his fingers, and it seemed as if her very being curled through him, entangling him just as surely.

He kissed her lips, trailing across to nip at her ear, as his hand moved up to cup her breast. Through the soft fabric of her dress, he could feel the warmth of her skin, the tautness of her nipple, and desire shot straight down through him, exploding in his abdomen, turning him hard and eager.

Verity's hands were on him, as well, sliding beneath his jacket and across his chest, and when she pressed up against him, her leg hooking around his, it almost shattered his control. He made a soft noise and began to kiss his way down her neck.

The iron taste of blood touched his tongue, slamming Nathan back into reality, and he jerked away, his arms falling to his sides. "Verity. My God, I forgot. Your throat." He reached out toward the red line across her neck but pulled his hand back quickly. "Are you all right?"

"What?" Verity looked blankly at him, her eyes a bit hazy. "Oh. That." She reached up and touched the cut. "It's nothing. I'm fine. I doubt it will even leave a scar." But she, too, stepped back, giving a little tug to her bodice to straighten it. "Well." She glanced around. "That was foolish. They could have come back." She walked over to pick up the knife again.

"Yes. I beg your pardon," Nathan said, feeling doubly guilty now. "That was very wrong of me."

Verity flashed him a grin. "It wasn't all on you, you know. I think I had something to do with it."

"Yes, well." He had no idea how to answer so he bent down and began to retrieve the coins.

Verity came over to help. When he stuffed a small iron bar into the pouch, as well, she let out an exclamation and reached over to grab his wrist. "Wait. What's this? You were hiding a weight?" she asked in delighted tones.

He nodded a little sheepishly. "Learned it from Sloane, and I found it handy when I was traveling on the Continent. One never knows when one's going to wind up in the wrong place. I'm no good with a knife, and a pistol is a bulky thing to carry around."

"Mmm," she said in a grave tone. "I can see that it would ruin the line of your jacket."

"And formal shoes don't hide a weapon as boots do." He sent her a dancing sideways glance.

Verity dumped her coins into the pouch and stood. "I think we'd better get inside the house before those men come back with companions."

They were only a few houses away from Verity's

home, and they were soon inside it. Verity locked the door behind them. Nathan watched, somewhat bemused, as she toured the rest of the downstairs, checking the windows and the basement.

"You think they were in your house?"

"I don't know. Obviously they knew where I lived since they were waiting for us." Verity shrugged. "I always do this anyway."

"Every night?" Nathan asked in astonishment, trailing after her as she went up the stairs and followed the same routine.

"It only takes one mistake," she told him.

He stood outside her bedroom as she checked it. It was impossible not to focus on the bed and equally impossible not to think back to their kiss a few minutes ago. Throughout the day, he had told himself he could not go down that path, and within only hours he had broken his vow. Nathan had always thought himself reasonably careful and in control. He was beginning to wonder whether he really knew himself at all.

## CHAPTER ELEVEN

WHEN THEY RETURNED to the parlor, Verity poured each of them a glass of brandy. She settled down in a chair, tucking one leg under her. Nathan sat down on the sofa across from her and tried to ignore the luscious picture she made—languid and relaxed, her hair in disarray, her lips reddened and faintly swollen from their kisses.

"Bravo on your performance, Mr. Dunbridge," Verity said. "I would never have expected you to put on such a show."

"I was a trifle afraid you wouldn't realize what I was doing." He felt unaccountably warmed by her compliment.

"Ha! I knew you were up to something though I wasn't sure what."

"You glared at me," he pointed out.

"You tossed me right into that helpless scared female role, of course I glared."

"Well, it seemed more distracting. I was just hoping they didn't know what you're really like." He paused. "The question is, who were they? Why did they attack us? At first I thought they simply wanted to steal our money, but clearly that was not the case. They were after something else."

"Yes. He said, 'Give *them* to me.'"

"Is that what he said?" Nathan replied. "Between that

scarf and his accent, I couldn't tell what he was saying half the time."

"I think those were his words. You're right—he was difficult to understand. I suppose it could have been 'give *it* to me.' Later he said something like 'tell me.'"

"The other man said that too," Nathan went on. "So... 'give them to me' sounds like they want something we have, but 'tell me' sounds like they want something we know."

"Maybe they aren't sure whether we possess it or just know something about it," Verity suggested. "But *what* were they talking about? And who hired them? Those two didn't act on their own—they were clearly hired bruisers. I would say it was something to do with one of my investigations, but I don't have any dangerous jobs right now. This Malcolm Douglas case is the only one I've been working on, but none of this fits with his previous comportment or aims."

"True—there's no need to stop us seeking the truth if his claims are valid. He shouldn't have anything to fear." The man had been a bit threatening the last time Nathan saw him, but it had all been about scandal; there had been no hint of violence in it.

"I suppose there could be some proof that your father married Margaret Douglas *after* your mother, which would make the marriage to Malcolm's mother illegal," Verity mused. "Malcolm might want to get rid of that."

"No," Nathan said flatly, standing up and beginning to pace. "If my father was already married to Margaret Douglas but fell madly in love with my mother, I could believe he might commit bigamy. But he would not have deceived a young woman just to have an affair." Nathan dropped back down in his chair. "Besides, it seems unlikely that Douglas is younger than I am."

"He definitely *looks* older. Really, more than a couple of years older. That's one reason I find it hard to believe that your father married Margaret on the date Malcolm told us."

"It must be someone else who hired the attackers, someone like...well, like Lord Arden, for instance." Nathan leaned forward, warming to the notion. "What if that guard you pummeled at the ball identified you to Arden afterward? Maybe he suspects you were the thief who stole his brooch, and that is the thing that those men were after."

"Well, the brooch wasn't *his*," Verity protested. "Anyway, I don't have it, I gave it back to Lady Bankwater."

"He doesn't know that. For all he knows, you're merely a common jewel thief."

"I'm an *un*common jewel thief," Verity corrected indignantly. "But you're right. The guard could have described me to Arden, and he could have figured out who I was and where I lived. I wondered about that a bit myself when I saw Arden at a party the next day. He had a rather fierce expression when he looked at me."

"There might be other people whom you have 'offended' with your past investigations," Nathan offered.

"Of course." She gave a little shrug of one shoulder. "A couple of weeks ago, I discovered that a grocer was selling adulterated flour."

"Flour?" Nathan quirked an eyebrow. "That seems a bit minor for you to deal with."

"It bothered my housekeeper," Verity replied. "Besides, I don't like cheats. A month ago I caught a banker who was unfaithful to his wife. He was quite angry at me, as her father is a very important man and is now uninclined to deal with him. Before that, I caught an embezzler. And of course there was the fellow who tried to steal the duchess's jewels. He swore he'd make sure I got mine in the end. He is in jail, but I imagine he has friends. And there was—"

"Good Gad, Verity. Perhaps I should have asked if there is anyone who *doesn't* want to harm you."

She let out a little laugh. "I'm sure there must be someone—it's quite a large country." She leaned forward. "The thing is those two men weren't there to hurt me. They were just threatening me in order to make us give them something."

"How do you know they weren't going to cut your throat after they got what they wanted?" Nathan asked.

"Goodness. You have a nasty turn of mind." Verity smiled. "I like that about you."

"Stop trying to deflect all my points with a quip. I'm onto you about that, you know."

She looked at Nathan, startled. "Well, I'm not trying to deflect anything here. It's just…" She broke off, dropping her gaze toward the fireplace. "There is another man who might want to hurt me."

"Who?"

"Lord Stanhope. I saw him at a party a week ago. I didn't think he saw me, but he might have."

"Stanhope? I don't think I know him. Who is he? Why would he want to harm you?"

"He's my stepbrother. The son of the man I killed sixteen years ago."

Nathan let out a long breath. "I see."

"I didn't think Jonathan saw me, and even if he did, there's a good chance he wouldn't recognize me. He was off at school from the time he was nine so we weren't around each other much. Besides, it seems likely that

Asquith's rumor of my 'death' would have made it to Jonathan at some point. Still, I have been careless. I've lingered too long in the *ton* as Mrs. Billingham."

"Perhaps you should drop the role," Nathan said.

Verity shrugged. "I've already used it on this investigation. I could hardly change roles now."

"Perhaps you shouldn't continue with this investigation."

Verity was taken aback for a moment. "Would you rather I didn't? Do you want me to leave?"

"No," Nathan said quickly. "No, I'd much rather you stayed with me." He realized suddenly how his words had sounded, and color flooded into his cheeks. "You're, um, vital to the investigation. It's just, you know, your safety…" He cleared his throat. "I understand that Lord Stanhope would be angry with you, but that's been a very long time. If he did discover you were alive, why not simply turn you into the authorities? Besides, it doesn't make any sense that the men would be asking you for something."

"Well, I did take my mother's jewelry."

"But surely that would be yours."

"I'm not certain a Stanhope would view it that way," Verity replied. "And there was a diamond ring among the others that had belonged to his mother."

"Even so, he couldn't expect you to have kept the jewels all this time," Nathan argued.

"Maybe not. But maybe he thought he could trace it if I revealed who I'd sold it to. Perhaps that information was what they wanted from me."

"Perhaps. But whoever it is, you're in danger. I don't like the idea of you going out tomorrow by yourself to the museum."

"Nathan, that's what I do for a living. I'm not going to back out on a client."

"I could go with you."

Verity rolled her eyes. "So my client will think I can't handle it on my own? I have to bring a man to protect us? No."

"But—"

She cocked an eyebrow. "Are you trying to tell me that I suddenly can't take care of myself?"

Nathan sighed. "No. Of course not. I just…it worries me."

"It will be in the daytime, not night, and I will be on my guard this time. I'll be fine." She poked a finger at him. "You better be on guard, as well."

"I give you my solemn vow." Nathan smiled.

He spent longer than he should have lingering over his glass of brandy. While Verity had good taste in liquor, it wasn't the quality of the drink that held him well past a polite hour. It was the woman herself; her golden eyes alight as they talked of the mystery of the attack. There was not anything to be said that they hadn't covered already, but Verity seemed happy to go over each detail and explore every option, and there was nothing that Nathan wanted more than to listen to her.

She was entrancing: her voice, her scent, her keen mind enveloped him, pulling him into her world. In the past Nathan had thought that the only reason any gentleman would work was because he needed the money— but seeing how fascinated Verity was by her profession, it made the parties and social engagements he was accustomed to seem boring in comparison. Of course, Verity made everything seem boring in comparison to her. She was the most alive person Nathan had ever known; when he was with her he felt more alive himself. And when they had kissed tonight it had been as if electricity was running through his veins.

Nathan watched Verity's lips as she spoke and it was all he could do not to pull her toward him again. Only the fact that he knew nothing would be there to stop them this time kept him from doing so. Even standing in the middle of a road he had barely been able to keep the reins on his passion. He could not risk going down that path now, here. Pulling his eyes away from her mouth took a physical effort, but Nathan finally swallowed the last of his brandy and bade Verity good night.

He was more alert walking home than usual. He even kept the small iron bar in his hand, just in case. If he was going to be around Verity, perhaps he should acquire a better weapon.

*Am I going to continue to be near her?* One way or another, this matter would be resolved, and he would have no more reason to see her. Back when they had been staying together at Stonecliffe, Nathan would have been glad to be rid of her, but now the thought was distinctly unappealing.

But he wasn't going to get tangled up in thinking about that now. There were more immediate things he needed to do. Right now there was someone sending miscreants after Verity. It was actually a good thing she had something to keep her inquiring mind occupied tomorrow; Nathan had plans for an investigation all his own.

He couldn't undo what had happened with Verity's stepfather—as much as it infuriated him. The man was dead now and beyond his reach.

But here and now he could protect her. This time, this man, whoever he was, was a villain Nathan would stop.

## CHAPTER TWELVE

THE MAN WHO opened the door to Sloane Rutherford's house the next morning didn't look like a butler—or, indeed, like any sort of servant. But naturally that was exactly the sort of butler Sloane would hire. Nathan handed him his calling card. The man looked doubtfully at it, then doubtfully back at Nathan, but he turned and disappeared into the rear of the house.

Nathan had never been inside Sloane's house before. He wondered if it had always been like this or if the attractive furnishings were due to Annabeth's presence. As he waited, Sloane's father, Marcus, came down the stairs.

"Nathan? My, this is a surprise," Marcus said, coming forward to shake Nathan's hand. "It's good to see you."

"I'm glad to see you, as well. Mr. Rutherford, could I ask you a question?"

"Of course, of course," Marcus said expansively. "Can't say I'll know the answer, though."

"Did you know Lord Stanhope? Around your age or a bit younger, perhaps?"

"Basil Stanhope? My goodness, I haven't seen him around for many years. Don't know where he is now. He was always a rum'un, though. You'll want to stay away from him."

"Yes, I'm sure I will."

Marcus went on, "If you've come to talk to Annabeth, I'm afraid she's gone to call on her grandmother."

"Lady Lockwood has returned to town?" Nathan asked in surprise. It hadn't been a fortnight since he'd seen her at Stonecliffe.

"Of course she has," Sloane said as he strolled up to join the two men. "Stonecliffe, even with a great-grandson, is boring compared to an illegitimate heir popping up."

"Yes, Eugenia always does love a mystery." Marcus smiled fondly.

"She brought Mrs. Dunbridge with her," Sloane added, a glint of humor in his eyes.

"My mother?" Nathan asked, startled.

"Mmm. And your aunt."

"Whatever for? She didn't tell them about Malcolm Douglas, did she?"

"Good Lord, no," Marcus replied. "Her ladyship loves holding a secret as much as she loves hearing one. Well, boys, I must be off. I promised Eugenia I'd take the ladies shopping."

He strode to the front door, picked up his hat from the stand, and left the house. Sloane and Nathan stood for a moment, looking after him.

"Eugenia?" Nathan repeated, raising his eyebrows at Sloane. "Your father seems to be terribly friendly with Lady Lockwood."

"Yes, they're thick as thieves. I can't explain it. But I'm not about to raise any questions. Lady Lockwood is the only person I've known who can control him." Sloane turned and started back down the hall, saying, "Come to my office. I assume this isn't a social call."

"No." Nathan followed him. He found it a little strange, as he had earlier at Lady Lockwood's party, to be around Sloane without feeling resentment or jealousy. Sloane was still sarcastic and arrogant, and of course it was galling to have to ask the man for help, but Sloane no longer seemed an enemy. Not that he was a friend, either. Nathan wasn't sure what they were anymore…which fit with everything else in his life these days.

Sloane closed the door behind them and went toward his desk. He stopped and turned toward the conversational grouping of two chairs, then finally sat on the edge of his desk, stretching his legs out to brace himself. Clearly he had as little idea as Nathan how to act around him now. "I assume you're here about Malcolm Douglas."

"No. It's about Verity."

"Verity Cole?" Sloane stared at him.

"Yes. She's helping me investigate Douglas."

"Oh. I see."

*Good. Then perhaps you can explain it to me.* Nathan didn't voice the thought but said, "The thing is, someone attacked us last night. They threatened Verity with a knife at her throat and wanted me to tell them something or give them something. We're not sure what."

"You think it's Douglas?"

"Not really," Nathan replied. "I can't see how it helps him. And there are others who have reason to come after her."

"I'm shocked." Sloane's lips quirked up derisively.

"Yes, well, I—there are some men from her past, but the likeliest to me seems Lord Arden."

"Arden?" Sloane arched an eyebrow.

"Yes. Verity says he's something of a blackmailer. The thing is, we stole something from his safe. It didn't bel—"

"Wait. You're saying you helped her steal something? Nathan...what has happened to you?" Sloane grinned. "Stealing? Chaps popping up claiming to be your brother?"

"Malcolm Douglas is hardly *my* fault," Nathan protested.

"Nor, I imagine, was stealing from Lord Arden. That has Verity written all over it."

Nathan ignored the remark. "So you can see that there are a number of people who could have hired these two men. I want to find them and question them. I want to know who paid them. That's why I came to you."

"Despite what you may think, I don't know every criminal in London," Sloane said drily.

"I'm sure you know more than I do," Nathan retorted. "And I'll wager you know where we should go to learn who they are."

"Nathan, you astonish me." Sloane looked at him for a moment, then stood up. "Very well." He went behind his desk and pulled out a drawer to take out a small pistol and stuck it into a pocket of his jacket. He followed up by removing a knife and sliding it into place inside his boot. "Did you come armed with anything other than your charm?"

For answer, Nathan removed his dueling pistol from the side of his waistband and a short club from inside a pocket.

"I'm impressed," Sloane said, closing the drawer and beckoning Nathan down the hall. "Let's go."

"Where are we going?"

"To see Parker."

"The man you threatened to murder a few months ago?" Nathan's voice rose in astonishment.

"The very same."

"But…why?"

"Because he *does* know every criminal in London." Sloane grabbed his hat and settled it on his head as he went out the front door.

"Are we planning to attack the man again?" Nathan asked.

"Nonsense. I'm a respected citizen now, didn't you know?" Sloane hailed a hackney to take them to the docks. "Parker and I have an understanding. I trade in legal items, and he trades in the illegal, and we stay out of each other's way."

Despite Sloane's assurance of a truce, Parker's men appeared none too happy to see them when they arrived at his headquarters. But, after a sullen glare or two, one of the men went into the back and returned a few moments later to lead them into Parker's office.

Parker didn't stand up or offer them a chair, merely folded his hands across his stomach and looked at them questioningly. Sloane returned the gaze steadily, also not speaking. *They'd be here all day at this rate.*

"We are looking for two men," Nathan said.

"What's it got to do with me?" Parker turned his truculent gaze on Nathan.

"We thought you might be able to help us," Nathan replied pleasantly. "One of them was my height and the other one short and square. They had on caps, so I don't know their hair color, and they had the lower halves of their faces covered."

Parker snorted. "Don't know much then, do you?"

"The tall, thin one had a rather distinctive scar on the back of his left hand." Nathan's eyes had been riveted to the hand holding a knife against Verity's throat. "Large.

Shaped like a crescent." Nathan traced the shape of the scar on the back of his own hand. "And I think he was left-handed because that was the hand in which he held the knife. His eyebrows were thick, almost grown together above his nose. He called the other man Shoe, I think—though that doesn't seem like a real name."

"They're none of my men," Parker said, shrugging his shoulders.

"I'm not going to press charges," Nathan said. "I just want to find out who hired them."

"Still don't know them."

"I imagine you *do* know Sir Philip Dobbs, of the Board of Customs." Nathan paused, pleased with the wary look in Parker's eyes now. "As it happens, so do I. A word in his ear about your business practices—"

"Here, now!" Parker protested, turning to Sloane. "We have an agreement."

"You and Mr. Rutherford have an agreement," Nathan told him. "You and I, however, have none. Of course, should you help me find whoever attacked my companion last night..."

Parker let out a long-suffering sigh, then said, "The tall one with the scarred hand will be Hill, and the short one's Shoemaker. They always work together, hire out to whoever pays them. They work out of the Blue Swan, up in Cheapside. That's all I know. You'll have to go there to find out anything else."

As they left Parker's office, Sloane murmured, his eyes glinting in amusement, "Nathan, I am impressed. Coercing Parker. You have unexpected depths."

"That would be the thing that impressed you," Nathan retorted.

THE BLUE SWAN turned out to be exactly the sort of tavern where one would expect ruffians to gather—a small, seedy, dim place that stank of ale and other unsavory things that it was probably better not to think about. Every eye turned to them the moment they walked in, no doubt sizing up their potential as marks to be robbed.

Sloane sent a long, assessing look around the place and nodded to one of the men. "Bellmont. I'd heard you were in Newgate."

The fellow let out a bark of laughter. "Not me, guv, it were me cousin."

They chatted for a moment in jargon that Nathan found largely unintelligible. After a farewell nod to the man, Sloane and Nathan wound their way through the tables to the bar.

"Rather impolite of you not to introduce me to your friend," Nathan commented. "Now that you're a respectable citizen and all."

"Yes, but he hasn't received his latest boots from Hoby's and I didn't want him to feel embarrassed when confronted by a dandy of your prominence."

The barkeep loudly disclaimed all knowledge of the men they sought and even shoved their coins back across the bar. Sloane shrugged and took Nathan's elbow, steering him out of the tavern.

"Damn it, Sloane, I need to find out where they are," Nathan protested, jerking his arm out of Sloane's grasp. "What the hell are you doing?"

"Negotiating." Sloane nodded his head to the left. "Come on." Once around the corner, they walked partway down the street and stopped at a narrow alleyway. "The barkeep can't be seen giving out information about his regulars."

After a few minutes the barkeep appeared, looking cautiously around him, and stretched out his hand. Sloane held up a gold coin, raising an eyebrow, and the man gave him the directions to a house.

"Third passageway off St. Mary Hill to the left. Before the Workhouse. Number's 8 but..." He shrugged, indicating how little one could rely on the flats showing numbers.

"Has Lord Arden ever hired them?" Nathan asked.

"Dunno. I've never heard of him hiring them. They're not the best, but he could have taken them in a pinch."

"But he does hire men of that sort?"

"'Course. Are you daft? A gent like him don't do his own dirty work."

"What sort of dirty work?"

"Here now...that's not enough coin for all this," the man whined.

"Just answer, Cartwright," Sloane growled.

He sighed. "He gets bruisers, you know, to make sure the marks pay."

"The people he blackmails?"

"Aye. And that's all I know." He plucked the coin from Sloane's hand and started to turn away.

"What about a man named Douglas?" Nathan asked, taking a step after him. "Scottish fellow, with an accent."

"No." The man pivoted back to face him and said in an aggravated tone, "No Scots. Now. Are you through?"

"Stanhope?"

"Who?"

"Never mind." Nathan handed the man another coin, which brought not quite a smile, but at least a less belligerent expression, to the barkeep's face.

It didn't take long to reach the pathway the barkeep had given them, but finding the correct place in the warren of houses was another matter. It took a good deal of fruitless wandering about and finally a few more coins to a street urchin to find the right flat.

The door eased open a crack at Nathan's knock, then immediately slammed. Putting their shoulders to it, Nathan and Sloane burst into the room, only to find that the sole occupant was a frowsy woman screeching at the top of her lungs. Her words were almost imperceptible at that pitch, but Nathan could make out one word. *Hill.* The man with the scar. The man that had cut Verity.

Nathan charged up a narrow set of stairs behind the screaming woman and Sloane followed.

The room above was empty, but a knotted rope hung out the open window. Nathan ran over and looked out in time to see a tall, lean man madly dashing toward St. Mary Hill.

"How'd you know he was up here?" Sloane looked surprised and impressed—an altogether irritating combination that Nathan unfortunately was getting used to seeing on the man's face.

"There wasn't anywhere else to go and she was clearly trying to alert someone," Nathan answered as he gave a sharp tug on the rope.

Sloane quirked an eyebrow. "Think it'll hold us?"

"It better," was Nathan's terse reply as he grabbed hold of it and backed out of the window.

Sloane grinned, and he followed Nathan's lead. Once on the ground, they took off at a run. When they reached the outer street, they spotted their quarry nearing the docks. They pursued him as he turned left at the Workhouse and cut across St. Dunstan's churchyard.

Swerving around people and dodging through traffic on Thames Street, they continued after him and were closing in on the man when suddenly he veered into a ramshackle building.

Sloane's jagged breathing matched Nathan's and the sound was all Nathan was aware of in the darkness of the room. The windows had been knocked out long ago, and between the dim light diffusing through them and a partially collapsed roof, his eyes adjusted enough to see a hinged wooden cover beside an opening in the floor. A faint light came up from beneath it.

"Trap door?" Nathan asked, his breath still coming in pants, and Sloane nodded.

They lifted the cover, peered into the hole and saw a ladder leading down to a dirt floor, with stone walls on either side.

"It's a tunnel." Sloane looked over at Nathan. "Shall we?"

"Of course we shall," Nathan replied and started down the ladder.

Nathan quickly moved aside so that Sloane could come down after him. The light, he saw, came from a spot ahead of them where the roof of the tunnel had caved in. The debris had been pushed to the sides, and the threat of collapse obviously didn't deter the man they were pursuing, for Nathan could see his form disappearing into the dark in the distance.

There was a narrow gap in the floor, but two planks had been laid across it. Nathan started toward it, Sloane on his heels, but before he reached the planks, there was a loud crack, and the floor gave way beneath Nathan. Sloane lunged forward to grab Nathan's arm, and for a moment Nathan dangled there. And then the floor completely collapsed beneath Sloane, and they both tumbled down into the dark.

## CHAPTER THIRTEEN

NATHAN LET OUT a groan. His head was pounding, and he was half covered in debris. He looked around him. "Sloane?"

There was no sign of the other man. Coughing from the powdered dust and crushed stone that hung in the air around him, Nathan called Sloane's name again. A string of curses from a few feet away reassured him that Sloane was alive.

"Are you all right?" Nathan began to dig out from the pile of dirt and broken planks that hemmed in his legs, visions of Sloane lying bleeding filling his head. The idea would have pleased Nathan in the past, but now he thought of the pain it would cause Annabeth; it was no longer an idea Nathan relished in any capacity.

"Of course I'm not all right," Sloane growled as he struggled to his feet on the other side of a pile of rubble. "I just fell ten feet." He brushed ineffectually at the white layer that coated his clothes. He looked up at the hole in the tunnel above him, and said, "Make that fifteen feet."

Nathan coughed and crawled out. There were various points of pain all over him that said there would soon be bruises, and something had sliced through one leg of his breeches, leaving a shallow groove of blood. The feel of wetness on his face made him suspect there was another cut on his head. But at least nothing seemed to be broken.

He walked over to stand beside Sloane, looking all around. "Where the devil are we?"

There was enough light from the collapsed tunnel above that they could see that they stood beside a shallow rectangular pit. It was floored in stone, and the remains of a stone wall marked its boundaries. Even with the rubble that had tumbled down on either side, it was clearly laid out in a pattern, with two smaller squares extending from it and a tiered sort of arrangement of blocks at one end, like a small pyramid. The opposite end of the rectangle was shrouded in darkness.

"I believe we have fallen into Londinium," Sloane replied.

"What?" Nathan's voice rose in disbelief, but as he looked around, he could see that the ruin before them looked very much like the remains of a Roman bath. "Good God. I think you're right. These are Roman ruins." He peered into the darkness, an urge to explore sparking in him. *What else lay down here?* "Blast. I wish we had a paraffin lamp."

"I wish we had that ladder."

Nathan turned to see Sloane staring up at the hole far above their heads, and for the first time, he considered the predicament they were in. There was nothing handy to climb, for one could see only more ruins around them—a walkway paved in stone, a collapsed wall, a taller stone wall rising at the edge of the darkness, adorned with some sort of mosaic.

"I'll be sure to bring a ladder for next time we fall through a floor." Nathan climbed up the pile of rubble.

At its highest, the unstable mound left many feet of space above his head. Not to mention the fact that the jumble of beams, dirt, and pieces of stone shifted precariously beneath his feet.

"Watch out," Sloane told him sharply, and Nathan jumped back to the ground. Sloane gazed up at the hole in the tunnel again, then sighed. "If we get out of here, Annabeth is going to kill me."

"Entertaining as that would be, it doesn't seem there's much chance of her getting to do so," Nathan replied.

"No." The two looked around, contemplating their situation.

"No one knows we're down here, do they?" Nathan mused.

"Not a soul," Sloane agreed. "I daresay there's little hope of anyone happening to pass by and see us."

"Since the only person we know who uses it is a criminal, I doubt they'd be much help, anyway."

"We've no food or water," Sloane continued the litany of their woes.

"No ladder or a rope."

"Not to mention the rats and snakes that are probably lurking down here."

"There must be some way out. We could try to move some of these blocks together here, build some sort of platform we could climb onto," Nathan suggested. It was an unlikely hope, he knew—the stones were either too large and heavy to carry or broken into pieces that did not stack easily. But he had no other solution. He wasn't about to admit that he and Sloane might very well be trapped here, unknown to the city above, for the rest of their suddenly abbreviated lives.

Sloane slanted a skeptical look Nathan's way, but shrugged. "Then let's get started."

The two men shrugged out of their coats, rolled up their sleeves, and began to build.

VERITY'S WORK WENT off the next morning without a bobble. The artifact was taken safely to the museum, and her client was grateful. It had taken no more than an hour, which left her the rest of the day to spend with Nathan—rather, working on his case, of course.

When she arrived home, Verity found a note from Lady Lockwood inviting Verity to call on her in the afternoon. No doubt Lady Lockwood was hoping to find out more about Nathan's purported half brother. Verity would have preferred not to go. She and Nathan had not made specific plans, but she had assumed they would work together. But with Annabeth's grandmother, an invitation was, in actuality, a command.

Verity hoped Nathan would arrive at her house before she had to leave, but he did not. As her carriage took her to Lady Lockwood's, worry began to nibble at Verity. It wasn't like Nathan to do anything rash, but last night when that attacker had drawn her blood, there had been a certain look in Nathan's eyes that in her experience with men usually preceded trouble.

Verity was shown into her ladyship's drawing room. Lady Lockwood's feisty pug jumped up and began to bark, though she didn't make any move to attack. Verity and Petunia had come to a truce many months ago.

Lady Lockwood banged her cane on the floor, and Petunia subsided. Verity made a proper curtsey to Annabeth's grandmother. "Lady Lockwood, I'm so pleased to see you again."

"One would think you might have called on me before nigh onto a year had passed," Lady Lockwood grumbled.

"I'm sorry." Verity was taken aback. "I, um, didn't realize that you would want—I mean, I was pretending to be Annabeth's maid in your house."

Lady Lockwood raised her eyebrows. "You aren't now, are you? I understand you're currently Mrs. Billingham, who has caught the eye of every bachelor in town."

Only Verity's years of spying kept her jaw from dropping. *How did Annabeth's grandmother manage to know everything?* "I apologize. I did not see you at any of the parties I attended, or I would have—well, honestly, I probably would have fled for fear you would unmask me."

Lady Lockwood let out a crack of laughter. "Nonsense. I always enjoy a good jest on the *ton*. Come in, sit down, girl, and chat with us." She nodded toward the window seat across the room, where a very pregnant woman sat.

Verity's eyes widened. "Annabeth! I'm sorry, I didn't see you over there."

"Ha! She's hard to miss," Lady Lockwood said.

"I know I am wide as a house, Grandmother," Annabeth said mildly as she shoved up to her feet and walked toward Verity. "You needn't point it out." She smiled and reached to take Verity's hand. "You can see why you haven't seen *me* at any parties."

"But how—I mean, when—" Verity's customary aplomb had deserted her. "I'm sorry. That was rude of me."

Annabeth laughed. "Don't worry. I'm accustomed

to the reaction. I'm truly not as far along as I appear. Sloane's afraid I'm going to have twins."

"It's Sloane's fault, he's entirely too large," Lady Lockwood decreed. "I have always maintained one should marry a small man."

Annabeth rolled her eyes at Verity, and Verity smothered a laugh. "I agree. We should definitely blame Sloane."

Verity and Annabeth sat down together on the sofa, and the next few minutes were spent discussing babies, a subject about which Verity admitted she knew very little. Lady Lockwood soon shunted such chatter aside.

"Mrs. Dunbridge and Miss Dunbridge are visiting," Lady Lockwood told Verity.

"Nathan's mother and aunt," Annabeth explained in an aside.

"Marcus was so kind as to escort them on a shopping expedition," Lady Lockwood went on. "But they're bound to return soon. Even Rose Dunbridge can only take so long dithering over ribbons and such. She can't know, of course, that you are looking into this Douglas—or supposed Dunbridge—for Nathan. So we must hurry to discuss the investigation before they come back. What have you found out?"

Verity took a deep breath. "My lady, I cannot discuss my clients and cases. I'm sure you understand."

"Quite right. It would never do for other people to know," Lady Lockwood said approvingly. Apparently Lady Lockwood did not consider herself to be "other people," for she went on, "Have you talked to the man yourself? I'm sure he's after money to keep his lips sealed."

Verity wondered if it should concern her that her thoughts ran so close to Lady Lockwood's.

"It's good that you're with Dunbridge," Lady Lockwood went on without waiting for a response. "Nathan probably won't think the man's a swindler—he has a disturbing belief in his fellow man's goodness."

"Mmm," Verity said noncommittally, but she couldn't help but smile.

"*I* could tell the scoundrel was lying—he had a weaselly look about him. What I wonder is whether he's after larger game. He'll claim to be legitimate, I warrant." She looked at Verity shrewdly, then nodded. "I thought so."

Verity sighed. She would have sworn her face had given nothing away. "My lady, please…"

Beside her, Annabeth laughed and said, "You might as well tell her, Verity. You know very well she'll have it all out of Nathan in an instant."

That was certainly true. And, actually, Lady Lockwood might be of more help than anyone. She knew everything about everyone and had probably been privy to such information for many years. So Verity told them about their meeting with Malcolm Douglas and what they had found out since then, ending with the revelation that the church where George Dunbridge and Margaret Douglas had supposedly been married had burned down.

"Well, that's certainly suspicious," Annabeth remarked.

"Yes, isn't it," Verity replied drily. "Do you know about any of his story, my lady? The girl, Margaret? Mr. Dunbridge going to Scotland?"

"No, I do not," Lady Lockwood said somewhat resentfully. "I never heard even a whisper about the boy getting entangled with some girl in Scotland. And I am always informed on the latest gossip."

"Yes, you are," Verity agreed. *The woman should have been a spy herself.*

"Nor can I think that George Dunbridge could have kept such a secret for so many years." Lady Lockwood paused, then added judiciously, "He probably did go to Scotland to fish or hunt grouse when he was young as a great many gentlemen do."

"Which makes it a handy thing to claim as part of Malcolm Douglas's story," Verity said.

"Have you checked the diocesan records yet?" Annabeth's grandmother asked.

Verity stared at her blankly.

Lady Lockwood smiled triumphantly. "Really, Miss Cole…and you call yourself a detective."

"But I've never—" Verity swallowed her excuses and said with all the humility she could muster, "I fear my knowledge in that regard is lacking, my lady. Perhaps you could tell me?"

"Churches are supposed to send a copy of the records to the headquarters of their diocese. That church would, of course, be in the London diocese." She added somewhat dishearteningly, "Though I understand they are not always diligent in reporting to the diocese. I'm sure there are a number of the records missing."

"But if St. Agatha did send in their records and if that marriage isn't among the records, it would be good evidence against Douglas's story," Verity said. She felt buoyed by the knowledge, and she would have liked to leave right then to find Nathan. But before she could say good-bye, voices sounded in the entry, and a moment later, two women swept into the room, along with Marcus Rutherford, and it was too late to escape politely.

"My lady." Marcus went to Lady Lockwood and made an elegant bow over her hand, and Verity noticed that he held it a fraction longer than courtesy decreed.

Verity expected a sharp set-down from Lady Lockwood, but the woman just smiled and patted Mr. Rutherford's hand. "I'm sure you must be quite worn out after squiring the ladies around. Do sit down and have some tea. Annabeth, ring for the butler." She cast a glance at her granddaughter then said, "Never mind. Rose, you do it."

"Indeed, yes. Annabeth, you mustn't tire yourself." One of the women smiled brightly and went over to pull the cord.

"I'm fine, Mrs. Dunbridge," Annabeth said with the air of one not expecting to be believed.

Lady Lockwood introduced Verity to the new arrivals as Mrs. Billingham, a friend of Annabeth's. It was imperative, of course, to keep the investigation a secret from Mrs. Dunbridge, and it scarcely mattered that Nathan's mother would know Verity under a false name, for once this case was over Verity would doubtless never see the woman again. Still, she couldn't help but feel a small pang of regret at the subterfuge.

Nathan's mother was the pretty middle-aged woman who had done Lady Lockwood's bidding, and the sharper-faced woman, his aunt. Mrs. Dunbridge launched into a long and rather silly account of their shopping, but her manner was so sweet and lively that even Lady Lockwood laughed instead of making a sarcastic comment.

As the conversation progressed, Verity began to wonder if Nathan's mother was as muzzy-headed as she appeared. There was a little twinkle in Rose's eye that reminded Verity of Nathan when he teased. Once, after Rose asked a foolish question that made everyone laugh, Verity carefully observed the woman's pleased expression, and Rose flashed Verity a small conspiratorial smile.

Though Verity was curious about Nathan's mother and would have liked to get to know her better, she was even more eager to spend time with her son. She wanted to tell Nathan what she had learned from Lady Lockwood, and the whole time she'd been here, she had been wondering if he had called on her, only to find her gone. Besides, there was that strange little tug in her chest, the faint nameless anxiety.

When Annabeth concealed a yawn with her hand and suggested that it was time for her to go home, Verity immediately rose. "Yes, of course you must be tired. Let me drive you home—I brought my carriage."

"Thank you." Annabeth smiled. "That will save me having to drag Grandmother's poor coachman out again."

"I'm surprised Mr. Rutherford didn't accompany you," Nathan's aunt said. There was a faint bite to her words. Verity suspected that the Dunbridge women nursed some degree of resentment at Annabeth's choice of Sloane Rutherford over Nathan.

"Sloane had some business to attend to this morning," Annabeth said, her own voice as smooth and placid as a calm lake.

"Yes, he and Nathan were doing something," Marcus added.

"Sloane and Nathan?" Annabeth and Verity chorused in surprise.

"Why, yes." Marcus looked slightly taken aback at

their response. "Nathan came to call as I was leaving this morning. I think it's good that the lads are becoming friends again."

Verity wasn't sure that Nathan and Sloane had ever been friends, let alone had grown closer after Sloane married the woman Nathan loved. She and Annabeth exchanged a look, and Verity asked Marcus, "Why did Nathan visit Sloane?"

Marcus tilted his head to one side, thinking. "I don't believe he said. We just chatted a bit and then I left."

The little tug in Verity's chest grew stronger, and she hurriedly made her good-byes, as did Annabeth. She expected Annabeth's grandmother to make an acerbic remark about their rushing through the courtesies of departure, but Lady Lockwood simply looked at them shrewdly and waved them away.

"What could Nathan want from Sloane?" Annabeth asked in a low voice, hurrying along with Verity to the front door.

"I don't know. But he's up to something. I'm sure of it." Verity swept through the door that the footman had hurried to open. She looked up and down the street and saw her carriage ambling along. Yanking off her gloves, she stuck her thumb and finger between her teeth and let out a piercing whistle.

Annabeth started at the sound, but the look she sent Verity was admiring. "I'd like to do that. Can you teach me?"

"I can try. It comes in handy." Verity tossed her a grin.

The driver turned the horses and started back to them at a much quicker pace. Still, Verity continued to survey the area as they waited.

"Why do you think Nathan is up to something?" Annabeth asked. "What do you suppose it is?"

"I'm not sure. He just had this look in his eyes—like he was planning some sort of mayhem and didn't want me to know."

"Mayhem? Nathan?" Annabeth said in surprise.

The carriage rattled to a stop beside them, and Annabeth climbed in, aided by the little boost from behind that Verity gave her. Verity gave a last encompassing look around and started to get in.

"Miss! Miss!" a high-pitched breathless voice called in the distance. "Wait!"

Verity stepped back and looked up the street to where a young girl ran toward her, waving her arms frantically.

"Sally!" Verity's heart sped up. *Something's happened to Nathan.*

Sally was the most reliable of the band of street urchins Verity routinely hired—the girl had a tenacity you couldn't teach—and Verity had given her the task of keeping an eye on Nathan today. Clearly her uneasy feeling had been justified.

Verity hurried forward. "What is it? Is Nathan all right?"

The girl reached her and doubled over, hands on knees, gasping for breath. Sally was small and dressed in worn clothing, her face and hands a sort of grayish color that spoke of little washing. Verity stifled her impatience, and after a moment, the girl began to gasp out her message, "Sorry. Late. Couldn't get a hack to take me, and then you wasn't home."

"That's fine. Just tell me—is he in trouble?"

The girl nodded. "They was chasin' a man—"

"They? Was a dark-haired man with him?"

Sally nodded. "That's him. I seen him on the docks afore. They chased this tall skinny fella into a place in Cheapside, and I waited, but they never come out. It's a bad place, miss, and gents like that... I don't know. I went in and couldn't see 'em. I think... I think they went down in the tunnels."

"That bloody—" Verity broke off. "I'm going to kill him."

"Which one, miss?"

"Both of them," Verity replied grimly.

"I left Ned there, 'case they come back out."

"Good girl. Climb up there and tell the driver where to go." Verity helped Sally clamber up to the coachman's seat, then jumped into the carriage herself. It took off with a lurch.

Annabeth, who had been watching the scene with her head out the window, said, "What's going on? I couldn't hear all of what she was saying."

"In short, Nathan and Sloane are fools, and they've wound up in a tunnel in Cheapside, and who knows what's happened to them. Of all the stupid things—" Verity broke off, then began to relate in a calmer voice everything Sally had told her.

"But why were they following this man? Is it Douglas?"

Verity shook her head. "I think it's perhaps one of the men who attacked us." At Annabeth's alarmed exclamation at that statement, Verity went on to explain what had happened the evening before. As she talked, Verity pulled a pistol case out from a side pocket of the carriage and began to load it.

Annabeth settled back against the cushions of the

carriage, looking somewhat stunned. "Well…Nathan's life has certainly taken a new turn."

"Yes. It's my fault. I shouldn't have let him help me with the case." Verity sighed. "Well, at least he has Sloane with him, thank heavens."

Annabeth sent her a wry look. "Yes. Because we all know how cautious and peace-loving Sloane is."

Verity looked at her for a moment, then leaned out the window and called, "Drive faster, Russell."

# CHAPTER FOURTEEN

NATHAN SET THE long block of stone on the base they had made and pushed it into place in the center, flush against another stone. He straightened up, stretching his back, and wiped his hand across his forehead. Though it was cool in this cave-like place, the exertion of carrying stones and fitting them together had made him sweat. He, like Sloane, had long ago discarded his jacket, waistcoat, and neckcloth, rolled up his sleeves and undone the ties of his shirt. But none of it was enough to make him cool; his thin lawn shirt was plastered to his chest and sweat ran down his face, smearing the dirt and grime that covered it.

Sloane, too, stood looking at the pile of stone before them, his hands on his hips, and it made Nathan feel somewhat better that the other man looked as weary and discouraged as Nathan felt.

From above them came a woman's voice. "Hello, lads. Need some help?"

"Verity!" Nathan's head snapped up and he saw Verity lying at the edge of the hole, braced on her elbows. His intense relief was overwhelmed by the fear that stabbed through him. "Get back! That floor just caved in on us."

"I can see that. But here it's still solid rock beneath me. I just leaned over and looked." She twisted and spoke to someone behind her, then disappeared for a moment.

Nathan's heart slowed down a notch, though it still made him cringe to think of Verity climbing out there to look over. Verity returned with a lantern, holding it out to shed light on the men below. With the lantern's light, he could see that Annabeth's face appeared beside Verity's.

"Annabeth!" Sloane thundered, scowling. "What the devil are you doing here? Good God, did you climb down that ladder? Have you taken leave of your senses?"

Annabeth rolled her eyes. "I'm with child, Sloane, not on my deathbed. And I must say, I would think you two would be a little more glad to see us."

"Of course we're glad to see you," Nathan protested. "It's just…" Verity, he knew, could handle herself, but not if there were more than several attackers to fight off. A very pregnant Annabeth would be of little help—not that he was foolish enough to tell her that.

Sloane, however, had no such reticence. "It's *dangerous*. God knows what sort of villain you're liable to run into here. They aren't going to back off because you're pregnant."

"That's why I have this." Annabeth held up a pistol.

"God save us," Sloane groaned.

Nathan sympathized with Sloane, but he had to stifle a little laugh.

"Since we are the ones currently saving your hides—" Verity knelt beside the hole again "—you might try addressing your prayers to *us* for the time being."

Sloane glared at her. "I can't believe you dragged Annabeth into this with you. You should have stopped to think."

"I'll remind you that *I* wasn't the one who decided to go charging through Cheapside and follow a man down into a tunnel," Verity retorted.

This remark served to shut Sloane up, and Verity tossed one end of a knotted rope down to them. "The ladder's too short to reach you, and in any case, it's attached to the entry. You're going to have to climb this rope."

Nathan eyed the rope. There was no way Annabeth and Verity could counter either his or Sloane's weight. "But how—"

"My coachman Russell is here with us," Verity answered his unspoken question. "And we've wrapped the rope around the ladder for leverage. But perhaps you should come up first, Nathan." When Nathan took a step toward the rope, she added drily, "You might want to bring the rest of your clothes. Not that we don't admire the view."

"Good Gad." In the excitement of the moment, he'd forgotten his state of undress. He was certain he was blushing from his chest to his hairline as he retreated, retying his shirt as he went. Well, at least he was more clothed than Sloane, who had shed his shirt entirely— not, of course, that Sloane would care.

Sloane laughed, proving Nathan's point. Nathan haphazardly pulled on his waistcoat and jacket and stuffed his neckcloth in his pocket. He went back to the rope and looked up. "Ready?"

"Yes," came a chorus of voices from farther back in the tunnel.

He couldn't quite dismiss the image of Verity being pulled down here with him. "Well, if you start to slide, let go."

"Nathan, would you just climb the rope?"

Nathan stepped up onto the foundation he and Sloane had laid—at least it was worth something—and began to climb. It had been years since he had done this, but it turned out he was still able to pull himself up, even though he was a good bit heavier than his twelve-year-old self.

He reached the top and crawled onto the tunnel floor, Verity rushing forward to help. Flopping onto his back, Nathan simply lay there for a moment, soaking in the relief of being out of the ruins.

"Are you injured?" Verity knelt beside him, peering down at him with an expression he'd never seen on her face before. She brushed the dust from his face and ran her hands over his chest and arms. *Well, this was rather pleasant, actually.*

"I'm fine," he said somewhat reluctantly and rolled to his feet. That look on Verity's face had been anxiety. Verity had been worried about him, which both surprised and warmed him. He would have liked to take her in his arms and just hold her. But of course he couldn't with Russell and Annabeth watching and Sloane waiting to be rescued.

Nathan took his place along the rope with the others and called Sloane to climb up. After Sloane reached the top, there was a great deal of him and Annabeth hugging and kissing in between bickering, while the others rolled up the rope and carried it and the lantern up the ladder. Sloane and Annabeth followed more slowly.

Verity's coach had been guarded by a group of street urchins, whom she rewarded with coins. There was no hack in view, so they squeezed into Verity's town coach, with Annabeth sitting on Sloane's lap and Nathan choosing to join the driver on his high seat rather than folding himself into the small space in front of the other passengers' feet. Verity suggested that she sit there, being smaller, but Nathan sent her a fulminating look and climbed up onto the coachman's seat. A man had to have some pride, after all, and he wasn't about to let Verity sit on the floor after he had already had to be rescued by her.

There was some compensation to the choice, anyway, as the breeze blew away some of the dust that had settled on him. It also cheered him a little to remind himself that Sloane, the former spy extraordinaire himself, was also nursing his damaged pride after their failed attempt to question, or even catch, the man they'd fallen into a pit chasing.

When they reached Verity's house, Nathan and Verity disembarked, and the carriage rolled off to take the other couple home. As they walked to the front door, Nathan tried futilely to rub away the streaks of dirt on his face and neck where his sweat had mingled with the dust.

"Oh, stop that," Verity said in an exasperated tone. "Come in and wash up. You and I need to talk."

That sounded faintly ominous, Nathan thought, but he had a few questions to ask Verity, as well.

Verity turned him over to her housekeeper, who, after an appalled exclamation, showed him upstairs to a wash basin and pitcher and ordered him to give her his jacket and waistcoat to clean. Nathan washed his hands and face, as well as his neck and lower arms, and finally wound up pouring the rest of the pitcher over his head. The result was less than perfect—he could only finger-comb his wet hair into some order and his shirt was still somewhat dirty, and now wet around the neck and the end of his sleeves. But he felt a great deal better. He would have liked to have his jacket, but, really, what did it matter at this point? Verity was hardly one to insist on proper attire, and she had already seen him in only his shirt, anyway. *Had she meant what she said about admiring the view?* He couldn't quite stifle the little rush of pleasure that thought brought.

He left the upstairs chamber and ventured down to the parlor, where he found Verity eating cakes and drinking tea. "Sit down. You must be hungry."

Nathan's stomach agreed. His questions could wait. He joined her, polishing off the rest of the food and drinking two cups of tea.

Verity waited until he'd drained the second cup before she crossed her arms and said, "Why were you two running around Cheapside, falling into holes?"

"We didn't actually intend to fall into a hole," he shot back, nettled by her description of his efforts. "We were chasing one of those men who attacked us last night so I could find out who hired them."

"So of course you turned to Sloane."

Nathan wasn't sure why, but there was a distinct tone of resentment in Verity's voice. "He's the only person I know who is familiar with the criminal underworld." When Verity raised one eyebrow he added, "Besides you, I mean. And I was trying to keep you out of it."

"Keep me out of it?" She stared. "I was well in it last night."

"And that's why. I think they targeted you, and I think Arden is highly suspect. I wanted to find out if I was right so I could stop him."

A number of emotions flitted across Verity's face so

quickly he could not be sure what they were. "I—well, that's, um, kind—no one's ever…" Verity paused, pressing her lips together, then squared her shoulders and lifted her chin a bit, saying, "Well, I don't see why you didn't ask me to help. It isn't as if I'm useless."

"No," he answered quickly. "Of course not. It wasn't that. It—I thought—I was trying to protect you," he finished lamely. He didn't want to think about the notion, more centered in his chest than in his brain, that he had wanted to slay the dragon of Lord Arden and lay it at her feet. To divert her from any further questions, he said, "Whatever I was trying to do, clearly I failed. The most information I got was from a barkeep who told me that Arden has hired men at his tavern. He couldn't say, though, if he had hired those two particular men. We tracked them down to a house, but I imagine they won't be going back there now."

"Still, that's useful. It gives us some other places to look for them and Douglas. Douglas could have hired them, too."

"Yes, it seems to be a common transaction there."

"Did Sloane know anything about them?"

Nathan shook his head. "No, we found out about that tavern from that man Parker."

"Ah, Sloane's former enemy that he sold off his illegal businesses to when he went legitimate."

"Of course you know all about that."

Verity gave a coy little half shrug.

"Then we found out where those men stayed from the barkeep. And that's when the chase started." He shrugged, then asked her the question that had plagued him the whole drive home. "What I want to know is, how the devil did you track us down?"

"Oh. Sally told me—one of those children who were guarding my carriage. She's bright and I use her to follow people fairly often. As I said before, no one notices street urchins."

"You had me followed?" Nathan's voice rose. She nodded, and somehow the lack of embarrassment or guilt on her face added to his quick anger. He jumped to his feet. "Why? Do you think I'm so untrustworthy?"

"No, of course not. I was worried about what you might do—after last night, I just thought you might get into trouble."

"And of course I'm too incompetent to take care of myself," he said bitterly.

"No." Verity stood up, her voice rising, too. "What is the matter with you? Would you rather I hadn't found you today?"

"That's not the point."

"Do you *have* a point?"

"The point is that you obviously think I have to be taken care of instead of being a help to you."

"Oh, you mean the way *you* thought *I* had to be taken care of and was of no help to you when you went after our attackers?" Verity's eyes took on a dangerous glint.

"I was trying to protect you!"

"And why is it fine for you to want to protect me, but it's not all right for me to want to protect you?"

"You do it because you think I'm useless." Somewhere in the back of his mind, Nathan knew that he should not start down this path, but he could not stop the words that came pouring out. "I have known what you thought of me from the start—that I was a bumbling fool who only got in your way. But I had begun to think you might have changed your view a bit now that we've…that we know each other better. But you still regard me as incompetent."

"I don't think you're incompetent." Verity fisted her hands on her hips and glared at him. "That's not why I worried about you. It's not why I wanted to protect you."

"No? Then why did you do it?"

"Because I care—" She stopped abruptly, looking faintly alarmed, then said, "Because you are my client. I cannot have my clients being knocked over the head or falling down holes. It's bad for my reputation."

"That's not what you were about to say." He narrowed his eyes at her. "You were going to say because you care about me."

"Don't be absurd."

"It's not absurd." His anger and hurt had drained out of him in an instant at her words. "That's exactly why I wanted to protect you."

Verity made a scoffing sound and looked away, apparently now fascinated by the view outside the window.

Nathan smiled to himself, warmth stealing through him. "Admit it. You've come to like me." He took a step forward.

Verity turned her head to face him, raising her chin a little, but Nathan noticed that she did not move back. He thought it was strange that the stubborn set of her chin made him want to kiss her.

"Come, Verity, you might as well say it." Nathan stepped close to her and put his hand on her waist. "You care about me."

She raised one shoulder in a shrug. "Perhaps…a little." And once again she made no effort to move away.

"A little?" His thumb began to make little circles upon her waist. "Is that all your kiss counts for?"

"That was a momentary aberration." Verity placed her palms flat on his chest as if to hold him back, but she applied no pressure. And the feel of her skin through the thin material of his shirt shot sparks all through him.

"Twice?" he asked, raising an eyebrow. "One kiss might be an aberration. Two is a habit."

She glared at him, annoyed. "Very well. *Yes*, I kissed you. And, *yes*, I liked it. I even like you, heaven help me. But that's not enough."

"Enough for what?" he murmured and bent to softly kiss the corner of her mouth. The little dimple there deepened, and she made a soft noise, part laugh and part pleasure, so he kissed the other side. And, finally, his lips came to rest fully on her mouth, his arms going around her.

Verity curled her hands into the cloth of his shirt, and when he lifted his lips, she sighed, "Oh, Nathan… this isn't wise."

"Not at all," he agreed and kissed her again.

"We're nothing alike," she murmured as she wrapped her arms around his neck and went up on her toes for another kiss.

"Clearly." Nathan began to kiss his way down her neck. *God, but she tasted delicious. Smelled delicious.* He was quickly losing his train of thought, but he managed to add, "You're rash and unpredictable."

She slid her fingers into his hair, and his passion spiked. "And you are stodgy and…" Whatever she was about to say died in a soft moan as his hand slid up to cup her breast.

Verity was so very sweet and pliable in his arms, her jagged edges melting away in heat and hunger. That is until Verity clenched her fingers in his hair and gave it a sharp tug.

"Ow." Nathan raised his head and looked down at her dazedly. "You could have just said stop." His arms fell away and he stepped back.

"Stop." Verity's eyes were bright, her face flushed, and her hair in some disarray. All Nathan wanted to do was take her back into his arms. "Nathan, what are we doing?"

"If you don't know, then I was obviously doing it badly," Nathan retorted.

A little smile tugged at her lips. "You were doing it very well. That's the problem. We need to think about this."

His instinct was to dispute her words. Nathan really wasn't interested in thinking right now. But she was right, of course. If they continued, they'd soon wind up in bed. And that would be a mistake. Really. It would. Even if he couldn't think of the reason why right now.

Nathan sighed and moved farther away, shoving his hand through his hair. "I apologize. I was, um…" What had he been? Impolite? Discourteous? That seemed far too tame. Filled with lust would be more like it. "Ungentlemanly."

Verity giggled.

*Of course she would.* He ought to know by now not to expect a typical response from her.

"I don't care about that." She made a dismissive wave of her hand. "The problem is—I do like you."

"Excuse me?"

"It would have been entirely different two weeks ago. Then it would have been easy. Just for fun. But now it would mean something. So I have to be careful.

I don't…" She looked away for a moment, then set her jaw and turned back. "I don't want to lose you. Lovers are easy to find. Friends are hard to come by."

"Of course. You're right." Nathan would have come up with words about propriety and being influenced by the high emotions of the day, about respect and regret and how very wrong they were for each other. Verity had summed it up in a simple statement. And it stunned him a little to realize how very much *he* did not want to lose *her*. "Well. I should go home now. It's been a wearing day."

"Yes. But tomorrow…" There was the faintest tinge of question in her tone.

He nodded. "I'll return tomorrow."

# CHAPTER FIFTEEN

OF COURSE HE would return tomorrow, Nathan thought as he walked home—and every day after that if the way he felt right now was any indication. His thinking was muddled, his emotions every which way, and he churned with desire for Verity.

He was well aware that he had no idea what he was doing. The only things he was certain of were: first, he very much wanted to make love to Verity, and second, he was doubtlessly acting like a fool. The latter concern was easily overcome; he had acted the fool around Verity so many times that he was beyond embarrassment.

Much more worrisome was his desire for her. Though Verity didn't seem bothered by what people might think of her, Nathan cared about her reputation. No doubt she would laugh at that concern and tell him that no one would either know or care what they did. But Nathan had been on the social scene far longer than Verity, and he knew exactly how much the *ton* delighted in the slightest bit of titillating gossip.

He liked Verity too much to make her his mistress, but the only other course was marriage. Nathan had grown content with the idea of living as a bachelor during his months abroad. And, given his financial state, the only marital options he had were to marry an heiress as his aunt wanted or drag a woman with him into a life of genteel penny-pinching. He didn't wish to do either. Even when he had been eager to marry Annabeth, he'd felt guilty, knowing that all he could give her was a chance to leave Lady Lockwood's house.

Verity, he was sure, had no interest in becoming anyone's wife. Any romance with her was destined to be blazing but brief. The desire that had flamed in him tonight was too fierce to last. And whatever had made Verity respond to his kisses would quickly fade as she came to realize that he was no more interesting than she had judged him to be when they first met.

In any case, they were completely unsuited for each other. Verity was prickly and suspicious and held her secrets close to her, whereas Nathan was practically an open book. Her idea of a pleasant evening wouldn't be sitting by the fireside, reading. Well, that wasn't really appealing to him, either, when he thought of it.

Nathan wasn't sure what Verity's idea of a perfect evening would be—breaking into someone's house, perhaps, or fighting a ruffian in a dark alley. Whatever it was, it probably was not making the social rounds—that got boring even for him. And there was that little matter of her killing Lord Stanhope years ago. However much the snake had deserved to die, murder was illegal, and it could be dangerous for her to be seen moving in aristocratic circles without a disguise. Someone would be bound to identify her at some point. And then what would she do? Flee to the Continent?

Which only went to confirm that spending a lifetime with Verity would be downright dangerous.

The right thing, the smart thing, was to do as Verity had suggested: carry on as they had been doing, working together but *not* falling into bed together. Nathan would be friendly but contained. Not stand too close or touch her. The only problem was that the prospect of doing all those things was distinctly unappealing.

Despite his turmoil, Nathan was too tired not to fall asleep as soon as he fell into bed. However, his night was filled with long, lascivious dreams, and he awakened the next morning in a sorry state, as confused and torn between lust and reason as he had been the night before.

As he shaved and dressed, his mind continued to churn, so much so that he had to retie his neckcloth three times before he got it right. To distract himself from such fruitless thoughts, he turned his mind to the events of the day before.

Admittedly, his venture yesterday had not ended well. Even if Nathan ignored the fact that he and Sloane had fallen into the ruins, they still had lost the man they'd been chasing *and* alerted him to their pursuit. The man wouldn't be going back to his home or other old haunts anytime soon. Instead he and his partner had doubtlessly gone to ground in the stews of London or left the city altogether.

Still, the fiasco had not been a total loss. The barkeep hadn't seen Lord Arden talking to the men who had attacked Nathan and Verity, but he had said that Arden came to that tavern to hire ruffians for his misdeeds. In comparison, the man had shown no recognition of Malcolm Douglas's name or description or of Stanhope's, which made Arden the much more likely person to have hired the men. The pair might move around from tavern to tavern, but people were generally creatures of habit.

As Nathan and Verity had discussed, there seemed little that Malcolm Douglas would gain by incapacitating them. Nor did it seem likely that Stanhope had recognized Verity from a brief glimpse at a party. She had been only a girl of fourteen at that time. And after sixteen years, would the man's blood have run so hot for revenge that he would have Verity killed? It seemed far more likely to Nathan that Lord Stanhope would have turned her in to the authorities.

Not to mention the undeniable fact that the men were asking about something they thought Verity and Nathan had or knew. This pointed strongly to Lord Arden as the culprit: he must have learned Verity's identity from the guard she had fought, and now he wanted back the brooch Verity and Nathan had taken from his house.

And Lord Arden was a problem Nathan could take care of. In fact, he rather looked forward to it. He went first to the man's house, where the butler informed him that Arden had gone to his gentlemen's club. Given the early hour, Nathan presumed it was the more ordinary club Arden was visiting rather than the scandalous one, the badge to which Nathan had seen in Arden's little box of treasures.

The hushed club, with its heavy dark furniture, plush carpets, and hovering butler was a milieu as familiar to Nathan as the docks were to Sloane. Nathan's father had introduced him to White's when he reached adulthood. Nathan had chosen a club more frequented by the younger set, but in essence they were all the same—a retreat from home and families for men of the higher classes, and Nathan was easily recognized as a person who *belonged*.

The place was half-empty at this hour: a couple of old men snoozing in their chairs, a few others talking in hushed tones, and various men perusing one of the newspapers. In truth, it hardly seemed the sort of place Arden would like, but perhaps it was good for picking up gossip to use for blackmail.

Nathan found Lord Arden sitting near one of the windows, sipping a cup of tea. Arden's brows rose a little when he saw Nathan heading toward him. They had never been anything but the merest of acquaintances.

"Dunbridge." Arden rose to greet Nathan, his expression guarded, and gestured toward the chair across from him. "Sit down. Shall I ring for tea?"

"No. This isn't a pleasant little chat."

"Indeed? How interesting. Do go on."

"I know about Lady Bankwater and the brooch. Your profitable little business."

"I'm afraid you know more than I, then." Arden gazed at him coolly.

"That is probably true in general, but you know this particular subject quite well. I was in the Blue Swan yesterday."

"That rat hole? Hardly seems the place for you."

"True, but it is apparently a place for you," Nathan replied. "I believe you're familiar with two men named Hill and Shoemaker?"

Nathan watched Arden carefully, and he was sure he saw a flicker of recognition in Arden's eyes, a second's hesitation before his languid reply. "Who?"

"You know, the men you hire from time to time to ensure payments by the people you blackmail."

Arden rose to his feet, eyes flashing. "That is an insult, sir. I should call you out."

"I wouldn't advise it," Nathan said calmly, rising to face the other man. "I will not brook someone threatening those close to me. And surely you know *my* reputation is that of a marksman. I could make my point without shooting you through the heart. I believe there are other parts of your anatomy that matter to you more." Nathan gave a careless shrug of one shoulder. "Besides, the subject of my insult to you would inevitably get out, and you wouldn't want that, would you?"

"I don't know what you're on about. You must already be in your cups," Arden said. "It's time you left."

"What I'm *on* about is that you hired those two men to attack Mrs. Billingham. And I cannot allow that to stand."

"What?" Arden's eyes widened a fraction. "I did not hire anyone to attack your little paramour."

Nathan grabbed a handful of Arden's shirt and shoved him back into the corner formed by the wall and a bookcase. They were partially shielded from the view of the rest of the club, but at this moment Nathan didn't care if everyone could see them.

"Do not insult Mrs. Billingham," Nathan said, his voice hard as granite. "Don't come near her. Don't send anyone after her. If you do, I will ruin you."

Arden had paled, but he attempted a sneer. "As if you could do that."

"Don't tempt me. Look around you." Nathan nodded toward the rest of the room. "This place, these men— you enjoy being a part of that, don't you? Are you willing to risk being banished from your club, unwelcome at any gathering, all for the sake of some petty revenge? Because that's what will happen if I tell everyone about your blackmail schemes and the sexual perversions you engage in at your other club. I told you: I know about you. I saw your membership token to the Devil's Den."

Arden's jaw dropped in surprise. "It was you who took—"

"Yes, it was I." Nathan let go of the other man's shirt and took a half step back, adjusting the cuffs of his jacket. "Lady Lockwood would be the first person I'd tell about your secret activities. That should ensure that all the *ton* would know."

Arden narrowed his eyes. "You have no proof of any of this."

Nathan smiled. "I don't need proof. You know that. All I have to do is say it."

Nathan saw frustrated acknowledgement flare in Lord Arden's eyes. Arden might be of higher rank, but he hadn't the liking or reputation in the *ton* that Nathan had.

"I won't do anything to your—Mrs. Billingham," Arden growled.

Nathan turned to leave, and Arden sent a last parting shot after him, "I never did in the first place."

Nathan didn't give the other man the satisfaction of pausing or turning back to question him. It was pointless; the man would only lie. And Nathan couldn't prove Arden had hired the men any more than Arden could prove he hadn't.

He continued out of the club, frowning in thought. Arden was the most likely culprit. Nathan didn't trust him, but on the other hand, Arden's eyes had shown the faintest flicker of surprise when Nathan had accused him of sending his men to attack Verity. His reaction was slight; Arden was good at hiding his true self. But had Nathan been mistaken?

If he had just warned off the wrong person then all he had done was put "Mrs. Billingham" in Arden's sights. And Verity was still in danger.

## CHAPTER SIXTEEN

VERITY WENT TO her office the next morning. She told herself that she had been neglecting her business the last two weeks, and she needed to catch up on reports and requests. However, when she arrived, instead of heading to her desk, she dropped into a chair beside Mrs. Malloy and said, "I think I've made a terrible mistake."

Mrs. Malloy's eyebrows went up. "With a case?"

"No. Well, I mean, I haven't accomplished anything there, either. But it's about Nathan."

"The man himself?"

"Yes. You see...well, yesterday I had him followed."

"Why? Do you think he's lying to you?"

"No, never that. He—I better start at the beginning." Verity launched into the entire story, starting with the attack and running all the way through rescuing Nathan and Sloane.

By the time she finished, Mrs. Malloy was laughing so hard she had to take out a handkerchief to dab at the tears in her eyes. "Oh, I'd have paid a penny to see that."

"It was rather amusing," Verity agreed. "But that's not the problem."

"Ah. Mr. Dunbridge's manly pride." The other woman nodded in understanding. "It's a devil of a thing to deal with. Was he angry?"

"He wasn't angry about the rescue, that just embarrassed him. But he was annoyed that I'd had him followed. We quarreled a bit, and, well, the long and short of it is that I told him I cared about him."

"What!" Mrs. Malloy looked at her in astonishment.

"Yes, and, then he began to kiss me, and…" Verity let her voice trail off.

"Oh, my. You went to bed with him?"

"No."

"Why ever not?" Mrs. Malloy exclaimed. "He's a handsome lad—that smile. And such elegant manners. If I were twenty years younger, I'd have snatched him up myself."

"You should have seen him yesterday in only his shirt and breeches." Verity's smile curved up reminiscently. "All sweaty and his shirt hanging open."

"Oh, my." Mrs. Malloy wielded an imaginary fan.

"As you can imagine, my defenses were down after that scene. And he was teasing me, his eyes twinkling in that way he has."

"I repeat—why did you turn him down?"

"I'm not a trollop, Bettina. I've turned down lots of men."

"I am aware of that. You're the choosiest woman I know. I've told you many times, you need to let go and enjoy what life has to offer. It's my opinion your Mr. Dunbridge has a lot to offer."

"He does." Verity's chest tightened. "For some woman who suits him. But I'm not that woman."

"It sounds as if he thinks so."

"It was done in the heat of the moment. Normally he doesn't—well, except for that once—ah, twice. But those were in the heat of the moment, too."

"It sounds to me like you two have a lot of heated moments."

"While we're on this case, yes. But normally we would not even be around each other, let alone attracted. We're thousands of miles apart in every way. He's so... nice. So thoughtful and such a gentleman. A true gentleman, I mean, not an aristocrat. And I am none of those things."

"What rubbish. Honestly, Verity, I've never known you to discount yourself before. You're very nice. And I don't think he's looking for a true gentleman."

Verity laughed. "You know what I mean. A true lady. Someone like Annabeth."

"Rutherford's wife?"

"Yes. Nathan was madly in love with her a year ago. I suspect he still is—or at least holds her as his ideal woman. Annabeth and I are nothing alike. I'm brash and have a wicked tongue. Not to mention, a positively lurid past. More lurid than even you know." *And yet I told Nathan all about it.* "He could never marry a woman like me."

Mrs. Malloy stared. "You want to marry him?"

"No!" Verity said quickly. "Of course not." She looked down at her hands, considering her next words. "I don't know what I want to have with him. But I feel a way I've never felt with any other man. I feel like I want to...*keep* him. And it scares me a little how much I want him to stay. I hate to think about what will happen when we take care of the Malcolm Douglas problem."

"The end of the case doesn't mean the end of you and Mr. Dunbridge."

Verity shook her head. "When the case is done, it will be different, even if we start an affair. He'll be doing the sort of things the upper class does, the things he's always done. And I cannot keep up the pretense of Mrs.

Billingham much longer, so I won't be in his world after this. Once the case is gone, the excitement will leave, as well. There won't be any rescues or attacks or things to discover. There won't be those 'heat of the moment' moments."

Verity smiled a little, remembering, then sighed. "Even if that emotion doesn't die, eventually there will come a time when Nathan will want to marry. I cannot imagine him not wanting a wife and children. It's simply his nature. Nathan is not the sort of man to keep a mistress on the side." Verity's eyes hardened. "And I'm not the sort of woman willing to share him. Someday, even if it's not soon, *someday* he'll leave."

Bettina Malloy studied her for a moment. "I'll admit I don't know much about marriage. I'm not the one to give anyone advice about that. What I do know is passion. Once it's burning, it's hard to stop."

"I know." Verity nodded. "It's not passion I fear."

"Then what?"

"I'm not in love with him—really, I'm not—but I'm afraid I could be. No, that's not quite right. I'm afraid because I know I *would* fall in love with him. And when we part, it will break my heart. I have to be sure that what I feel for him is worth the pain it will cause."

"So you've finally found a risk Verity Cole won't take." The older woman's smile softened her words. "What did he say when you turned him down?"

Verity lifted one shoulder in a half shrug. "I didn't exactly turn him down. I told him I don't want to lose his friendship. Which is true—once you start, the friendship is gone. While you're in the affair, it's so much more than friendship, and after the affair ends, it's so much less. But now I worry that last night already damaged what we have. Nathan was a perfect gentle-man, just as one would expect of him. He didn't argue or try to persuade me, he agreed to continue as friends. But after that, it was awkward between us. Neither one of us quite knew how to act. What if that is how it will continue to be? What if I've ruined it? I shouldn't have kissed him."

"It would have happened sometime," Mrs. Malloy said flatly. "The feelings were there whether you kissed him or not. And you weren't the only participant. I warrant Mr. Dunbridge encouraged you along the way."

A faint smile touched Verity's lips. "Yes. He was rather good at it, too."

Mrs. Malloy reached over and patted Verity's arm, her voice comforting. "I have the feeling this will all work itself out. Mr. Dunbridge doesn't sound to me like he's going anywhere. You need to trust your instincts. I've never seen you so discombobulated."

"That's because it's never been real before."

"I know, dear. And that's why this is a good thing."

"A good thing to be at all sixes and sevens?" Verity frowned.

"Of course." Mrs. Malloy smiled. "That's the way love is, dear. And now you know."

Verity had tried to concentrate on reports for her cases the remainder of the morning, but she could think of nothing but Nathan. It was thoroughly irritating. How romance-obsessed ladies in the *ton* ever got a single thing accomplished was beyond her understanding. Of course, most ladies of breeding had few things they needed to get done, and the things they *did* were prob-ably all in service of landing that dashing beau they thought of constantly. Well, she wasn't going to join their ranks. Standing up from her desk, she told Mrs. Malloy she was going for a walk. Busying her body often freed Verity's mind and brought her clarity on a case.

Before she knew it, she was walking to a place she'd been just recently. And though Verity told herself it had nothing to do with Nathan, deep down she knew if she was not considering some sort of entanglement with him, she would not be so fixated on checking on the home where she had killed the late Lord Stanhope.

Verity knew she shouldn't be here again; she wasn't even in disguise this time. But perhaps she could use that to her advantage. The young girl she'd talked to originally had seemed loose-tongued—it was only her superior that had kept her from saying too much about Stanhope. And the girl had been working outside the house last time. Maybe if Verity waited around for a while she would come back out. She'd probably be even more willing to give information to someone who was dressed as Verity was now—in a proper day dress and not tattered rags like the last time—and could offer her a few shillings for her trouble.

But she couldn't just stand on the sidewalk for however long it might take for the girl's chores to take her outside. Surely then Verity would draw the attention of the older woman and ruin her chance at getting more information. Verity discreetly studied the house as she walked past, continuing around to the street that formed the back border of the park. There was no entrance on this side—the pleasant bit of greenery in the middle of the city was intended for only the residents of the crescent row—but the wrought iron fence was little impediment to Verity.

Several of the trees in the park branched outside it, and after a quick glance around her, Verity made a running jump and swung up onto an overhanging tree limb and shimmied along it to the trunk and down on the other side of the fence.

Shrubbery grew along the fence, shielding the park and its occupants from the view of passersby. Verity crossed the grass to the other side and sat down on a bench where she could see the house without being seen herself.

Nothing of any note happened for the next hour, and Verity felt herself growing drowsy. But she came alert in an instant when a man opened the gate and stepped inside the park. Her pulse quickened and for a moment she thought it was Lord Stanhope, back from the country estate. Verity quickly slipped off the bench and ducked into a cluster of greenery that bordered a large tree nearby.

On closer inspection of the man, she could see that not only was he shorter and heavier than Jonathan, he had the beginnings of a bald patch—he certainly did not possess her stepbrother's thick hair. She was more on edge than she had realized if she'd thought this man could be Lord Stanhope.

Verity was well hidden on two sides by the shrubbery and sprawling tree—not that the man would have noticed her anyway. He didn't glance around the park, keeping his eyes on the gate, only looking away to check his watch occasionally. It was obvious he was waiting for someone, and Verity cursed her bad luck. She'd hoped to catch the attention of the girl if she came out of the house, but Verity could hardly pop out from her hiding place like some sort of deranged jack-in-the-box with this man here.

Her mind was busily working through scenarios—perhaps she could feign that she had dropped a piece of jewelry and been searching for it all this time—when the person the man had been waiting for walked through the gate. This time it *was* Jonathan Stanhope. Verity's eyes widened. She melted further into the shrubbery behind the tree and peered out through the branches.

Stanhope's face was stony, and he greeted the other man shortly—*Milsap. One of the most renowned Bow Street Runners.* Stanhope had some serious business if he had hired Milsap. Verity could not hear what the two were saying from this distance, only the tone of their voices. Stanhope was clearly angry, and the other man looked taken aback.

Verity cast about for a way to draw nearer while remaining concealed, but at that moment, Stanhope swung around and began to pace, his words reaching Verity in snatches as he walked back and forth. "...what I paid you for...excuses...you swore to me that she was dead."

Though her name was not mentioned, Verity felt a deep certainty that Stanhope was talking about her. Had he recognized her at the party last week after all?

Milsap followed him, saying, "Sir, she was. She is."

"Don't lie to me, Milsap," Stanhope snapped, his voice as cold as his expression. "I will not brook deception."

Verity's stomach tightened. *I will not brook this behavior, young lady.*

The other man stiffened, his voice turning frosty. "Sir. I do not lie. I have a reputation to uphold."

"I don't give a damn about your reputation." Stanhope swung around. "I want you to do the job you didn't do sixteen years ago."

He strode toward the gate, the other man at his side, talking in a cajoling tone. They stopped at the gate, and Stanhope made a curt remark, then strode off. Milsap turned sharply and walked in the other direction.

Verity didn't move from her hiding place, her heart racing. Milsap walked straight past her, muttering, "Just like them, blaming me 'cause he's seeing things. Bloody aristocrat."

Verity waited several minutes to emerge from behind the tree to make sure neither of the men returned— and to let her rapid pulse slow. There was no mistaking Jonathan Stanhope's anger at the prospect that Verity might not be dead, and he was just as obviously determined to find her if she was alive.

A craven impulse to run bloomed within her, followed by a desire to find Nathan and...*and what*? Tell him she was afraid? Not strong enough to fight her enemies? A fragile flower who needed his protection?

Something like a growl sounded low in her throat, and Verity steeled her spine. This was her problem. Her danger. She'd been fighting her own fights all her life, and she wasn't about to stop now. She had no doubt that Nathan would feel he ought to protect her if she told him, but he had enough of a burden as it was, trying to protect his family's reputation. And she refused to appear weak in front of him—that was not the woman he knew. Not the woman she wanted him to know.

Verity walked briskly out of the park, keeping careful watch for Stanhope or Milsap to turn back even as she began to logically consider the problem.

The rumors of Verity's death that Asquith had planted had worked in the past if a hunter as renowned as Milsap had believed them. But would that subterfuge still hold? Even though she now used a false last name and was frequently in disguise, Verity had been in London long enough and engaged in enough cases that she was known to many people. She, too, had a reputation.

It had been a mistake to keep the name Verity; it was not a common one. A mistake, too, to have worn so little disguise in her role as Mrs. Billingham. She had been overconfident, too certain that her past was well behind her, and it had been sheer self-indulgence to move among the *ton* looking like herself.

But there was nothing she could do about that now. She wasn't going to waste time in regret. The question was how likely was Milsap to discover her, given those missteps on her part?

The fact was that very few people knew her by her real first name, and those who did would never betray her. And the truth of her past was something she had entrusted to no one. *Well, except for Nathan.* But there was no one more honorable; he would be silent.

She owned her home under a different false name, and she had kept its location secret from Mrs. Billingham's suitors. Though she had met Malcolm Douglas there. Verity was noticing a distinct connection between her recent lapses of letting her guard down and her further involvement with Nathan. Was she really becoming as frothy-minded as the ladies she had belittled in the past?

However, Milsap was not going to be moving among the people of the *ton* asking questions. His milieu was the criminal world, where Mrs. Billingham was unknown. Unless, of course, he happened upon Lord Arden during one of his blackmailing schemes. She could only pray Arden was unaware of her involvement with stealing back the Bankwater brooch. If he knew her, even as Mrs. Billingham, Lord Arden would be in a position to undo all her secrets in one fell swoop.

# CHAPTER SEVENTEEN

NATHAN APPROACHED VERITY'S front door with some unease. He had the distinct impression that she would not appreciate his warning off Lord Arden this morning, so he had to be careful not to give that away. And he found it damned difficult to hide anything from Verity. She didn't pry usually. And it wasn't that he was an abysmal liar—after all, he was quite adept at politely denying that a dress was wildly unflattering or agreeing that the excessive padding in a man's jacket looked natural. And he had never given away anything told to him in confidence.

But somehow, he found himself wanting to tell Verity all sorts of things. Memories from his childhood. Things he liked or disliked. Random notions that popped into his head. He was sure that they held no interest for her. And yet somehow he wanted her to *know*. Almost as much as he wanted to *know* Verity. Which was another thing he didn't quite understand. He'd always been interested in people, but he'd never been as curious as he'd been about Verity—even from the beginning, when he thought she was Annabeth's peculiarly rude maid.

It was as if she was one of those Russian dolls— when opened, one found another inside and another after that. It was always that way with Verity—another layer, another piece of her to fit into the puzzle, another conundrum to figure out, until he reached the core of her. Although he wasn't quite sure he ever could.

After what had happened last evening between them—the heat that had swept them, the awkwardness as they parted—he wasn't even sure how to act with her. Should he be more formal? Or would she interpret that as aristocratic coldness? He'd vowed not to pursue a romantic relationship, but he had serious doubts about his ability to keep his eyes from drinking her in.

Then he walked into the parlor and saw her, and all his thoughts flew away. She looked a bit subdued in a plain brown carriage dress—well, as plain as anything Verity would wear—and her flaming hair was bound in braids and wrapped around her head in a conservative style. And still the sight of her sent his pulse racing. Clearly he was going to have a problem keeping his vow.

He greeted Verity, pleased that his voice conveyed nothing of the messages his senses were sending him. She was so lovely. She smelled so divine. His fingers itched to caress the satin-smooth skin of her cheeks. He curled his fingers into his palm and said lightly, "I'm eager to hear your news."

"What?" She stared at him, startled. "How—what do mean?"

A little taken aback, Nathan said, "Yesterday you said you had something to tell me. Something you'd learned about the case, I thought."

"Oh!" Verity said. "Yes. Of course. Yesterday when I was visiting Lady Lockwood, she told me—"

"Good Gad, you had to suffer Lady Lockwood yesterday too? Searching the streets of London must have seemed quite peaceful after that."

She grinned, the little dimple beside her mouth making its appearance. Nathan remembered kissing that spot.

"Oh, she's not so bad," Verity said. "You just have to take her as she is. That's where I saw Annabeth. I met your mother and aunt, as well."

"Did you like them?" Nathan asked. *Not that it should matter.*

"I think it would be difficult *not* to like your mother," Verity replied. "But the part that pertains to you is that Lady Lockwood told me that marriage records are supposed to be sent to their diocese's office."

"So you think the London diocese would have them?"

"Yes. If they exist. Though I have to warn you that she also told me that some churches were careless in that regard."

Nathan waved that away. "It's a chance. Let's go."

"I already ordered the carriage brought round."

It took a bit of talking to get the clerk at the diocese to search for the records from thirty-five years ago, but finally he turned and went back into the shelves behind him. They waited for him in silence.

Nathan watched Verity as she glanced about, then fiddled with the buttons of her gloves. It occurred to him that it hadn't been merely her plain clothes and hairstyle that had made Verity appear subdued. During their ride over here, she had been unusually quiet, spending most of the time gazing out the window, and he had had to repeat a statement to her a time or two. Then there was that way she had reacted when he asked about her news—overly surprised, almost alarmed— and he was sure that it had been relief he saw in her eyes when he explained his question.

"Verity, is there something wrong?" Nathan asked. "You seem...distracted."

"No, of course not." She looked at him, a tiny frown forming between her eyes, then said, "Nathan, I—this morning—"

The clerk dropped a record book down on the counter in front of them, making them jump and sending up a puff of dust from its worn cover.

Verity whirled and reached eagerly for the book, pulling it closer. Nathan leaned in, excitement welling up in him. Now they would actually have proof that Malcolm Douglas was lying.

Verity flipped through the pages until she found the right date, then ran her finger down the lines. She stopped abruptly, breathing in a little gasp.

"What?" Alarmed, Nathan looked over her shoulder at the words above her fingertip: *July 29, 1787—George Dunbridge m. Margaret Douglas.*

"My God. He was telling the truth." Nathan stared at the page, stunned. Turning, he walked out the door, moving automatically though he noticed little of the world around him. He felt as if he were in a fog, like nothing was real. Behind him, Verity hastily closed the record book, handed it back to the clerk, and followed Nathan.

Outside, he stopped and turned to Verity. "My entire life has been a lie."

Verity said only, "Come, let's get you home." Linking her arm through Nathan's, she steered him to her carriage.

Verity was uncharacteristically silent as they rode home. Nathan just stared out the window, flooded with thoughts and emotions and not really seeing anything they drove past. It wasn't until they reached her house and Verity reached over him to open the door that he realized that Verity had been holding his hand between both of hers throughout the drive. His hand felt very empty when she let go.

Nathan walked with her into the house, and Verity went to the liquor cabinet in the parlor, saying, "If you aren't in need of a glass of whiskey, I certainly am."

"I need it. Believe me." Nathan took the glass from her and downed it quickly.

"Another?" Verity asked, taking the glass and starting back to the decanter.

"No. I'm in enough of a fog as it is." But his brain was working again now—even if he still felt strangely disconnected—and he was gazing into a heart-wrenching future. "It was all a lie—my whole life. Everything I've thought, everything I believed—none of it was true. I'm not my father's only son and heir. Hell, I'm not even legitimate. The manor, the land—Good Lord, my very name—are not mine."

"I'm sorry, Nathan. I should have been less optimistic, but I was certain Douglas was lying."

Nathan nodded. "I knew in my head that this might be what we found out, that it was possible he was telling the truth. But deep down, I didn't really believe it. I couldn't believe that of my father. I was certain he was too good a man, too honest, to—how could he have done it?" Nathan's stomach churned.

Verity came to him, wrapping her arms around him and leaning her head against his chest. Nathan clutched her to him, as if anchoring himself to the only thing in his world that seemed real at the moment. When he finally released her, he gave her a small crooked smile. "Perhaps I will have another whiskey after all."

Verity poured him another drink, and they sat down. Nathan said, "I don't understand how he could have married my mother, knowing he was already married. Making her his mistress, not his wife. Knowing any child she bore him would be a bastard. He and Mother always seemed so devoted to each other. How could he have lied to her that way?"

"People in love will do extraordinary things. Things opposite to their nature. Perhaps he wanted so much to marry your mother that he was willing to commit bigamy, but he felt he couldn't tell her because she would have rejected him. Maybe he thought that no one would ever find out. That he could get away with it, and your mother would never know."

"He certainly did a good job of that. At least for thirty-three years." Nathan sighed, rubbing a hand over his face. "I don't know how I can tell her. I don't know what to do about the estate. Or Malcolm." He let out a short, bitter laugh. "Hell, I don't know what I'm going to do about anything. Where we're going to live. *How* we're going to live."

"You don't have to do anything right now. Give yourself a little time."

"You're being very kind."

"As opposed to my usual cruelty?" Verity teased lightly.

"No, of course not. I didn't mean that—I just…" He sighed. "I know you must think I'm utterly feeble—nattering on about this when you had to overcome more horrible things in your life. You gave up your sister, your home, sacrificed your entire life, and I am whining about finding out my father was a bigamist."

"It isn't a contest, Nathan." She leaned toward him.

"And if you think I wasn't complaining the entire time about my troubles, you are sadly mistaken. No one is calm and composed about having their world turned upside down. No one expects you to be a saint."

"I'm far from that. I'm just a man." Nathan stared into the amber liquid in his glass. "What's appalling is I am realizing that I am a *useless* man. I've lived off an inheritance all my life. I've earned nothing and have no skills that are of any value to anyone. I have to pay for myself and my mother now, and I haven't the slightest notion how."

"You do have skills."

"What? My talents lie in dancing well, carrying on a polite conversation, being charming to the old ladies, and agreeable enough to take the wallflowers out onto the dance floor. I'm a valued guest. That's all."

"That's not nearly all you are, Nathan. You are also loyal and honorable and kind—and I can assure you that those are qualities not possessed by many people. You know how to make people feel at ease. You're smart. You speak well. You're confident."

"I'm not entirely sure I have any reason to be the last."

"Stop that." Verity left her chair and to his surprise, she knelt in front of him, her hands on his knees, and gazed earnestly up into his eyes. "Do not pretend you have no value just because you aren't named Dunbridge any longer. You're still you, and you are all those things I just listed. You think that honor and trust are not valuable? How many people want an untrustworthy banker? Or bookkeeper? Or lawyer?"

"Certainly not me. I learned that lesson." He grimaced at the memory of his former attorney.

"The knowledge of their professions are all things that can be taught," Verity continued. "That's where your intelligence is useful. Your ability to win people over is quite handy. You are resourceful. You can plan. You have courage."

"Perhaps you should hire me," he joked.

"Maybe I will," she tossed back.

Nathan leaned down, cupping Verity's face in his hands, and gazed into her eyes. "You are all of those things and more, yourself." *Not to mention beautiful and desirable.* "And I very much appreciate all you just said." He kissed her forehead lightly, then couldn't resist brushing his lips against hers, as well. He was filled with the urge to lift her up into his lap and kiss her much more fully. The thought of sinking into her warmth, her comfort turning to desire, tempted him beyond measure.

*But no. I cannot do that.* Nathan refused to play upon her sympathy and warm heart in order to pull her into something she was uncertain about, something which would now be even more foolish for her. Verity was so much more than just a balm to his pain, a quick way to fill the emptiness that now opened inside him.

He was already indulging himself a great deal by staying here and pouring out all his doubts. They had found the proof. The whole matter was over, and he should simply walk away, even though the thought made his heart clench in his chest.

Nathan's hands fell away and he started to sit back, but Verity reached up and grabbed his lapels, jerking him back. "Oh, no, you don't. You don't get to cry off that easily."

"I wasn't—"

She stopped his words with a kiss. Her kiss was

long and deep, leaving no more uncertainty as to what she wanted, and every good intention Nathan had flew away from him. He went down onto the floor with her, his knees on either side of her legs, and pulled her up into him. The momentum threw them off balance, and they toppled over.

Nathan twisted to take the brunt of the short fall, pulling Verity atop him, never breaking their kiss. Verity laughed and sat up. She moved so that she was astride him, his rigid flesh pulsing against her. That was exactly where Nathan wanted to be…only without all the bothersome clothes between them.

He looked up at Verity. Her face was flushed, her eyes glowing, a few stray strands of her hair loose and falling around her face. Nathan knew he had never seen anyone as beautiful. His entire body ached for her. But he struggled for one last shred of sanity and said, "No, we shouldn't—"

"Shh…" Verity said softly, laying her forefinger across his lips for silence. Her smile was pure temptation. "I don't care what we should." She bent and kissed him.

"You don't want—"

She kissed Nathan again, longer this time, then murmured, "What I want is you."

# *CHAPTER EIGHTEEN*

NATHAN LET OUT a shaky breath. "I don't know."

"You don't want me?" Verity raised an eyebrow.

"No. God, no. I want you. But I don't want your pity. I don't want you to…just because you feel sorry for me."

"Well, now you're just being daft." Verity had wanted to lose herself in Nathan. To ignore all that had happened today. She had wanted to give Nathan comfort, wanted to take away her own worries, if just for a little while. And when he had kissed her so softly, she would have tossed away her doubts and taken him to her bed just for that.

But when he had sat back instead of trying to seduce her with her own sympathy—in that instant, Verity had *known*. It wasn't about drowning out her swirling thoughts or even about making Nathan happy. Verity felt fairly certain that she would at some point have exactly the opposite effect on him.

Nor did it matter what might happen, how this affair might end, or whether her heart would break. The only thing that was important was being with Nathan. She wanted to melt him with her kisses, to make him groan with desire. She wanted to feel his breath on her neck as he moved within her. To know that she drove him to distraction in the same way he did her.

Nathan couldn't be hers in the future. But right now, at this time and this place, he was.

She gazed into his eyes—those heart-melting, good intention–destroying eyes—and murmured, "Make love to me, Nathan."

He smiled then, a lazy, sensual, almost smug smile, and his hands slid over her dress slowly, up her thighs and onto her torso, moving with a deliberateness that made her ache for more and at the same time filled her with such pleasure that she wanted it to last forever. Nathan cupped her breasts, his thumbs brushing over the fabric lightly, teasing her nipples into hardness. Verity leaned her head back, arching her chest against his hands.

She heard him suck in a little breath, and she looked down at him. His eyes were dark with desire, a flush rising in his face, but still his fingers moved languidly on her, slipping beneath the neckline of her dress to tease at her bare flesh. *Two could play at that game.* She circled her hips against him. Light flared in his eyes, and he shot up, one hand curving around the back of her neck, and kissed her.

And then, with a twist of his body, Verity was on her back, and he was kissing her as if there was nothing in the world but her mouth and this moment and the hunger that roared through them. He kissed her mouth, her cheek, her throat, his hands tangling in her hair. His lips moved across her skin, exploring her throat, working downward to the swell of her breasts above her dress.

Verity's hands slid under his jacket, but it wasn't good enough. Wasn't close enough. She wanted to feel Nathan's skin beneath her fingers, to learn each contour and line of him. Frustrated, she tugged at his neckcloth, undoing the intricate folds, then moved on to the buttons of his waistcoat. *Why did gentlemen wear so very many clothes?*

She pulled at the ties of his shirt, and there, at last, she found what she sought. His flesh was warm and smooth, and it jumped a little beneath her touch, a low moan sounding deep in his throat. Her hands glided up his front, over the hard ridges of his ribs and the padding of muscle, finding and circling his flat nipples.

"Verity…"

He rose up a little, bracing himself on one forearm, and with the other hand began to undo the buttons of her dress. The brush of his fingertips between her breasts as he worked his way down her bodice sent sensations so exquisite they were almost painful spiraling through her. Nathan tugged at the ribbons tying her chemise, in his haste pulling one of them into a knot. He let out a soft curse, and yanked at the ribbon, snapping it.

He sent her a slightly startled look. "I'm sorry."

Verity laughed softly. "Really?" She crossed her arms beneath her head, the bodice and chemise sliding to the sides. She felt aflame, and she knew it shone in her eyes, in the catlike smile she sent up at him.

"No. Not really." He pushed the clothes completely away and gazed down at her for a long moment.

It seemed to Verity that she could feel the heat of his eyes tracking across her. She reveled in that heat, the desire that stamped his face pushing her own hunger higher. Nathan slowly ran his finger across her breasts, tracing the circle of her nipples, his eyes darkening as he watched. Then he bent to kiss the tops of her breasts, his lips as light and soft as butterfly wings, teasing, and she arched up, wanting more, and at last he took her nipple into his mouth. The pull of his lips, the stroke of his tongue sent a long, slow surge of passion through her.

Verity could not hold back a moan, and she dug her fingers into his hair, urging him on. She wrapped her legs around him, aching to take him inside her and frustrated by the barrier of their clothes. Nathan reached beneath her skirt, shoving it up and gliding his hand up her thigh.

But still, her clothes impeded them. Verity wanted to feel his fingertips on her skin, to have him flush against her. She pushed his jacket back from his shoulders, and Nathan reared up, shrugging out of jacket, shirt, and waistcoat all at once and flinging them aside.

He came back to her and took her lips in another deep kiss. Verity roamed her hands over his shoulders and back, her fingers digging into his flesh whenever his mouth sent some new tremor of delight through her. Her fingers followed the curve of his buttocks, and then she slipped one hand around to his front, dipping inside the waistband of his breeches. She felt the pulse of his response against her pelvis.

She fumbled at the buttons of his trousers, and Nathan let out a low growl of hunger and frustration. He rolled away and began to remove his boots and breeches, and Verity seized the opportunity to peel off the rest of her clothes, as well.

Nathan turned back to her, his eyes smoldering as they drifted down her body. "You are beautiful."

"So are you," Verity replied.

"Beautiful?" He quirked an eyebrow.

"Yes." She reached up and combed her fingers through his hair. "Such wonderfully mussed curls." She traced his eyebrow. "Eyes women swoon over."

Her forefinger dropped to follow the curve of his lips. "Very kissable mouth." She trailed her fingertips down the side of his neck and over his collarbone onto the muscles of his arm, her touch light as a feather. "Very kissable everything."

She demonstrated by sitting up and brushing her lips against his mouth, then his throat, then the bony point of his shoulder, as she flattened her hands against his chest and slid them down over his sides. Casting a little sideways grin up at him, she said, "You don't like me saying you're beautiful?"

"Oh, I like it." He curved his hand around the back of her neck and kissed her. "Very much." He nibbled gently at her earlobe and let out a soft chuckle. "Though somehow it doesn't seem very manly."

Verity closed her eyes, the touch of his teeth on her skin vibrating through her. "Of course it is." She slid one hand downward to take him in her hand. He sucked in a breath. "And you're quite manly."

Nathan took her mouth in a fierce kiss, his hands on her shoulders bearing her back down to the floor. Verity felt as if he were consuming her, and she loved it. She kissed him, claiming him as much as he claimed her, and she opened her legs for him in silent invitation.

She could feel him, stiff and pulsing, probing at the soft center of her, the movement teasing and arousing until she felt as if she might go mad, and then, at last, he slid into her with aching slowness, stretching and filling her in the most elemental way. It was everything she wanted and yet not enough.

Verity wrapped her legs around him, and he began to move, still with that same unhurried sensual stroke that was both delightful and frustrating. She dug her fingers into his back, urging him on. Then, at last, his movements quickened, matching her urgency, and the coil of desire in her grew ever tighter, until she was panting, aching for release. She gasped as pleasure exploded within her, and Nathan shuddered, letting out a hoarse cry as they tumbled together into the shattering depths of passion.

Nathan collapsed against her. He nuzzled into the crook of her neck, murmuring her name, then rolled to the side, taking his weight from her. Verity wished he had not been so considerate; she had liked feeling his body against hers, warm and substantial. But she felt too replete, too stunned, to even make a coherent sentence.

He curled his arm around her, and she snuggled against his side, her head on his shoulder. Was this really her—feeling so soft and warm, as if she could melt into him? So lacking in thought or alertness, so drifting in happiness and pleasure?

Nathan idly stroked his hand up and down her arm, his body growing lax against her. His hand stilled, his breathing slowed, and he dozed. Verity didn't mind; she liked this unguarded moment, when she could smooth her hand over his skin and breathe in the scent of him unnoticed, when she didn't have to be strong or pragmatic or skeptical. When she could be the vulnerable creature that usually hid inside her hard outer shell. She could be soft and calm without worrying about what danger she was opening herself up to.

Verity rose onto her elbow and looked at Nathan. His face was slack with sleep, lashes shadowing his cheeks. It was unfair for a man to have such thick lashes. And hair that curled in such loose soft waves—a stray curl was always tumbling down onto Nathan's forehead in a boyish, appealing way. It made concentrating on anything but him very hard to do. He was eminently appealing asleep like this. But even more so when he was awake and she could look into his eyes, see his smile, hear his laugh.

*What does he see in me?* she wondered. She wasn't modest enough to deny that she was attractive or that men often desired her…at least until they came up against the cold iron in her. But Nathan was well aware of her nature, had come up against her hardness and her blunt speech. She had teased him into frustration—and clearly enjoyed doing so. He knew her past, knew more than anyone else had.

Though she wore bold colors to suit her pose as Mrs. Billingham, the truth was Mrs. Billingham's style was not far from Verity's own. She had long chafed under the necessity to dress so that she went unnoticed.

Verity was too bold and unladylike in every way. And Nathan wasn't the sort to sleep with a woman just because she was willing. Yet he wanted her. Indeed, she felt rather sure he went against his better judgment in making love to her. But he had.

Well, she might not understand it, but she wasn't about to argue against her good fortune. Verity smiled to herself and lay back down, nestling against Nathan and looping her arm across his chest. Closing her eyes, she too fell asleep.

She was quick to wake up, though, when she felt Nathan stirring. She turned onto her other side, facing away from him, suddenly feeling a little shy. There was another thing she wasn't accustomed to feeling, but everything was so different with Nathan. She closed her eyes and lay there, wondering what he would do, what he would say. Perhaps he would kiss her shoulder or caress her back, telling her…

"I'm sorry. Verity, I'm so sorry."

"What?" Verity shot up to a sitting position, her dreamy thoughts exploding. Pain pierced her chest, and she was barely able to push back the tears that wanted to well in her eyes. "You're sorry?" At least her voice had sounded more indignant than hurt.

Nathan's eyes widened in alarm, and he said hastily, "No, God, no, not sorry for this—this was beautiful. Wonderful." He sat up, reaching for her arm, but she jerked away from him. He groaned, pushing his hands back into his disordered hair. "*Why* do I always say the wrong thing to you?"

"Because sometimes you blurt out the truth before you can manufacture a polite lie?" This was better, she thought. She always preferred blunt speech. She would appreciate that…later.

"No. It's not a polite lie that what we just had was… was…the devil!" Nathan cursed. "I can't think of anything adequate to express what it's like to be with you. To be in you, to taste you, to feel you. Surely you cannot think that I did not enjoy making love to you."

"I don't know what else I'm supposed to think when the first words out of your mouth were that you regretted it." Still, Verity softened a little inside at his words.

"But I didn't. I didn't regret it. Not for a moment. I was apologizing to you because it was reprehensible of me to pull you to the floor in the middle of the drawing room as if you were a…"

Verity stared. "You mean you're apologizing because you weren't gentlemanly enough?" She was swept with relief. Her eyes began to dance, her lips curving up.

"Dammit, now you're laughing at me."

"No. Never." Verity leaned over, looping her arms loosely around his neck, and kissed him lightly. She sat back, bracing her hands behind her and crossing her ankles, as if settling in for a friendly chat. It gave her a little thrill that his eyes went to her naked breasts. She no longer felt shy at all.

"I would never want to be disrespectful to you." Nathan's jaw tightened.

"You weren't disrespectful. I rather liked your…eagerness. Though I will admit my bed is more comfortable. We'll have to try that next time."

"Next time." He wiped his hands over his face. "Verity, no. We can't do this again."

Verity sighed. She should have known. Nathan's noble nature was rearing its head. "Now you're going to turn saintly on me?"

"No, of course not. Trust me, I feel anything but saintly." He reached for his clothes and began to dress. "What I'd like to do right now is try that bed out."

"That sounds like an excellent idea to me." Verity smiled up at him. Even as he stood and pulled on his breeches, he couldn't keep his eyes off her body, and whatever his mouth said, the noticeable bulge in his breeches was telling a different story.

"Verity, would you please get dressed? I'm trying to have a reasonable discussion here."

Verity blew out a sigh and picked up her chemise. She pulled it on, leaving the top ribbon untied, and stepped into her petticoat. She turned and faced him, crossing her arms. "There. Satisfied?"

He looked anything but satisfied, and his gaze went to her underpants, still lying where she'd thrown them earlier. "You're not..." He stopped and cleared his throat. "Verity, I was in a weak moment, and I let myself be carried away. I had promised to give you time to think about things, to decide whether you wanted to go any further down this path. But I didn't give you a chance to consider all the ramifications."

Verity rolled her eyes. "Nathan, for pity's sake, it's not as if your advances were unwanted. As I remember, *I* was the one who pulled *you* down to the floor and kissed you."

"Yes, you were." A faint smile touched his lips, his eyes warming. "But that's not the point. The point is that there's your reputation to consider, and you deserve more than being someone's mistress. And what if... what if you became pregnant? You couldn't—I would of course—but marrying would be wrong. I have nothing to offer. No prospects, no estate, hell, I don't even have my name anymore."

It shouldn't hurt that he dismissed so easily the idea of marrying her. He was right, of course; she knew as well as he that marriage was out of the question. How could she be offended when she had as little desire to marry as he did? How could she argue against it?

But neither was she going to let him get away with using that as an excuse. "Nathan, if you don't want to have an affair with me, just say so. But don't tell me you're doing this because it's better for me. *I* decide what's better for me. *I* decide who I let in my bed. I'm not some fragile flower. I know how to protect myself in every way. I have my *own* name and my *own* prospects. And I have no intention of getting married—to you or anyone else." She planted her fists on her hips, her eyes flashing. "For whatever bizarre reason, I want you in my bed. So the only question is, do you want to be there?"

Nathan's eyebrows shot up and then, surprisingly, he began to laugh. "Only you could be so bellicose in saying you want someone."

"Not someone. You."

"Yes. I understand." He moved toward her, smiling. "And I am very glad of that." He stopped in front of her and gazed down into her eyes. "To answer your question, yes, I want to be in your bed." Reaching up, he began to idly play with a loose strand of her hair. "And you look very beddable right now."

Verity smiled and said teasingly, "Again? Already?"

"Yes, again. Already." He leaned down and kissed her lightly on the lips. "And every time you'll have me." The kiss that followed was longer, and when he lifted his head, his eyes were heated.

"Then I suggest it's time we go upstairs." She took his hand and led him from the room.

## CHAPTER NINETEEN

NATHAN AWOKE, disoriented at first. He blinked and glanced around, and everything that had happened last night came flooding back into his mind, with the result that he was immediately hard. *Again? Really?* Not that he minded. A faint smiled touched his lips.

He was in Verity's bed. He couldn't remember ever awakening in a woman's bed. He'd never kept a mistress. He hadn't had the money to pay for another household, let alone all the expected jewels and dresses and so on that his acquaintances had complained about. Besides, he had pined for Annabeth, however unlikely it was that she would marry him, and no other woman had ever been more than a flirtation to him.

Brothels and lightskirts didn't appeal to Nathan. He'd dallied with tavern maids when he was at university, but he'd given that up as he became an adult. His friends had joked about him being a romantic, wanting love instead of simply a willing body. But the truth was that he'd found the transaction demeaning—on both sides.

Over the years he'd had short affairs mainly with widows—women wise to the world who, like him, expected nothing more than some nights of pleasure. However, he had never actually spent the whole night in their beds; instead, he had left before dawn in order to preserve the woman's reputation.

But last night, when he had finally forced himself to leave her bed, Verity had, as always, laughed at his concerns for her reputation and had proceeded to convince him to stay in a most enjoyable way.

Nathan linked his arms behind his head and gazed up at Verity's ceiling as he considered how very good he felt. He was far too happy, really, for a man who had discovered the day before that he was illegitimate and was suddenly out of a house or, indeed, even money with which to live.

The door opened and Verity sailed in, carrying a large tray. "Get up, slugabed. I've brought you food."

"Mmm. You're a jewel." Nathan sat up to inspect the goods on the tray she set on the bed, but his eyes lingered on her first.

She wore a dressing gown which was not in any way immodest, but Nathan wanted to slide his hands across the smooth, shining satin and under the lapel. He wondered what she had on beneath the robe.

"Uh-uh," Verity laughed. "You're not leading me astray."

"I didn't do anything," Nathan protested, feigning indignation.

"I knew what you were thinking," she replied lightly and sat down on the bed beside the tray, curling her legs under her. "I'm a detective, you know."

"And an excellent one." Nathan took a piece of bacon from a plate and devoured it. "Tell your cook she's a gem."

"I thought *I* was the jewel."

"Oh, well, you are, of course. Of an entirely different sort."

"A diamond?" Verity asked, tearing apart a roll and slathering it with butter.

"No, you're much too rare for a mere diamond." He considered the matter. "An emerald, I should think. Cleopatra wore them, you know."

"Goodness. I am impressed. You know your jewelry."

Nathan chuckled, shaking his head. "Not in the least. I have simply spent far too much time in the presence of Lady Lockwood."

"Now I'm impressed by your fortitude."

"I haven't seen that you are very much in fear of her ladyship," Nathan retorted.

"Not in fear," Verity agreed. "More in awe."

They continued to eat in silence, but Nathan noticed that Verity glanced at him more than once, a thoughtful look in her eyes, but said nothing. He had the suspicion that she wanted to talk about his situation but hated to spoil his mood. His stomach dropped. He hoped Verity was not about to tell him that with what they had learned at the diocese the case was all wrapped up. It still seemed unfinished. Though Nathan had to admit he was less upset about the possibility of her closing his case than he was the idea that might also end this exceedingly brief affair. However he felt about last night, it didn't mean Verity necessarily felt the same.

With an inward sigh, he laid down his fork and said, "What? I can tell you're thinking of something."

"I'm not certain that this case is solved."

Her words were so far from what he expected that he could only stare at her for a moment. "What do you mean? It seems very clear cut to me. We saw the record—my father married Margaret." He managed a faint smile. "Are you sure it isn't just that you don't want to admit you're wrong?"

"Well, that *does* take some getting used to—it so rarely happens." Verity sent him a twinkling glance. "But all my instincts told me Mr. Douglas was lying, and my instincts are very good. I have trouble believing that Malcolm Douglas wasn't here to extort money from you. Everything about him—his gestures, his voice, the things he said—all seemed so memorized. Rehearsed. I've known a number of liars and mountebanks, and he fit the role."

Nathan looked doubtful. "I don't know…"

"I'm not relying only on my feelings. There are several peculiar things about this whole matter. Why does he go by the name Malcolm Douglas instead of Malcolm Dunbridge? I realize that his family hates the English, but surely that's better than being thought illegitimate. Why did he slip out of the inn where he was staying and disappear? And if he has a legitimate claim as the heir, why didn't he hire an attorney to press his claim in court? Why come to you with these hints about coming to an understanding?"

*More than hints.* Nathan thought of the thinly veiled threats the man had made to him privately. But even those threats didn't disprove the man's paternity. "Maybe… maybe he just didn't want to get embroiled in a scandal. If his uncle is any indication, he comes from a family with a good name. He might not have wanted to embarrass them."

"If he wanted to avoid a scandal, all he had to do was not make the claim at all. As you said, his uncle seems upper-class and with some degree of wealth. It's not as if Malcolm really needs the money. And speaking of his uncle, why did Malcolm not tell his uncle what he was doing? Why did he not stay with him or at least let Robert know he was in the city?"

"Maybe he thought his uncle would disapprove."

"I imagine he would, given all the gossip that will result. But his uncle, indeed everyone, will know about it soon enough. He'll have to take it to court to establish his legitimacy. Most perplexing is the fact that he seems to have disappeared. Why has he not contacted you again?"

"Yes, those things are oddities, and I don't know how to explain them," Nathan admitted, but determinedly quashed the little bit of hope her words raised in him. "But we cannot ignore the fact that Margaret Douglas and my father married two years before I was born. It was right there in the records."

"But how do we know that they were married before *Malcolm* was born? We agreed that Malcolm looked older than you. There's a touch of gray at his temples, and lines at his eyes and mouth."

"Some people turn gray early. And he has that fair Scottish skin—if he spends much time outdoors, he'd have lines."

"And some couples marry *after* they have a child. I'd put him nearer to forty than thirty-four."

Nathan looked at her. "I don't know. Even if they got married afterward, they were still married, which means my parents were not."

"Not necessarily. Your father could have been a widower when he married your mother. Margaret could have died. Women often die in childbirth."

"That's true. I could just be the second son." Nathan paused, thinking. "But if that were true, why would my father have kept it a secret? Why would he have let his heir be raised in Scotland instead of at the manor? He would have known my mother would have treated the boy well. Mother has the softest heart one could find."

Verity shrugged. "That is one of the many inconsistencies in this tale."

"Do you really think there's a chance that this isn't true? Or are you just trying to lift my spirits?"

Verity leaned forward, putting her hand on his. "I wouldn't try to raise false hopes in you, Nathan. That would be cruel. But neither can I ignore the oddities here, and I wouldn't want to advise you to give up without investigating further."

Nathan quirked a smile. "Do you *ever* advise giving up?"

Verity grinned back. "Only when there's no one still standing."

Whether she had been trying to cheer him up or not, Verity had made him curious, even a little hopeful. And, really, today almost anything seemed possible. He wouldn't admit defeat this easily, no matter how great a blow yesterday's discovery had been. "Very well. How do we find the answers to your questions?"

"The first thing we have to do is learn Malcolm Douglas's age. I want to see the records. So we need to find out where he was born."

"His uncle is the best source of information on that score," Nathan said.

"I agree. We must discover Robert Douglas's address." She paused. "Though calling on him and asking about Malcolm's birth might make him suspicious of us. It's an odd thing to do, and even if he isn't aware of his nephew's scheme, he would have to wonder."

"I can see him at his club. He did extend an invitation to me to visit him at White's anytime."

"Where I am not allowed to enter, being a mere woman." Verity scowled.

Nathan's eyes gleamed with amusement. "I am afraid that this time you are simply going to have to trust me."

"Don't be silly. Of course I trust you. And you're right—a chance meeting is less likely to arouse his suspicions, even if it is an odd topic."

"I'll think of some way to work it in." Nathan reached over and took her hand. "But first I might need a little distraction from such heavy matters."

"Oh, I know just what will help—a game of whist!" Verity looked around the room. "Where *are* my cards?"

"I have something else in mind."

He tugged her to him, and Verity went easily, opening her eyes wide in faux innocence and saying, "You do? Why, whatever can that be?"

"This." He kissed her lips.

"Oh, that." She smiled, curling her arms around his neck. She took his mouth in a long, drugging kiss. "That doesn't seem very responsible when we have a case waiting."

Nathan slid his hand under the lapel of her dressing gown, cupping her breast, and nuzzled the side of her neck. "It appears I am becoming quite reckless."

Kissing her, he bore her back down on the bed.

ROBERT DOUGLAS WAS not at the club when Nathan arrived, which was a bit deflating. But Nathan was well-known there, so he took a seat and picked up a news sheet, pretending to read it as he kept an eye on the door.

It would probably be more natural seeming this way, less intentional.

After what felt like an eternity he saw his quarry enter the club, handing off his hat and decorative cane. Nathan looked back down at the paper in his hands as if absorbed, intending to look up at the last moment and recognize Douglas.

However, Mr. Douglas started the conversation himself before Nathan could do so. "Good day," he said cheerfully. "Mr. Dunbridge, isn't it? We met at Alan Grant's not long ago."

"Yes, of course." Nathan stood up to shake his hand, offering him a friendly smile. "I remember quite well. Do sit down."

"Thank you, sir." Douglas settled into the chair across from Nathan's, and for a few minutes they exchanged casual remarks about the weather.

The butler brought Douglas a cup of tea, and in the lull after the other man took a sip, Nathan asked, "I believe you were awaiting your nephew's visit when I saw you last."

Douglas nodded. "I was. But he never came. I don't suppose you've run into him anywhere, have you? As I remember, you were looking for him, were you not?"

"I was indeed. It's too bad." Nathan feigned a look of disappointment. "I'm thinking of purchasing a cottage in Scotland, and Alan told me your nephew was born in a picturesque spot. But he couldn't remember the name. I was hoping Malcolm could tell me."

"Gairmore?" Mr. Douglas's eyebrows flew up in surprise. "Are you sure? It's just a little spot in the Highlands where the family was…um, visiting for the summer."

His normally open and gregarious expression shifted and he glanced away.

"That's exactly the sort of place I'm looking for," Nathan said with delight. "A pleasant summer house where I can retreat when summer in the city becomes too much. Did they own a house there?"

"No. Margaret and her mother, um, just happened to be there. Taken by surprise a bit, you see. It sounded to me like a rather *primitive* place. Well, no matter." Robert smiled brightly at Nathan. "I'm sure your friend was talking about the family estate, not far from Aberdeen. They live in Edinburgh most of the time, but the estate is where the Douglas heirs are usually born."

"Yes, no doubt I misunderstood," Nathan replied smoothly.

"Now, *that* is a lovely spot. Excellent fishing," Douglas went on, and Nathan joined him in a discussion of hunting and fishing and the best locations in Scotland for doing either of those things.

After a long enough time to conceal that his motivation had been only to ask about Malcolm Douglas's birthplace, Nathan took his leave of Robert and returned to Verity's house. Verity had not returned yet, but the housekeeper let him in and offered tea while he settled down in the front room to wait for her.

It hadn't been long since they'd last been together, but after checking his pocket watch for the fifth time in less than a half hour Nathan had to admit that he was eager to see Verity again. He had already felt oddly close to Verity and after the night they spent together there was now a vague sense of unease in his gut when she wasn't nearby. As though he'd forgotten something or was missing a cherished heirloom he was accustomed to wearing every day.

Not, of course, that he would have told Verity that. Her teasing about being as important to him as his favorite pair of cufflinks would be relentless. And she was so much more than that to him. It was simply such a new feeling that he knew no better way to describe it.

Apparently he wasn't the only one who was already used to him being here. Nathan reflected that the housekeeper was beginning to treat him like a member of the household. And with all the time he'd spent here lately, the place was beginning to seem almost like home.

He decided not to continue that line of thinking. With Verity he could have only the present. No plans, no future. He thought again of her adamant rejection of marriage. It wasn't that he wanted to marry her, either, but still, her words had stung a little. Nathan had to wonder if she truly did not want to marry...or if she just didn't want to marry *him*.

## CHAPTER TWENTY

VERITY SAILED OUT of the house not long after Nathan left. It was irritating of course, that she couldn't join Nathan in questioning Robert Douglas, but she felt too cheerful this morning to let anything dampen her spirits. Besides, she figured she should avoid her Mrs. Billingham character, as well as any place that Lord Arden might frequent. Verity still suspected that Milsap, the Bow Street Runner who was sniffing about, had the most chance of finding her through the Bankwater case.

Verity had almost told Nathan yesterday about what she had learned in the park despite her decision not to—the man seemed able to take down her walls with ease. She was thankful the clerk had interrupted her—given the tremendous blow the marriage records had dealt Nathan, he certainly hadn't needed to be loaded down with her problems, as well.

Indeed, it would be quite selfish of her to tell him about Stanhope now—especially since, as she looked back on the scene she had witnessed, Verity suspected that she had reacted too strongly. She'd let panic overtake her. All she had really learned was that her stepbrother had thought her dead years ago, or, at the least, tried to find her years ago, and was now looking for her again.

But she didn't know what he wanted: revenge, justice, jewelry that he thought should have been part of his inheritance? One thing she was certain of was that he could not have been the one who set those two men upon them the other night. He didn't even know whether Verity was alive, let alone where she was.

So Stanhope currently presented no danger to Nathan and was utterly irrelevant to his case. However, that could all quickly change if Nathan thought Stanhope was a threat to Verity. Then Nathan was all too likely to go after the man himself—and a Stanhope was always more dangerous than they seemed on the surface. She couldn't let Nathan become part of a vendetta against her.

No. It was the best course to keep Nathan out of the situation. She would take care of the problem herself—it was, after all, the way she had always handled everything. She would just have to be more careful than she had been of late. She would be on the alert whenever they went out, and she would avoid the *ton* as much as she could. As she had done yesterday, she decided to wear a plain brown dress and she wound her hair up in tight braids, taking the extra precaution today of topping it off with a mobcap.

As Verity dressed, her mind wandered back to Nathan. Waking up beside him had been so—well, she didn't have a word for the feeling. *Nice? Wonderful? Sweet?* They were all too vague and colorless to describe the thrill that had run through her when she looked over at him, sound asleep, his chest bare, his hair delightfully rumpled, and to know that she could smooth her hands over his body and kiss him awake, and they would once more have that soul-shaking experience, that lovemaking that seemed to tear her apart and put her back together again.

But it hadn't been only desire that stirred in her. There was the simple pleasure of having breakfast with Nathan, talking and laughing as they made plans for the day. She wasn't sure why it warmed her deep inside to see him comfortable and at ease there in her bed—hair tousled, jaw stubbled, without his perfectly arranged neckcloth and exactly correct attire. There was a certain intimacy to it, a closeness that she had never shared with anyone.

Verity admitted few people to her house, and even fewer men to her bedchamber. She suspected that Nathan thought she was worldly wise and experienced when it came to sex. She was, she supposed, compared to the ladies of Nathan's world—girls innocently virginal till their wedding night. But the truth was that Verity had not been with many men—only a few brief affairs, usually in the heat of some dangerous adventure.

She was quite adept at flirting and pretending interest she did not feel. She had enticed more than one man with behavior that promised more than she would ever deliver, but that had been part of whatever role she was playing. None of it was real, and she never traded her favors for information despite her spymaster urging her to do so.

Her mother's marriage to Lord Stanhope had given her a poor view of men and marriage, and her first lover had tried to betray her to the French—she had Sloane to thank for stopping him from doing so. For several years thereafter she had sworn off men altogether.

She had learned to split herself into two parts: the person that she presented to the world and the secret self she hid, the true Verity. Men belonged solely in that first world. And it had operated well enough.

*Until Nathan.* Nathan, it seemed, was an exception to all her rules. A risk she had never taken before, but one she wouldn't give up now for anything. She'd meant what she said to him last night. She had thrown away her reservations. It didn't matter what lay at the end of their affair. Right now she was going to enjoy it.

She smiled a little to herself as she started down the street. She had planned to go to her office and from there to talk to a lawyer about illegitimacy laws, but instead she found her feet turning toward Hyde Park.

Verity had not gone there to catch a glimpse of her sister in several days. She had been too busy—or perhaps too happy; she wasn't entirely sure. Today she was a trifle late, and Poppy and the nanny were strolling back toward her house.

Verity stopped and edged back to the partial shelter of a tree. As always, there was a little ache in her heart at seeing her sister. It had been so many years, but Verity could still see traces of the seven-year-old Poppy in the grown woman.

She wondered what would happen if Poppy glanced over and saw her. Would she recognize Verity, even with her recognizable hair hidden? Or was Verity too much a stranger to her now? Did Poppy remember her? Did she despise Verity for leaving her with strangers?

For an instant, she thought of walking over to Poppy and telling her the truth, as Nathan had mentioned. However good Verity was at imitating people's physical characteristics, Nathan knew people's hearts much better than she. Maybe he was right and Poppy would be happy to see her.

Or maybe Poppy would berate her. Or, worse, simply ignore Verity and walk away. Verity's stomach knotted at the thought. She wasn't a coward, she'd never been a coward, Verity told herself. And yet this she could not do.

She watched as the two women walked out of the park, pushing the baby carriage. Maybe there would be no blissful future for Verity, but she wasn't going to dwell on the past anymore.

She was going to do her job and talk to the solicitor about the laws of legitimacy, and then she would go home. To Nathan. Verity turned and walked away.

WHEN VERITY WALKED into the house hours later, Nathan was sitting in her drawing room, which pleased her much more than seemed reasonable. He stood up, smiling, and started toward her, and Verity went into his arms, lifting her face for a kiss. It was not a polite kiss of greeting, and one kiss led to another until it was several minutes before they parted and sat down to talk.

"How was your meeting with the attorney?" Nathan asked.

"Boring," Verity replied. "I want to know what you found out. Did Uncle Robert give you the name of the town? Was he suspicious?"

"He seemed surprised when I asked, but he didn't appear suspicious or question my reason for asking. Gairmore is the name of the town. Here's what I found interesting: Douglas said that Malcolm was not born at the Douglas estate, which is where their heirs are *traditionally* born, but in a remote village in the Highlands."

"That *is* interesting." Verity, who had been nestled against Nathan's shoulder, sat up straight, her eyes gleaming.

"And right after he said the name, he got flustered. He said they just 'happened' to be there, that they were caught by surprise. He assured me that it was primitive and not the sort of location I'd want to summer at."

"A remote village in the Highlands seems an unlikely place to visit when one is about to have a baby, don't you think?" Verity mused.

Nathan nodded. "But a good place to hide an inconveniently early birth."

"Exactly. And why was he born anywhere in Scotland, for that matter? Why not at your manor or here in London? That's where they were married."

"Yes, and why was it only Margaret and her mother who were there? Why was my father not there to see the birth of his son? Robert didn't mention my father at all. Just quickly changed the subject and started telling me about the Douglas estate."

"That indeed sounds smoky."

"Do you think he's part of it? That he knows what his nephew is doing?"

"If so, Robert's a very good actor."

"I wouldn't say he's that—he certainly didn't hide it well when I asked him about the town where Malcolm was born."

"Yes, it would seem that he knows he shouldn't talk about Malcolm's birth, but I'm not sure that he knows who the father was." Verity frowned. "When we met him, I didn't see any reaction to hearing your name, and one would think he would recognize it immediately."

"I don't see what we can do except follow the only lead we have." Nathan grinned. "Care for a trip to the Highlands?"

THEY TOOK THE carriage along the Great North Road to Edinburgh, then turned northwest to climb into the Highlands.

It should have been a boring, even arduous trip, but instead it seemed an almost magical time. Each night was filled with desire as they explored each other's bodies, learning what titillated, what pleased, what sent the other soaring into an explosion of passion.

They spent the long days talking. Little was said about Malcolm Douglas and his claim or the men who had attacked them, and Verity pushed her worries about Jonathan Stanhope to the back of her mind. Neither of them wished to spoil this time alone together. Nathan told amusing stories about Lady Lockwood and her dog Petunia. Verity taught Nathan how to mark cards and fuzz dice and gave him tips on breaking into houses.

"I knew it. You really *are* a criminal," Nathan told her.

"I have to know how one cheats in order to catch those who do it," she retorted. "I've been hired to catch thieves. And sharps at gambling clubs. To spot mountebanks and charlatans."

"Such as someone pretending to be a wealthy widow?"

Verity laughed. "Just so. But only if they're an adventuress intent on swindling. One learns all sorts of things in this business—once I was hired to catch a poisoner. He thought it was his wife who wanted to do away with him, but it turned out to be the cook who'd been paid by his nephew to put it in the man's nightly posset. So I had to study all sorts of poisonous plants and chemicals."

"You didn't learn that when you were working for Asquith?"

"I was a spy, Nathan, not an assassin," Verity retorted. "But yes, I learned a bit about arsenic and such back then just in case it became necessary to use it. But I was more likely to give a man something to put him to sleep. Much easier to steal secrets when he's unconscious."

"Mmm. And none of the messy aftermath," he offered drily. "So you broke in and doctored a drink and then waited for him to fall asleep?"

"Usually I managed to get inside houses without breaking in." She adopted a coquettish attitude, looking up at Nathan through her lashes. "A little of this. And a little of that…" She changed to a worshipful look, clasping her hands together at her breast. *"Oh, my, you must be so important. And at such a young age—how very clever you are."* She grinned. "Flattery and flirting usually got me in the door. And if I brought a guard a warm grog on a cold night, who was going to turn that away?"

"Especially if you offered to chat with him while he drank it."

"But of course. Sometimes I was the distraction, and Sloane or someone else got inside, and sometimes only I could work my way inside and take whatever it was Asquith wanted. That was a good bit more exciting."

"You never got caught?"

"Of course I did. But luckily I always managed to get away. You'll have to learn these things if you intend to be a detective."

"To charm women or to break into a house?"

"I think you know how to do the former," she retorted. "The rest you can learn."

His eyebrows went up a little. "Are you serious?"

"Why, yes. Did you not mean it when you said you could work with me?"

"Yes, but I didn't assume *you* did."

"It makes sense. You would attract more wealthy clients—men who would never hire me would trust you. You're one of them, no matter what comes out about your birth. You can go places I cannot—gentlemen's clubs, for instance." Verity hesitated. "But of course if you were only joking, I wouldn't press you."

"I wasn't—I mean, yes, I was joking, but only because I didn't think you would actually consider it. I would in fact very much like to work for you."

"Good." Verity slanted a glance at him, her eyes taking on a glint. "Though, I do have to warn you that I am a very demanding employer."

"Are you?" Nathan settled back, looking a bit uncertain but ready to play along.

"Indeed." Verity swung one leg over him, straddling his lap. She felt his flesh surge beneath her, and she smiled, moving a bit as if finding the exact position. "I like things done just the way I want." She trailed her forefinger down the center of his chest.

A pulse leapt in his throat, sending heat through her. "I think I can follow orders."

"Can you?" She cupped his face between his hands. "Then kiss me."

He did, his mouth firm and hot on hers, seeking, coaxing, and a sweet ache formed between her legs. He cupped her breasts, caressing her through her dress, and she moved against him again, frustrated by the material between them.

It was absurd, but Verity felt as though she could not get enough of Nathan. They had made love only this morning, and it wasn't as if they had been celibate any other night on this trip. But already she was hot and wet, eager to feel his length slide into her, filling her in the most delicious way.

Verity slipped off him, and he reached for her, but she scooted away and reached under her skirts to pull off her undergarments. Tossing them aside, she lifted her skirts and straddled his legs once more. She unbuttoned his breeches, freeing his pulsing erection; he was clearly as ready as she.

Going up on her knees, she slid down onto his shaft, closing her eyes at the exquisite satisfaction. She moved up and down, the vibration of the coach beneath them adding to the sensations. Nathan gripped her hips, his fingers digging into her, and as she rocked faster, he reached beneath her skirts, finding the slick nub between her nether lips, and stroked her.

Verity arched back, her body taut in that final moment where she hung at the edge, aching and eager, and then she went over it, her body shuddering as Nathan thrust into her, letting out a hoarse groan as he reached his own release.

She went limp against him, laying her head on his shoulder.

"Did I impress my future employer?" Nathan's rumbly low tone tickled Verity's ear and she shivered a bit.

"Oh, you are very impressive in this regard." She added a feigned coolness to her voice. "But I'll still have to see how you are at filing."

"Cheeky." Nathan grinned. "I like that."

Verity could feel him getting hard again inside her. "You certainly seem to. And I must say, I enjoy your work ethic." As the pulsing heat between them sped up again, words, cheeky or otherwise, flew from her mind and Verity's sole thought was that she was happier than she'd ever been before.

## CHAPTER TWENTY-ONE

EVENTUALLY THEY HAD to proceed on horseback, lest the carriage break an axle on the rough pathways the Scots termed *roads*. It took them over a week to reach the village of Gairmore, tucked away deep in the Scottish Highlands. Even on a summer day, washed in sunshine, the community was not a prepossessing sight. A few rutted narrow roads and squat dark cottages made up most of the place, with a very plain kirk at one end and the banks of a loch at the other.

Nathan and Verity looked at each other, pulling their horses to a halt. "This is where Margaret Douglas chose to have her lying in?"

"Perhaps Mr. Douglas was telling the truth, and they just got caught here." Nathan looked around doubtfully.

A woman stood in the doorway of her house, staring at them, and within moments, two other women and a man emerged from the houses around, clustering in the lane. Verity glanced at Nathan, handed him her reins and dismounted, then walked over to the group.

Verity launched into her Scottish act, and within moments, the others were chatting away with her in accents even more difficult to understand than Verity's. Nathan decided not to bother with dismounting; there was little chance he'd understand a fraction of the conversation.

There was much nodding, and now and then, the

Scots glanced over at Nathan, and at one point, all of them laughed. Nathan had the distinct feeling that Verity had made him the butt of some jest, but he just smiled pleasantly. Verity had clearly won them over.

Soon followed pointing in several different directions, along with more chatter, and Verity went into a long round of thanks and farewells. She strode back to him, and Nathan swung down to join her. Verity took his arm, pulling him with her as she started down the street.

"How do you do that?" Nathan asked. "It's not only that you can sound like them. You were immediately their friends. They didn't so much as nod in my direction."

"Och, weel, now, you're a Sassenach, aren't you?" Verity said lightly.

"How did they know that? I never opened my mouth," Nathan protested.

Verity sent him an amused glance and changed to her usual voice. "Nathan, anyone could tell that just by looking at you. I didn't sound just like them, it seems. They were sure I was from Glasgow."

He grimaced. "Still, they were willing to talk to you. They *wanted* to talk to you. Somehow you manage to be one of them."

"You can go into a gentlemen's club or a gambling den and talk with ease to anyone there, which I cannot."

"Yes, well, that's because I *am* one of them."

"And you grew up watching them, imitating them. You learned how to be like them. All one has to do is study one's subjects and blend in. Make their gestures and expressions. I didn't do it overnight. I had trouble not acting and talking like a gentleman's daughter when we were living on the streets, but I watched everyone else and imitated them, and I discovered I had a talent for it. It's become second nature to me now, I suppose. I adopt other people's gestures and expressions. Though you have to be careful there, or they might assume you're mocking them." She shrugged. "It helps to give them something they want, as well. They were clearly dying of curiosity about us. There aren't many visitors in Gairmore, apparently."

"Imagine that."

"So few, in fact that the older man recalled everyone who's stopped here in the last forty years."

"The Douglas women?" Nathan asked.

"He thought so. But he went to ask his sister, who was older than he and might recall it better. One of them went to talk to Mrs. McCready, who owns a 'fine house' beside the loch, where she lets out rooms to visitors."

"That sounds promising."

"I thought so. I would venture to guess it's the only house that does. Unfortunately, the woman who had been midwife here for many years passed. Her daughter is carrying on her work, but she was probably too young at the time to remember. So we are going to visit the Reverend Mr. Gordon at the kirk to look at the records of births."

"What did you tell them we are doing?"

"I told them you were actually a Scotsman, but your poor mother had died when you were young and you had been given to a couple in England. You grew up thinking they were your parents, but you've heard that you are not, and now you want to find your true Scottish parents. All you know is that you were born here."

He raised his brows. "Why not tell them the truth?"

"What would be the fun in that?" Verity tossed back.

"Of course." He grinned. "How silly of me."

They continued to the plain church, but found no one inside. The parsonage beside it, however, opened to their knock, revealing a stern-looking man wearing a dark suit and a white collar with preaching bands.

Verity sent Nathan a sideways glance and nodded slightly. He took it to mean she had decided the man in front of them would react better to a gentleman's questions, so Nathan said pleasantly, "Reverend Gordon?"

"Aye. And who are ye?" The man frowned, which did not seem promising.

But Nathan took heart in the fact that at least Gordon's accent was not as thick as the earlier villagers. Nathan went on to politely explain that they were looking for the records of births in the village thirty to thirty-five years ago.

"Thirty-five years! To what purpose?"

Nathan launched into Verity's story of his own supposed birth, which only made the man scowl more.

"There's no English born in Gairmore," the cleric said.

"That is my point," Nathan said, struggling to keep the sharpness from his tone. "I believe it was a Scotswoman who was my mother."

"Humph. No outsiders of any kind in Gairmore."

Nathan drew himself up, assuming a haughty face, and there was an expectation of obedience in his voice as he said, "Still, I would like to examine them. I believe these *are* public records."

The other man sent him a resentful look, but said only, "Aye, well, follow me."

He led them back to the church. Verity squeezed Nathan's arm. "Good work. You were terrifyingly lordlike."

Mr. Gordon pulled out a leather-bound journal that looked as if it had been there for a century and began to thumb through the yellowed pages. "What is the name you're searching for?"

"Douglas." Nathan itched to grab the book from the man's hands. One would have thought it contained vast secrets the way Gordon shielded it. "It would have been 1787 or 1788, probably."

"Hmm." The reverend gave him a suspicious look and returned to his slow perusal of the pages. "I don't know of any Douglases. Ah." His finger stopped its journey down the page. "Ah. Well. Here it is. 'February twentieth in the year of our Lord 1787. Malcolm Andrew Ramsay Douglas.' How peculiar."

Nathan and Verity exchanged a glance. "That's be-fore—"

The rest of Verity's sentence was cut short by the other man reading on, "'Mother Flora Ramsay Douglas, father John James Douglas.'"

"What?" Nathan's gaze snapped back, and he yanked the book from the cleric's hands.

"Sir! That is church property."

Nathan paid him no attention, just ran his eyes down the page to the name in question. Beside him, Verity leaned against him to peer at the book. "Well. That's a bit of a twist."

"What in the—I don't understand." Nathan recovered from his astonishment enough to hand back the book and gave the minister a coin for the church in thanks, then took Verity's arm and swept her out the door.

"What is going on? Margaret's *mother* had the baby? Margaret is Malcolm's sister?"

"I have trouble believing that. Why would Malcolm

pretend that he was your father's son with Margaret? The truth would have been bound to come out at some point. He would have had to prove his birth in a court of law."

"Perhaps he *was* just looking for a bit of blackmail and didn't intend to go to court," Nathan mused. "He knew my father had married Margaret, and he made up the rest of it just to get me to pay him off."

"Or perhaps Malcolm didn't lie about his parentage." Verity stopped and turned to Nathan. "Maybe it is the record that's false."

"You think Reverend Gordon falsified the information?" Nathan's brows soared. "Why would he do that?"

"Money," Verity replied succinctly.

Nathan sighed. "I suppose you will think I'm terribly naive to be shocked at the idea of a clergyman lying."

"I think most people would assume a clergyman would tell the truth. But there are churchmen who love money. And it might not necessarily have been for personal gain. New pews for the church or a bell tower repaired could have been the lure."

"He *was* suspiciously reluctant to let us see the record of the birth."

"Yes, but I'm afraid he's not old enough to have been here at that time."

"So you think his predecessor accepted the bribe?"

"Perhaps. Or the clergyman could have been the one lied to. Did you notice the names of the witnesses?"

"No," Nathan admitted.

"One was a Dr. Joseph MacPherson. The other was Mrs. Donald McCready."

Nathan looked at her blankly, then remembered. "You mean the woman who lets out her home to visitors?"

"Seems likely, doesn't it? She takes paying guests. Flora and Margaret had to have a place to stay. Her house may not be as fine as the villagers said, but obviously it must be nicer than any other house in Gairmore."

"So she paid her landlady and the physician to lie?"

"Do you think this village has a doctor?" Verity asked skeptically, and Nathan shook his head. "Neither do I. I think they brought a physician with them. One whom they knew would say whatever they wanted."

"If Flora Douglas brought a doctor along with her, she clearly planned to have the baby here instead of at the family estate—which makes no sense. The family had no connection here, and it's difficult to get to. And who in her right mind would choose to give birth in the Highlands in the winter?" Nathan said.

"Exactly. There had to be something questionable going on."

"It seems to be a common occurrence in this family."

"If Malcolm was your father and Margaret's son, he was not legitimate because he was born in February, months *before* Margaret married your father. So… let's say you are Margaret's mother and you wished to hide that your daughter had an illegitimate child, but you didn't want to give the child to a foundling home. And let's say you are young enough that it isn't entirely unbelievable that you yourself could have a child at your age."

"Then you might whisk your daughter away before anyone knows," Nathan completed the thought. "Go to a remote place for the final months and the birth, and then pretend that the baby is yours."

"Such things do happen," Verity said. "A relative taking an illegitimate child and raising it as their own to protect the unwed mother."

"But we know that my father married Margaret."

"Several months later. The Douglases might not have known that he would marry her."

"But after that, surely he and Margaret would raise the boy, not his grandmother."

Verity shrugged. "I don't know. Perhaps they felt they couldn't reveal that the original story was untrue."

"I suppose." He sighed. "Well, we've no idea who or where this doctor is, but…"

"We *can* find Mrs. McCready," Verity finished for him.

As it turned out, finding Mrs. McCready was easy, for Verity's newfound friends had talked to the woman in question and revealed that she did, in fact, have rooms to let. Getting information out of her was another matter.

Mrs. McCready was a soft, plump woman with a sweet smile. Her white hair peeped out around the edges of her ruffled mobcap. Nathan was reminded of the cotton cap that Verity had worn when he first met her as she pretended to be a maid in Lady Lockwood's house, and he smiled a little to himself. Verity's cap had been almost comically large in order to cover her hair and partially conceal her face. He remembered, too, the golden eyes beneath its edge.

At the time she had thoroughly irritated him in almost every way. And now…well, he had to admit that she still had the ability to irritate him, but somehow he didn't mind. Indeed, he almost enjoyed it, which he suspected meant there was something seriously wrong with him.

Mrs. McCready greeted them with pleasure, assuring them that she had rooms for both of them. "Mr. Dunbridge on the floor above your room, of course. We're always verra careful with the proprieties. It wouldnae do to…" She leaned in a little, lowering her voice. "Appear at all questionable, if you know what I mean."

Nathan wished Verity had set them up with a different story instead of using the one she'd already told the townsfolk of her being employed to help Nathan find his true parents. The role of a married couple would have been much more agreeable.

"I do," Verity said, sending Nathan a twinkling glance that told him she knew precisely what he was thinking. She went on to inquire into their supposed mission. Nathan noted that the warm brogue Verity had been using with the townspeople had become a fainter gloss of a Scottish accent, her tone crisp and authoritative as she spoke to the landlady.

The other woman looked flustered. "Och, nae, lass, I cannae remember that far back."

"They were a bit unusual," Verity said in an apparent attempt to jog her memory. "Flora and Margaret Douglas. Two refined ladies from Edinburgh, accompanied by a doctor."

"I dinnae remember." Mrs. McCready shook her head vigorously, sending the several bows of her cap fluttering, and gave them an apologetic smile. "My memory's not what it was."

Nathan reflected that he had grown cynical enough the past few weeks that he was sure the sweet old lady was lying.

"I'm sorry I cannae help you," Mrs. McCready went

on. "Janet can see you to your rooms. Janet!" She raised her voice.

"Yes, missus, I'm here." A middle-aged woman moved out of the shadows of the staircase. In contrast to her employer, she was a dour-looking woman with iron gray hair wrapped up in a tight knot at the crown of her head. She nodded at Nathan. "This way, sir, miss."

Janet clomped up the stairs, leaving them little choice but to follow her. She moved down the hallway and opened a door. "Here ye are, miss. Ye have a view of the loch." She waved toward the windows along the opposite wall.

"Thank you." Verity drew a breath, and Nathan knew she was going to question the maid about the Douglases.

But before Verity could speak, Janet said, "I remember them."

"The Douglases?"

"I dinnae remember their names. But I was here when they came—like ye said, two high-and-mighty ladies from Edinburgh and Dr. MacPherson. They brought their maid, as well, and they didnae like the food. The bread was too coarse, the mother said, and the haggis too dry. I remember 'cause I was an undermaid working in the kitchen, and Mrs. Fleming, the housekeeper, was in a snit about it."

"Well, I suppose since the mother was carrying a child, her taste might have—"

The maid let out a snort. "Carrying? Not her. It was the lass that had the babe. Poor lass—she was quiet. A weepy little thing. 'Course, who wouldn't be? Her mam was stiff as a poker and never had a smile to offer. Weel, it was a bastard, poor wee babe, so her mam was angry at her. That's the way it is, isn't it, the lass always gets blamed, and the man's off enjoying himself."

"Yes, unfortunately, that's often the way it is," Verity said sympathetically. "Did the daughter ever say anything about the baby's father?"

"Nae. They didnae talk to the likes of us, ye ken." She paused, tilting her head a bit. "Though—now that I think about it, there was that once the lass stood up to her, and I ken it was about a man."

"Do you remember what they said?" Verity asked.

Janet shook her head but continued to look thoughtful. "It was—the mam said—" She shot a quick glance at Nathan, then went on, "Sassenach."

"An Englishman?" Verity could not fully suppress the excitement in her voice. "They were arguing about an Englishman?"

The other woman nodded slowly. "I think so. I cannae be sure—I just remember because it surprised us all." She shrugged. "I'm sorry. That's all I know." She gave Nathan a little bob of a curtsey. "Now, sir, your room is up the stairs."

"Yes, of course." Nathan pulled out a gold coin and pressed it into her hand. "Thank you. You've been a great help."

Janet smiled broadly and quickly pocketed the coin. "Thank ye, sir."

"One other thing…" Nathan said. "You didn't remember the two women, but you knew the doctor's name. Was he local?"

Janet's eyebrows went up. "Oh, nae, sir, he was from Inverness. I knew him because he's the missus's brother."

"Mrs. McCready's brother?" Nathan's eyebrows shot up.

"Aye. The missus's name was MacPherson before she married Donald McCready."

Verity gave Janet a thin-lipped smile and said, "While you show Mr. Dunbridge to his chamber, I believe I'll give Mrs. McCready another visit."

"Oh, nae, miss." Janet's eyes opened in alarm. "Dinnae tell her—"

"Don't worry, I won't tell her you told us," Verity assured her.

"I'll go with you," Nathan said quickly.

"No, dear." Verity patted his arm. "This is something I'll do better without you."

Nathan sighed as he watched Verity trot down the stairs.

"Oh, sir...the missus is bound to know." Janet turned her worried gaze on him.

"Don't worry, she'll make up an entirely different story," Nathan told Janet. "She's quite good at that."

## CHAPTER TWENTY-TWO

AFTER JANET SHOWED Nathan to his bedchamber and he again reassured the woman that Verity would manage not to reveal her help, he went outside. There was a stone bench that looked out over the loch, and he sat there waiting for Verity.

When Verity emerged from the house, he stood up and went to meet her halfway. "I trust Mrs. McCready is still in good health."

Verity smiled and patted his cheek. "I didn't harm a hair on the woman's head. I'm not entirely a barbarian, you know."

"Mmm. Only half of one?" He cocked an eyebrow.

"Nonsense. No more than a third, I'm sure." Verity was clearly pleased at Nathan's hearty chuckle and gave him an answering smile before continuing. "Anyway, I didn't need to resort to anything so crude as violence. I simply pointed out how very distressing it would be to Mrs. McCready and her brother if the British Foreign Office came to investigate their aid to the French."

Nathan choked. "Their what?"

She lifted a shoulder. "I had to have some reason for already knowing what Janet told us. So I told her we already knew about the suspicious circumstances of the Douglases residing here."

"You do know that Malcolm was born before the war with Bonaparte."

"Oh, the Scots are always conspiring against England." Verity waved away that problem. "And England is always at war with France."

"Actually," Nathan said in a musing tone, "I suppose we were at war. His birth would have been during that first little spat with the colonies."

"You see? So I went on to say that we had hoped that she might provide us information that would clear up the reason she was housing known Anglophobes like Flora Douglas, and I was going to give her another chance to tell her side of the story."

"As always, I bow to your wisdom," Nathan said, offering his arm. "Now why don't we take a stroll along the loch and you can tell me what you learned. I think it's better to discuss it away from all the ears in the house."

Verity linked her arm with his. "You are wise, as well. Unfortunately, Mrs. McCready had little to tell that we didn't already know. Margaret and her mother came here to conceal the birth of Margaret's illegitimate child. She didn't know the exact circumstances, such as who the father was. All she cared about was that she was getting several months of paying guests in return for not asking or answering any questions about the whole thing." She paused for a moment, then said, "I did learn one piece of new information, though."

The tone of her voice made Nathan stop and turn to look at her. "Good information?"

Verity nodded. "Well, not good for Margaret, but definitely good for you. Apparently Margaret died only a few months later. Mrs. McCready didn't know the details, unfortunately, but she was positive it wasn't longer than a year after the birth."

Nathan let out a long breath. "Then my parents' marriage was legal. I'm very glad to learn my father didn't deceive Mother like that."

"It also means your birth is legitimate. And since we now know that Malcolm was born before George Dunbridge married his mother, he is not legitimate and therefore has no claim to your estate."

"None?"

"Remember the day you spoke to Robert Douglas at his club? I went to talk to an attorney."

"Yes, I remember. We never talked about it, did we?"

"No. Your discovery of Gairmore was far more interesting. The lawyer told me that if the parents marry after the child is born, the child can share in the personal property but not the real estate. And since the thing you have of value is the real estate, he would get nothing."

Nathan frowned. "That seems rather unfair. I mean, he's older and my father did do the right thing and marry her, even if it was a bit late."

Verity chuckled. "Only you would feel sorry for the man who is trying to steal your estate from you."

"Well, he *is* my brother, despite all that." They began to walk again. "I can't help but think how different my life would have been if I'd grown up with a brother."

"I think with a brother like him, it would not have been an improvement."

He glanced at her and smiled faintly. "You're probably right."

"I, um, I suppose our case is over now," Verity said.

"I suppose." A fist clenched in Nathan's chest at the thought of not being with Verity all the time, of leading separate lives. It didn't mean he would lose her, but... Anyway, there were things that needed to be done, loose ends to tie up—surely there were. He cleared his throat. "But first I think...I think that we should go to Edinburgh and talk to the Douglases."

"Why?" Verity stared at him, and Nathan had a swift pang of doubt—*does she not feel the same desire to stay together that I do?*

"Well, um, to talk to Malcolm's parents—or, really, his grandparents." He warmed to this idea. It made sense, really, when one thought about it. It wasn't simply an excuse to extend his time with Verity. "It's possible Malcolm has returned to Edinburgh, given that we haven't been able to locate him. He might have realized that his charade was destined to fail and went home to lick his wounds. Surely, if we can speak to him, he will see that the proof we have would make a shambles of his claim."

"Whether he is there or not, I'd like to discover if his parents are privy to his scheme," Verity added. "If they are, we can show them what folly it would be to continue the plan. To thwart Malcolm's blackmail, we would be forced to expose his family's own lies, and that would plunge not only him but his grandparents as well into a terrible scandal."

"Exactly." Nathan nodded. "If they aren't aware of what he's doing, it would seem to me that they have a right to know that he is about to destroy their reputations. I'm sure they would do their best to dissuade him. I would much prefer to settle all this quickly and quietly. Even though Malcolm cannot succeed, it would cause my mother a good deal of heartache to find out about my father's secrets. It would damage my father's reputation—*I* find it rather unsavory that he didn't acknowledge his son, that he let someone else raise him. I can imagine how the rest of the *ton* will seize on that. I'd hate for Mother to have to face the gossip."

"You would have to face it, as well."

"I don't care about that, really. I've realized the past few weeks that the *ton* isn't all that interesting to me. Still, I think it's worth trying to avert a scandal that can only hurt both the families."

"You're right." Verity nodded. "It doesn't seem likely that Flora has any part in Malcolm's plans. Given all the trouble she went to in order to hide the facts of his birth, I doubt very much that she would want it spread about now. She is probably the best person to control Malcolm. She certainly sounds like she dominated Margaret."

"Yes. Good. Then we'll leave for Edinburgh first thing tomorrow." Nathan stopped and turned to Verity, taking both her hands in his, and smiled down at her. "I don't care for our sleeping arrangements here."

Verity linked her arms around his neck, her golden eyes glinting up at him in that way that never failed to stir him. "Ah, but you have to remember—sneaking into forbidden places is what I do."

She stretched up to kiss him.

VERITY GLANCED OVER at Nathan as their carriage made its way through the streets of Edinburgh. It hadn't been hard to learn where John and Flora Douglas lived. They appeared to be a prominent family.

Verity and Nathan had dawdled a little on their way to the city. The last three days had been bittersweet, for every touch, every kiss, every shared smile or laugh had been countered by the knowledge that they would soon return to London, to the lives they had established long before they met each other.

She knew Nathan would still come to her even after they returned to London; there had been no slackening in their passion. But it would not be the same. Nathan's calling on her, even spending the night in her bed, would not match the time they had spent in each other's company, the moments, both mundane and monumental, that they shared.

*Was this love?*

Was love wanting to be with him all the time and missing him when he wasn't there? Was it this desire to have him in her bed, to see him last thing at night and first thing in the morning? Was it the way her heart lifted when he came into the room?

Verity wasn't the kind of woman who fell in love. She was free and independent—accountable to no one, responsible for no one. Needing no one. But at the moment all she could think was *I cannot bear to lose him.*

And there was the small matter of Jonathan Stanhope and the Bow Street Runner. Verity had managed to be busy enough with Nathan and the case to not give it too much thought, but she knew that snare was also awaiting her in London, at home. Home had just recently started to feel like a safe concept to Verity and now here she was, back to feeling as though laying down roots would invariably mean being entangled by them.

More than once during the trip, she had been tempted to tell Nathan about Stanhope. She wanted his advice—Nathan knew more about those in the *ton* and perhaps he'd have some way out of the mess she hadn't thought of. But more than that, she had simply wanted to share her thoughts and feelings with him, to wrap herself in his warmth and ground herself in his steadiness. She wanted to believe it wouldn't be too selfish of her.

They seemed to be nearing the end of Nathan's problem, so her concerns would not be adding so much to his burden. And she no longer balked at the idea of him witnessing her fear or weakness. Still, the possibility that Nathan might confront Stanhope frightened her. She would never forgive herself if something happened to Nathan because of her.

*How did I let myself get caught up like this?*

But Nathan wasn't impulsive; he would listen to reason. And perhaps it was time to just trust him with the knowledge without parsing it over herself first. After all, she had already trusted him with her heart.

"Nathan…" Verity began. "There's someth—"

"This must be it," Nathan said at the same time, gazing out the window. The carriage had rolled to a stop in front of a large, elegant house. "Why would Malcolm have wanted the Dunbridge estate?" Nathan murmured.

"I don't know. Another puzzle. Hopefully we'll find out."

He turned to her. "Sorry I interrupted you. What were you about to say?"

"Oh. It was nothing," Verity replied, smiling at him. This was no time to bring it up. This was the second time she'd been stopped from saying it. Maybe it was a sign it was better left alone.

They went up the few steps to the front stoop. The butler who answered the door at their knock told them Mrs. Douglas was unavailable, but when Nathan told him his name, the butler's eyes widened slightly and he said, "I'll see if Mrs. Douglas will receive you."

The man went into the first room in the hall and they

heard him say, "There is a Mr. Dunbridge who wishes to speak to you, ma'am."

"What?" A feminine voice rose in a shriek, and an instant later a woman charged out of the drawing room. She was silver-haired and straight-backed, and her attire was fashionable and expensive, if somewhat staid. Verity thought she would have appeared regal if it had not been for the wild look in her eyes and the way she twisted a handkerchief in her hands, as if to tear it asunder. "Dunbridge! How dare you!"

She strode straight toward Nathan, her eyes flashing, her face twisted in hate. Verity had to admire Nathan's courage for not stepping back. She had visions of having to wrestle the old lady to the ground, but the woman pulled up abruptly. "It was *you*, wasn't it? *You* took Malcolm!"

Nathan's brows soared up. "I beg your pardon? Malcolm? What are—"

The woman plowed on, ignoring him. "If you hurt him…if you so much as touch one hair on his head, I will *kill* you."

"Mrs. Douglas," Verity said crisply, moving forward to draw the other woman's gaze to her. "You must calm yourself."

"Calm myself? Calm myself?" Mrs. Douglas repeated, her voice rising with hysteria. "When you have kidnapped my son?" Her words left both Verity and Nathan gaping at her, and she went on, her voice frantic and high, stumbling over her words. "Give him back to me. I swear—let him go. I'll see you hang for this."

"Stop!" An older man emerged from the drawing room and walked toward them, leaning on a cane. "Flora, you must not disturb yourself this way."

The woman whirled. "John…they have Malcolm." Her voice broke and she went to the man, whom Verity assumed to be her husband.

"Shh," he said gently, taking her hand. "Dinnae fash yourself. We must remain calm. They want to negotiate or they wouldn't be here." He looked toward Nathan, and his voice turned hard and cold. "What do you want? How much will it cost?"

"I assure you we did not kidnap your son," Verity said sharply.

"Mrs. Douglas, Mr. Douglas," Nathan said in a soothing tone. "Please believe me when I say that I have no desire to disturb you. Why do you think Malcolm has been kidnapped?"

"Because his valet told us," John Dunbridge snapped. "He saw Malcolm abducted on the way to London."

"Then you should question his valet again," Verity retorted. "Because *we* saw Malcolm *in* London—when he came to Nathan to tell him that he was the son of your daughter Margaret and George Dunbridge."

"Malcolm would never have said that," Flora protested. "He *despises* your father. I am his mother, and he would never—" She broke off, tears again spilling out of her eyes, and looked over at a portrait on the wall. "Malcolm is the most loyal of men."

Verity's gaze followed the other woman's to a large painting of a young man dressed in a tartan. His hair was a reddish blond, and his features were attractive, though his jaw was set in a stern, even defiant, look akin to the expression on Flora Douglas's face. Verity's insides turned cold. "Is that—"

"Malcolm. My son." Mrs. Douglas's voice rang with pride.

Nathan stared at the portrait with the same dumb-founded expression Verity felt on her own face. "My God. That's not—"

He and Verity looked at each other. She nodded. "He was an imposter."

# CHAPTER TWENTY-THREE

"WHAT NONSENSE IS THIS?" Mr. Douglas asked in a nettled voice. "Who's an imposter?"

"The man who came to me in London, sir," Nathan answered. "He told me he was Malcolm Douglas, and he claimed to be my father's legitimate heir."

"That's ridiculous," Douglas said crisply. "Malcolm is *my* heir."

Nathan glanced at Verity and she shrugged. There seemed little point in continuing that argument right now. The entire case had been turned on its head.

Nathan clearly thought the same, for he said only, "Nevertheless, a man approached me, making that claim. Clearly, he was not actually your son." Nathan gestured toward the portrait. "But I had no way of knowing that. In tracking down his claim, we wound up here."

"The devil you say," the older man blurted.

"It's true. I was there," Verity told him.

"And who are you?" Mr. Douglas frowned at Verity.

"I'm Verity Cole, and I am an investigator."

"A female? I never heard of such a thing." This statement seemed to nonplus John Douglas as much as the rest of their news.

"Why would anyone pretend to be Malcolm?" Flora Douglas asked in a bewildered tone.

"Our thought was that he was trying to get Mr. Dunbridge to pay him in order to avoid a scandal," Verity explained. "If your son was taken, then perhaps the imposter did it to keep the real Malcolm Douglas from showing up and ruining his scheme." She paused. "Have you received a demand for ransom?"

"No." Flora Douglas began to twist her handkerchief into knots again. "And it's been weeks."

"If you'd tell us exactly what happened, perhaps we could try to help you find him," Nathan offered.

Both the Douglases stiffened, and Verity suspected they would have liked to refuse anything from a Dunbridge. But then the woman sagged, leaning against her husband, and Mr. Douglas sighed and said, "Come in, then." He looked across the entryway to the servant who still hovered there. The servant's expression was placid, but Verity had spent enough time pretending to be a maid in Lady Lockwood's household that she knew there would be much gossip in the staff's quarters tonight. "Bring us a pot of tea and send Cummings to us."

Mr. Douglas ushered Nathan and Verity into the drawing room and gestured toward a sofa. "What is it you want to know?"

"Where exactly was your son taken, Mr. Douglas?"

"In Delbourne, Cummings said. Malcolm was on his way to London."

"I knew he should never have gone to London," Mrs. Douglas put in bitterly.

"He was going to visit his uncle?" Nathan asked. At the other couple's surprised looks, he added, "We talked to Mr. Robert Douglas after the imposter came to me with his claim."

"And Robert said that was Malcolm?" Douglas asked in amazement. "He didn't set you straight?"

"He never saw the man, and we didn't ask him about the claims the man made. It was rather a delicate subject, you see. We merely wanted to find out if he knew Malcolm. He told us that he hadn't seen Malcolm, but he assumed it was simply because his nephew was a young man who wanted to see London without an uncle hanging about."

Flora snorted. "He *would* think that. I knew he wouldn't look after Malcolm properly."

Her husband smiled at her indulgently. "Malcolm is thirty-four, my dear, hardly a child. He's been on his own for some time."

"Yes, but he was in Edinburgh then," Flora retorted. "Look what happened as soon as he left Scotland."

A man walked into the room and said diffidently, "Sir, you wished to see me?"

"Ah, Cummings. Yes." Mr. Douglas turned to Nathan and Verity. "Cummings is Malcolm's valet. He was traveling with Malcolm when he was abducted." He looked back at the valet. "Tell them what happened, Cummings."

"Yes, sir. Master Malcolm and I took the Great Road. We spent the night in Delbourne—that's a village just before Stevenage. It was going to be our last stop before the city. And then…" He swallowed. "The next morning Master Malcolm walked down the road a bit, just to stretch his legs, you see, as he gets restless in the coach. I took his things to the carriage and when I turned back and looked for him, I saw these…these two *scoundrels* jump out and grab him." He looked over at Mr. Douglas and said earnestly, "There was nothing I could do, sir. I tried—"

"Yes, yes, Cummings, we understand. I know you wanted to help him."

The valet swung back to face Nathan. "There were two of them, and they were so quick. They knocked him over the head and threw him into a carriage, then took off. I shouted at them to stop and ran after them. By the time I got back to our coach, they were nowhere in sight. We followed, but when we reached Stevenage, well, there was no way to know where they'd gone. We didn't know what else to do, so we came back." Cummings sent Mr. Douglas another apologetic glance. "I'm so sorry, sir."

"I know. No one blames you, Cummings," Douglas said. His kind words raised him a little in Verity's view.

"Where exactly did these men come at him?" Nathan asked.

The valet stopped and cast his eyes up, thinking. "They charged out from a hedge at the edge of the village, just past the tavern on the right. Um, the Bull and Bear, I think? Or maybe that was the one by our inn. The Green Lion?"

"That's fine. As long as it's the last tavern going toward Stevenage, I'm sure we can find it."

Nathan turned to the Douglases as the servant slipped out of the room. "We'll inquire in that village and do whatever we can to find Malcolm. I think our best hope will lie in finding the man who is impersonating him." He cast a glance at Verity, perhaps remembering that she was the detective, but she merely nodded. Normally, with Sloane or some other man she would feel the need to wrest control of the investigation back. But it was nice seeing Nathan work—he really did have a head for this.

"Mrs. Douglas," Verity spoke up, "it would help us a good deal if you had a likeness of Malcolm that we could show people when we inquire about him. Perhaps you have a small portrait of him?"

The other woman closed her hand protectively on the locket she wore around her neck. "I…" She cast a pained look at her husband. "No. John…"

"I promise we will give it back to you when we find him," Nathan told her, and apparently the woman could see past his father's name enough to recognize the honesty in Nathan's face.

Flora took in a short breath and lifted the chain over her head. She rubbed her thumb over it once, then handed it to Nathan. He and Verity made their brief farewells and exited the room quickly.

Verity was surprised to see the butler standing by the door, a basket in his hands. He held it out to them, saying, "Here's a bit of food for the road. We hope and pray you will find the young master."

There was a glimmer of moisture in his eyes, and it touched Verity. The true Malcolm must be a decent sort for the servants to truly care. She took the basket from his hands and hooked it over her arm. "We will do our best. Thank you."

Outside Nathan draped the locket around Verity's neck, then took the basket and opened the carriage door, giving her a hand into the vehicle. It struck Verity that this was another thing that ruffled her feathers with other men, but she didn't mind when Nathan did it. It was simply a part of Nathan's good nature. *Or maybe I have changed*, she thought.

It made her a little uneasy to think that Nathan might have such influence over her, so she started to talk about business as soon as Nathan sat down beside her. "I knew there was something off about him. I should have thought of the possibility that he was impersonating Malcolm Douglas."

"I don't see how you could have figured that out," Nathan replied. "We'd never seen the real Malcolm."

"Well, we certainly should have been more specific with his uncle than saying Malcolm was tall, blond, and blue-eyed. That could fit any number of men." She paused. "But his impersonation makes sense of several oddities in the matter." She began to count them off on her fingers. "He didn't arrive at his uncle's, as he had said he would. The idea of scandal staining his name—either one—didn't bother him. He didn't pursue the matter in court because he knew he couldn't even prove he was Malcolm, let alone prove that Malcolm was your father's heir. All he wanted was to get some blackmail money from you."

"And leaving his inn, that always bothered me. But the imposter wouldn't want to make it easy to find him. I could have brought someone with me who knew the real Malcolm. His uncle, say. Or even if I just told his Uncle Robert where he was, that would have been disastrous for him."

Verity nodded, then straightened. "Those men. The ones who attacked us. He could have sent them."

"The imposter? Why? It wouldn't have benefitted him to have us harmed."

"Maybe he grew alarmed because we met Malcolm's uncle at that Scottish party. He was afraid Robert Douglas would look for him." Verity chewed the inside of her cheek, thinking. "Or he may not have expected us to investigate his claim. But when we did, he realized that we might discover that he wasn't really Malcolm. Consider the timing. The attack on us was after we'd talked to his uncle *and* after we'd tried to track Malcolm down at his inn."

"True. But that doesn't explain why they were asking us 'where.' Still, we have not been set upon again, so I will not complain. The most important thing to me is that you are safe."

Verity slid over to snuggle against his side and Nathan's arm went around her shoulders.

This was so very nice. She didn't want it to ever end. Verity had never had permanence, nothing to make her stay. There was nothing in her life she could not change just as easily as she slid from one role to another. Even her house, satisfying as it was to have a home, was something that she could sell and leave. But Nathan... Nathan anchored her. Whatever flight of fancy she pursued, Nathan was still there, so sure, so even, so very much himself, and her heart quailed inside to think of him not being there, of living a life without him.

It was dangerous to want something so much. Verity tried never to do it. But she wanted this life with Nathan. And she would continue to ignore the knowledge that sat darkly in the back of her mind: the truth that their time together would end, that Nathan could never be hers.

"We'll have to look in the village where the real Malcolm was abducted, of course—Delbourne. But it's been some time, and I can't imagine we'll find anything helpful there," Nathan mused. "I think the surest way to locate Malcolm is to find the imposter and make him take us to Malcolm."

"You are very set on finding him, aren't you?"

"Yes, of course. He's my brother." Nathan turned his head to look down at her.

"Half brother. One you've never known, from a household that despises your name."

"That doesn't change the fact that he's family."

Verity sat up and looked Nathan in the face. "You do realize that he may not be imprisoned."

"You mean the imposter might have killed Malcolm."

Verity nodded. "It's easier to simply get rid of a man than to hide him somewhere and bring him food and water. Less risky."

"I know." Nathan sighed. "And believe me, I don't want to be the one who carries that news back to his mother."

"Grandmother." Verity nestled back against his side. After a moment she said, "Do you think Malcolm knows?"

"That he is really Margaret's son? Or that his father was George Dunbridge? That he has a brother?"

"Any. All of it."

"I think—the way his mother said he would not have come to me and claimed to be my father's son, I think he must know the truth and he's been raised to despise my father. But however much he knows or doesn't know, I think that to him and Flora, they are mother and son."

"It will devastate her if we don't find him. Even if he's dead, it would be better to know than to spend the rest of her years wondering."

"We'll find him," Nathan said firmly. "We could learn something in this village. I doubt his valet investigated—his thought, of course, was to chase after the other vehicle."

"Perhaps we will," Verity agreed, though she doubted it. Even if there had been some evidence, after all this time, it wasn't likely to still be there.

WHEN THEY REACHED Delbourne two days later, her doubts were justified. They asked first at the inn where Cummings had said he and Malcolm had stayed. No one in the inn remembered Malcolm, even after they showed them the miniature portrait in the locket.

"Good-looking chap, in't he?" the girl at the tavern said, but shook her head. "But I don't remember him. It gets terrible busy in here some nights."

The ostler in the stables said, "Oh, aye, I remember his valet running in, all upset and shouting that someone had been kidnapped," the ostler said. "Don't remember his name."

"Was this the man who was kidnapped?" Verity showed him the locket.

"I don't know, miss. I didn't see him. The fancy folk don't come in the stables, just the drivers or post boys."

They walked down the street to the tavern Cummings had mentioned, the Bull and Bear. A hedge grew just past the inn, and they followed it to a narrow break in the shrubbery. Verity walked through the break with Nathan behind her, and they looked over the ground behind it. There were scuff marks and footprints, but no way to tell whether the marks were old or new.

"Look." Verity's voice rose a little bit in excitement, and she bent to pick up a small crumpled bag caught in the tangled branches at the bottom of the hedge. Straightening out the bag, she showed it to Nathan.

"Fairborn's Confectionary," Nathan read, and he glanced up sharply at Verity. "Just like the bag of lemon drops that fell out of our friend Hill's pocket during the fight."

"Curious, isn't it?"

"Very. Let's check inside the tavern next door. Surely

these two didn't spend all their time out here in the bushes eating lemon drops."

Inside the tavern, the barkeep raised his eyebrows. "Two men who were here a month ago? Nay, how could I remember that?"

"They were from London," Verity said in an attempt to prod his memory. "Dark-haired. One short and square and one tall and thin."

Nathan held up the small bag. "The tall one was fond of these sweets."

The man still shook his head, but a customer sitting beside the bar spoke up. "I remember those two. He was fair devoted to those lemon drops." He nodded toward the bag in Nathan's hand. "Not sure when that was, though. At least a fortnight ago."

The tavern owner gave his customer a skeptical glance. "And how do you remember that, Walt? You're foxed by nine o'clock every night."

"Because that short one bumped into me and spilled half my glass," Walt answered, his voice filling with indignation at the memory. "I would've drawn his cork, I'll tell you." He pantomimed a punch, then added candidly, "Only he looked like a bruiser." He turned to the barkeep. "Don't you remember?"

"Oh, aye, I remember you whinging on about somebody spilling your ale. Didn't know it was them."

"Well, they were just here that once," Walt said generously.

"Did you speak to them?" Verity asked the customer.

Walt snorted. "Are you daft? He gave me such a black look when I told him to watch where he was going—I wasn't likely to chat with 'em."

"Did you happen to hear anything they said to each other?"

"Nay." Walt looked disappointed. "They were too far away. They sat in that corner by themselves all evening." He pointed across the room. "And then they left. Haven't seen them since."

"So you've no idea where they went afterward? An inn, perhaps?"

The other man shook his head. "But that's worth something, isn't it?"

"Yes, you've been very helpful." Nathan dug out some coins. "This should see you through this evening."

"I think we can be certain now that Malcolm—the real Malcolm—was abducted by the same men who attacked us," Verity said to Nathan as they walked out the door.

"Yes, I think it's unlikely there are two sets of ruffians who fit the same description involved."

"This means they must have been working for the false Malcolm," Verity said.

"Yes, I have to admit I was wrong. It seems unlikely that Lord Arden would have hired the exact same ruffians that kidnapped Malcolm Douglas," Nathan agreed.

"It makes our task easier. We at least know their names, which is more than we have for Imitation Malcolm. All we have to do now is track down Shoemaker and Hill."

Nathan let out a groan. "Not another visit to the catacombs."

Verity laughed. "This time we'll take a ladder."

# CHAPTER TWENTY-FOUR

THEY ARRIVED IN London late that evening, tired from their journey. Verity's house was a welcome sight, and Verity sank onto the couch with an enormous sigh.

"I should have known better than to wear new shoes on a trip," she said, unbuttoning the red leather half boots and pulling them off. She dropped them on the floor and lay back on the sofa, resting her head on the arm of the couch and idly watching Nathan kneel to light a small fire in the fireplace.

When he was finished, he joined her on the couch. Lifting her feet, he set them on his lap and began to massage them.

"Ahh." Verity let out a blissful noise. After a moment she said, "You've been very quiet today."

"Have I?" He glanced at her, the corner of his mouth lifting in a faint smile. "No doubt I've been nursing my wounds after having my theory about Lord Arden squashed."

The truth was he had been feeling strangely let down, the feeling increasing as they drew nearer to London. It was absurd. He should feel overjoyed that they'd proved that he was his father's legitimate son and heir.

He was glad of that, of course, and it was even a bit heartening to learn that his actual half brother was not the one threatening to bring scandal down on the Dunbridges. His world had been restored; he could go on just as he always had. And yet…

There was something in him that mourned a little. The prospect of a new life had been exciting, even if it was somewhat alarming. He was sorry to let go of the plans he had daydreamed about—becoming a detective, working with Verity…*being* with Verity. In short, continuing to live as they had the last few weeks.

But he wasn't going to tell Verity that. He wasn't sure he wanted to know how she would react. So he said only, "I've been thinking about what we should do tomorrow. Where to start. I can't think Shoemaker and Hill would return to the places where we found them before."

"You're probably right, but it's worth a try. Old habits are very hard to break, even when you know they're foolish. I could set 'my' urchins to looking for any of those three men. They can roam around everywhere without rousing any particular notice."

"Perhaps we should get out and about tomorrow, make calls, go shopping. The theater—we should go to a play."

"Why?" She looked at him quizzically. There was something else in her expression—something guarded. Nathan wondered if he would ever look at Verity and not be curious as to what secrets lurked behind her eyes. *Probably not.* But it didn't bother him as much as it used to. Perhaps there was something to be said of a relationship where the past was not known, unlike his courtship with Annabeth. A certain allure of mystery and continual discovery.

"Well…because I want to. It'd be nice, don't you think?"

Verity hesitated, and Nathan felt a pit in his stomach

as he waited to hear the words he had been dreading for days. *Their affair was coming to an end.*

"Yes," she finally answered. The cloud he had seen before left her eyes, and her face grew relaxed and warm. The foot rub was obviously having a good effect on her. He wondered if it was awakening feelings having nothing to do with her feet, as it was him. "I'd like that."

"And, to be practical about it, we have been out of town a good while, so if our blackmailer has tried to call on us again, he's had no luck. He may be on the watch for us."

"For *you*." Verity's tone was one of correction. "You are the one the imposter will be looking for. I think perhaps I will wear a disguise. A wig, at least."

"Really?" Nathan wasn't sure why he cared. Yes, he loved the brilliant hue of Verity's hair, but it wasn't as if she looked any less beautiful as a blonde or a brunette. Still, it felt…as if she was hiding herself from him. "Why?" He frowned.

"I've stayed quite long as Mrs. Billingham, I think. I worry that I might become a bit too well-known amongst the *ton* at this rate. I still need to be able to do work for other clients."

"But the *ton* already knows of our courting. I can't very well just be seen out with someone that looks strangely like Mrs. Billingham. No wig could hide your beauty. And I'm assuming you aren't suggesting I take a street urchin to the theater."

Verity laughed. "No, I suppose that would draw even more attention. It can't hurt to take out Mrs. Billingham once more."

"How about twice?" Nathan paused, then added, "I also thought we might pick up some sweets."

"Fairborn's Confectionary." Verity gave him a croc-odile smile, all teeth and wicked intent. "Clever boy."

"I thought so. If we want to catch sight of our targets, it's one place we know at least one of them goes regu-larly." Nathan pressed his thumbs into the instep of her foot, and Verity let out a soft groan, sounding so much like a woman in the throes of passion that it sent a lance of fire through Nathan. He drew a shaky breath and con-tinued his work, though now he was less rubbing away the soreness as tracing idle patterns on her skin.

Nathan studied Verity's face as he stroked her feet and ankles. She'd closed her eyes, her lips faintly parted, and a blush tinged her cheeks. Her breath was a trifle faster, and he could see the throb of the vein in her throat. His loins tightened. "But right now…" He slid a hand far-ther up her leg. "I have something much better in mind."

Verity sucked in a little breath as he teased at the soft skin of her inner thigh. She opened her eyes and cast him a demure look. "Why, Mr. Dunbridge, are you trying to seduce me?"

"Am I succeeding?"

"Hmm. Let me think." Verity crossed her arms be-neath her head and sent him a tantalizing smile. "It might take some effort to convince me."

"In that case, perhaps I should try harder." His hand went up, sliding beneath her undergarments and over her skin to the juncture of her legs. His finger moved over the sensitive skin, hot and slick, flooding with moisture at his touch. "Why, Verity…I do believe you're lying. You seem very receptive to me."

Her only response was to bend one leg at the knee, opening herself more to him. Desire pulsed through him now, but Nathan was patient, reveling in the buildup of hunger inside him, the knot growing ever tighter, as he watched Verity's face. He could see every new pleasure as it went through her, each soft gasp and sensual smile, the golden eyes growing ever more lambent and dreamy.

Nathan pulled his hand back, and Verity's eyes flew open. "Don't stop."

"Trust me, I won't go far." He leaned over, bracing one arm on the back of the couch and ran his hand slowly down her body, caressing her breasts and stomach.

His hand went to the ties of her dress, undoing them and shoving back the bodice. Her nipples were dark beneath the thin cotton of her chemise. He trailed his thumb over each one, then bent to suckle them through the cloth. Nathan lifted his head and gazed down at Verity's breasts, the cloth now wet and transparent, clinging to her pointed nipples.

"Nathan…" Verity moved her hips beneath him. "Aren't you going to do more than look?"

"Oh, yes, a great deal more. When I've had my fill of looking."

Nathan unfastened the bows of her chemise and pulled the loosened cloth down so that it cupped her breasts. He trailed his forefinger down the hard center line of her chest until it met the cloth.

"You should have ties all down the front of this, as well."

"You could just tear it apart."

Heat surged in him at her words, and he clenched his hand on the back of the couch, fighting down the demand of his hunger. "I think not. This is a very nice view."

He ran his finger slowly over her breasts, circling the nipples, then gently squeezed them. He laid a soft kiss on each one before he straightened. Shoving her skirts up to her waist, he grasped her underpants and pulled them off, leaving her legs clad in her stockings and garters. And that, he thought, was a very nice view, as well.

He was hard as a rock, his erection straining against his breeches, but still he took his time, caressing her legs, sliding close to the juncture of her legs, but not quite touching. Verity said his name again, urgency in her voice.

"Patience, love, patience."

Verity let out a low growl that made him smile, and he went down on his knees beside the sofa, his hand moving up at last to caress the soft and vulnerable flesh between her legs. His fingers roamed the hot wet core of her desire, first exploring, then stroking with sure rhythmic movements. She moved beneath his touch, the tension mounting in her.

"I want you inside me," she whispered, her voice thin with the strain of control.

"Not just yet, love." He pulled his hand away.

Verity shot him a fierce look. "I will get you for this."

He chuckled softly. "I hope so."

Nathan slipped his fingers inside her, his thumb sliding over the slick nub. He could see the climax building in her—the tightened cords of her neck, the short sharp breaths as she pushed up against him. Then it burst upon her, a blush sliding up her chest and neck, her back arching, face taut as the wave of pleasure rippled up her body. She was glorious, so beautiful it made his heart clench, and he was torn between the joy of watching her and the ache of the desire to be inside her.

She let out a long groaning sigh and went limp, every part of her soft and yielding in a way Verity almost never was. Her chest rose and fell rapidly, and she opened her eyes to look up at him, her gaze glowing and a little dazed. She was, he thought, the very vision of a woman well pleasured.

Nathan positioned himself between her legs, his hands on her thighs, sliding slowly up to touch her hipbones with his thumbs, then back down, as he gazed at her. He bent to kiss her lips softly and murmured, "Are you satisfied?"

Verity shook her head slowly, her smile full of sensual promise, and her fingers teased lightly over his hands and arms.

"Ah, well, we shall have to see what we can do about that." Nathan's thumbs slipped between her legs, opening her more fully to him, and he leaned down to kiss her in that most intimate place.

Verity let out a little yelp of surprise and delight, and her fingers slid into his hair. "Nathan…"

After that, she uttered no more words, as his mouth worked on her, emitting only little sounds that pushed his own arousal into a searing mixture of pain and pleasure. She came quickly, and he eased back, caressing her with long, lazy strokes, then drove her to the heights again.

Nathan straightened and looked down at her, taking in the glow that radiated from her. He buried his face against her chest. "Sweet heaven, but you are beautiful."

His arms went around her and he rolled onto the floor, taking her with him. His fingers fumbled with the buttons of his breeches, but Verity sat up, straddling him, and pulled his hands away. "No, no, no," she said, her voice light and teasing. "Now it's my turn. I intend to have my way with you."

Verity smiled wickedly as she settled in, wriggling

a little. Nathan had thought he could feel no fuller or hotter, but he found his limits went far beyond that.

She shoved the sides of his jacket down to his elbows, then untied his neckcloth and draped it around her own neck, the cloth skimming over her breasts, tantalizingly concealing and revealing the points of her nipples with her movements. It looked, he decided, infinitely better on her.

After unfastening the buttons of his waistcoat, she pushed the cloth aside and went to work on the ties of his shirt. The second one knotted, defying her efforts, and she simply ripped it apart, and the sound went all through him, nearly shattering his control.

Baring his chest, she was true to her word, kissing and stroking every bit of his exposed skin, pausing to nibble his flat nipples into life. Nathan felt as if a volcano was building in him, and he throbbed with hunger, aching to plunge into her and find his release, but he clamped down on his control, wanting even more to feel the full extent of Verity's sensual revenge.

She sat up, lightly dragging her nails down his chest, provoking such a shot of desire through him that he bucked beneath her. Verity smiled, tightening the grip of her legs around him, which immediately inflamed his senses even more.

Scooting back a little onto his legs, Verity unbuttoned his breeches, freeing him at last. "My goodness," she made a face of amused surprise. "Eager, aren't we?"

"Yes," he told her through gritted teeth.

She gave him her seductress smile again, her eyes gleaming, as she grazed her fingernails along his shaft. At his choked noise, she laughed softly and bent to kiss the soft skin of his stomach, her tongue making tiny swirls across it.

Stripping his breeches down his legs, Verity journeyed over his legs and abdomen, tasting and teasing, her touch so light it made him shiver, then stroking him with a firm hand or her agile tongue.

Nathan groaned, his fingers digging into her thighs. "You'll drive me mad."

"Mmm. You know I always like to win."

"Then I yield." Sweat bedewed his brow, and his entire body felt aflame. "I have to be inside you."

Verity's eyes were molten gold as she moved forward and slid slowly down onto him. She moved with exquisite slowness, and finally, with a growl, Nathan rolled over, taking her under him. His thrusts were hard and fast, hunger riding him. He was desperate to have her, to meld with her. At last he came in an explosion of fierce pleasure and utter release and collapsed against her, his breath ragged. He rolled onto his side, still holding her, unwilling to let go.

Verity held him, laying a soft kiss on his shoulder, her voice barely audible as she murmured, "I love you."

Later that night, lying in bed with her, Nathan played that moment over again in his mind.

*Had Verity really said she loved me?*

It had been so brief and soft, and he had been so dazed, sated, and still spellbound, that he'd been incapable of stringing a thought together, much less asking a question or making a reply.

He had fallen asleep, of course, and when he had awakened a long time later, he found himself alone, one of the pillows from the sofa under his head and an afghan thrown over him. Verity had also left a glass of wine and plate of cheese for him and taken his clothes. She'd certainly been busy while he slept, all without waking him up. The woman could be as silent as a ghost. It was a little disquieting.

Nathan had been glad for the food and drink, as he'd awakened starving, and he had downed them as he wrapped the afghan around him and went in search of Verity. She was asleep in bed, her hair a cloud upon the pillow, dark in the dim light of a low-burning lamp. He slipped into bed beside her and propped himself up on his forearm, watching her and thinking.

He wasn't sure whether she'd been too kind to awaken him or if she had wanted to be by herself after the intense intimacy. He knew her body well now and was rarely astonished anymore by the things she said or did, but Verity was still a mystery to him in so many ways. *She'd left a lamp burning for him.* He wished he knew exactly what Verity thought, what she wanted of him, how she felt. If she had indeed murmured that she loved him, had she regretted it? It seemed too late, too awkward to bring it up now. He was sure he would get an unwelcome response if he awakened her to question her, and tomorrow in the light of day, Verity was likely to slide out of it some way. She held her feelings close, guarding them like a treasure.

Which made what she had said tonight even more important. His instinct was to respond to her, to tell her that he loved her, too. Because, God help him, he did.

It wasn't the sort of love he had felt for Annabeth, that low yearning, but a seemingly insatiable desire to be with Verity, a compelling need. He had fallen into passion with Verity at first, but Nathan had known from the beginning that there was no future for them. Still, in the past few weeks, all his preconceptions had fallen by the wayside.

They had been together almost constantly on this journey to Scotland and back. One would think he would have felt constrained by the close quarters or irritated by something Verity did or said, that they would have quarreled or their passion would begin to pall.

But it had been both thrilling and comfortable being with Verity, and it seemed as if his desire for her only grew with each passing day. They were close in a way he'd never felt with any other woman. It had been almost as if they were married.

That thought brought him up short. *Did* he want to marry her? Was that even a possibility? Verity had told him most decidedly that she would never marry anyone. And no matter how much he loved her, he couldn't deny that Verity was in no way the wife he had always imagined—the mistress of his house, the mother of his children.

His chest warmed as he imagined her in his home, sharing his life, and, really, a brood of wild red-haired children would probably be the menace he had once imagined, but they would be *fun.* Just like their mother. And he would love them beyond all reason. Just as he did their mother.

It made perfect sense that he had never imagined a wife like Verity—he had never met anyone like Verity.

Could he be happy with her for the rest of his life? He gazed at her, studying her profile, the curve of her eyebrow, the line of her jaw. She turned toward him, as if sensing his presence, and snuggled close to him, and his heart stuttered in his chest.

The real question was: Could he be happy for the rest of his life *without* her?

## CHAPTER TWENTY-FIVE

NATHAN SPENT THE next morning going very visibly from one place to another, establishing that he was once again in the city. Verity had managed to beg off in order to check on the cases she had neglected while they were in Scotland. In the afternoon, however, she couldn't resist joining him to visit Fairborn's Confectionary.

Though Nathan was intent on making sure Malcolm knew that he was back, Verity was able to convince him to stay in their carriage to keep an eye on the shop. It would not do if their quarry saw Nathan or Verity first. And the men were already distinctly aware that Nathan was onto them after the chase with Sloane.

The coachman alternated between driving up and down the street—Russell asked no questions, having long ago become accustomed to Verity's odd requests—and pulling up in front of some other business for a time.

Watching the shop was, all in all, a rather boring exercise, and Verity spent much of her time planning what to wear that night at the theater. She was still uncertain about going out undisguised, but she hadn't known what to say to Nathan when he had pressed her on why she had wanted to wear a wig, so she had decided against it. The time for telling him about overhearing Stanhope in the park had passed. At this point her "not telling" looked more like hiding what she'd learned.

Nathan seemed the forgiving sort, but he was also an honest man. An honest man that just had his whole life undone and thrown back together by a lie. Verity wasn't sure how he would respond to her withholding what she had known for so long.

Besides, no one had discovered her in all this time that she'd been playing Mrs. Billingham. What were the chances that she'd be discovered during one more night out? And she desperately wanted one more night with Nathan. *Who knew how many we have left together?*

"Do you do this sort of surveillance a great deal?" Nathan asked as the afternoon wore on.

Verity let out a little laugh. "Unfortunately, yes. It can be a bit dull."

"I can see why you wanted to dress up as a crossing sweeper last time."

"Yes, but this street is really too busy to do much of any activity. We can return tomorrow—or prowl around the area where you found Hill before. We can hardly expect the man to buy lemon drops every day."

"I suppose not," Nathan agreed.

It was something of a relief when the shop closed and they could return home. It took Verity some time to get ready for going out—trying this style and that, changing her mind about the evening gown she had chosen and therefore having to come up with an entirely different set of accessories. She even dithered over which fan to carry.

Verity told herself she was being ridiculous, but she wanted everything to be perfect. She wanted to strike just the right tone that would both stir Nathan's senses and be stylishly elegant.

The way Nathan's eyes lit up when he saw her was

reward enough for her efforts. In that instant, all that mattered was Nathan and the little world that they had created.

When they walked into the theater, however, it was apparent that they would not be in a world of their own. Lady Lockwood stood near the stairs with Marcus Rutherford and Nathan's mother and aunt.

Nathan came to a halt and turned to retreat, but it was too late. They had been spotted.

"Dunbridge," Lady Lockwood called, and as they drew nearer she added in an offended tone, "I didn't know you would be here."

"Yes, well, here we are," Nathan replied, forcing a smile.

"I am so happy to see you again," Rose Dunbridge said to Verity in her sweet way. "We haven't had a chance to talk since we met at Lady Lockwood's, oh, that must have been a fortnight ago or more, wasn't it? Now we can have a nice chat."

Verity's stomach sank at the prospect of talking with Nathan's mother and aunt. Any conversation with them was bound to be full of pitfalls, given what they had learned about Nathan's father, and she didn't like the idea of having to lie to Mrs. Dunbridge. She was glad she had decided against wearing any disguise tonight so at least she didn't have to explain a change in her appearance to the two women.

"Yes, yes, plenty of time for that," Lady Lockwood said impatiently. "Come along, it's almost time for the curtain to go up. You'll sit with us, of course." She nodded to Nathan and Verity.

"Of course." Nathan and Verity trailed after the others to Lady Lockwood's box. He bent his head toward Verity, murmuring, "I'm sorry."

"Lady Lockwood is a force of nature," Verity replied. "I can hardly expect you to go against that. Though I do wish we had arrived a bit later."

Lady Lockwood waited for Nathan and Verity at the door. "We cannot speak about it now, naturally," she said in a low voice, casting a regretful glance inside the box at Rose. "But I want to hear everything that happened. You must come to the dinner I'm having on Saturday."

It would have been useless to disagree so Nathan nodded, and they took their seats. Fortunately, the curtain rose before any more conversation could take place. Everyone knew that Lady Lockwood disliked conversation during a performance—except her own comments, of course—so the first act passed in relative silence.

When the curtain fell, there was the usual visiting between boxes; Verity thought it might be this activity that brought the *ton* to the theater more than the play itself. But she was grateful for the custom when three middle-aged gentlemen almost immediately squeezed into the box, clearly intent on wooing Nathan's pretty mother, thus precluding any conversation with Rose. It was amusing to watch the suitors jockey for the position closest to Rose while Nathan loomed over them, scowling, but after a time, Verity took pity on the men and slipped her hand into the crook of Nathan's arm and tugged slightly.

"Shall we take a stroll?"

"Yes, of course." Nathan abandoned his surveillance of the men and went with her. They strolled along the corridor, and Nathan was stopped twice to talk, only nodding at a few others.

It brought home to Verity quite forcibly just how many people in the *ton* knew Nathan—and how many of them were now wondering who was the woman on his arm. Coming undisguised tonight had been a mistake. She had been able to ignore the threat of Milsap, the Bow Street Runner, during their trip to Scotland. But it was altogether different here in London; she was being far more unwise than she had even let herself acknowledge. She felt sure there were already several women jealously trying to find out exactly who had caught Nathan's eye and how his mystery lady could be defeated.

Nathan went to fetch them a glass of champagne, and Verity strolled over to a potted palm against the wall, where she would be less visible. When Nathan started to walk back to where she had been, Verity went to meet him, but stopped as her eyes fell on Lord Arden. He stood only a few feet away from her, deep in conversation with another gentleman. The other man glanced over, as if feeling her gaze.

*Jonathan Stanhope.* Verity's heart leapt into her throat.

Stanhope's dark gaze met hers, and any hope that he might not recognize her vanished when he exclaimed, "You!"

Verity whipped around and took off, running for the stairs.

"No! Wait!" Before she could reach the stairs, he reached her and grabbed her arm. "Verity, stop."

Out of the corner of her eye, she saw Nathan drop the drinks he carried as he ran toward them. Panicked, Verity stamped on Stanhope's foot with the heel of her slipper, wrenched her arm away and ran down the stairs. Stanhope came after her. There was a crash behind her, and Verity turned at the landing, glancing back. Stanhope was rising from the demolished potted palm and charging at Nathan.

*No, no, no! Nathan couldn't be involved in this.* She started back up, then stopped. The worst thing she could do was make it clear that she and Nathan were close. Nathan could hold his own, and others would jump in to stop the brawl. The best thing she could do was get as far away from Nathan as fast as she could.

Verity turned and flew down the remaining steps. She heard rapid footsteps pursuing her, but she lifted her skirts and darted through the crowd and out the front door. Running across the street, she disappeared into Covent Garden.

She took a twisted route through the darkest of streets, and only when she was certain that she had lost anyone following her did she hail a hack and head back to her house. When she reached it, she saw her own carriage rolling away and Nathan banging at her door.

He whirled at the sound of her hansom. "Verity! Thank God." He started toward her, but she was already running up to unlock the door.

Nathan followed her inside, saying, "I looked all around for you."

"I wanted to lose him," she explained, turning back to face him, and for the first time she got a good look at Nathan. His hair was in disarray, his clothes rumpled, and there was blood on his cheek. Her voice rose in alarm. "Nathan! What did you *do*?"

"I hit him. Threw him into that ugly potted palm, actually. Who was that fellow, anyway?"

"It was Lord Stanhope," she flung at him. "Oh, Nathan, why did you do that?"

Nathan stared at her. "Because he was chasing you.

Do you think I'd just stand around and let him grab you again?"

"You shouldn't have."

"For pity's sake," Nathan snapped, nettled. "I know you think you never need any help. But I'm not useless."

"That's not why—don't you understand? That was *Stanhope*. He saw me, recognized me, can connect me to you! It won't take him long to find out everything about Mrs. Billingham. Especially with Milsap on his side. I probably have a day—two at most."

"Milsap? Who on earth is that? Verity, what is going on?"

Verity sighed. "He's a Bow Street Runner that Jonathan hired to find out if I was really dead." She still wasn't ready to tell Nathan, to see the anger in his eyes when he found out she knew all this for weeks. But everything was unraveling. There was no point in hiding something for fear of it tearing them apart. That had already come to pass. "I've been checking on the Stanhope house here in London. I wanted to remain Mrs. Billingham, to stay with you, but I had to know if Jonathan had recognized me. A couple of days before we left for Scotland, I overheard him. I learned he was looking for me again."

"Why didn't you tell me?" Nathan's look of hurt was worse than the anger Verity had been expecting. "We could have… I don't know. Stayed in Scotland, bought Milsap off. Something."

"I wasn't positive about what I heard. Jonathan never said the name Verity. And I didn't want it to be true. I clung to that possibility that it wasn't about me. And so I didn't tell you. I tried my best not to think about it. I just wanted to go on as if it had never happened."

"So you didn't hide it because you don't trust me?" Nathan's eyes searched hers.

"No." Verity's throat tightened. "I didn't want to leave. But now I have to. Go to France or Germany or somewhere."

"Leave?" Nathan's eyebrows shot up and he took a step forward. "No, Verity. You killed his father in self-defense. To protect your sister."

"Don't be naive. He's a lord. I am a nobody. They won't take my word over his."

"But I will stand up for you. I—"

"No, you won't," Verity said flatly. "You will tell them you scarcely knew me. Lady Lockwood and the others will back you up. You hit Stanhope because you saw only that he was accosting a woman whom you thought was a lady. You were fooled by me just as everyone else in Society was. You had no idea I was a fraud."

"You can't be serious. I'm not saying anything like that. You obviously don't know me at all if you think I would."

Verity let out a loud noise of frustration. "Nathan, be reasonable. For once in your life, don't be honest and courageous. If he knows that you are with me, if you oppose him, he will go after you, too. Yes, you are a gentleman and you're popular among the high and mighty, but you aren't a *lord.*"

"What can he do to me?"

"Besides drag your name through the mud?"

"I don't care about that."

"We just spent the past month chasing leads around trying to protect your name!" Verity shot back. *Why was he being so obtuse?*

He waved her words away. "People know me. They

respect me. They—" He stopped, gazing off into the distance, then said, "Marry me."

Verity's jaw dropped. "What? Have you lost your mind? Marrying me would ruin you."

"No. It will give you status. You wouldn't be a nobody, you'd be my wife. You'd belong in the *ton*. All you have to do is deny what Stanhope says. Say that you didn't kill his father. Someone else did, and you ran in terror. Carlisle and Noelle will back us up. And Lady Drewsbury— she's a countess. And Lady Lockwood. You know she'd do it if for no other reason than she loves a good fight."

"*That's* why you want to marry me?" The idea hurt more than Verity would have thought possible. "So you can protect me? It wasn't enough that you heroically gave up Annabeth so she would be happy? Now you're going to sacrifice yourself again in order to save *me*?"

His eyes widened, and he quickly said, "No! No, that's not what I mean. It's not only to protect you. I mean, I'm not sacrificing myself. I want to marry you. This is just…hastening things. I know you don't want to marry, but look at how we've been the past few weeks together. How happy and…and *good* it's been."

"Passion doesn't last, Nathan. 'Good' and 'happy' aren't enough."

"It's not just passion," he protested. "I love you."

"The way you loved Annabeth a year ago?" Verity shot back. He looked stricken at her words, and she immediately regretted them. "I'm sorry. I was angry. I didn't mean it."

"I think that's precisely what you meant," Nathan replied. "You don't trust me. You think I'm fickle and shallow. You've always discounted me—I'm naive, I don't know what I'm doing, I simply float through life."

"No." Verity was aghast. "That's not what I think. Maybe at first, but not anymore. I can be aware of how very different our lives have been, how very different *we are* without it being a judgment on you. Just because I keep some things private, it doesn't mean that I don't care for you."

"You see? *Care.*" Nathan let out a bitter little laugh. "You can't even say the word *love*. You *want* to be alone. You're scared to commit yourself for a lifetime. You like things the way they are because it means you don't have to give anything of yourself to me."

"What the devil do you think I've been doing the past weeks but giving myself to you?" She was suddenly furious. "I've let you into my life. Into my house. Into my bed."

"But not into your heart," Nathan said quietly. "You have given me your body, you have made space for me in your life—and I am very glad that you did so. But I want more than that, Verity. I want everything. I want marriage or nothing at all."

"Then leave." Verity felt ice all through her. "I'm not marrying you."

Nathan's face tightened. For a moment, she thought he would argue, but instead he turned and walked out the front door. The door slammed, leaving only silence behind.

Verity's knees were suddenly weak, and it was hard to breathe. She sank down on one of the risers at the foot of the staircase. *He was gone.* She felt as if some vital part of her had been torn out, and she wanted to run after him, to tell him she would marry him, that she'd throw herself into his care and let him protect her.

But she would not do that. She *could* not. She wrapped

her hands around her knees and rested her head on them. She couldn't be weak. She couldn't give way to tears and regret. Verity had learned long ago that the only way to stay alive was to keep moving. Do what she had to. *Don't look back.*

Nathan didn't understand what danger he would be putting himself into. He had always lived a privileged life. Perhaps he hadn't had as much money as some of his friends, but he had been protected from want, from fear, from condemnation. He didn't know, as she did, what it was like to be vulnerable. So easily overwhelmed by the powerful.

Verity felt sick, remembering Stanhope's face, astonished and sharp and somehow gratified. He was glad he'd found her; he wanted to see her punished. She had faced down men with weapons without a qualm, but just the sight of him, so similar to his father, just the feel of his hand grabbing her arm, sent shivering terror through her.

He would see her dead, she was certain, and he would ruin Nathan as well if Nathan crossed him. And no matter how very much Verity wished Nathan were with her right now, his arms strong and warm around her, she would not subject him to Lord Stanhope's revenge.

She was being sensible. She was doing the right thing. She was being strong. *But, oh, God, why does it have to hurt so much?*

## CHAPTER TWENTY-SIX

NATHAN'S FURY CARRIED him halfway home before it turned to heartache. *Was I born under some unlucky star?* Every time he loved a woman, she broke his heart.

Nathan thought about drinking himself to unconsciousness, but he couldn't see what a raging headache tomorrow would do to improve his situation. It was the sort of showy and unreasonable thing Sloane would do, not him. So he spent a sleepless night fruitlessly thinking of all the things he'd said wrong and the things he hadn't said, all the ways in which Verity was utterly in the wrong, and all the days that stretched out in loneliness before him.

He decided he would go back to her the next morning. He'd say he was sorry and tell her that he would run away to France with her—or anywhere else she wanted to go. He would say he didn't need marriage or her undying declaration of love.

Only it wasn't true. His heart had shriveled inside him when she could say nothing more than she "cared" for him. One cared for a friend or for one's aunt. It wasn't what you felt for the love of your life. And he could admit that to himself even if Verity wouldn't hear it—Verity *was* the love of his life.

It was unfair to expect her to feel as he did, given that he had only realized that he loved her last night.

But he had been in love with her long before he awoke to that fact. Surely she knew that—women often seemed to know what a man felt before he did. And certainly they knew what they felt themselves.

Of course, Verity was not like most women. Maybe she didn't recognize her feelings any better than he had. She had said she loved him, but that had been in the aftermath of passion, right before slumber. Was it possible she had not even realized what she'd said?

And of course she was frightened. With Stanhope grabbing her tonight, how could she not be? She'd had bitter experience with a man's protection in the past, but, still, it hurt that she obviously didn't believe Nathan could keep her safe. It wasn't his fault that she assumed she could not trust a man, but he supposed it wasn't her fault, either.

And there he was, being reasonable again. But reason didn't fill the hole in his chest. He could tell himself that he would put her out of his mind, that he would go on with his life, that he would get over her, just as he had with Annabeth.

The problem was that he felt much worse than he had when he called off his engagement with Annabeth. Then he had felt sad but—admittedly—also a bit righteous in his sacrifice. Now, with Verity, he felt as if his guts had been ripped out of him.

Trying not to think about Verity was like trying not to think about a knife in his chest—she was all he *could* think about. He wanted to know if she was sleeping or lying awake like him. Did she regret what she'd said? Might she change her mind—or was that just wishful thinking? Was she over there packing her bags, getting ready to run? And where would she run to? At least when you fell in love with someone with roots, you knew where they'd be. That was some sort of comfort—you could avoid them or seek them out, whichever was salve for your wound. But someone like Verity…Nathan really might never see her ever again. And that thought was more terrifying than anything else he could imagine.

Far earlier in the morning than was polite, he went to her house. He did not simply enter as he had become used to doing, but knocked and waited for the house-keeper to answer. Whatever hopes Nathan had that they could fix what had occurred last night were second-ary to his most fundamental wish. *Please, just don't let her be gone.*

Verity was walking down the hall, tucking some-thing into a reticule, and she looked up, saw him, and stopped. She was dressed in severe black, and her face was pale, her eyes a bit swollen and red. Clearly she had not emerged from last night unscathed, either.

It gave him a little burst of bitter satisfaction, which was no doubt petty of him—but, dammit, he was getting tired of being the only one who got hurt. Though, even as he thought it, it squeezed his heart to see her unhappy.

"Nathan." There was surprise in Verity's voice. *Did she really think that I would simply walk away from her and never give her another thought?*

"Verity." He hoped he wasn't imagining that there was a moment of happiness in her eyes that sparked when she saw him. He glanced at her attire. "Are we mourning Herbert again?"

Her face relaxed. "Hubert. Really, Nathan, one would think you would remember your best friend's name."

"Ah, but he was only a classmate."

She sighed. And both of them said in chorus, "Poor Hubert."

*It was so much the same, so painfully different.*

"It's my new disguise," Verity went on, taking a black bonnet from the hat rack and putting it on. She pulled down the black veil attached to the hat.

"Deep mourning indeed. I can hardly see you through that veil."

"That's rather the point." Verity pushed the veil back up atop the brim. "I doubled the gauze."

"It's conspicuous, though," he pointed out. "People will remember you."

"They'll remember a *widow*. That's all people see."

An awkward silence fell. All Nathan could think of was how lovely Verity looked even like this—fine-boned and fragile, her golden eyes made somehow more luminous after her tears. He pulled his thoughts back. "Um, I came by to see…have you…are you leaving soon? Do you know where you're going?"

"I can't leave yet. I must find Malcolm Douglas first."

"What?" He hadn't expected this. "No. I don't want you to put yourself in danger. I will continue to look for him myself."

"I don't leave a job unfinished," Verity said, iron in her voice. "I am a professional." She paused, then added, "Are you terminating my employment?"

"Well, that would be difficult since I'm not paying you. You're doing it as my friend, remember? And I will always be your friend."

"Nathan…" Verity said through gritted teeth. "You make it exceedingly difficult to remain angry at you."

He smiled faintly. "I try my best."

Verity rolled her eyes, and he supposed it was a sign

of just how far lost he was that it warmed him to see it. She went on, "Lord Stanhope can find out who I am— or, rather, who I'm pretending to be—fairly easily, but no one in the *ton* knows where I live. Except you, of course, and I think I can trust you not to reveal it. He'll discover where I am eventually, but it's bound to take him at least a few days. We don't have much time to find Malcolm, anyway. I don't want the imposter deciding the scheme's not going to work and getting rid of him."

"Of course." Nathan thought he should try again to get her to leave. It was selfish of him to want her with him. *What if Stanhope* did *find her?* He looked at her set chin and almost smiled. *As if he could stop Verity from doing exactly what she pleased.*

They drove again to Fairborn's shop, first touring all the streets and lanes around it before settling across the street from the sweets store. Verity sat close to the opposite wall, inches of room between them, stiff and poised as if ready to jump out of the carriage. Nathan missed the feel of her body against his side, and it was hard not to reach out to touch her arm or take her hand, as he usually did.

He wished Lord Stanhope seven ways to hell for bringing all this on them. He wanted badly to confront the man, to have it out with him, force him to leave Verity alone. But Verity was right in not wanting Stanhope to connect Nathan to her—he might use Nathan to track Verity down. Right now, there was the chance that he didn't know who Nathan was. After all, Nathan didn't know him.

And that was a bit odd, now that he thought about it. Nathan didn't know everyone in the *ton*, of course, and Stanhope had looked a few years younger than he, but still… Perhaps he ought to investigate Stanhope, find a lever he could use against him, as Nathan had with Lord Arden. If the son was anything like his father, there was probably something wicked in his past.

He considered asking Lady Lockwood, the fount of all social knowledge, about Stanhope, but there he'd run the risk of revealing Verity's secret. Her ladyship was a bloodhound—she would figure it out. Perhaps he could just ask around casually at his club about the man.

"Nathan!" He was pulled from his thoughts by Verity clutching his arm, her voice rising in excitement. "I think that's Hill."

"Hill?" Nathan straightened and peered out the window.

"Yes." Verity dug a lorgnette out of her reticule and held it to her eyes. She handed it to Nathan. "Look."

"I think you're right." He looked at her. "I never really expected this to work."

"Sometimes you get lucky." Verity slid out of the carriage and, after a word to her driver, she walked in the same direction as Hill, staying somewhat behind him and on the opposite side of the street.

Nathan joined her, letting Verity keep her sights on their quarry through the shield of her veil while he gazed in shop windows and the streets ahead, mapping where they were going in his mind. It was no surprise when Hill made his way into the narrow streets of less prosperous areas. No longer having the distance of the wider thoroughfares between them and the man they pursued, Nathan and Verity hung farther back.

Their attire made them stand out more here, and more than one person looked at them oddly. Nathan glanced pointedly at her veiled hat, which made them even more conspicuous, and Verity nodded, and, with a little sigh, pulled it from her head and handed it to an astonished woman standing at a cart.

Fortunately, Hill never even glanced behind him, but continued at an unhurried pace. He stopped to buy a meat pie from a cart, which caused them a moment of anxiety as they did their best to disappear by squeezing into a doorway. Then their quarry continued on his way, carrying the pastry but not eating it.

He crossed a broad street into the area of the docks, and Nathan exchanged a surprised look with Verity. He had expected the man to return to a residence. If Hill was just going to work on the docks, they would have a difficult time keeping themselves hidden the whole while.

Hill turned before he reached the busiest area and made his way toward an old dilapidated warehouse. He entered the building, and Nathan and Verity trotted after him, cautiously easing open the door and peering inside. The large building was empty but for a few crates, all coated with dust. A set of sagging stairs led upward, but the ruffian had passed the stairs, continuing toward the opposite end of the building.

Nathan and Verity glanced at each other. There was no cover for them here, but they had to follow. It seemed unlikely that the imposter they sought was here, but it did seem like a perfect place for a prisoner to be hidden. Verity slipped across the floor, noiseless as a cat, and Nathan emulated her as best he could. Hill, ahead of them, still seemed completely unaware of their presence.

Just then there was the sound of feet and a short square man rounded the corner, saying, "Bloody 'ell, man, I thought you was never com—"

*Shoemaker!* Verity and Nathan froze at the sight of him, but there was nowhere to hide nor time to do it. Shoemaker saw Verity and Nathan, and yelled, pointing his finger at them. "It's them! Hill, you bloomin' idiot."

He charged toward them as Hill swung around, gaping. Shoemaker pulled out a knife as he ran, and Nathan rushed forward to meet him.

"Duck," Verity called out and Nathan hit the ground instantly. He heard a whizzing sound above his head and looked up in time to see the knife Verity had thrown hit Shoemaker in the arm. The man roared, turning toward Verity at this attack, and Nathan used the distraction to leap forward the last few feet, crashing into Shoemaker and taking him to the floor.

The two men grappled, rolling across the ground, and Verity dived for her knife. There was the sound of footsteps running—apparently Hill had taken the opportunity to flee, leaving his companion to fend for himself. Out of the corner of his eye, Nathan glimpsed Verity half rise, twisting, and fling her knife at Hill, but the knife clattered onto the floor and Verity cursed. The outer door crashed open, and Verity took off running.

Nathan hadn't the time to look over to see where she went. He was too busy struggling to his feet, pulling Shoemaker up with him. Shoemaker swung, but Nathan dodged and the man's meaty fist only grazed the side of Nathan's ear. Nathan punched him in the stomach, following it with a forceful jab to the jaw. Shoemaker's head snapped back and he staggered, windmilling his arms to avoid falling. Nathan risked taking his eyes off the man to glance over, looking for Verity.

Neither she nor Hill were there, only her knife and pieces of a smashed meat pie on the floor. Nathan's opponent took advantage of his momentary inattention and darted for the door. Nathan pursued, but before he could catch Shoemaker, Nathan saw Verity limping back to the warehouse, and he ran to her instead of chasing his man.

"Verity! Are you all right?" He skidded to a halt beside her.

"I'm fine," she said in a disgusted tone.

"You aren't fine. You're limping."

"I broke the heel on my shoe, that's all. I fell, but I couldn't have caught him anyway. That blasted Hill is fast."

"I know," Nathan said drily. "Sloane and I chased him through Cheapside."

Verity sighed, putting her hands on her hips, and looked around. "So they're in the wind again."

"'Fraid so. But…" Nathan took her arm and started back into the warehouse. "I think we may find Malcolm here. There's bound to be a reason they're hanging about in an abandoned warehouse. It's not a pleasant venue, but a good place to hold a prisoner. No one around to hear him or see him. Shoemaker sounded impatient, as though he'd been waiting for Hill. Maybe Hill was coming to take over his watch. And bringing the prisoner's meal."

Verity grimaced. "That blasted meat pie. I threw my knife at him and it hit the pie. I ask you, what are the chances of that?"

They walked through the warehouse, stepping around the splattered pie, to the hall where they'd seen Shoemaker emerge. It had three doors. Two of them stood open, revealing empty rooms. But the last door had a wooden bar across it.

With a mixture of excitement and trepidation, Nathan lifted the bar and pulled the door open. They peered into the dim room, lit only by two barred windows high on the wall. They could see a bed with a thin mattress and a chain attached to its heavy iron frame.

The chain stretched out of sight, and when they stepped farther into the chamber, they saw that the chain led to the ankle of a tall thin man with shaggy blond hair and a reddish beard as unkempt as his hair. One eye had a fading yellow bruise beside it. He was dressed in a shirt and breeches, both liberally sprinkled with dirt and stains. Even though he was thinner and wilder looking, he was clearly the man in the portrait of Malcolm Douglas.

He held a wooden bucket above his head, clearly about to throw it, but at the sight of them, he stopped, looking astonished, and lowered the bucket. "Who the devil are you?"

"Well, actually, I'm your brother," Nathan said.

# CHAPTER TWENTY-SEVEN

DOUGLAS GAPED AT NATHAN, then scowled and said flatly, "I don't have a brother."

"You are Malcolm Douglas, are you not? I am Nathan Dunbridge, George Dunbridge's son." Nathan felt a twinge of unease. Flora Douglas had sounded as though Malcolm knew about his parentage, but what if Nathan had just revealed a family secret?

However, Malcolm's next words reassured him that Malcolm was fully aware of the circumstances of his birth. His lip curled into a sneer. "Dunbridge. I might have known. Then it's *you* behind this."

Nathan sighed. Apparently every Douglas thought of his family as villains. "No, I am *not* the one who kidnapped you."

Verity moved forward pugnaciously, saying, "What is the matter with you people? Nathan is rescuing you, and in case you haven't noticed, with physical harm to himself." She gestured toward Nathan.

Douglas looked down at the small woman in some bemusement. "I...um..."

Verity crossed her arms and continued. "Now, would you like to be freed or stay here and nurse your stupid resentment of the Dunbridges?"

Douglas sighed and set down the bucket. "I, uh, apologize for my lack of courtesy. But I haven't the slightest notion what is going on, and I'm getting bloody well tired of it. Excuse my language, miss. I am very grateful for your rescue." He gave Nathan a pointed look. "But Flora Douglas is my mother, and I want nothing to do with George Dunbridge."

"Understood," Nathan replied equably and went over to examine the chain padlocked around one leg of the iron bedstead. "They certainly went to the extreme to keep you locked up."

Malcolm shrugged. "They chained me up after I tried to escape."

"One might think the bar on the door would have sufficed."

The other man shook his head. "They put that there after the second time I tried to escape, because I broke the lock. The third time, I knocked out the skinny one, but the short fellow was right outside the door with a gun, unfortunately."

"And the first time?" Verity asked, looking intrigued.

"That was when I woke up back at the beginning, right after they kidnapped me, and they knocked me on the head again. When I came to, they had bound and gagged me."

"Perhaps I like you after all," Verity said, a smile tugging at the corner of her mouth.

Nathan squatted down beside the bed. "If both you and I lift the frame, Douglas, Verity can slip the chain from the bed. We can deal with the leg iron when we've gotten you to safety."

"No need to break your backs," Verity said cheerfully. The morning's events had obviously improved her spirits. She whisked two short metal rods from her upswept hair, and knelt, making short work of the lock on the leg iron. "Now, gentlemen, I suggest we leave before those two return."

"I wish they would," Douglas growled. "I'd like to get my hands on them."

"You wouldn't if they come back with guns," Verity told him. "Or comrades."

They walked quickly through the warehouse. Malcolm glanced at the smashed meat pie on the floor and said a little mournfully, "I suppose that was my breakfast."

"I beg your pardon," Verity said. "It was a casualty of the battle."

When they stepped outside, Malcolm pulled in a deep breath, looking all around, though he squinted and had to shade his eyes, unaccustomed to that much light. "How did you find me? Why were you looking for me?"

"We weren't at first. It wasn't until your parents told us you were missing that we began to search for you," Nathan replied.

"My parents?" Malcolm said in alarm. "I had hoped perhaps they might not know. Did they pay a ransom?"

"No. There was none asked."

"Then why—"

Nathan told him the whole story, beginning with the man arriving at Stonecliffe saying he was George Dunbridge's son. By the time Nathan reached the end of the tale, they had left the docks and found a hansom.

Malcolm looked from Verity to Nathan and back, a little more enlightened than he had been to start with. "But why? Why would he think he could escape notice? He couldn't have carried that off for years. My parents would have known it wasn't me. My uncle would have—" He turned toward Nathan. "Does Uncle Robert know about all this?"

"Not that I know of. Since we thought the imposter was you, we didn't want to discuss the blackmail with your uncle," Nathan explained. "Certainly your uncle said nothing about it to us. He put you not arriving down to a young man's desire not to be burdened with an uncle while he sowed his wild oats."

Douglas snorted. "I think I'm past the wild oats age."

"The imposter was the right height and had blond hair and blue eyes, but he wouldn't have been able to fool someone that knew you, even at a distance. He stayed well hidden and played a convincing Scotsman." Verity paused, then added, "Though now that I've met you, I have to say his accent was a bit too thick for someone raised as you were."

Malcolm looked at Verity, faintly puzzled. "And who are you now? Another Dunbridge?"

"No," Nathan said somewhat sourly.

Verity shot Nathan a repressive glance and replied, "I am a detective, and I am helping Nathan with his inquiries. Now to get back to the subject, this man obviously knew about at least some of the, um, circumstances of your birth. Who would know that?"

"No one." Malcolm shook his head. "It's certainly not common knowledge. It would be a terrible scandal. We are a very small family. I don't have any cousins, my sibling—well, Margaret—died when I was a baby, and Uncle Robert is my father's only brother. My parents' social circle is quite small, as well. They were always very private, especially after I was born."

"Obviously someone knew," Nathan pointed out.

"Most likely it came from the Dunbridge side."

"That's impossible. I'd never heard any of the story until this chap came along. And basically, I *am* the Dunbridge side. Our father is dead, and he didn't produce any children other than the two of us."

"I told you, I'm not a member of your family." Malcolm's scowl returned.

"That's clear. *My* family is actually pleasant," Nathan shot back.

Verity rolled her eyes. "That's more than enough of the fraternal squabbling. I want to ascertain who kidnapped you. You or your parents or a servant must have told *someone*."

Douglas set his jaw stubbornly, but finally, as one tended to do under Verity's gaze, he went on, "I suppose it might have been that chap at the inn."

"What chap? What inn? The one where you were kidnapped?"

"Yes, the night before they knocked me over the head. I'm afraid I don't remember it all that well." His forehead knotted in thought.

"Getting hit on the head can affect your memory," Nathan said.

"Yes, and I do remember that we had a good bit to drink. He was an amiable fellow. He was blond and had light-colored eyes—I guess they were blue, as you said. About my age. We talked a great deal. He was very interested in Edinburgh and so on. I don't remember exactly what I said—we had more brandy than I am accustomed to drinking. I believe we talked about where I went to school and my parents and such." He sent Nathan and Verity a fierce look. "But I wouldn't have told him *that*. Not a casual stranger."

"Do you remember what his name was?" Verity asked.

"Um…Tidwell? No, that's not quite it. His first name was Will. Topper? Tolliver!" he exclaimed. "That's it."

"Of course, there's no assurance that was his real name," Verity added.

"Speaking of—" Nathan reached into his coat pocket and pulled out the locket Flora had given him "—your mother didn't want to part with this, but did in the hopes that it would help us find you."

"Thanks." Malcolm looked at it a moment before tucking the locket away.

They arrived at Robert Douglas's house, and the servant who answered the door inspected them warily—not an unreasonable reaction, given the way the three of them appeared.

Nathan thought the man was about to send them on their way, but at that moment Malcolm's uncle came out of a nearby room. "Ridley, who—" He stopped and stared in astonishment.

"Hello, Uncle Robert."

Robert opened his mouth and closed it, then managed to say, "Malcolm? My heavens, lad, what happened to you? You look—" He floundered, apparently finding nothing adequate to express his nephew's condition.

"I was kidnapped before I got to London. These two found me and let me out," Malcolm summarized succinctly.

"I—I—don't know what to say. Goodness." Robert came forward. "Well…do come inside, Malcolm." He shook his nephew's hand, then Nathan's. "Thank you, Mr. Dunbridge, for returning our lad to the bosom of his family. And the lovely Mrs. Billingham." He nodded graciously at Verity, then returned to Malcolm. "I do hope that you will provide me with a somewhat more detailed story."

"Yes, of course. But I'd very much like to clean up first. And eat."

"Of course. I'll pour you a wee dram of whiskey, as well."

Malcolm turned to Verity and Nathan. "Thank you seems inadequate. But I am truly most grateful."

"Perhaps in a day or two, we could call on you. You might have remembered something about this Tolliver fellow to help us find him."

Malcolm frowned. "I don't want word of this getting out. The scandal would hurt my mother terribly."

"We won't say anything," Nathan replied. "I give you my word. I would prefer to avoid the scandal, as well."

"Thank you." Malcolm looked relieved. He paused, then said, looking a trifle abashed, "And I'm sorry for what I said, you know, about your family. It's just, well, I'll always be a Douglas."

A few minutes later, after they left the Douglas house, Verity said, "You don't seem to be destined for a warm relationship with your newfound brother."

"No, I fear you're right," Nathan replied. The lack of that possibility was too little to bother him with the weight of Verity leaving dragging him down. "I don't suppose I'll miss what I never had."

They rode back to Verity's house, silent most of the way. Nathan could think of nothing but the fact that with Malcolm back, their case really was over. Verity could leave now, her duty done. Nathan's stomach knotted at the prospect. He couldn't just let her go like this.

Verity was frowning as she looked out the window

of the carriage, and Nathan wondered if she, too, was dreading the end of their time together. That hope was dashed when she said, "I hate that this Will Tolliver—if that's even his name—will get away with everything."

"So do I." Nathan hadn't been thinking about it, but he felt the same way. "Not to mention Shoemaker and Hill."

"Look at all the things they've done—attacked us, abducted Malcolm, tried to blackmail you—and we're going to let them just walk off?"

"I don't like it any better than you," Nathan said. "I'd like to go after them, too, but I don't see how we can charge them without bringing Malcolm and my father into it and setting off exactly the scandal we were trying to avoid."

"I know." Verity sighed. "Malcolm has suffered enough—though I must say, he was certainly ungracious to you, so I find it harder to care about his reputation. But I do care about yours."

Her words warmed Nathan. But there was that word again: *care.* He would like to think that she simply found it difficult to say the word *love* rather than believe she didn't feel it. Verity had learned in a hard school to keep her emotions buttoned up. But his doubts warred with that hope.

They reached her door, and she turned to him. Nathan thought of all the other times they had arrived here and he had entered as if he belonged. It hurt to stand here like a stranger and bid her good-bye. "I…um, well, I suppose you will be leaving soon now. Since we found Malcolm."

Verity nodded and looked away. Nathan might never see her again. He wanted to plead with her to stay, to tell her that he would go with her wherever she wanted, married or not. But if she didn't love him, he couldn't make her. He had to let her go.

He opened his mouth to say good-bye, but the words that came out were, "Lady Lockwood is expecting us at eight this evening. I'll be here to escort you fifteen minutes prior."

Before she could protest, he turned and strode off down the street. He expected her to come after him to argue or to call out a refusal after him, but she did not. He wasn't sure what that meant; he hoped it meant he had a chance. He was *not* going to lose Verity.

# CHAPTER TWENTY-EIGHT

VERITY KNEW SHE should have told Nathan no. There was no reason, no excuse for going to Lady Lockwood's. She needed to go upstairs and start packing. She would be leaving soon, now that it was all over. It was too risky to continue operating anywhere near Stanhope, now that he knew she was alive. It hurt to leave her business, though it paled beside the hurt of leaving Nathan. She'd have to trust that Poppy would be fine, even if Verity couldn't check in on her sister herself anymore.

Only nothing felt over. Not the case, not her life in London, and most of all, not her relationship with Nathan. Today had been the strangest tangle of emotions—happy, sad, excited, nervous—one moment awkward silence and the next sweet familiarity and comfort, followed by a sudden stab of pain and longing. *How can I bear to leave Nathan?*

She loved him. Maybe she couldn't say it to him—outside of that one unguarded moment where it had accidentally tumbled from her lips—but Verity had to admit it to herself. She loved Nathan and wanted to be with him. Part of her wanted to throw caution to the winds and marry him as he'd asked. But that would be an entirely selfish thing to do; she would ruin Nathan's life. It was one thing to put herself in danger, but it was quite another to lay waste to Nathan's name, staining him with her crimes and even putting him in danger.

Verity didn't regret what she had done in the past—she'd do the same thing today if it meant saving her sister from Stanhope—and she had accepted the consequences. But Nathan didn't deserve that. She wasn't going to ask him to sacrifice himself for her.

Which was exactly why she should not go with him to Lady Lockwood's tonight. She shouldn't have agreed, shouldn't be thinking of what dress she would wear and how she would arrange her hair and whether she would try that new perfume she'd bought the other day.

She told herself that after tonight, she would be stronger. Firm. This evening, when they left Lady Lockwood's, she would make him see that marriage was out of the question.

But surely it would be all right to let herself have this last evening with him. To spend a few hours near him, committing every expression, every gesture, every smile or laugh to memory, to be taken out and pored over when she was alone.

Having tossed away her widow's veil, Verity chose that evening to wear a half mask as they went to Lady Lockwood's, and she kept a careful lookout for anyone lurking around her house or following them, as she had earlier today. She didn't think that Stanhope had tracked her down yet, but she wasn't about to take any chances. Especially not when she was with Nathan and his family.

Nathan was charming, as he always was with women of every age and status, not pushing Verity to any familiarity, but not treating her with the awkward stiffness that he had shown earlier that day. He treated her, in short, like a casual acquaintance, a stranger, and Verity could not decide whether he had decided to accept her decision and distance himself from her or was setting out to woo her as if they had only met. Whichever it was, she found it a trifle unsettling…and perhaps that was his purpose. Nathan was being conniving, and for some reason, she found it as endearing as it was irritating.

Nathan's mother and aunt were at the dinner, along with Sloane and Annabeth, and, of course, Marcus Rutherford, Sloane's father and Lady Lockwood's frequent companion these days. In her role as Mrs. Billingham, Verity had learned that their relationship was the subject of much speculation among family and friends, not to mention the entire *ton*. But no one had the courage to broach the subject with her ladyship.

Verity knew that Lady Lockwood was brimming with curiosity about the trip they had made to Scotland and what they had found there, but the presence of Nathan's mother and aunt kept her silent on that score.

But partway through the third course, Marcus Rutherford asked, "How was your trip to Scotland, Nathan?"

"Oh, um…it was quite pleasant." Nathan glanced at his mother a little apprehensively.

*"Ow."* Marcus cast a wounded look at Lady Lockwood and reached down to rub his shin. "Why did you ki—oh…"

Verity brought her napkin up to her mouth to muffle the laugh that threatened to tumble out. Clearly Sloane had not inherited his skill at deception from his father. Verity glanced down the table to see that Annabeth was focused intently on her plate, her shoulders shaking a little. Sloane closed his eyes in a resigned way.

Under Lady Lockwood's fierce gaze, Marcus scrambled to cover his mistake. "Now, Brighton is the place to visit for me. Don't you agree, my de—um, Eugenia?"

Before Lady Lockwood could respond, Rose Dunbridge said, "Scotland?" She looked at her son in surprise. "Did you go to Scotland, dear? I didn't know that."

"Briefly, yes. Went to, um, visit a friend of mine."

"Oh." His mother looked disappointed. "I hoped you might have gone to meet your half brother."

Nathan dropped his fork, and everyone at the table froze, staring at Rose. Finally Nathan choked out, "You—how—you knew about Malcolm Douglas?"

"Why, yes, dear, of course. I'm sorry. Were you not aware? I assumed your father had told you." Rose glanced around the table at all the startled faces. "I thought everyone knew the story."

"*I* never knew it," Lady Lockwood said in an affronted tone.

"No, Father didn't tell me," Nathan said. "I had no idea."

"Oh, dear." Rose looked guilty. "I am so sorry. I shouldn't have—though I don't know why George would—"

Nathan broke into his mother's floundering words. "How did *you* know, Mother?"

"Why, George told me, of course," Rose replied, as if the matter should have been obvious. "He wouldn't have married me without telling me everything about his first marriage."

Verity stifled a groan. Nathan looked bereft of speech.

"Well, don't just sit there, Rose," Lady Lockwood barked. "Tell us what happened."

Rose quickly obeyed. "It was a tragic story, really.

Quite romantic." She turned to her sister-in-law. "Did you not know either, Jossy?"

"No, I didn't." Aunt Jocelyn sounded as offended as Lady Lockwood. "I knew there was some sort of trouble with a Scottish girl, but that is all."

"George went to visit a friend who had a lodge in Scotland. Goodness, I can't remember his name," Rose said. She looked again to Jocelyn. "The fellow he knew from school—you remember him, don't you? Had some sort of accident when he was still young."

"Never mind him," Lady Lockwood said sharply. "Stay with the story, Rose."

"Yes, of course. George was quite young, only nineteen, and he met a Scottish girl there. Their ancestral home was near Duffy's lodge—Duffy—yes, that was his name."

Lady Lockwood cleared her throat loudly.

Rose hurried on, "Her name was Margaret, and she came from a good family, but her parents were dead set against the English. And I must say, that seems terribly unfair. George didn't have anything to do with all that. He didn't even know what Culloden *was*. Anyway, her parents forbade her to see him. But that sort of thing never works out the way one intends, does it? The two of them simply met in secret. After a time, well, you know…" Her cheeks turned pink.

"Yes, yes, she became pregnant," Lady Lockwood put in. "We're all aware of that. What happened? He married her?"

"Not then. When he left Scotland, they didn't know about the baby. He was madly in love with her, though. They sent letters to each other through Duffy, but then George stopped receiving any from her, and Duffy told him that Margaret had gone somewhere with her mother. George believed that she no longer loved him. He was quite sad, of course, but he accepted it."

"But he must have found her," Annabeth said, clearly caught up in the story. Verity had to admit the whole thing sounded much like a novel—one of those where the woman who'd sinned suffers a terrible life full of tragedies and dies at the end. Which seemed, really, rather unfair.

"Yes, George saw Margaret one evening at a party. Apparently she had not been well since the birth of the baby. *I* think it was that she was wasting away from grief—losing the man she loved and then her son."

"The baby died?" Jocelyn interrupted. "But you said Nathan had a half brother."

"No, the boy didn't die, but to avoid the shame of her daughter bearing a child out of wedlock, her mother, Flora, moved them to some remote place in the Highlands for the birth, and when they went back to Edinburgh, they pretended that it was Flora who had borne a child. Margaret had to appear to be only his sister, and of course it grieved her. But what else was she to do? Label her child illegitimate?"

"I would think she would have fought to keep her child," Annabeth said with all the emotion of impending motherhood.

"Yes, but she wasn't a strong woman like you, dear. I gather she was quite cowed by her mother. She pined for her son and got paler and more downcast, so finally her parents let her go visit some cousins in the hopes she would improve. The cousins brought her to London for the Season. And she and George met. Of course, when she explained it all, George told her she should have sent for him—he would have whisked her away from her family and married her. Then they got married in London and went racing back to Scotland to get their baby. But along the way, there was a terrible accident— the coach went off the road, and poor Margaret died."

"How sad," Annabeth said.

"Yes, isn't it?" Rose nodded. "I always felt very sorry for the poor girl."

"But if they were married, why did Father keep Malcolm a secret?" Nathan asked. "Why wouldn't he have brought him back and raised him?"

"George wanted to, but the Douglases were terribly against it. Flora loved the baby and everyone thought he was her son. The boy was almost a year old by then. Your father realized that to take him away from the only mother and home the child had ever known would be cruel. John and Flora doted on him."

"But couldn't he, I don't know, have had Malcolm come to visit us sometimes?" Nathan sounded wistful.

Rose smiled fondly at him. "George and I would have loved that. I so wished you had a brother to play with. It always grieved me that I could have no more children. But Margaret's parents were adamant. You see, John—that's Margaret's father—was glad to have a son who could inherit his estate. If Malcolm spent any time with us, people would start to wonder why, especially given the Douglases' aversion to the English. There would be gossip, and it was all too likely that the true story would get out. Even if it wasn't proved, the rumor would follow him all his life. And Margaret's memory would be irreversibly besmirched. George couldn't do that. He understood it would be better for everyone that way." Rose sighed. "I really believed George had told you and I had hoped that perhaps when you were adults, you and Malcolm might get to know each other. Become friends."

"I don't think that's very likely," Nathan said.

"Why not, dear?" Rose asked. "I mean, now that you know, you could meet each other."

"I have met him," Nathan replied and began to explain the whole story to his mother. The others had heard the first part of the tale, but everyone hung on his account of Malcolm's kidnapping and their subsequent rescue of him.

There was a long silence after he finished, then Rose said faintly, "Oh, my."

"Well, they're Scots," Lady Lockwood declared, as if that explained the matter. "What can one expect?"

"Not *that*, one would think," Sloane replied sardonically.

Nathan snorted out a laugh, quickly covered with a napkin, and Lady Lockwood favored both of the men with a stern look.

"I rather like the Scottish myself," Marcus said mildly. "You remember that chap McSweeney, don't you? Capital fellow."

"Sean McSweeney?" Rose said. "I thought he was Irish."

"He was," Jocelyn said.

"Six of one, half a dozen of the other," Lady Lockwood put in, and from there the conversation devolved into a discussion among the older group about their various acquaintances of both nationalities.

Verity, struggling to suppress a grin, looked across at Nathan, and he grinned back, and a pain pierced her at the thought of never again sharing a thought with him without even needing to speak. She swallowed and looked away.

Nathan and Verity left as soon as the meal was over—even Nathan couldn't summon up enough so-cial graces to remain long enough for a properly cour-teous departure. Verity thought about the fact that this was the last time she would be with these people, and her throat tightened with tears. She had never before felt this way—at least, not since she had left her sister with her new parents. After that, Verity had come and gone, slipping in and out of lives without a regret. But, then, she had never had a group of people she was close to before. That had been the wiser course, she thought. She hated the way this felt.

"I can't believe it!" Nathan exclaimed as soon as they were in their carriage. "All this time, all the effort we made to keep Mother from learning about Malcolm Douglas—and she knew all along."

"It would have been a bit easier just to have asked her to begin with," Verity agreed, glad to be distracted from her blue mood. "I'm glad, to hear the whole story though, even if it is late."

Nathan smiled at her. "It's much more in keeping with the father I knew. I'm glad he wasn't aware Marga-ret had borne his baby and that he married her as soon as he found out. He wanted his son, he didn't abandon the boy, but instead did what was best for him."

"Many men would have hidden that knowledge from their wives."

"Yes. He trusted my mother enough to be honest about the matter—and she loved him enough to accept his past."

What must it be like to be that certain of love? Verity

wondered. To know that the person who held your heart took you as you were, to believe that your love would hold even through your troubles? Verity had never seen the likes of it.

She had seen infatuation that turned into indifference or dislike. She had seen young love, but there was no assurance that it would last a lifetime. But Nathan's parents had had that sort of love; they had known each other's faults and loved each other still, had weathered their troubles together.

It was no wonder that Nathan was the man he was, growing up with their example. Verity had more than once considered him naive, too ready to trust, too prone to leave his heart unprotected. But it wasn't naivete; it was seeing that love between his parents all his life that made him believe in things she didn't dare hope for.

It was a subject she didn't want to dwell on.

"I have been thinking about this case," she said. "There's something odd about it. And it's not just that I hate to see those three villains get away with what they did."

"Just one thing odd about it?" Nathan raised an eyebrow.

She smiled a little. "No, the whole thing is peculiar from beginning to end. First, why was there no ransom note? Why did Tolliver kidnap Malcolm and not ask for ransom?"

"I presume he abducted him just to get him out of the way so Tolliver could impersonate Malcolm. It would have been awkward if the real Malcolm had suddenly shown up."

"But why not try to get both blackmail *and* a ransom? It's not as if he would have had any moral qualms about it."

"True. And the Douglases would have been much richer marks. Why didn't he choose to blackmail them instead? He wouldn't have even had to put on a charade for them, just threaten to tell everyone what they'd done." Nathan sat forward, his eyes alight. Verity knew that he felt the same compulsion she did to unravel this whole tangled web. "I cannot believe that this Tolliver chap just happened to run into Malcolm at an inn and decided to kidnap him and impersonate him in order to fool me into believing he was my father's legitimate heir."

Verity nodded. "Exactly. It had to be planned out. He would have had to know about Malcolm's background. Even if Malcolm had had a great deal to drink, it's hard to picture him letting out a lifelong family secret to some stranger he happened to meet on the road."

"Yes, it would make more sense if Will Tolliver already knew Malcolm," Nathan agreed. "But why would Malcolm lie and say the man was a stranger?"

"Maybe Tolliver *was* a stranger. We don't know for sure the man at the inn had anything to do with the kidnapping or the impersonation. It's very possible that Tolliver was not the same man we met. All we really know is that he had drinks with Malcolm and had the same coloring as the imposter."

"And even if Tolliver was the man we met with, he may have just been hired, as Shoemaker and Hill were," Nathan offered. "He could have just met Malcolm in order to study his speech and mannerisms."

Verity nodded, pleased that Nathan was thinking along the same lines she was. "I think the real culprit was someone who knew the Douglases better than that. Malcolm said he'd never told anyone, that it couldn't be someone close to him. But I think he's being naive."

"He wouldn't want to believe that someone he knew would do such a thing," Nathan agreed. "I wouldn't, either. But it makes more sense." The carriage had pulled to a stop in front of Verity's house, but neither of them made any move to leave.

"It wouldn't have to be a close friend," Verity went on. "That sort of knowledge gets out, no matter how much one tries to keep it a secret. A maid has intimate knowledge of the women she tends to. All of their servants and acquaintances knew that Margaret and her mother went on a trip for several months and came back with a baby. There were bound to be people who were suspicious about the tale. Flora was childless from Margaret's birth and then suddenly, late in life, she had a baby?"

"A number of people could have dug into the matter and found out the same things we did—I wish we'd asked the people in Gairmore if anyone else had made inquiries."

"Will Tolliver is the only one who can answer these questions," Verity said.

"But he's taken to his heels," Nathan pointed out.

"That doesn't mean he left the city. A Londoner could just as easily hide here in the city. I think we need to speak to our attackers again."

"Hill and Shoemaker? Shall we look for them tomorrow?"

Verity nodded. "They're the only ones who can tell us who they were actually working for." She wondered guiltily if she was only making excuses to be with Nathan again.

"And you hate that they escaped us twice." Nathan's eyes twinkled.

"Yes, I do." She scowled at the memory. "I'd really like to have another go at them." Verity looked at him. "Don't tell me you wouldn't."

Nathan grinned a little wolfishly. "You're right. I would."

*That look. That smile.* In that moment, Verity ached to kiss him. Instead, she opened the door and slipped out of the carriage. Nathan followed, but she was at her front door in a flash and already unlocking it when he came up behind her.

Verity opened the door but twisted back to face him, as if barring the door. Her pulse leapt in her throat, and she wasn't sure whom she was thwarting, Nathan or herself. Still, she stood fast. "Good night, Nathan."

"Verity." He gave her a little formal nod.

She tried to read his face, but for once she could not. Was that disappointment in his eyes? And how wicked of her to wish that it was.

"Tomorrow then," he said and turned to leave.

"Tomorrow," Verity murmured as she watched him walk away.

# CHAPTER TWENTY-NINE

VERITY SLEPT LITTLE, just as she had the night before. *Am I never going to be able to sleep again without Nathan beside me?* It was a ridiculous thought. She'd slept fine alone for all her life, but now she found her bed cold without his warm body pressed against her. Worse, she couldn't seem to control either her mind, which circled endlessly over all the reasons she had to leave Nathan, or her heart, which ached to be with him.

Long before Nathan arrived, Verity was up and ready to leave, the little breakfast she'd managed to force down sitting like a lump of lead in her stomach. She was not going to do this anymore, she told herself. Today would be the last time. If they didn't find their two attackers, she would give up. She'd come home and pack, even if she did get tears in her eyes every time she started to do so.

She would go to France. Or Italy. Or maybe all the way to America. She would start a new life. She would... well, she didn't know what she'd do, but surely there was something that would fulfill her.

Nathan's knock startled her out of her thoughts, and she went to answer it, relieved to shove all that aside. She told herself Nathan could not possibly look thinner or wanner than he had the day before, but somehow he seemed to. It made her heart ache, and all she wanted was to take him in her arms and comfort him.

Verity never should have taken up with him. She should have known she would only hurt him. In fact, hadn't she known? But she had done it anyway—and that just proved she was not the right woman for a man so kindhearted. It had been wrong and cruel to pull him into her life. Worse, she knew that if she had the power to do it all over again, she would do the same thing. She couldn't resist Nathan.

"Good Gad, Verity," Nathan said, staring at her. "I—you—I'm at a loss for words."

She laughed, her spirits lightening as they always did around Nathan. "I decided not to reprise my widowhood." Verity patted her abdomen, which was substantially larger than normal. "Padding."

"But you look like you're with child. You'll be so... so noticeable. I can't think that this is a good idea."

"I thought you were at a loss for words." Verity smiled. It felt so nice, but also bittersweet, to be trading teasing barbs with Nathan again.

"Apparently I recovered." He grinned back at her.

"I got the idea last night when I saw Annabeth. When you're pregnant, no one sees anything but that." Verity pointed at her stomach. "They don't look at your face. And I put on my old 'Judy' wig, which does nothing for my skin. It's amazing how much that conceals one. If you'll remember, you never noticed me when I wore it."

"Oh, I noticed you." The look in Nathan's eyes made her heart do a little flip.

Verity could feel herself blushing, and she went on hastily, "The padding is practical, as well." She slipped her hands into the concealed slits in her skirt and pulled out a gun and a knife from beneath the false stomach and brandished them in the air. "And I put on these old worn clothes so I'd fit in at the taverns."

"Yes, I hear the taverns are often frequented by heavily armed pregnant women in dowdy frocks."

She grinned. "Just so. The knife proves quite useful when strangers try to pat one's belly."

He began to laugh.

"Stop that. You'll hurt poor Bertha's feelings. She does her best, you know."

"Bertha?"

"Yes. Bertha Goodbody, washerwoman." Verity made a little curtsey.

"Such a pleasure to meet you." Nathan sketched a bow and extended his arm to her. "I am at your disposal, Miss Goodbody."

"*Mrs.* Goodbody," Verity corrected as she tucked her hand into the crook of his elbow. "I'll have you know I'm a good woman."

"My apologies. Of course you are. Indeed, you're the best."

*How in the world am I going to be able to part from this man?*

They took a hack, her carriage being too noticeable in the former haunts of Hill and Shoemaker. Once in Cheapside, they proceeded on foot, questioning patrons of taverns and setting Verity's band of street urchins loose to ask questions all around.

Nathan was somewhat surprised to find that, despite his doubts, Verity didn't draw attention from the people they met. The low, rough voice and East End accent she adopted fit in, and most of them seemed too tired or too wary, too incapacitated by gin or simply too ground down by life to look at anything but the coins Verity and Nathan offered.

One or two people acknowledged that they'd seen the two men Verity and Nathan sought in this area, but none knew where they lived or who their companions were. They went to the flats where Nathan and Sloane had found Shoemaker and Hill before, but they were now occupied by other residents who disclaimed all knowledge of the former tenants.

Finally, after many fruitless hours, they returned to Verity's house for afternoon tea. They were just about to return to the search when the leader of Verity's crew of youthful informants knocked at the door.

"There's not much, miss," Sally said as she ate the remainder of their tea and cakes. "Nobody knows those blokes—or at least, they won't own up to knowing them. I think some folks are dead scared of 'em. But…" She paused to take a gulp of tea. "There's talk."

"What kind of talk?" Verity asked.

"About men in the tunnels. Like where that bloke fell in the hole." Sally jerked her head toward Nathan.

He sighed. "That's how I'll always be known, isn't it? The bloke who fell in the hole."

"That's likely," Verity agreed with a little grin. "Go on, Sally—what about these men? You think they're Hill and Shoemaker?"

"I dunno, miss. But people say something bad happened down there. And some just say it's safer to stay out of the tunnels." She shrugged. "Sorry. That's all, miss. People are tight-lipped about it. But they always bring that up when anyone asks 'em about the men you're after."

"That's good, Sally. Thank you." Verity dug into her

coin purse and handed the girl several coins. "Now you'll remember to share with the others, right?"

"'Course, miss," the girl said somewhat scornfully. "I always take care of me own. You taught me that."

When the front door closed behind Sally, Nathan and Verity looked at one another. He sighed deeply and said, "Back down to the tunnels, then."

After loading a rope ladder and lanterns into their carriage, Nathan and Verity returned to the dilapidated building where Nathan and Sloane had fallen into the ruins.

When they climbed down into the tunnel, they found that someone had laid two planks across the gaping hole into the Roman ruins. Nathan eyed the narrow make-shift walkway with some suspicion, but he followed Verity across it.

They proceeded down the tunnel, though Nathan soon had to stoop not to knock his head. They came upon another branching passage, but it ended in a pile of rubble, so they continued on.

"Wait." Verity lifted her light to peer into an offshoot. "Is that a door?"

"Perhaps it's a hole where someone else fell in," Nathan said acerbically as they started down the exceedingly narrow corridor, which had a ceiling even lower than the one they had just left.

"No," Verity laughed. "This looks more recently built—and not as well. I think someone made it to reach the main tunnel."

Even Verity had to duck down to go through the opening, but once through, they found themselves in a more spacious underground room.

"A cellar," Nathan said. "They dug it out from an old cellar."

"Look, there are some stairs. Maybe this is how they exit the tunnels." Verity started toward the far side and the steep set of steps leading up to a doorway.

The door had long since fallen from its rusted hinges and lay in pieces, and the inside was in similar disrepair, with piles of trash and broken pieces of wood scattered around. An outside door was boarded up, and the only light aside from their lanterns came from a small square in the wall where a window had been made of chunks of old opaque glass in varying colors. A few rats ran squealing at their entrance.

"Ugh," Verity said, pulling out a handkerchief and covering her nose. "What a stench."

"Yes. People have been building fires here." Nathan gestured toward the scorch marks on the stone floor. He, too, pulled out a handkerchief, adding, "And obviously using it as their 'facilities' as well."

"But there's another odor besides that. It smells like..."

"A dead animal," Nathan finished. They looked at one another. "It's just an animal, surely. A rat, probably."

"I think it's coming from up there." Verity moved toward a set of rickety stairs leading upward. "The smell gets stronger." They exchanged another long look.

"What if it's not—" Nathan sighed and said in a resigned tone, "We have to see, don't we?"

"Unfortunately, I think so." Verity lifted her skirts a little and started up the stairs. "You needn't come."

"You have to be joking," Nathan said, climbing up after her.

They stopped abruptly as they reached high enough to see the floor above.

"Bloody hell," he said, his voice muffled by his wadded-up handkerchief. "It's a man."

Verity nodded, dread growing in her stomach. "Those boots…"

She forced herself to climb the rest of the way so that she could see the man's face. Her stomach lurched, and she swallowed hard and turned away. Nathan was right behind her, and she buried her face in his chest.

"Good God!" Nathan exclaimed. "It's Will Tolliver."

Verity pushed at his chest. "Let's go. Leave."

"But surely we should see if we can figure out how he died."

"I don't care how," Verity retorted. "All I need to know is that he's dead."

They hurried back down the stairs and out the way they had come, not stopping until they'd crossed the planks over the ruins and climbed back up into the abandoned building.

"We should tell someone," Nathan said.

"Who?" Verity asked, blowing out the lanterns and starting toward the outer door.

"I'm not sure," he admitted. "I've never found a dead body before."

"Well, I'm not in the habit of it either. The only bodies I've seen were during the war, and my main concern was always getting as far away as I could, as quickly as possible."

They went outside, and Verity drew in a deep breath. "I've never thought of London air as fresh before."

They stowed their gear in the carriage, but Verity's nerves were jumping so that she couldn't stand the thought of getting into the vehicle. "I have to walk."

Gesturing toward the coachman to follow, she set off at a brisk pace, Nathan beside her.

"Why would someone kill Tolliver?" Nathan said. "I suppose there might be any number of other people he was trying to swindle. But his sort of criminal activity hardly seems something one would *kill* him for."

"Maybe if one was desperate enough, unable to pay him say, one might. Or furious enough at what he'd done to—" Verity stopped and swung toward Nathan. "Like Malcolm Douglas, for instance. He'd been knocked over the head and imprisoned by Tolliver for weeks. That might be enough to make one want revenge." She whipped around and began to stride briskly forward again.

"Malcolm?" Nathan hurried after her. "He wouldn't kill someone."

"How do you know? Just because he's your half brother doesn't mean he is like you. He could be a terrible person. Terrible people must get kidnapped, as well."

"But he's been locked up all this time," Nathan pointed out. "He couldn't have killed him."

"We rescued him yesterday morning. He's had a day—more than a day—to do him in."

"But how did he track him down? We've been trying to find Will and weren't able to until just now—and Malcolm didn't have your little gang of urchins to run all over looking for him."

"Maybe he knew Tolliver. If you'll remember, I thought it was suspicious that he said Tolliver was just some fellow he ran into in a tavern."

"You just don't like Malcolm."

"He was rude to you. And not terribly grateful, given

that we'd rescued him." She frowned. "Maybe Malcolm was part of the scheme, after all."

"Verity," Nathan said sternly.

"Oh, very well," Verity said grudgingly. "That does seem unlikely."

"Besides, the man has been dead longer than a day, hasn't he?"

"I don't know, Nathan. I'm not an expert in dead bodies."

"And here I thought you would be," he teased, and Verity had to smile.

"Well, I'm not, and apparently finding one puts me on edge." She started walking again. "Still, I'm not entirely crossing Malcolm Douglas off the list."

"My thought is that it was likely a falling out among thieves," Nathan mused.

"You think it was Shoemaker and Hill?"

"We know that they are prone to violent methods. They could have argued over the money. Maybe Tolliver didn't give them the payment he promised. After all, he never got any money out of his scheme with me."

"He certainly wouldn't pay them if he was dead."

"Yes, that puts something of a hole in that argument," Nathan admitted.

"Or maybe someone else paid them to do away with Tolliver."

"Are you going back to the real Malcolm again?"

"No, no. But what if…I just can't get away from the idea that someone else was involved besides Tolliver, someone who knew Malcolm better."

Nathan nodded. "It makes sense, though I'm not sure how we'll find out who that person is. You think that it was this other man who killed Tolliver? Or hired Shoe-maker and Hill to kill him?"

"Yes. Not asking for ransom wasn't the only pecu-liarity. Shoemaker and Hill attacking us the first time doesn't fit either, really."

"I thought we decided it was because they were try-ing to discourage us from finding out the truth."

"But that makes little sense. It happened shortly after you asked for my help, when Tolliver first talked to us. We'd barely begun to look into anything. There's no reason he'd want to keep us from investigating the mar-riage records—they supported Tolliver's claim. He had no idea we would go to Scotland."

"But it's too coincidental for the same two men to kidnap Douglas and also attack us for some other per-son like Arden or Stanhope." Nathan frowned. "Though I still don't see why they would have been asking us where something was unless it was Arden and the brooch."

"Exactly. It doesn't fit." Verity paused, trying to ex-press the theory that had begun forming in her brain. "Maybe Hill didn't ask about 'them,' maybe he said 'him.' What if Will Tolliver was the thing they were trying to find?"

"Very well, I'll give you that. It's easy enough to confuse 'em and 'im. And I suppose there was some reason to think we might know where Tolliver was. I had been in contact with him. He had come to your house. But why would his own henchmen not know where the man was?"

"What if they weren't *his* henchmen?"

Nathan looked at her for a long moment. "So your thought is that this other fellow, the Scotsman that knows the Douglases' secret, hired all three of the men. Or he—Mr. Unknown—and Tolliver were in partnership. And Mr. Unknown sent those two to find Tolliver. But why would he have been looking for Tolliver? Why wouldn't he have known where the man was?"

"I'm not sure. I haven't fully thought this out. Perhaps they argued about something or Tolliver cheated him some way. But we know Will left the inn where he was staying. Maybe he didn't tell our mystery man where he was going."

"Tolliver could have had second thoughts, I suppose," Nathan mused. "Decided whatever he was getting paid wasn't worth the risk of committing fraud. Or he realized the scheme wasn't going to work. He certainly hadn't convinced us. But would this man kill Tolliver just because he did a bad job? Because he fled?"

"That seems unlikely. But he might kill him because Tolliver could identify him. If this mystery man is someone the Douglases knew, he would be afraid of that."

"Yes…"

"But you aren't convinced," Verity said.

"Are you?" Nathan asked.

"Not really. There doesn't seem to be an important enough motive to warrant the whole subterfuge."

"Yes, why would someone—" Nathan stopped abruptly, and stood for a moment, staring blankly into space.

"What?" Verity asked, excitement beginning to stir in her. "Nathan, what are you thinking?"

"What if…what if we have been looking at this thing the entirely wrong way? What if we turn it upside down?"

"I don't understand. What other way is there?"

"Maybe the scheme was never really to prove Malcolm was my father's heir. Maybe it was to reveal that he *was* illegitimate."

"Who would want to do that? Oh!" Her face cleared. "It's the *other* inheritance someone wants—the Douglas inheritance that the real Malcolm will get when his father, or, rather, grandfather dies."

"Yes." Nathan's eyes lit with enthusiasm as he followed the idea out. "You found out that an illegitimate son couldn't inherit the family estate, and I suspect the Douglases' estate is worth much more than my manor."

"So when the scandal breaks, that land would go to the person who would be the rightful heir. Which is…" Verity looked at Nathan, her eyes widening.

"John's brother," he said grimly.

"Uncle Robert," Verity said softly.

"It would have to be. There weren't any sons from their marriage, just Margaret. And it wouldn't pass through her even if Malcolm weren't illegitimate. Malcolm told us it was a very small family. I recall Robert is his only uncle."

"Robert would inherit, and he wouldn't appear to have had anything to do with taking it away from his nephew. He wouldn't look like the villain. His family wouldn't hate him for it."

"No. They'd hate me. The wicked Sassenach."

"Everything makes sense now. Robert doesn't want to physically harm his nephew, just keep him from interfering with his plan. He hires a couple of ruffians to kidnap him and keep Malcolm locked up, then he finds an actor or mountebank who fits the general description and can pretend to be a Scotsman. Uncle Robert then gives the imposter all the information that he wants provided to us. Maybe he also hoped for some blackmail money, but it wouldn't have mattered, really. His eye was on the larger prize."

Nathan added, "It also explains why he didn't ask for ransom—Robert wouldn't have wanted Flora and John to know that Malcolm had been kidnapped. And who knows whether Shoemaker and Hill realized that Malcolm's valet saw the whole incident."

"Even if they were aware they'd been seen, they wouldn't have told their employer."

"Robert probably thought his brother had no idea. I'm sure he wouldn't have wanted the Douglases to come to London and create a huge stir."

"Exactly—" Verity wagged her finger back and forth to indicate the two of them. "You and I might have been accosted by them and learned that our Malcolm was a fake."

"When I look back at it now—" Nathan's gaze was hazy as if actually trying to see into the past "—it wasn't an accident when Robert told me the name of the village. He's clearly too good a liar to have slipped up. Good enough, in fact, to make it *appear* as though he slipped up, which would make me even more certain that there was a family secret there. He wanted us to have the name of the village, wanted us to go there and find out what really happened."

"He's an excellent liar," Verity said. "He certainly fooled me."

"He asked me more than once to tell him if Malcolm turned up, which adds weight to your idea that he lost track of Tolliver."

"Where he slipped up was underestimating you," Verity told Nathan. "He assumed you would have no concern for your brother, that you would be happy to spread it around that Malcolm was illegitimate."

"I don't think family loyalty is something Robert understands well," Nathan said drily.

"What do we do now?" Verity asked. "If he killed Will Tolliver, we can't just let Robert get away with it."

"No. I don't know how we'll convince anyone of our theory, though. Malcolm and his parents won't want to believe it, especially coming from a Dunbridge." Nathan scowled. "And we have no proof, just conjecture. Still, we have to warn Malcolm about his uncle. Robert failed with this scheme, but that doesn't mean he won't try something else. Though I'm not sure how he could claim the inheritance without killing him." Nathan's head snapped up, and he and Verity stared at each other in alarm.

"He may have cared enough about Malcolm to go after the fortune by other means. But if murdering him is the only way—well, Robert's already done away with one man."

"And we left Malcolm alone with him."

## CHAPTER THIRTY

THEY TURNED AND ran for the carriage.

It took fifteen minutes to reach Robert Douglas's narrow redbrick house, and Nathan spent the whole time careening between deep satisfaction at unraveling the mystery and frustration at not figuring it out earlier. "Why didn't I think of this before?"

"You aren't omniscient, Nathan," Verity told him. "I'm the supposed investigator—if anyone should have realized it earlier, it was I. You have to admit that it was a rather convoluted motive."

"Yes, but who would have had such intimate knowledge of the details of Malcolm's birth besides someone in his family?" Nathan shook his head. "Truth is, I took Robert at face value. I should have been more suspicious."

"Don't fret. We'll save Malcolm," Verity said confidently. "Surely his uncle won't have done away with him this quickly—not after everything that's happened."

They tumbled out of the carriage and raced to the front door. Nathan's knock was thunderous. It was only a moment before Douglas's butler opened the door. He looked startled at the sight of them, dirty and disheveled from their explorations in the tunnel, and his eyes widened as they went to Verity's suddenly augmented stomach. But he managed to keep his voice smoothly polite. "Sir. I'm afraid Mr. Dou—"

Nathan stepped into the entry without waiting for an invitation. "I have to speak to Malcolm."

"But, sir, Mr. Douglas has guests—" He stepped back, gaping, as Nathan and Verity swept past him toward the sound of voices and laughter coming from the drawing room. He hurried after them. "Sir. Miss, er, ma'am, there is a gathering in—"

Verity and Nathan rushed through the open double doors and stopped. There were several people in the room, dainty teacups in hand, and they all turned toward the couple at their sudden entrance.

It took only a glance to see that Malcolm was not among them. His uncle was, and Robert came forward. "Why, Mr. Dunbridge. And, ah, Miss, Mrs., um…"

"I need to see Malcolm. Where is he?" Nathan asked.

"Ah, well, you see, he's not here at the moment. We were just having a bit of tea and cakes while we wait for him to return. Why don't you come in and have a bit of refreshment?" Douglas's eyes went to Verity again in some horror. "Or perhaps you'd rather wait for him in another room."

"I'm sorry, sir, but I only want to speak with Malcolm. If you could tell me—"

"Oh, I'm sure he will be back any moment," Robert went on in a tone of forced joviality. "The dear boy wouldn't want to miss you. Why don't we just go over here—" He took Nathan's elbow in one hand and Verity's in the other and tried to steer them toward an alcove in the rear of the room. "You must be tired, uh, in your condition, Mrs., um… I'll just have some refreshments brought for you, and you can wait right here for Malcolm."

Nathan resisted his pull. *Why is the man so intent on us remaining here?* "I wouldn't want to disturb your party. If you'll just tell me where he went…"

"Not a party, really, just a few of my friends who want to welcome Malcolm to London."

"Yes, where is the lad, Robbie?" one of the men asked. "We're all eager to see him. I haven't seen Malcolm since he was a schoolboy."

Robert's smile was fixed. "Yes, I am so sorry. Malcolm had to run an errand. I'm sure he will return before long."

"What errand?" Nathan said flatly, no longer even trying for a polite veneer.

"Well! That's a bit rude," one of the women murmured.

"I'm sorry, madam," Nathan said, sending a nod her direction. "But at the moment, Malcolm's safety is my uppermost concern." He looked straight into Robert's eyes, his own usually warm gaze now stony. "I am certain Mr. Douglas will agree with me."

"Safety?" another guest said, puzzled.

"I urged him to visit my doctor," Robert replied. "I'm sure *you* understand *that*."

"Then we shan't bother you anymore," Verity said cheerfully, turning and going out into the entry hall, where the butler hovered, and asked him, "Could you tell us where Mr. Douglas's doctor is located?"

Nathan followed her, but Robert was right on his heels. "Really now, you mustn't disturb the good doctor."

"No, I'm afraid we must." Nathan looked at the butler, his voice steely. "The lady asked for his address."

The man's mouth opened and closed, and he glanced over at his employer, then quietly gave them an address.

Verity and Nathan started out the door. Nathan had thought that Robert might give up his efforts to keep them there, but, as was evident by the footsteps behind them, that was not the case. Nathan turned to see Robert hurrying out of the house after them.

His suspicion deepened. It seemed very much as if Robert wanted to delay Nathan's talk with his half brother—though he couldn't know what they planned on telling Malcolm once they found him. Nathan had the uneasy feeling that Robert's actions meant that something was happening to Malcolm right now, and Robert didn't want Nathan to interrupt it.

Clearly Verity agreed. "There's some mischief here," she whispered, moving more quickly to the carriage. "Who has a welcome home party in the afternoon?"

"And then sends the honoree off to the doctor before guests arrive?" Nathan added as he opened the door to the hansom. He turned to give her a hand up, and he saw Malcolm down the street, walking toward the house. Nathan relaxed in relief. "Thank God."

Malcolm was still a good distance away, and Nathan started toward him, Verity by his side. Unfortunately, Robert Douglas followed only a few steps behind them.

"Malcolm," Nathan called as they grew closer. "I was looking for you."

"Dunbridge." Malcolm looked disgruntled, and Nathan assumed his displeasure was at seeing his half brother until Malcolm went on, "Uncle, why the devil did you send me to Dr. Norton? His surgery was closed." He glanced toward the front of the house, where his uncle's guests had gathered, watching curiously. "And who are those people?"

Verity pinched Nathan's arm, and he nodded, positive now that Robert had had something planned. Perhaps he was establishing an alibi for himself while someone else did away with Malcolm?

"Oh. Well…" Robert glanced toward the gathering and back to his nephew, then gave a little chuckle and said, "I'm sorry, my boy, but I had to get you out of the house. I invited a few of my friends over to see you, and I wanted to surprise you."

"Oh," Malcolm said unenthusiastically. He looked at Nathan. "Is that why you're here?" Noticing Verity for the first time, Malcolm goggled at her miraculous transformation. Verity was too busy looking around for signs of danger to notice.

"No, I came to talk to you," Nathan said.

"Come, let's go inside," Robert said with hearty good cheer. "You must meet everyone." He clamped a hand on Malcolm's arm and urged him toward the door.

Nathan stepped into Malcolm's path. "Stop. I'm serious. There is something important I need to discuss with you."

"Why are you acting so strangely?" Malcolm asked, frowning. "Both of you." He looked from Nathan to Robert, then turned to Verity. "And why in the world are you, um—" He made a vague gesture toward her, finishing lamely, "whatever you are?"

"I'll explain everything," Nathan told him. "But I need to speak with you. Now. Without your uncle."

"What?" Robert looked offended. "How very odd."

"Would you please just tell me?" Malcolm asked

crossly. "I am tired. I'm not quite back to myself and I'd like to sit down."

Verity seized the reins of the conversation, saying bluntly, "Nathan's afraid your uncle is going to kill you. He is just too polite to say so in your uncle's presence. I am not." As Malcolm gaped at her, she went on, "Robert Douglas is behind everything that happened to you. He hired the two men who kidnapped you. He hired Will Tolliver to pretend to be you. It was all his scheme."

"Have you run mad?" Malcolm stared. "Nathan, what—I don't understand."

"We found Will Tolliver's body this afternoon," Nathan replied. "We believe he was killed to keep him from revealing who paid him."

"I—why—"

"The story Tolliver told us would never have stood up in court," Nathan said. "It would have resulted in nothing except to prove that you are illegitimate, that Flora is really your grandmother."

"What does that have to do with Uncle Robert?"

"For pity's sake, Malcolm," Verity snapped. "Think. If your illegitimate birth came out, who is the one person who would benefit?"

"Is there nothing a Dunbridge won't do!" Robert thundered, his face reddening. He turned to his nephew. "Malcolm, don't listen to him. He's trying to cause trouble, just as his father did."

"Stop." Malcolm held up his hands. "Stop. All of you. I don't know what you're doing, Dunbridge—if you believe this nonsense or you're playing some bizarre prank. But this is ridiculous. I'm going inside." He started away.

"Malcolm, wait." Nathan took a step after him.

Malcolm turned, his eyes flashing. "No. Go away. Leave me alone."

Sending a triumphant glance at Nathan, Robert Douglas turned and sauntered after his nephew. Nathan let out a curse, watching his half brother walk away.

"Blast it. How do I convince him?" Nathan said.

"Well, now that you've accused him of it, Robert may decide he can't kill his nephew after all without looking incredibly suspicious."

"Only if we spread it around. And even then, we'll have no proof of his scheme, with Tolliver dead."

"Rumor is a powerful thing," Verity said. "One doesn't have to prove anything. If we tell Lady Lockwood, it would be all over town within days."

"Yes, but the scandal would hurt all of them, not just Robert."

"I suspect Malcolm would rather be the topic of scandal than dead. And if he's too stubborn and foolish to— Nathan!" She broke off midsentence and pointed, but before he could turn to look in that direction, Verity had broken into a run.

A team of horses charged down the street toward them. They were moving at far too great a clip for both the busy thoroughfare and the large wagon they pulled. A man crossing the street dodged out of the way, and the driver of another carriage shook his fist and shouted as they sped past him.

Nathan knew at once what Verity was thinking. He sprinted after her, calling out to Malcolm, who was walking near the edge of the pavement, his head down. Robert, trailing some distance behind his nephew, stayed suspiciously close to the row of houses.

Nathan hadn't quite caught up to Verity when the

wagon suddenly veered across the street, heading straight at Malcolm. Nathan yelled his brother's name again, and Verity called, "Watch out!" but their cries were drowned out by the shrieks of the party guests.

For the first time Malcolm raised his head and saw the horses bearing down upon him. Nathan was still too far away; he knew he wouldn't reach Malcolm in time. Then he saw Verity jump, and the two of them went flying.

## CHAPTER THIRTY-ONE

"VERITY!" NATHAN'S HEART was in his throat and he ran toward her.

The horses swerved back onto the street, and Verity popped back up from the shrubbery into which she and Malcolm had jumped. She brushed debris off her fake padded belly, and Nathan was swamped with relief. Whirling, he ran after the wagon and leapt up to grab the back side of it. He dangled precariously in midair for a moment, but his toes found purchase on the wood, and he pushed off, swinging up and into the empty wagon.

Nathan planted his feet wide, bending his knees so he was partially crouched to better accommodate the rocking of the vehicle. Two men—one tall, one short, just as he expected—sat on the driver's bench. With all the commotion, neither one of them seemed to have noticed him yet. The man not driving, whom Nathan recognized as Shoemaker, clutched the bench with both hands, screaming at the top of his lungs, as the wagon rocketed on. Hill, obviously inexperienced at driving, was shouting at the horses as he sawed at the reins, trying to steer the team.

As Nathan carefully made his way forward, holding onto the side of the wagon, the back end slid sideways and clipped a lamppost, then ricocheted back. Nathan, losing his grip, bounced from one side to the other but managed to stay upright. Regaining his footing, Nathan lunged forward and hooked one arm around the driver's neck, jerking Hill back tightly so that the man was immobilized against him.

With the other hand, Nathan wrenched the reins from Hill and hauled back on them. It would have been better to use both hands on the reins—better still to reach the braking lever—but Hill was struggling so much Nathan couldn't release him. He only hoped that all the other drivers on the road had the good sense to pull out of the way.

Finally, Nathan felt Hill grow heavy as if he was losing consciousness. Nathan dropped the arm around Hill's neck and shoved him over against Shoemaker, then lunged, reaching over the dividing wall, and pulling back hard on the brake. The combination of the brake and a firm hand on the reins slowed the horses, but Hill sucked in a large gulp of air, which revived him and he whirled around, swinging at Nathan.

Hill's fist collided with Nathan's cheek, snapping his head to the side and sending him staggering back a step, releasing the brake. The horses, however, apparently had enough and simply came to a stop, lathered and tossing their heads, blowing out air.

Nathan grabbed Hill by his arms and hauled him into the wagon bed. The two men grappled, and Shoemaker started over the back of the driver's bench to join his partner.

Then suddenly Verity was there, clambering up to the driver's seat and throwing herself at Shoemaker. Clasping her hands together, she swung them into his face. Stunned, he reeled back, and she gave him a hearty shove, sending Shoemaker tumbling off the wagon onto the ground.

She turned to help Nathan just as he slammed his fist into Hill's gut and followed it up with a hard right hook. Hill's eyes rolled up, and he collapsed. Nathan swung around, panting, and grinned at Verity.

"Glad you had my back," he said, the elation of victory pumping all through him.

"Always," she replied, pulling a handkerchief out of her pocket and handing it to him.

Nathan dabbed at his split lip as he took in the sight of her. The sleeve of Verity's dress was torn and her arm and cheek were scratched. Her padding had twisted around to her hips, and her wig had slid to one side of her head, wild red strands of hair escaping from it.

"God, you're beautiful." He stepped forward and pulled her into a kiss, ignoring the twinge of pain in his lip.

Malcolm trotted up, his uncle and the entire party trailing him. "Nathan, are you all right? God, when I saw you'd jumped on that wagon—" He shoved his hands back through his hair. "And you, ma'am. You saved my life. You have my eternal gratitude. That driver must have been drunk or insane. It was as if they aimed—"

"Right for you?" Nathan suggested. He nodded toward Shoemaker, who had recovered his wind and was wobbling to his feet, groaning.

"Oww, me 'ead." He looked up at Verity accusingly. "I think you broke me rib."

"You should be glad that's all I broke," she retorted.

Malcolm gaped at Shoemaker. "You!"

"Now, it wasn't me," Shoemaker whined, backing

up a step at the fire in Malcolm's eyes and holding out his hands placatingly. "I didn't…"

Malcolm strode forward and punched him on the point of his chin. Shoemaker slid back to the ground, unconscious, and Malcolm turned to Nathan. "The same men. But why? And how—have they been lying in wait for me?"

"Easy enough to do when they know what time you'll be walking into your house after an unsuccessful trip to the doctor's," Verity said scornfully. Nathan had untied his neckcloth and she took it from him, kneeling down to bind Hill's hands.

Malcolm stared at Nathan for a moment, then looked over at his uncle. He turned back to Nathan, saying uncertainly, "But, no, that couldn't…maybe one of the servants…"

Nathan climbed down from the wagon and went over to him. "Malcolm. You have to face the truth or you'll wind up dead. Your uncle sent you to the doctor even though he knew the man wouldn't be there."

"It was to set up the surprise party for my nephew," Robert said indignantly and came forward to join them. "I resent your implication, Dunbridge." He jabbed his forefinger at Nathan. "*You* were the one who was insisting on talking to Malcolm. *You* went outside to stop him and hold him there."

"It was you who arranged for your nephew to visit London," Nathan shot back at him. "You knew when and where Malcolm could be abducted. You had him locked up because you still had enough family feeling not to kill your nephew. But when we broke him out of his prison, when we ruined your plan, you had no choice but to do away with him so you could get to his inheritance."

"I've never heard anything so preposterous," Robert sputtered.

Nathan continued, raising his voice a tad more. "So you went back to the men you had hired and arranged for them to create an 'accident' for your nephew in front of the party you planned. That way you'd have multiple witnesses who would swear that you had nothing to do with Malcolm's death. Oh, and then there was Tolliver. Did you have to kill him to keep him from revealing what you'd done? Did you hire these two for that task as well?" He swung a hand toward Shoemaker. "Or did you do it yourself?"

"This is all nonsense and lies," Robert retorted. "If anyone wanted to do away with my nephew it would be you. Don't listen to him, Mal. He's merely trying to hurt you. I am your family. He's just…"

"My brother," Malcolm said heavily.

"Use your head," Verity said, joining them. "Nathan has no reason to do anything to you. He's done nothing but help you."

Malcolm looked from Nathan to Robert, his eyes troubled. "Rude as she is, she's right. Nathan had no reason."

"A Dunbridge will say anything. He is just a smooth talker like his f—" Robert's voice faltered as Malcolm's eyes flashed and he took a step toward him. "Malcolm. I didn't hire Hill or Shoemaker. I never saw them before today."

The air was suddenly silent as Malcolm and the others looked at him. Nathan said quietly, "How did you know their names, then?"

"What? Why, you told me, of course."

"No. We didn't," Nathan replied.

"Then Malcolm must have told me." Robert forced a little chuckle, but his eyes took on a hunted look, and he took a step backward.

"No." Malcolm's voice was sad. "I didn't. I thought that his name was Hall."

Robert stepped back and suddenly he reached down to the unconscious Shoemaker and snatched a pistol from the man's belt. He aimed it with shaking hands at Nathan. "Damn you! Damn all your family. You ruin everythi—" Verity began to edge toward him, and Robert swung the gun and fired at her.

Nathan jumped, taking Verity to the ground, his body covering hers. "Verity!"

Robert gaped, his eyes wild. Malcolm surged toward him, and Robert whirled and darted into the street. It was hard to tell if he turned his ankle on a pothole or just lost his balance, but one moment Robert was standing and the next he was down on the ground—directly in front of a horse drawing a carriage. The driver let out a shout and hauled back on the reins. But there was no time to stop, and the awful muffled sounds of the horse's hooves on Robert's body were followed by the wheels of the carriage.

There were shouts from all around, and Malcolm rushed out into the street, crying out, "Uncle! No!"

The others hurried after him. A man exclaimed, "My God, he's dead!" A woman screamed and fainted, and more than one man turned away from the sight of Robert Douglas's lifeless form.

The horse reared, and the driver of the carriage dropped the reins and jumped down from his seat. "He ran right out! I didn't see him!"

Chatter and movement were all around him, but the tumult didn't pierce Nathan's awareness. He had eyes only for Verity.

"Verity!" Nathan ran his hands over her frantically. Her eyes were wide and frightened and her chest was still. "Where were you hit? Don't you die on me."

Verity's hands flew to her chest, and her face was panicked. Finally she sucked in a huge breath. "I couldn't breathe!" She sat up, pulling Nathan close and holding on tightly. "I'm all right now. It was just the wind knocked out of me."

"Thank God," Nathan said fervently, raining kisses across her forehead and hair. "I thought you were dead. I thought—" His voice choked off and he tightened his arms around her convulsively.

"I'm not. I'm fine. I wasn't hit."

"Are you sure?"

"Positive." She pulled back a little and glanced around. "What happened? Did he get a—oh." She saw the body on the street. "Is Robert dead?"

"I think so. I wasn't paying attention to anything other than you." Nathan relaxed his arms, letting her go and sitting back on his heels. He lifted a hand to push back his hair. "Ow." He looked down at his arm, aware for the first time of a searing streak of pain. The sleeve of his jacket was sliced through and blood stained the material around it.

"Nathan!" Verity gasped. "It's you! You've been shot." She shoved back his jacket and pulled it off, eliciting a little yelp from Nathan.

"Have a care, would you?"

She ripped his shirt sleeve farther apart, revealing a streak of red across his arm, and let out a sigh of relief. "Thank heavens. The ball didn't go into your arm, just grazed you."

Nathan peered down at his arm and said mournfully, "Another jacket ruined." He sighed. "I'm growing rather tired of getting shot."

## CHAPTER THIRTY-TWO

"STOP WRIGGLING." An hour later, Verity knelt beside Nathan on her parlor floor, washing the dirt and gunpowder residue away from his wound.

Her touch was as gentle as she could make it, but her tone was sharp. The sight of Nathan bleeding had scared her down to the bottoms of her toes. For an instant she had been unable to breathe again, and then her nerves had spiked, and she'd had to clamp down hard on her emotions to keep from dissolving into hysteria.

Nathan had not been a cooperative patient. She had managed to keep him from going with Malcolm to take the prisoners to jail, but he had flatly refused to let a doctor look at his arm. Finally she'd given up and brought him back to her house.

He had stripped off his shirt, which, frankly, had not helped to calm Verity. It no doubt showed some lowness in her nature that tingles of lust could spring up in her at a time like this, but it seemed somehow a natural part of the wild tangle of emotions inside her.

"I can't help but flinch when you keep poking at me," Nathan said.

"I'm not poking." She paused and scowled into his face. "Though it would serve you right if I did. I don't know what you were thinking, jumping in front of me like that."

"I was trying to keep you from being shot," he retorted.

"And you got yourself shot instead." She tossed the rag aside and dabbed the ointment on the burn.

"What is that green slime?" He cast a doubtful look at the ointment in the jar.

"It's good for burns, and that's more what this is." She began to wind the strip of cotton around his arm. Tending to him had helped her nerves, and when she tied off the bandage, she sat back on her heels and looked at him, a teasing smile beginning on her face. "Not to discount your heroism, but I got shot anyway."

"What?" He straightened in alarm. "Where? How—"

"It deflected from your arm right into my padding." She picked up the padding she had worn, discarded with her wig on the floor, and dug her fingers inside it, pulling out the spent ball and holding it up. "It turned out to be an even more useful disguise than I had anticipated." She moved back to kiss him gently. "Thank you. You shouldn't go about sacrificing yourself like that, but I'm very glad you did. If you hadn't done that, Robert might very well have killed me."

Nathan cupped her face between his hands. "I will have nightmares about that moment for years." He kissed her, his lips lingering for a long, sweet moment, then pulled her up to sit on the sofa with him. He turned to her, his face earnest. "I want to say something to you."

Verity's heart skipped a beat. What if he'd decided to let her go?

"The other day, when I asked you to marry me, I was angry because you reminded me that only a year ago, I'd been in love with Annabeth. I was—I don't deny that."

A little pain pierced her heart, and she said quietly, "I don't want to be the woman you settle for."

"You're not. There's no question of settling. Verity, *you* are the woman I want. My feelings for you are entirely different than what I felt for Annabeth. She...she was my lifelong friend, and I loved her in a quiet way. It was a peaceful, sweet sort of love. We didn't argue. I never got angry with her. She was perfect."

"This is hardly the way to convince me you love me instead of Annabeth," Verity said drily.

"Let me finish. *That* was what I thought love should be. It was what I wanted—our lives fit. We matched. It was easy."

Verity raised an eyebrow.

Nathan hurried on, "But love isn't easy. Love isn't just getting along or being comfortable or matching. It's wild and intoxicating and uncertain. You and I argue and I worry, and I'm never smooth and adept with you. There's no handling you, no way of tying you down. And I have absolutely no defense against you. You can cut straight through my soul." Nathan ran a hand back through his hair, searching for the right words. "When I hold you, when I kiss you, when we make love, it's the most exciting—no, exciting is too tame a word for what I feel. I feel as if everything inside me changes, as if I am torn apart and made whole again." He gave her a wry smile. "I'm sorry. I'm not saying this very well, am I?"

She shook her head quickly. "No, I think you're saying it just right."

Nathan took her hand between his. "I'm not asking that you feel the exact same way. I just want you to know that you are in no way my second choice. You're the most wonderful thing that's ever happened to me. With Annabeth, I played the noble part and broke off the engagement. I could never do that with you. I am not going to be the gentleman this time. If you move to Paris, I am going with you. If you won't marry me, we'll live in sin. I refuse to lose you."

Warmth spread through Verity, and her lips curved up in a teasing smile. "You mean you would hold me against my will?"

Nathan sighed. "Blast it, Verity, you make it very difficult to issue grand romantic statements. No, of course I wouldn't force you to stay with me if you didn't want to—I could not bear to be the reason for your unhappiness. But I'd bloody well try to convince you to stay. I'd never stop trying to woo you. I certainly wouldn't *offer* to break it off to make it easier for you. I'd do my best to make it damned difficult for you to leave."

Verity smiled. "Then it's a good thing that I intend to marry you, isn't it?"

Nathan had drawn breath to speak, but at her words, he stopped and stared. "What did you say?"

"I want to marry you. I accept your proposal—and don't think I'll let you out of your offer. I'm not nearly as good a person as you. If you left me, I promise I'd make your life a living hell."

Nathan relaxed, letting out a soft laugh. "Would you?" He pulled her to her feet, smiling down into her face.

"Of course. I would haunt you. Send evil notes to any woman who caught your fancy. Cut up all your neckcloths. Set Petunia on your best boots."

"You *are* wicked." Nathan put his hands at her waist.

"I am. Because, you see, you are mine. I love you, and I'm never letting go." Verity laid her head against Nathan's chest. Nathan pressed his lips to Verity's forehead and said, "You knew, didn't you? Before I started my grand statement, you'd already made up your mind to marry me."

Verity smiled. "Yes."

"Yet you let me blather on."

"Of course. I liked hearing it."

"I think you just like to torture me." He stroked his hand across her hair.

"There is that, as well."

"Why did you say yes? Not that I'm objecting, mind you, but you were so against it. Why did you change your mind?"

"Well, you're a very good catch, you know," Verity said.

"Ha. What a bouncer. I am a terrible prospect, and you know it—a man with an estate mortgaged to the hilt, nothing to offer you."

Her face turned serious, her eyes steady on his. "I have a house. I have a business. I have money—what I'm lacking is the man who holds my heart in his hands. You are the kindest, most handsome, *best* man in all of England, and I love you madly. You were right. I was scared—not just of what Lord Stanhope might do, but scared of risking my heart. Scared of reaching for the life I wanted, the man I loved, just because it might all turn to ash in my hands. Now I finally understand that without you, ashes is all my life would be. You are everything to me, Nathan. None of the rest of it matters."

"Verity." Nathan swallowed hard, and his hand cupped her cheek, his thumb stroking lovingly across her skin. "I love you so much—I can't tell you a tenth of what's in my heart for you."

"I already know it." She smiled and reached up to brush back a strand of his hair that had fallen across his forehead. "This evening, when you looked at me in my torn dress, covered in dirt and stains I'd prefer not to identify, sweating and gasping for breath, that dreadful wig tilted over my ear, you told me I was beautiful and kissed me. I knew." Her eyes began to twinkle and the corner of her mouth turned up in a teasing smile. "Only love could make you that deluded. And I realized I had better grab you before you came back to your senses."

"If love is a delusion, then I promise to never regain my senses. I will love you until the end of time," Nathan told her.

"I'm not sure if that means you'll be wearing a tailcoat or a straitjacket to our wedding. But, honestly, I don't even care."

## EPILOGUE

NATHAN AND VERITY stopped in the street, looking up at the sign above her office.

"Dunbridge and Dunbridge," Verity read with some satisfaction and tucked her hand into the crook of Nathan's arm. "It looks perfect, don't you think?"

Of course, everything had looked perfect to her for the past month. They had solved the case. Shoemaker and Hill had confessed to being hired by Robert Douglas for the kidnapping of Malcolm and the attack on Verity and Nathan—though the men had told the authorities that they had only been planning to scare the couple into giving up Will Tolliver when Nathan and Verity attacked them and the men had been forced to defend themselves. Which, Verity, had to admit, was not *entirely* untrue.

Shoemaker and Hill had also disavowed any knowledge of Tolliver's murder. Verity found that claim less convincing. Robert Douglas did not seem the sort to empty his own chamber pot, so to speak, but since there was no proof on either side and Robert was dead and therefore beyond punishment, Verity had to satisfy herself with the knowledge that Robert's two henchmen would spend much of the rest of their lives in prison.

The Dunbridge name remained unstained, and though the Douglases' reputation had suffered from the gossip surrounding Robert's actions before his untimely demise, at least Malcolm's paternity was still a secret. And Malcolm himself had changed enough in his attitude toward Nathan and the Dunbridges that he had attended Nathan and Verity's wedding.

Even Lady Lockwood and Nathan's mother and aunt taking over what had been intended as a quiet little wedding in Verity's parlor—turning it into an extravaganza of white lace and flowers and candles in Lady Lockwood's ballroom—had not dented Verity's good humor.

It had been sweet of them, really, and it had been good to have all their friends and family there—not to mention a bit of surprise to see how many friends and family she seemed to have picked up over the course of the last couple of years.

*It was really rather embarrassing to be this utterly happy.*

"Are you sure you don't want to name it Cole and Dunbridge?" Nathan asked. "I feel as though I'm taking over your business."

"Ha. As if I'd let you," Verity shot back. "I like this. Besides, Cole wasn't even my real name."

"It wasn't?" He let out a chuckle. "I suppose I ought to be inured to surprises from you. What *was* your real name?"

"Cowhill," Verity said. "All in all, I prefer Dunbridge." She grinned up at him. "Besides, I'm beginning a new life. It seems appropriate to have a new name."

"As long as you don't change Verity."

"You said the name was a misnomer when you met me," she protested.

"Now I find I quite enjoy the irony."

Verity smiled and leaned her head against his arm. "It's all been wonderful, hasn't it?"

"If this is what marriage to you is like, I shall have a

very happy life." Nathan paused. "Others might think it odd to spend one's honeymoon breaking up a ring of jewel thieves, but I thought it added a certain liveliness to the venture."

"Well, I could hardly let them steal that poor woman's necklace—it was a treasured family heirloom."

Nathan bent to kiss her softly on the forehead. "No, I don't suppose you could."

"Besides," Verity said with a wicked look, "chasing people wasn't *all* we did."

He matched her grin. "No, there was quite a bit more. And it was interesting to actually *be* husband and wife instead of pretending we were." He looked up at the sign again. "Shall we go see what mayhem has occurred while we were gone?"

"Wait." Verity put her hand on his arm. Her stomach was suddenly dancing with nerves. *But she wasn't going to let herself back out.* "There's something I need to do." She drew a shaky breath. "I don't want any shadows hanging over us and our life together. I've lived in fear of my past for too long. I've faced guns and knives and even, once, a sword, and not flinched. Yet when it came to my past, I have been a cowering little girl. But no more. I'm going to face Stanhope."

"Very well." Nathan took her hand, and his calm confidence steadied Verity.

"And I want—I *need* to visit Poppy. You once told me that I should give her the chance to decide whether or not she wanted me in her life. You were right. The only reason I stayed away so long was that I couldn't face her rejection. But you give me strength, Nathan. With you, I am braver."

He cupped her cheek with his hand. "My love, you are

braver than anyone I know, and stronger. However, I'm very glad you feel I help you. Do you want me to go with you?" There was a certain wariness in his eyes, and she knew he thought she would insist on doing it by herself.

In the past, she would have, but now she said, "Yes. I want you by my side."

"Then that's where I'll be."

WHEN THEY ARRIVED at Poppy's house, Verity was doubly glad Nathan had come with her. His quiet presence steadied her as she left the carriage and started up the short walk to the house. But before they reached it, the front door opened, and Jonathan Stanhope came out.

Verity came to a dead halt, stunned, her stomach turning to ice.

He was putting on his hat, his eyes on the steps in front of him, but he looked up and saw Verity. He went still, his gaze suddenly intent—like a hound that had scented his quarry, Verity thought.

Beside Verity, Nathan muttered, "What the devil is he doing here?"

Verity's thoughts flew to her sister. *Had he hurt Poppy? Threatened her?* And suddenly the ice was gone, and a hot determination flooded her.

"Nothing good," she snapped and tightened her grip on Nathan's arm.

"Verity." A smile started on Stanhope's face—not the fierce triumphant one he had shown her at the play, but an uncertain curve of the lips that matched the faint wariness in his eyes as she marched up to him. Before she could speak, he said, "I wish to apologize for startling you at the theater. I had been looking for you for a very long time, and I was so surprised that I fear I lost my manners. I should have guessed that you might not know who I was."

"Oh, I know you, Lord Stanhope."

"I see." He looked taken aback. "Well, um…I'm not Lord Stanhope yet. Merely Mr. Stanhope—Jonathan, I had hoped, to you. My father still holds the title."

Verity stared. She felt as if all the wind had been knocked out of her. "He's *alive*?"

"Yes. Were you not aware?"

"No," she said faintly, feeling a little breathless, and Nathan slipped his arm around her waist.

"He still lives. But he is much changed. He spends most of his days in a chair on the terrace, looking at the garden. His memory is very poor. He wouldn't know who you are."

"I thought—all that blood—I thought I killed him." Verity was grateful for Nathan's supporting arm. She was bombarded by conflicting emotions—relief, joy, disbelief, regret over the years lost—and she turned to Nathan, her eyes shimmering with unshed tears.

"I know, love," Nathan said to her, tightening his arm around her waist. He looked over at Stanhope. "Verity thought that she had been blamed for his murder. That evening at the theater, when you appeared, well, we presumed that you were going to accuse her of exactly that."

"That is why you ran?" Jonathan said. "You thought I wanted revenge?" He shook his head. "I don't. Frankly, I am grateful, as are all the servants. Father seems content and is in no pain, and the household is now peaceful. No doubt I sound as cold as he, but what you did made my life a great deal more bearable. I was under his rule just as you were. I was still at school…the servants found him. Money and jewelry were missing, so the assumption was that thieves had broken into the house and when he tried to stop him, they attacked him."

"But Poppy and I were gone."

"We decided that whoever assaulted him also abducted you and your sister." A faint smile touched his lips as he saw the skeptical expression on Verity's face. "I didn't believe that, you understand, but it seemed the best solution. I did try to find the two of you, but not because I wanted you punished. I thought to simply bring you home. But we could find no trace of you."

"We were hidden by an expert," Verity said drily.

"Eventually, I found Poppy, but you were much tougher to locate. I hired a Bow Street Runner—"

"Milsap," Verity cut in.

"Yes." Jonathan frowned, but didn't ask her how she'd known. "He told us you were dead. However, Poppy never believed it. She said you were the toughest, most resourceful person in the world and we would eventually find you. Still, several years in, I gave up searching. But when I saw a redheaded woman at a party not long ago, it relit the question in my mind. I contacted Milsap again, but he proved as useless as he had been the first time. And then, by the merest chance, I saw you at the theater. After that, I was able to discover where you lived, but no one was there."

"We were on our honeymoon," Verity said. "I'm sorry—I haven't introduced you to my husband, Nathan Dunbridge."

The two men shook hands, and Jonathan went on, "Please, you must come inside. Poppy will be beyond delighted to see you."

They followed him to the front door, where a puzzled-looking maid let them in, then, bobbing a curtsey, led them to the drawing room. Verity's sister was seated, stitching on an embroidery hoop, and she looked up in surprise. "Why, Jonathan, you're back. Did you forget something?"

Her eyes went past him to Verity, and she drew in a sharp breath. Poppy jumped to her feet, her embroidery falling unnoticed to the floor. "Vetty!"

Verity nodded, her throat clogged with tears at the sound of the childhood name that only Poppy had called her.

Poppy ran to Verity and flung her arms around her. "Oh, Vetty, you're finally home!"

Verity hugged her tight, half laughing, half crying. "Yes. I'm home."

Jonathan soon left, giving Verity and Poppy the chance to chat together. They talked for over an hour, recalling their childhoods and relating their histories since last they saw each other. Poppy proudly brought out her three-month-old son to show Verity and Nathan, and they made appropriately effusive compliments.

Eventually, making promises to call on one another soon, Verity and Nathan left.

"Well…that was…" Verity said as they walked along, her hand tucked into the crook of Nathan's arm.

"Unexpected?" Nathan guessed.

"I was going to say like something out of a novel," Verity replied wryly. "If anyone else told me this story, I would have been sure they were lying."

"Sometimes good things happen, Verity." Nathan smiled. "You didn't see enough of it growing up, but you deserved to. You deserve all the joy we have now."

She smiled back at him, her eyes a little misty. "I suppose I will have to get used to that now that I am married to you."

"Yes. Because I intend to do everything I can to make you happy."

"For a moment, when I learned how wrong I'd been about Jonathan and what happened—well, about everything—I was angry at myself for simply assuming I'd killed Stanhope and fleeing. Everything would have been all right. My stepfather wouldn't have remembered. I wouldn't have had to give up Poppy or join Asquith's organization or do all the things I've done."

"I think we have both learned how foolish it is to assume we know things without finding out," Nathan said lightly, then went on in a serious tone, "But you cannot blame yourself. You couldn't have known the future. You were only fourteen, and you were scared. You did the best you could."

"The important thing is…" Verity stopped and turned to Nathan, looking up into his face, her eyes glowing with love. "I am glad I did what I did, despite all that happened. However hard, however dangerous the course I took, it was the path that led me to you. If I had stayed, I would have had a completely different life. I wouldn't have met you, and you are the one thing that I could not bear to lose."

"My love." He smiled down at her. "I would have found you. No matter where our lives went or what we did, I know that somehow I would have made my way to you. You are my North Star."

"My words will never be a match for yours. So you will just have to settle for this," Verity said and kissed him in a way that made certain that even Nathan didn't have a coherent thought left in his head.

\* \* \* \* \*

# ACKNOWLEDGEMENTS

So MANY PEOPLE put time and effort into this book, and I would like to thank them all. Thank you to all the folks at Canary Street Press, from the copy editor to marketing to the art department that designed the lovely cover. And a special thanks to my editor, Lynn Raposo, whose suggestions always improve the story.

Of course, thanks are due, as always, to my wonderful agent, Maria Carvainis, and her team.

Most of all, I am so very grateful to Anastasia Hopcus, for helping me bring Nathan and Verity's story to life.